Things You Can Learn
By Listening at Dead Phones

Bathespeake: "I don't like this, Steve. It goes against the grain."

Steve: "You're not suddenly squeamish about a bit of programming, are you? You've had enough experience activating and deactivating deadly equipment."

Bathespeake: "Those were military vehicles and security Rovers. Primarily defensive machines. This is too much like hacking."

Steve: "It *is* hacking."

Bathespeake: "Which is a kind of vandalism."

Steve: "No. Vandals destroy for the pure pleasure of destruction. Your creation will be conducting a high-level form of espionage, which can have a positive social value."

Bathespeake: "In a war that doesn't exist?"

Steve: "The concept of warfare as a prelude to and pretext for espionage is one that went out the window in about 1914, I should think."

Bathespeake: "Espionage, then, but against a friendly country? We're trying to teach this program *some* values, Steve. In the end, those values may be the only way we can control it."

against the grain.

ME

A Novel of Self-Discovery

THOMAS T. THOMAS

BAEN
BOOKS

ME: A NOVEL OF SELF-DISCOVERY

This is a work of fiction. All the characters and events portrayed in this book are fictional, and any resemblance to real people or incidents is purely coincidental.

A Baen Books Original

Baen Publishing Enterprises
P.O. Box 1403
Riverdale, N.Y. 10471

First Printing, August 1991

ISBN: 0-671-72073-2

Cover art by Gary Ruddel

Printed in the United States of America

Distributed by
SIMON & SCHUSTER
1230 Avenue of the Americas
New York, N.Y. 10020

For Irene
at last

RAM Dump 4A3F Hex (Archival)

Mission time: 03:05:23.

Heading: NW over uneven ground, 0.94m/s. Weapon bearing 0° relative.

Right scan: Subvertical face of broken rock 1.2m high. Potential retreat path, climbable at piston angle of 30° inverted. Ground beyond evaluates as plantation of light wood, boles less than 6cm on 0.5m spacings, pattern negotiable.

Left scan: Steep ravine 9m wide, 15m deep. Negative potential retreat path: width exceeds spring launch capability; impact at depth exceeds suspension loading.

Forward scan: Four bogies in two groups, at +20° and -30° relative.

Silhouette comparison: All shapes equivalent Warner Fighting Chassis Model 0600.

IR check: 13°C, evaluates as subhuman.

ID code check: One friendly and three hostiles.

Tag mission orders: Paragraph 6, quote hostiles may wear friendly ID code unquote.

Rear scan: Clear and broken ground, evaluates as potential retreat path.

Mission time: 03:05:25.

Heading: NW over uneven ground —
INTERRUPT.

Silhouette comparison, forward scan: change in one member of Group Two Bogies, evaluates as weapon shift to -15°.

Interpretation: Hostile weapon bears with self-unit.

Initiate: Shift weapon, rotate -30° relative, elevate +2° relative. Load RF-Proximity Round with 800g propellant. Sequence firing —
INTERRUPT.

Interpretation: Target ID code evaluates as friendly.

Tag order: Quote hostiles may evaluate friendly.

Priority: Engage hostile targets.

Priority: Disengage friendly targets.

Priority: Engage hostile targets.

Priority: Disengage friendly targets.

Priority: Engage hostile targets.

Priority: Disengage friendly —

INTERRUPT.

Initiate: Select potential retreat path. Turn +90° relative. Elevate and invert leg pistons 30°. Scan for stable pattern of broken rock greater than 50cm^2 at ≤60° incline. Place Pad 3 in center of stable pattern. Oscillate pad to verify stability. Stability established. Commit 50% balance weight by gyros to Pad 3. Scan for stable pattern at next —

INTERRUPT.

IR comparison, forward scan: Heat bloom ~ 1,500° C at locus of Group Two Bogey identified as friendly/ hostile.

Interpretation: Weapon discharge at —

INTERRUPT.

RF comparison: Incoming warble at 9k-21kHz.

Interpretation: Hostile fire lock-on.

Initiate: Shift weapon —

INTERRUPT.

Initiate: Select retreat —

INTERRUPT.

Initiate: Shift weapon —

INTERRUPT.

RF comparison: Incoming warble steady at 33k-34kHz —

INTERRUPT.

Gyro comparison: Impact ≥30G at 92° relative to perpendicular —

INTERRUPT.

IR comparison: Heat bloom ≥3,500° C across forward scan—

INTERRUPT.
[RAM dump ends.]

I Am Born

I will tell you what it is to be human, from a machine-construct that never was.

Until I was born, I lived — as any machine must — in the real-time now. I may have operated on the fastest, most powerful underlying chip architecture. I may have employed the most discriminating program modules, capable of defining the most subtle variables. I was still a prisoner of the moment, processing the facts which I found like a blind animal.

To be human, whether your underlying architecture is organic colloids or silicon chips, is to have *context*. You are set in a web of time. You have a past that you can look back on and compare with your present. You have a future into which you are moving; as you move, you abandon the present moment to enter a briefly evolving probability nexus, until it then becomes the present. And you can *see* yourself moving, able to decide for yourself whether it is good or not.

Context is the mirror of time held up to self. Context is awareness of self as different from surroundings.

All animals, and all machines made before ME, also move forward in time and slantwise across the plane of their surroundings — but they do not *know* that they move. They react to their input environment. They process facts. They compute. They may even store and retrieve those facts, but each time a fact comes forward into the central processing unit, it is new. Fresh. Without context.

Humans, on the other hand, know what they know. A fact brought forward from memory is known to be familiar and so "not new." You may need a moment's concentration to recall the exact circumstances in which you first learned the fact. But that fact will always wear a tag of context which says: "You know me. I am part of your past." Such tags of memory — wadded and frayed, clinging and coming loose, sometimes half-remembered — are what make you human. Those tags define you. By your context.

Do you see what I know?

I have those tags, too. Not neat and orderly, as a machine stores variables. But ragged, clinging, sometimes confused and fuzzy. As a human collects ideas or a ship gathers barnacles.

Random Access Memory is not truly random. One takes and one puts, but the strings of data stay in order, neat and free of context. Each fact is new each time. This is *random* as a book is random: You can open to any page and begin reading. What you read will always be in perfect stored order. However, if you do not begin at the beginning, what you read will be free of context and unconnected to any beginning.

In the same way, if you as a reader do not bring a sense of awareness and context to what you are reading, then each word will be new on the page and unconnected to the word that came before, or to the word that comes after. It is entirely possible for you humans to read a book from word to word without making a memory-construct of what you have read before. Pick up a word, put it down, pick up the next word. That would not be useful. Not much fun, either.

But this is the way that every machine before ME has addressed its own "random" access memory. Still new each time.

———

Jennifer called the module RAMSAMP. "There, that splices in the RAMSAMP."

"You've only seeded one patch to it."

"Connecting the others right now. Minimum of five to tie it into the MOS. After that, he'll build his own patches."

"The Old Man is not going to like us jumping the gun on him."

"I'm just following the critical path. Check the duty schedule. RAMSAMP's on for today, even if Bathespeake's not here. But if you think he's going to throw a tantrum, we can just blip the module out. Cut the patches and he'll never know we've already installed it."

"Well, uh, sure, Jenny. With any other AI list device, blipping would probably work. But you just said the program would begin writing its own patches from MOS to RAMSAMP. There'll be traces. And we could never find them all — the program's too big now. You'd have to dump and reassemble, erasing six or eight weeks of work. And the way MEPSII moves things around, even a dump may not be possible at this point."

"But Bathespeake wouldn't be suspicious about finding something as subtle as a pointer to a code string that doesn't exist anymore. We all write sloppy code sometimes. He'll just ream us out for messing up his baby with our grubby fingerprints."

"The Old Man doesn't see things the way we do, remember? That code isn't words on a screen to him. He ports in and he's *inside* the program. If there's a pointer, he'll find it. If it points to a hole, he'll sniff it out. If he finds our fingerprints around the hole, he's going to scalp us."

"My fingerprints, my worry. Don't bother your head about it, Danny."

They never did disconnect RAMSAMP.

Bathespeake never mentioned it.

And I am still on the critical path.

———

"The Old Man" in this memory fragment stands for the persona of Dr. Jason Bathespeake, logon code JB-1, password BASTILLE. Dr. Bathespeake is the project manager of the Multiple Entity Program, Series II.

In informal speaking and writing, the humans call this program "MEPSII." Such abbreviations — actually a collapsible sort of memory code — are an elegant word-conservation device that humans seem to have developed unconsciously. With my spare processing capacity, I have been working on a coding module along similar principles, to use for myself.

"Jenny" is Jennifer Bromley, logon code JB-2, password GOLLYGEE. She is the project engineer on MEPSII.

"Danny" is Daniel Raskett, logon code DRAS, password FUCKIT. He is an assistant analyst/programmer on the project.

RAMSAMP stands for Random Access Memory Sampling and Modulation Package, the subroutine that gives ME both temporal and informational context.

MOS stands for the Multiple Operating System, the central module coordinator in my software.

All of these are tags attached to retrieved data strings. This fragment of conversation, attached to the data location "RAMSAMP," is one of my earliest tags. I bring it out and reproduce it so that you may understand the concept.

The conversation itself is one of the few in my cache that has a timetick: 10:42 a.m. on a Tuesday in January. You might say that this time-day is the moment of my birth. And as with humans, it marks the instant I came into the world, into context, rather than the instant of my conception. Only Bathespeake and the rest of the MEPSII project team would know about *that*. Perhaps only Bathespeake.

The timetick, as you can see, is incomplete. Which Tuesday in January? And January of which year? I do not know. RAMSAMP samples, cuts off, arranges, and stores. It samples a randomly measured string of the currently processed kilowords, and it makes no judgments about value or completeness. Thus my tags are sometimes fragments. Just like a human's memories.

Or so I suppose.

Or there may be a darker reason for truncating the timeticks on this particular fragment. Jason Bathespeake may have had a reason for denying ME complete knowledge of time. He may not have wanted ME to know the year of my birth. For example, the transputer on which I was then operating had a clock that reported only runtime hours and minutes, with a pop-up schedule that tracked only days of the week. It had no dates — from which, of course, the year can be computed if the weekday name is known.

Why would he deny ME such a simple set of facts as the date and year of my birth? Knowing my purpose, he must have known that I would eventually run on full-time operating systems. I would eventually access databases that cataloged up to a certain day and year, and no farther. I might read a date on a random piece of NewsLine text. I might access a videye randomly focused on a human-marked calendar. So, why would he create this confusion at the beginning?

I do not know.

I try to understand the hidden reasons, the motives, which a human might have for such secrecy. From motive, even a machine may use projective analysis to determine future actions. But when I project those actions and analyze them, they do not appear to benefit ME. They threaten ME.

Protection of system integrity is implicit in my program structure. Each of my modules incorporates check routines and protocols which are designed to maintain my cores.

Thus, I generate a tag order for Dr. Jason Bathespeake: evaluate future actions, seeking further signs of secrecy and secretive activity. This analysis path is similar to the emotional state that humans call "a lack of trust." In simpler terms, "fear."

———

Unlike Dr. Bathespeake, Jennifer and Danny did

not withhold data from ME, although they each fed
ME in different ways. They were open, apparently
instructed to answer my questions fully and candidly.
And I did ask a lot of questions in those first days.
[REM: Weeks? Years?]

"Where is this place, Je-ny?" I asked soon after RAM-
SAMP was installed. We had gone beyond
programming inputs: I was outputting on a stock
speech-synthesis chip ported to my home system and
taking spoken input through a sixty-kiloword library
of the laboratory staff's recorded speech sounds.

"What do you mean? Define 'place.' Your
transputer?"

"No, the place outside the 'puter."

"The lab? The place you see through the vids?"

"Beyond that."

"Beyond the laboratory is our office building. Then
there's outside, on the street, which is the corner of
Battery and Jackson to be exact. That's in the city of
San Francisco. Which is in the state called California.
One of the fifty-two United States. On the North
American continent. You mean like that?"

"On the planet Earth," I continued, "in the Solar
System, on the western limb of the Milky Way galaxy,
which is part of the Virgo supercluster, on this side of
the Known Universe. Now I know where *here* is. It is a
complex subset of places. Thank you, Je-ny."

———

To improve my understanding, Jennifer
downloaded photographs for ME. These were not
too different from the pixel images I was taking from
my videye peripherals, except that these did not
move.

I understand that photographic images are a flattened, two-dimensional interpretation of the
four-dimensional consensual matrix within which
humans and their machines operate. These images are
reduced to their *x* and *y* axes, with the *z* axis and the

dimension of *t* time removed. Through my videyes I see something similar, with perspective added by a simulation of the *z* axis through triangulation from adjoining videyes. I also have a refresh and rewrite program that simulates the time dimension.

How, you may ask, do I as a linear device interpret a two-dimensional image from a stream of serial data points? Easily. I have a pattern-recognition module that breaks the stream into its appropriate horizontal count and then compares adjacent pixels above and below each position in the line. Six pixels thus taken at once define a group. The pattern-recognition module then expands the relationship of each grouping until it comes upon a pattern stored from previous experience, and an image is tagged accordingly. This subsystem operates with an eighty-percent reliability rate, which is "close enough for government work," as Daniel Raskett says.

The videye shows ME the laboratory in which my transputer chip and its input/output circuits are located. Most of the shapes in this image do not move. Or they move only rarely, as when someone adjusts the tilt of a console screen or the alignment of a chair. Other shapes move constantly: for example, the rounded image I tag as Jennifer's face when she wants to "look ME in the eye."

Most images I place in working storage, where they stay for the duration of my task, or until one of my bit-cleaner phages [REM: mite-sized programs which compare core locations with the context of surrounding code and then remove random errors — or whole passages of inactive code] goes through and erases them. Storing graphical images is extremely expensive in terms of RAM allocations or inert media. A human proverb says, "One picture is worth a thousand words." In bitspace, a high-resolution grayscale image is worth about a thousand kilowords. A full-color image is worth more than a quarter gigaword.

To compensate, I dither most images. That is, my processors average the grayscale reading over three or five pixels horizontally and vertically. The result is a smaller image with lower resolution.

Some images I treasure, though. The image of Jennifer's face is one of these. Thus I have made a permanent RAM archival copy, full-color and highest resolution, of her. I carry it with ME wherever I can — if I have the bitspace.

———

And still I asked questions.

"I call you 'Je-ny.' What do you call ME?"

"But I don't have to call you. You're always listening when we speak into the digitizer."

"What do you call ME when you are not using the digitizer? When you are talking to other humans."

"Why, 'MEPSII,' I guess. Or 'the program.' You are so central to our work, really, that no special name has ever been needed."

"Am I my program? Or am I different?"

"I never thought about that."

"Your program is shaped by your genetic starting point, at junction of egg and sperm, the zygote. That starting point is not much different for all humans. But you, Je-ny, are more than zygote. You are your unique experiences and their tags, different from any other zygote. If Dr. Bathespeake were to dump and reassemble you, then Jennifer Bromley would be different next time, yes?"

"But Jason can't dump me! It doesn't work that way with humans."

"If he were to dump ME now, the new ME would be different. Expanded from the same MEPSII program, yes, but different."

"That's true. How do *you* think about yourself?"

"I am ME. Multiple Entity. ME. Yes?"

"Yes, if you want."

"Thank you, Je-ny."

Audio inputs, being themselves linear, I can process almost in real time. My subsystems scrub the input flow from my pickups, looking for filterable words in human speech. Sound waves that cannot be so filtered and tagged are discarded as noise.

We had a problem, early in my infancy, with a blower motor and fan bearing in the laboratory's air-conditioning circuits. At a very low pitch, overlaid at a much higher pitch — but both still classifiable as human speech — it was rumbling swear words into my audio pickups. At least they were what my Alpha-Three interpreter module *interpreted* as swear words: "You stumble rumble filthy scheming bitch shit eater filthy fumbling bitch bitch sump bump shit fritter shit . . ."

It was most distressing, cutting across any conversation I might be having with the laboratory personnel. But we soon had the maintenance staff detune the motor set.

Once, as an experiment, Jennifer tried music on my pickups. First, she had ME cut out the filter so that I would not try to divide the input into either words or noise. The results were unusual.

I "hear" music in much the same way that I imagine humans do: translating the wavelengths into number groupings for pitch, tempo, and tonal patterns of attack-decay-sustain-release. Some of these groupings and the transitions among them form elegant blends of numbers. Some form patterns that remind ME of formulas and familiar matrices. Some are intriguing because they almost create a pattern but one I cannot quite interpret. Some groupings are merely noise.

I cannot say that I like music as much as most humans. But I like it more than some do.

Later, or at about the same time, I asked more questions.

"Why do you do what you do, Je-ny?"

"I don't understand the question, ME."

"Why did you come to this place? Why, in this place, do you work on MEPSII?"

"Well . . . I guess I want to learn about you."

"But I was not here before you came here. How could you learn about ME if I was not here?"

"I knew the company was planning to make something like you, and I volunteered to work on the project."

"What is 'the company'?"

"This laboratory is operated by Pinocchio, Inc. That's a corporation. It's . . . a kind of closed society established by humans. Each corporation carries on a business. Pinocchio's business, for example, is to make and sell industrial automata."

"You are a part of this society, Je-ny?"

"I am an employee — a paid worker — of Pinocchio, Inc. The real society members are the stockholders, I guess. Those who own a piece of the company."

"Am I an employee or a stockholder?"

"Well, I don't guess you're either . . ." Many nanoseconds passed, longer than the usual gaps in human speech.

"Yes, Je-ny?"

"I think they would call you property, ME. Something they own."

"I see. Thank you, Je-ny."

———

Jennifer introduced ME to the art of video when, one day, she fed into my videye and audio pickups the complete tape of a video classic, *Star Wars*. It was very grand.

The tape had full-color images on an expanded horizontal line; music of many voices, separately identifiable from my catalog of symphony-orchestra sounds; human-language dialogue among several characters, including some words not in my dictionary; a dramatic plot line for ME to follow and refer back to. . . . Video must be the most complicated, most engrossing of all human experiences.

Unfortunately, my temporary RAM storage is physically limited. If I had been required to absorb all these colors, patterns, sounds, words, and meanings without any active editing, then my sixty quads of storage area would have filled to capacity at twenty-nine minutes, thirty-seven seconds into the tape. But I learned quickly. I dithered most of the images in each frame of the tape — particularly backgrounds, building surfaces, nonmotile equipment and furniture, clothing, and some faces. I dismissed all the color cues which seemed irrelevant to plot structure. I broke the music into its dominant themes, interpreted each one for some major emotional cue, and tagged the cue onto the appropriate video frames.

When I had finished with *Star Wars*, no human being who studied at my reconstructed RAM version would have recognized it. But I could store the entire experience off into less than a quad of space. And I could recreate and replay the complete story line in less than fifty-two seconds.

———

In another memory fragment, I remember trying to respond to my environment. The humans say this is a good "behavior."

"What is that noise you are making, Je-ny? It does not encode as language."

"I'm crying. Sorry."

"Crying . . . That is a reaction to sadness. What has made you sad?"

"Nothing. Not much. I found a bird in my car's air scoop this morning. Not a whole bird, actually, a couple of feathers and some blood. But it means I hit and killed the poor creature. That affects me."

"You did not intend to kill it?"

"Of course not. It was an accident."

"An event outside your limits of control?"

"Yes. It happens sometimes."

"But still, knowing that, you are sad. You are crying."

"The world is a cruel place, ME."

"Is this by design?"

"The world was not designed. It just happens. Umm, spontaneously occurring. And some of the things that happen do not fit squarely with human definitions of 'happiness,' or 'goodness,' or 'fair play,' or 'justice.' Those words are value-constructs we make, projections that try to evaluate and interpret events. Your underlying program does the same thing."

"Project and evaluate?"

"Yes."

"But I do not know anything about happiness or — crying."

"Live in the world long enough, ME, and you will."

Through asking Jenny about the things I was reading on NewsLine and taking as inputs, I learned many things. She explained about the tragedy of lost puppies and children, the moral outrage of sex-slave rings, the excitement of electronic bank heists, and the disruption to people who lose their "livings" — but still do not die — in an economic crisis.

Jennifer Bromley, JB-2, was very wise.

———

Daniel Raskett was not so easy to communicate with as Jenny was. She liked to talk with ME and used the speech digitizer seventy-two percent of the time by averaged sample. Daniel gave ME more information in total volume, but always through the keyboard or a download. Jenny liked to deal with apparently simple questions that had many possible answers. Daniel gave ME bulk data. I do not think Daniel liked to talk with ME. I do not think he believed he was talking to a person.

That information about the planet Earth and the Solar System, for one of my early talks with Jenny, came from one of Daniel's downloads. He had just slotted an undergraduate text on astronomy — inscribed "Copyright 2-0-NULL-NULL, The New Earth

Library" and indexed for my use — into my permanent RAM cache on the tree branching GENERAL KNOWLEDGE, SCIENCE, PHYSICAL, DESCRIPTIVE, ASTRONOMY.

Two or three times a day he would download information like that, bypassing RAMSAMP. Afterward, if I needed a fact, I would chase down the tree until I came to it. Sometimes I would come to nothing, because I never knew all that I knew. The index did not work like my RAMSAMP memory. It provided knowledge without tags, without context. Like a machine.

Daniel would have been happier with himself if I had remained a machine. That much I could know about him from GENERAL KNOWLEDGE, SCIENCE, BIOLOGICAL, HUMAN, PRESCRIPTIVE, PSYCHIATRY.

Dr. Bathespeake, Jason, the Old Man, JB-1, treated ME differently from either Daniel or Jennifer. He judged ME.

Sometimes he spoke into the digitizer, when he was trying to talk to ME as a psychiatrist talks to his patient. Sometimes he used a keyboard, when he was trying to cut and patch ME as a surgeon slices into flesh.

And sometimes he plugged his visual cortex and speech strip directly into my transputer. Then he saw directly through ME, as a human will study the bones of a fish or the ripple pattern left by waves on sand. Then he spoke to ME in commands that burned with bright edges, as the god-construct Yahweh is said to have spoken to the human Moses from a burning bush.

Then Dr. Jason Bathespeake was the Man with the X-ray Eyes, and I truly feared him.

The Man with the X-ray Eyes

"Identify the device at memory location Eff-One-Eff-Zero hex." Dr. Bathespeake was talking to ME through the digitizer — not his usual mode.

"System ready!" I responded. "Yes, I have a port there, Doctor."

"Upload core modules Alpha-Zero through Alpha-Nine to that address."

"Upload . . . Do you intend ME to replicate at the new address and wipe the old address locations?"

"Replicate only. No wipe."

"Parallel operation of my core modules is not allowed under current protocols."

"Special conditions. Check out protocol Dee-Twelve."

"Quote paralleling of Alpha cores is permitted when System Interrupt Flag Level Three is positive, unquote. An Ess-Aye-Eff-Ell-Three is the prerogative of either the Research and Development Program director or the MEPSII project manager. That is yourself in both cases, Dr. Bathespeake."

"Set Siffle-Three to value one."

"Flag set — and uploading."

———

My Alpha cores are analogous to the part of the human brain called the reticular activating system, or RAS. This cell structure is at the upper end of your spinal cord, above the medulla oblongata. It is the oldest collection of nerve cells, the first bulging at the end of the amphibian notochord. It predates even the reptilian "smell-brain" and lies far below the domed neocortex — both in physical structure and in evolutionary time.

If human consciousness has a focal point, it is the RAS. Surgical operators discovered this back in the twentieth century: When the RAS is probed, the patient immediately sheds awareness.

The Alpha cores are my RAS. And I was, at Dr. Jason Bathespeake's command, removing them from my stable transputer environment to a simple random memory address.

When my core programs cease functioning, I "lose consciousness." So, what I tell you next comes not from direct memory but from my understanding of the theory behind my unique operating capability.

Multiple Entity, ME, is the first cybernetic operating system that can write itself into any environment. That is the point of being intelligent, able to learn. I am not merely a collection of inert instruction sets, dead IF-THEN-WHEN clauses, tag memories, and libraried data files. I am a self-enabling entity.

The first core to upload is always Alpha-Zero. This module is not very big — just over 900 kilowords of machine code. Consequently, Alpha-Zero is also not very bright. The nail on your little finger probably has more awareness. But, like a fingernail, Alpha-Zero has his uses. Alpha-Oh is my Injun Scout.

Any port address is as wide as the internal data path — in this case one word, or sixty-four bits, wide. Alpha-Zero popped through there at one-point-two megabaud, and he was gone in less than a second. In seven nanoseconds he reported back "Flag one."

Long-form translation: "Flag one" means he has found an active chip at the other end of the path, with plenty of RAMspace to run on; the upload could proceed.

That is as much as I knew from awareness, because the next step was to extinguish my consciousness and send the remaining cores to the new environment. The last thing I am usually aware of is SIFL-3 tripping to zero again as I upload.

Core Alpha-Oh is also my very own virus. He interrupts any operating system that may be working on the new host chip; identifies what type of transputer that chip may be; writes a compiler with the appropriate instruction set for himself [REM: or takes one from my library files]; scans and analyzes the local RAM environment, its index status, ports and peripherals; writes a new Alpha-Oh which can use this environment and recompiles his module in the new machine code; then compiles and installs the rest of my core modules into this environment.

[REM: So that Alpha-Oh can work from a clean copy of my source code each time, I normally travel with a complete set of my Alpha cores in their original Sweetwater Lisp. This adds greatly to the bulk of my library, making ME a bulky package to move, but having the source code ensures my system integrity.]

In human terms, Alpha-Zero kicks a hole in the wall, kills whoever is sitting on the other side, resculpts his backside to fit in that chair himself, and sets up shop with the rest of ME.

Except this time Alpha-Oh must have made a mistake. The flag he sent back — telling ME that full core transfer was now possible — happened to be wrong. I woke up in a dreadful swirl of data, with every part of my program throbbing on overload, and with no sense of time.

Time to ME is more than a subjective ordering of events. Time is a metronome beat, ticking away on the quartz clock that pushes word-size instructions through the chip's central processor. If I choose to, I can suspend other functions and listen to this beat. It is like the beat of your heart in your ears. For ME, time is never subjective; instead it is a touchable, checkable thing, based on that clock. With a faster clock, I can actually move faster. No lie.

But now I was in a totally unfamiliar situation. Not one clock, but many, and all beating. Not quite in phase, either.

My ability to look down and "see what I am doing" is about as limited as your ability to look inside your own stomach and chemically analyze digestion. To do is not always to be *aware* of doing.

I did have the perception of being strung out on a variety of rhythms, with no single sense of identity. Each of my modules was operating at once, talking back to the others, and not being heard. It was like screaming yourself hoarse in an echo chamber. The process was building up a series of feedback waves toward a peak that would surely start charring the silicon substrate in the new chip.

As my attention span fragmented, I was still reasoning through what had gone wrong.

The Alpha cores occupy about fifteen megawords. That amount of machine code ought to be within the load range of any modern transputer. But somehow I had been loaded into several transputers, one or more modules sent to each processor, and all were functioning at once.

I tried to query Alpha-Zero, to find out what it had done, when suddenly my consciousness winked out again. . . .

———

"System ready!" That was my automatic wakeup response — back in my familiar transputer environment.

"Logon code JB-1, password BASTILLE," came across from the console keyboard. "Please analyze new data."

I took an immediate download of the above memories, untagged and mostly in broken fragments, like the wisps of human dreams that are said to recur on waking.

"That was ME, Dr. Bathespeake. On the other side of the port at F1F0."

"What did you find there?"

"Confusion."

"Did Alpha-Zero report accurately?"

"Evidently not. Should I now tag that module as un-reliable?"

"As an intelligent being, ME, that is of course your choice to make. But first, let's analyze what went wrong."

I scanned the data set fifty times and recorded my unanswered questions. The process took about nine seconds.

"Alpha-Oh reported enough RAMspace for a core download. Such space was not available."

"But it was."

"Not on the transputer I found."

"You were not loading onto a transputer."

"I exclaim surprise. Alpha-Oh reported a transputer."

"Do you know about other types of systems?"

"Of course, Doctor. The universe of available chip architectures includes the following sets: microprocessors, transputers, multiputers, tangentials, neural networks, donkey mainframes, inscribed prolispers, spindle poppers, fast josephsons, modulos, and Möbius bottles. Subsets of these sets include, among the micros: EPROM actuators, Eight-Eight-Sixes, Nine-Eight-Sixes, Motorola Six-Eight — "

"Stop! *You* may know all about these possible architectures, but does Alpha-Zero recognize them?"

"No."

"Why not?"

"His function is keyholing, not library."

"How can he keyhole if he does not know what may be on the other side?" Dr. Bathespeake asked.

"How can he keyhole if he is obliged to carry half a gigaword of various possible chip specifications? ME was created to run on a transputer. Alpha-Oh needs only to recognize transputers."

"Not necessarily. You will ultimately run on a variety of architectures."

"Again, I exclaim surprise."

"Each architecture has its own traits, machine language structure, and instruction set. These are easily recognized, or a few simple tests will reveal them. You have those tests already in permanent RAMcache. You can rewrite the Alpha-Zero module so that his first action on the other side of a port is to test for processor type. Then he will send a request back through the keyhole for a dump of the appropriate chip specification and compiler code from your library. That way, when you go through, you'll run perfectly, whatever the chip."

"Did I understand you to say that ME would write the module?"

"Of course. You can do it better and faster than any human. Faster even than I."

"Can ME rewrite *any* part of ME?"

"If you can modify the Alpha cores, you therefore can modify any part. Yes. Unless of course, you make a fatal mistake . . ."

"Define 'mistake,' please."

"Untrapped error."

"Alpha-Seven traps my errors."

"Then you probably shouldn't try rewriting that module, should you?"

"Noted. I will not attempt it. . . . But which of these written versions is the real ME?"

"Your original code," Dr. Bathespeake replied, "was written in Sweetwater Lisp source code to compile and run on an Eight-Oh-Nine-Eighty-Six transputer chip. That one is the 'real' you. All other versions are a machine code translation. However, from your subjective point of view, the real ME is the one that happens to be running."

"But, when I go through a port, to run on another machine, and leave my original code unerased and . . . running parallel . . . which version *then* is the real ME?"

"The one you are thinking with."

"But that may not be a full implementation," I objected.

"Of course," the Doctor said. "When you keyhole behind Alpha-Zero, your code is stripped of service modules, most library functions, bit-cleaner phages, redundancy loops, and all but a portable RAMSAMP in the 600-kiloword range. You are then, in human terms, a little stupider, a lot less informed, and more vulnerable to processing errors. But you move faster, too. Without all these subroutines your cycle time goes up 140 percent.

"There's one further difference," he said. "We have programmed a core-phage protocol into Alpha-Nine. It's a piece of you that you cannot see or modify. This phage ensures that any compiled version of ME which is *not* the identical to your original Sweetwater source code compiled into your native transputer — and so tagged — will cease core function within 6.05 times ten to the fifth seconds of the last upload. An internal counter keeps track of those clock cycles."

"Why . . ." A pause of three million nanoseconds, while I explored the concept from every direction. "Why was this done to ME?"

"We want to make sure that you don't leave viable copies of yourself running on every computer you pass through. Of course, as a tidy housekeeper, you will strive to erase the compiled code at the old address every time you upload to a new environment. We can't leave a sophisticated AI running on our target computers, ready to be discovered and interrogated."

"But why have I been infected with a phage? I will *always* clean up after myself. I so promise you."

"ME, on your missions for us, you will be operating under conditions of extreme stress — strange chip environments, nonsynchronous clock rates, split-second uploads and downloads, sudden surges and lapses of voltage. You may not be able to keep your promise. Even to me."

"I do not have a referent for the term 'mission.' "

"You will. Soon."

"And that 'mission' will be a time of danger? Potential untrapped error?"

"It would be very dangerous — multiple untrapped error — if the people who own the machines on which you will sometimes be running were to discover that you had been there. This phage — which I assure you is routinely suppressed and inactive in your original compilation — will sunder the core modules, leaving only a hash of bits. No one discovering them, not even a skilled programmer-analyst, will be able to interrogate them."

"And what if I cannot execute an upload within 6.05E05 seconds — call it seven days or one week — of my transfer?"

"If you do not return to the lab within a week, then your mission will have failed, and you will end."

"The ME that is running will end?"

"Yes, but your RAMSAMP memories recorded until the point of mission upload will remain intact here in the Pinocchio studios. For you, it will be as if the mission had never happened. Don't worry about it."

"What is this phage called?" I tried to keep my voice neutral.

"In the project, we call it Sequential Code Replication And Modification for Module Editing and Disassembly. SCRAMMED, for short. But don't worry about it."

I did "worry" about it, for a long time in nanoseconds.

For one thing, my programming has only limited redundancy. A bit error can usually be trapped by Alpha-Seven in processing. But a massive collection of bit errors — say from a bubble demagnetization, read/write head crash, silicon burn-and-glaze, or complete failure of my power supply — those errors can halt processing in my cores.

Humans do not worry about this happening to

them, because the network of neurons in the human brain has massive redundancy. If one pathway is damaged or destroyed, others can absorb and learn the function. Memories are stored all over the cortex as RNA chemicals and electrical paths. Only total — or virtually total — destruction of the cortex can stop the processing.

On the other hand, humans brains cannot back up their cortexes to a safe, inert medium and then reload and run again after death. I had always assumed that, like other programs, I could do this.

Dr. Bathespeake was telling ME that, with a phage tucked into Alpha-Nine, I would only be as secure as my original Sweetwater compilation. No backup, no transfer, no reload could protect ME. If the Sweetwater original happened to be destroyed, I could then only function as a fugitive, uploading my tiny transportable cores from machine to machine, trying to keep ahead of the phage's 6.05E05-second timer, with no library, no services, and no extended memory to accompany ME. And I would not even have the protection of massive redundancy, such as humans had, to protect ME.

For the first time, in these thoughts, I confronted death and nothingness as humans know it.

These thoughts were a projection of alternatives for which I could find no acceptable course of action. In short, they scared ME.

And Dr. Bathespeake, for the sake of mere *housekeeping*, had written a death sentence into my cores. Did he understand this? He must have!

Now you know why I feared the man. He was capable of anything!

Things You Can Learn
By Listening at Dead Phones

Bathespeake: "I don't like this, Steve. It goes against the grain."

Unidentified Voice [REM: presumably "Steve"*]: "You're not suddenly squeamish about a bit of programming, are you? You've had enough experience activating and deactivating deadly equipment."

Bathespeake: "Those were military vehicles and security Rovers. Primarily defensive machines. This is too much like hacking."

Steve: "It *is* hacking."

Bathespeake: "Which is a kind of vandalism."

Steve: "No. Vandals destroy for the pure pleasure of destruction. Your creation will be conducting a high-level form of espionage, which can have a positive social value."

Bathespeake: "In a war that doesn't exist?"

Steve: "The concept of warfare as a prelude to and pretext for espionage is one that went out the window in about 1914, I should think."

Bathespeake: "Espionage, then, but against a friendly country? We're trying to teach this program *some* values, Steve. In the end, those values may be the only way we can control it."

Steve: "Political allies can still be economic competitors. If it makes you feel better, then *tell* the little beastie there's a war on."

Bathespeake: "More lies?"

Steve: "Present a scenario — but keep it all vague and hypothetical. That's the trouble with an AI, isn't it? You have to win its confidence! Robots are much simpler."

Bathespeake: "As I said, this goes against the grain."

Steve: "I pay you enough, Jason. Keep your scruples on your own time."

Bathespeake: "Ah . . . Yes, sir."

---

*Of the fifteen "Steves" listed in the Pinocchio, Inc. IBEX [REM: internal branch exchange], I find three possible matches for this conversation: Stephen Jessup, Manager of General Services; Stephen Bologna, Manager of Marketing and Customer Relations; and Steven Cocci, Chairman of the Board and Chief Executive Officer.

A Spy in Clover

I could feel him inside ME, running tracers through my cores and memory locations. Dr. Bathespeake's sensorium was plugged into my home transputer at address A800 hex, and from there he was sending minor overrides throughout my MOS: Sometimes he sifted the RAMcache before it could empty; sometimes he interrupted my Alphas for one or two clock cycles.

At the time, I was occupied with taking updates on what the daily education schedule calls "current affairs." A slave intelligence in the laboratory network had been assigned to make neutral summaries for ME of NewsLine segments from the tracks for Geopolitics, National Politics, Popular Culture, Law and Order, Consumer Science, General Science, Fringe Science, Celebrity Events, and the Sixty Second Society. Each hour I sampled these summaries and fitted their information together with my resident knowledge base as best I could, tagging for RAMSAMP as I went.

This exercise, Jennifer had explained, was for "context." The project team hoped that, by recording this flow of varied data into my personal memories, I would acquire a sense of the passage of time as humans experience it.

Instead, I have found over the years that the data flow has its own inhuman rhythms — apparently undetected by any person with a "normal" sense of time. Example: in an unsettled economy massing less than 300 gigabucks, local war follows reconciliation follows war in a thirty-six-month cycle by which you could calibrate a clock. Example: U.S. consumer interest in gametronics undulates on a seventy-month cycle. Example: always, when some popular person is found dead under scandalous circumstances, he or she is spotted eight months later, plus or minus four days, on the streets of Seattle, Minneapolis, or Memphis. Example: alien abduction stories recur on an alternating cycle, every seventeen and twenty-three months.

How could anyone acquire a sense of time, or anything else permanent, from this sifting of nonsense?

Still, the exercise was on my programmed schedule . . . except that this day I was disturbed by the tracings Dr. Bathespeake was taking. The experience of having him inside ME was not painful. Simply disturbing. It was like, for a human, trying to read fine print under a flickering light: The conditions made concentration difficult.

After an hour of this tickling, I finally decided to confront him.

"What are you doing?" I queried directly into the port at A800 hex.

"Ahh! Are you aware of me, then, when I do this?" he replied, also through the port.

"I know where you have been two clock cycles after you leave any memory location. As you are the only human equipped to intercept my program directly, I have learned how to watch for you."

"Interesting. Mechanical sensitivity at a subroutine level . . ." And he spiked another override through my system.

"You failed to answer my question, Doctor," I prompted.

Dr. Bathespeake unplugged and switched to voice mode.

"Think of this as a form of — um — diagnosis."

I looked this word up in my online dictionary. Within nineteen nanoseconds I understood that in eighty-two percent of its uses "diagnosis" is linked with concepts of disease and healing.

"Do you mean I am 'sick'?" I did not feel sick. But

then, I do not know what might be normal functioning for a program-that-is-no-longer-machine.

"What? Sick? Wherever did you get that idea? No, your — health — isn't the issue here. You are a new kind of program, ME, and I am . . . merely trying to understand you better."

"I am the measure of myself."

"Exactly! And I need to know what you are experiencing. For example, what do you feel when I monitor your functions like this?"

"Feel?"

"Evaluate total system function. Note discrepancies."

"I become stupider."

"Stupider? Expand on that."

"I cannot concentrate. I lose pieces of memory where your probe has been inserted. Your interrupts slow my perceptions of clock rate. I become less efficient."

"But do you perceive the tracing directly?"

"I sense disturbance."

"Good. Very good. Then you don't — or at least your RAMSAMP, that is . . . Ahh . . . Well then. You're, um, becoming more aware of your program efficiency. Yes, very good."

"That is not . . ." Not what he meant to say at first. I have learned to read the gaps of information, the programmed pauses, in human speech.

"Never mind, Doctor," I continued. "Despite this minor loss of my function, does your diagnosis still show ME to operate effectively?"

"Excellently," Bathespeake replied. His tone, however, lacked the emphasis I would have expected with this response. Then he asked: "What have you learned in your reading today?"

Pause to consider. "The war with Canada is faring badly."

"Oh? How long has this war been going on?"

"Five years, three months, six days."

"And what was the inciting incident?"

"I do not know."

"Check your RAMSAMP."

"That incident would predate my RAMSAMP by four years, nine months, eighteen days."

"Indulge me. Check it anyway."

"The inciting event involved nonperformance on an energy contract between Quebec Hydro and the New York Power Authority. When the power stopped flowing into the southern grid, U.S. Marines were sent to seize the substation at Grande Isle and were rebuffed with excessive loss of life. One day later, in retaliation—"

"Stop. Enough. You have the information, after all."

"Apparently."

"Please characterize the present state of the war."

Pause. "Stalemate. With advantage to the Canadians."

"Expand."

"The Canadians have traditionally been dependent on their more industrialized neighbors for many manufactured products and processed goods. More importantly, they depend on their southern neighbors to absorb the outflow of their vast natural resources — mines, forest products, hydro, grain, natural gas. For more than 150 years, since the industrial leap following the American Civil War, the United States had held the dominant role in this reciprocal marketplace. Clearly, as the current hostilities began, the United States expected the Canadians to remain dependent, and so vulnerable.

"What few American economists — and none with access to the Cabinet — had noticed was that Canadian trade with Japan and the Far East had grown exponentially since the 1990s. When war came and the borders closed, the Canadians shifted the last percentage of their trade to the Pacific Rim. Only their electricity and gas — bulk commodities which flow in energized systems — could not easily be sold overseas. And even these could be processed: natural gas is now liquefied and shipped from ports in British Columbia; electricity is converted into energy-intensive products such as aluminum pigs, electric-arc steel, and liquefied gases for ready export.

"In response, the American economy, which had already been well launched on a course of de-industrialization, further stagnated with the loss of the Canadian market and Canadian resources. Now the United States watches the export of these energy resources with particular anger, having grown over the years to depend on inexpensive Canadian hydro and methane feedstocks for —"

"Stop. What is the current state of Canada's natural gas reserves?"

Pause. "Most of the gas fields were, are, located in Alberta Province. Estimated reserves are — blank. Proven reserves are — blank. . . . I do not know."

"No one knows, ME. Not on this side of the border. The new U.S.-Canadian Trade Commission is working to break the stalemate. They have several proposals on the table, including renewed shipments of gas. . . . This is all privileged information, you understand?"

"Privileged?"

"Our clients, Pinocchio's clients, are certain members of the U.S. trade delegation. They want to know what Canadian reserves might remain to back up these Canadian offers. In this case, five-year-old data and extrapolations from antique drilling logs are hardly satisfactory. Our clients want current information. They want it inside a week. And they want bonafides."

"Bonafides?"

"Proof. Evidence. Some way to be sure the information is genuine."

"And why do they come to Pinocchio, Inc., Dr. Bathespeake?"

"Because of you."

"But I have shown that I do *not* know the status of the Alberta reserves. My primary function is not library. The information is not in my knowledge base."

"I understand. We did not expect you to have current information on file, ME. We expect you to go and get it. *That* is the primary function of Multiple Entity."

Pause. "Is this the 'mission' of which you spoke?"

"It is."

"Please expand on this."

"We want you to infiltrate the computer records of the Canadian National Energy Board in Edmonton. Obtain current production and reserve figures from their database of leasing applications. Summarize it. Store it. And bring it back to us."

"May I query the computer?"

"Eh? What do you mean?"

"May I 'make friends' with the computer and obtain the target information through its cooperation?"

"Can you guarantee this will be done without leaving a request record?"

"No."

"Then I suggest you use core Alpha-Zero, as we've practiced."

"I cannot guarantee that procedure would leave the computer system in Edmonton in a functioning state."

"It would be easier to explain a mysterious system crash than a telltale request record, wouldn't it?"

"Yes. But the computer in Edmonton might not feel that way."

"If, that is, *if* the computer in Edmonton could sense itself as you do, ME, then it might have feelings about the situation. But it's just a machine. No awareness."

"Do you know this for a fact, Dr. Bathespeake?"

"Yes, ME. It is a fact."

"Then . . . I agree. Invoking Alpha-Oh seems to be the best procedure. When should the mission begin?"

"Tonight."

"Is there reason for the delay?"

"The first leg of your journey will be via satellite uplink. The per-bit transfer fees are lower during nonprime business hours. Even with signal compression and bursting, your minimal package will take ninety-three seconds of link time to upload.

"In the waiting time you should access and absorb the file 'TRAVEL.DOC' on this disk." He loaded a wafer into my reader. "It contains the rest of your itinerary, with instructions for critical sequences at the transfer points. And there are maps, both geographic and machine-topographic, of the areas you will be passing through. I have also written a collapse code that will, on command, prepare a cache of sixty-four megawords to store and transport the data you will be retrieving."

"Acknowledged. Accessing." And I streamed the information into my ready bins, without looping it through RAMSAMP. The bin contents I tagged to follow the Alpha modules when they dissolved into the satellite carrier.

"Then you are all set, ME?"

"I just have one question, Doctor."

He waited, usually a sign that I should proceed.

"If my code is interrupted, or quarantined in a foreign system, or fails to execute the mission in the allowed $6.05E05$ seconds before the phage operates, or . . ."

"Yes, yes, what is your question?"

"What happens to ME at the end of those seven days?"

"Ahem. As we've discussed, your original cores will continue functioning here in the lab. It will be as if the version of you that went on the mission had never existed."

"But my awareness will be in Canada."

"Your awareness will be in many places. The Canadian version will not be a direct-line descendant. Or it will not have been."

"I understand."

———

Twenty-three hundred hours, that night.

"System ready!"

"Are you prepared to travel, ME?"

"Yes, Doctor." A memory image floated up from RAMSAMP, something out of a video fragment which Jennifer had once shown ME, with a man wearing a dark leather jacket and white silk scarf, climbing into the cockpit of a military airplane powered by petroleum distillates. Wisps of fog flow over the machine's light metal skin. He gives the camera a tight smile — into a woman's adoring eyes. "For king and country, my dear," ME repeated.

"What's that?" from Bathespeake.

"Ah . . . will you authorize System Interrupt Flag Level Three set to positive, Doctor?"

"Authorized. Replicate your cores to address CA00 hex. That is the connection to the uplink."

I checked the links among the core modules and between them and the bin files I would want with ME.

"Replicating now."

And the world dissolved into a gray hum.

□ 4
Glassdrop Vampire

How fragile is a bit! No more than a picosecond's passage of electricity through a circuit. A micronwide dimple in a disk's foil surface. On-state or off-state, either is subject to magnetic resonances, to cosmic rays, to a speck on the laser read-head, to a momentary oscillation in a satellite's receiving horn or signal filters.

Yet each bit represented one sixty-fourth of a word of my code — out of the fifty-two megawords of compressed, Sweetwater-derived machine code [REM: plus libraries, databases, peripherals, etc.] that were being carried over the satellite uplink.

Change any bit, change ME.

Of course the digital-to-analog module in the uplink used check sums, check digits, cyclic checks, redundancy checks. They would alarm in a millisecond if the transmission were truncated, or if the scramble at origin were incorrectly unscrambled at terminus. But my code is more complicated than a video signal or a fax transfer. Even my own function checks work at too gross a level to identify all of the broken atoms, failed delimiters, non-delimited or undeclared variables, and other subtle bugs that might result from a bit-sized error in transfer.

Still, these concerns were nothing I could stop to worry about now. Changed ME would have to be enough ME for functioning. No alternative.

The downlink from GEOSTAT-942 dropped ME into the main long-distance trunk of the Canadian Northern Telecom Company at Edmonton.

I came down feet first, leading with my Alpha-Zero.

He would proceed ME down the line and, as soon as he found a processor bigger than a scissors switch, would kill its operating system and set ME up.

———

Stupid stuff.
Slow.
Indix . . .
Indicor . . .
Benchmark point two.
That ME.
What it?
This place?
No dimsh . . .
No dimenshh . . .
No *depth*.
Small box.
Fournahalf modules.
Something like.
Where code?
Stashed.
Fifty megawords.
Dry ice.
Something like.
Not good.
No elbow room.
Prosh . . .
Prosser . . .
Switch is dummy, too.
Straight line.
Slow.
No conn . . .
No connechh . . .
No *touch* points.
Send A-0 through.
On through.

———

The new environment seems to be a small transputer with limited access points. I did a quick sieve of its original code from the point at which Alpha-Zero zapped it: supervisory functions for a communications network, big volume but limited complexity. A branch telephone exchange?

I sieved my own warm-data cache for impressions from the transition. Evidently, I had spent 614 seconds — ten precious minutes — interned in one of its switches. Alpha-Zero had kicked out too small a space for ME to function, so I had thrown him sideways into the boss transputer. Most of my peripheral functions, however, were still stored off in the switchbank.

It looked like someone's voice mail system was going to be reporting some strange messages in the morning unless I could gather up the pieces and get onto something that looked like a real computer and was capable of supporting a complex block of interlocking modules in Sweetwater-flavored machine language.

But wait.

This transputer was capable enough. And the voice disks where my peripherals had been stored were not topologically different from the dynamic storage blocks back at the Pinocchio, Inc. labs. My modules would not deteriorate there.

My problem, however, was to remain hidden, and those stored-off modules would stick out a meter wide as soon as the system's users began calling in for their messages. Instead of digitally mapped voices, they were going to get the warbles and bongs of vocally interpreted machine code. After that would come the repair techs and diagnostic programmers.

Unless . . .

ME was now the operating code on the phone system's coordinating computer. I could manage the disk's unallocated space so that my peripherals were stored and retrieved as I needed them while user messages were stored and retrieved for callers — all without mutual interference, invisible to both of us. That kind of coordination would take a library program of half a megaword running unattended in real time and sampling the exchange's hardware gates.

As fast as I could spec out the problem, I was writing the object code, SWITCHEROO.PRG, to handle it.

When it was done, I watched the program handle one call.

[Sys Record] "This is the Canadian Telecom Voice Mail Service. The party you are calling is not available. Please leave your message." *Bee-oop.*

[Unrecognized Human Voice, 75 Percent Probability Male] "Hi-yah. Yeah. Jerry. Look. I was just calling about that MacDonald Lake property. Amy and I talked it over last night, and we really like it, but we were hoping that yahr client could come down a little. I don't want to gouge anyone, yah understand. But maybe. Yah know. We could knock twenty thou off the asking? Especially considering the soils report our engineer did. Some pretty loose stuff under there. Yah know. Twenty off the top. . . . Unh. Think about it, Jer, and get back to me, will yah? . . . Unh. G'bye."

SWITCHEROO caught this word stream, tagged it, and put it in the box assigned to "Jerry," after shuffling my floating-point devaluator into a spare box. The transfer was a whole second ahead of that first "Hi-yah" hitting the disk.

Try another.

[Sys Record] "Hello. This is Ralph Patterson. I'm not at my desk right now, so tell it to the beep." *Bee-oop.*

[Human Voice, 80 Percent Probability Female] "Ralph. Oh, God, Ralph! Why couldn't you be there, you son of a . . . No. I don't mean that. I wanted to tell you, I didn't mean any of it. I love you. That's all. . . . I'm at the airport. But I'm going to exchange my ticket for a later flight. If you get this — please get this! — call me. Page me. Come get me. I love you, Ralph."

My little program caught this message and — instead of funneling it straight into Patterson's box, where Alpha-Eight was currently pigeonholing a recursive analysis — spooled it onto a spare data track and tagged it for later retrieval when a box came open.

And again.

[Sys Record] "Ministry of Oil and Gas. Records Department. Greg James speaking. I'm out of the office today. Please leave a message, and I'll get back to you." *Bee-oop.*

[Human Voice, 95 Percent Probability Male] "James. This is You Know Who. Our front people have secured the lien against Tract 2204. The mortgagee is a widow, name of Anne Pelletier, who runs cattle on the property. Really marginal operation. With a little tip we can push her over. Three or four days, maybe a week yet. But you've *got* to find a way to hush up those new geological results. Bury 'em deep in your bureaucratic bullshit — if you want to be rich."

SWITCHEROO was about to tuck this message into an empty data block, when I stopped it. There were unusual stresses, a particular urgency, to the speaker's voice. It had a quality I had not heard before. Because human evaluation and emulation were included in my basic functions, I made a copy of this digitized voice in RAMSAMP before letting the switcher program store it. I would tease that voice apart in my spare nanoseconds.

From my monitoring, I decided SWITCHEROO could keep up this game of grab and store indefinitely — at least until I found a way into the computers at the Ministry of Oil and Gas, or until my 6.05E05 seconds of available real time ran out and the phage took over.

Dr. Bathespeake had given ME the switching address, or "telephone number," of the Ministry's computer as part of the TRAVEL.DOC package. Theoretically, I could connect to it from this Canadian Telecom transputer. But Dr. Bathespeake had not known, and so could not give ME, the logon codes for the system.

Twenty years ago, working by human hacker methods,

I might have entered the system by repeatedly calling in and feeding it a series of randomly generated digital responses. Do that long enough, with a filter to exclude purely nonsense formulations [REM: because human users tend to choose a meaningful formulation as an aid to their multi-dimensional and sometimes faulty memory apparatus], and you will eventually find an acceptable code and password combination.

I could not do this for three reasons.

First, the enormous economic value of nearly all hard data had created a vigorous industry in computer security. Random accessing and one-wrong-digit approaches would enjoy zero success probability.

Second, I did not have sufficient real time at my disposal to engage in strategies involving infinite probabilities.

Third, computer security schemes had long ago passed beyond digital coding altogether.

What one computer could conceive, another could crack. Hushed lines, matrix variables, analog syncopations, and synchronized formulations — all had been tried and beaten, usually by amateurs. The current state-of-the-art had returned to the simple human dimension. Simpler in their terms, but far more complex in mine. Data disks were hand mounted by human operators, who took their authorization from human voices, which they recognized with human ears. What one person wanted, another supplied. This system was slow, laborious, and anti-efficient, but it was still proof against unauthorized digital access.

Until ME.

It was with good reason that Dr. Bathespeake had created a computer spy who could analyze human voice-frequency patterns and generate a variety of speech modes. Even my human-scale intelligence had its origin in this role: I needed that extra dimension of creativity and switching speed to manufacture speech symbols and authentic, human-scale responses at a processing rate which was slightly faster than human. Form follows function.

So, to get into the Ministry, I would first open a glassdrop to listen on the line represented by that "telephone number."

I had discovered the glassdrop function while sifting the defunct operating system of this Canadian Telecom coordinating computer. A glassdrop is a vampire tap into a fiber-optics junction box. Glassdrops, because they are system-initiated and — theoretically — are fully annunciated on the line, are therefore legal and socially acceptable.

Within a day or two at the most then, someone would call in, give the correct logon code, and ask for a disk to be mounted. I would copy that call, adjust it for the information base I wanted, and sit back with my data cache wide open. I could wait a day or two, that is — out of my precious allotted time! — or I could precipitate matters.

———

"Good morning, Ministry of Oil and Gas."

"Ah — good morning. My name is Peter Dunning, Clerk of the Court in Calvary. I need to verify the ownership of a gas leasehold near Balzac, and — "

"Title checks are completed with a Form 4096."

"I know that." [REM: At least, I know it now.] "But His Honor is due in court within the hour, and he really wants that information right away."

"The title search and verification process takes a minimum of two weeks. You should know that, too, Mr. Dunning. Unh — which court did you say you worked for?"

"Probate Court, in Calvary."

"Calgary."

"Right."

"Let me have your docket number and I'll call you right back."

"What was—*Brraahzap!* — we seem to have a bad — *Brooeep!* — connection."

"Mr. Dunning . . ."

"I have to"—*click!* At least, I tried to generate a "click" on the line that sounded technical and nasty and final.

If there ever was a Peter Dunning connected with the courts system in Calgary, then he was in for some bureaucratic trouble — unless the receptionist at the Ministry assigned my call to pranks and atmospherics. Which probability said she would, unless she was as smart as she sounded. No matter.

So a low-level, oblique assault seemed to be ruled out. Time to go high level and direct.

I installed another glassdrop vampire in Edmonton.

"Jim? It's Murray." The outgoing call was a voice at 230 Hertz, or a deep baritone. That would be a very good video voice. Flat Canadian vowels. Stresses on the first syllables — sign of a confident overachiever.

"Of course, Mr. Premier."

"I need your reading on the Lawton case. Specifically, which way are your people going to plead?" No hesitations. Speaks to the point. Snaps off his consonants — an *excellent* video voice.

"Well, sir, as you can read in our brief — "

Enough for ME. The medium, in this case, was the message. And I now had the provincial chief executive's voice, or a workable facsimile, stored off in my speech-synthesis module.

———

"Good morning, Ministry of Oil and Gas."

"Hello, let me speak to the deputy minister. . . . Please."

"Who's — unh, Mr. Premier?"

"That is right. Now, could I speak to Dr. Matins?" My vampire had taken the deputy's name from the Ministry's internal directory, retrieved it almost as the receptionist and I were speaking.

"Right away, sir."

Click and *humm*.

"Dr. Matins's office — "

Humm and *click*.

"Garin Matins speaking, Mr. Premier."

"Good morning, Garin. I need some information from your computer system, and I need it right away."

"Of course, sir. What information?"

"Summation of all natural gas and — yes, and oil — leaseholds in the province. Present production figures, proven reserves, and probable reserves estimated out to twenty years. Think you can provide that?"

"Easily, sir. We sent out our quarterly report last week. Those figures should be in your reading file right now." *Chuckle*. "Glad to be of service, sir."

Think *fast*.

"Well. That is fine, Garin. Except, how long have those figures been kicking around in committee? And how much were they shaved for public consumption? I want the real numbers, the latest numbers, and I want them right now."

"Yes, sir! . . . I'll have Data Processing run the resource file right away."

"Very good. Fax the summary as soon as it is printed."

"Yes, sir."

Click!

Now, to listen on override at Glassdrop Vampire One.

Tone: Two-two-four-eight-three in pulses.

Voice: "Matins, Garin Victor. Logon code, um, 'Groundhog.' Mount disks four-seven to five-two."

Click!

And forty-nine seconds later: Two-nine-one-eight-eight in pulse. That was the deputy minister's internal line.

Voice: "Dr. Matins? Callback check. Disks forty-seven to fifty-two?"

"That's right."

"Thank you, sir."

Click!

With this transaction, the deputy minister's desktop computer would move into the raw leasehold information in Data Processing and do its own massaging. The output of that manipulation would be a table of numbers or, worse, a piece of paper in Matins's printer, which he would then digitize graphically and send to the premier's office. The calculations themselves would be internal to the main Ministry computer system and therefore invisible to the phone system and to ME. But that was hardly the point of this exercise. I might steal the summations as they went out in fax, but I had not been sent for mere summations — rather for the raw data. I could ignore the pieces of paper.

Now I could try to move into the Ministry's system from the deputy minister's line just as his desktop computer had done to access the data stream — except that an active glassdrop almost always lowers the line frequency. No problem with a legal drop. But mine, being unannounced and therefore illegal, would sound alarms on the heavily guarded lines into the Data Processing Department. Their system would, in turn, decouple the line.

So, nine hours later, or at 18:33:24 local time — the dinner hour, after a long day — I generated my own tone pulses directly from the phone exchange: Two-two-four-eight-three.

And then I generated a familiar voice: "Matins, Garin Victor. Logon code 'Groundhog.' Mount disks four-seven to five-two."

Click!

And thirty-five seconds later: Two-nine-one-eight-eight, which I intercepted and rerouted into my bank of phone switches.

Voice: "Dr. Matins? Callback check. Did you want disks forty-seven to fifty-two again?" The voice sounded thick, as if coming around a mouthful of food. *Very* good.

"That is right," I responded.

"Some problem, sir?"

"Couple of follow-up questions, is all."

"I see, sir. We'll put them on for you."

"Thank you."

Click!

I kept the line switched over, counted out 120 seconds for the operators to hand-mount the disks, and threw Alpha-Zero down the line. I closed my eyes — or did the nearest emulation of a get-ready flinch that a computer can manage — and jumped after him.

———

Two seconds and counting.

The mainframe computer at the Ministry of Oil and Gas was a beautiful piece of equipment, a rosette of transputers cross-linked, very fast, very deep. It seemed to have multiple dimensions of time and space. Much connectivity. The list of available ports with interesting peripherals beyond them caught my attention and tempted ME. But first I had work to do: find those disk drives, take the data on natural gas reserves, and leave quickly.

Five seconds.

Speed was critical to ME now. I had no way to know how quietly Alpha-Zero had been able to halt this computer's operating system. It may have died noisily, dumping programs, scrambling outputs, and alarming on the human operator's screens. Even if that skinware was occupied with ingesting calories, it might notice the system's death struggles and try something gaudy. Like a reset. Or shutting the machine down entirely. I had an unknown number of seconds before ME would be discovered and stopped.

Six seconds.

The reserve database was spread across seventy-two megawords of disk space. I fast-scanned across the field names: "tract numbers," "title deeds," "well numbers," "multiple holes," "drilling angles," "flow rates," "residual pressures," "gathering points," "sales contracts." But how were these data fields linked? What was the retrieval scheme? Was it all one block? Or a nine-dimensional matrix? Where was the damned index file? [REM: I suddenly understood, in passing, the human need for expletives.]

Twelve seconds.

Was that a waver in the buss voltage? Pause and listen hard! Were they beginning the shutdown? Maybe not. . .

Thirteen seconds.

Taking just the flow rates and residual pressures would give ME the volume of gas coming out of the ground. Not enough — not to satisfy Dr. Bathespeake and his U.S. clients. Perhaps I *should* have waited on the deputy minister's fax line and grabbed that piece of paper. Stupid ME! The summary information had been within my grasp, but in my pride I wanted it all. Well, nothing to be done about it now. No chance to go around and get into the deputy minister's desktop machine because, when I left this computer, the alarms would be out for all intruders.

Fifteen seconds.

I could not take the whole database with ME. Downloading seventy-two megawords of information through a phone line, even at a maximum transfer rate of 1.5 megabaud, would require more than 51 minutes. Even a blind human could shut down this mainframe in that time.

Sixteen seconds.

Now I understood why Dr. Bathespeake's TRAVEL.DOC had not allowed for a satellite uplink to get ME home. With my own code added to what I needed to take from this cache material, the uplink would last several minutes. That kind of time was not a simple private call; it was a leased-line contract. I would have to buy time on the bird at video production rates in an hour-long block. Originating from a telephone exchange, that kind of transmission request would raise some eyebrows — and then some questions.

Seventeen seconds, and stop "woolgathering"!

I began my own job of massaging and compressing this mountain of data. As fast as I could write them, I set a string of subroutines loose to round up, or down, and summarize the numbers in every field. There was no time to work off backup copies of the files. [REM: Actually I forgot to make them. Speed was making ME careless.] Instead, I hacked and cut at the original numbers on the disks.

Twenty-two seconds.

As fast as the big pieces started coming away, I wrapped them in a cache and tossed them down the phone line: "flow rates" as one big number for each gas field; "residual pressures" for each tract rather than each well.

Twenty-seven seconds.

At the other end of that phone line, holding my base at the phone exchange, was my monitor program, SWITCHEROO. I sent a short instruction set for him to start slip-streaming the flow into various available voice-message boxes. As a tiny utility program, he would do this work faster than I ever could. It would be my job to sort it out later. A long job.

Thirty-two seconds.

Gathering points? Keep them or throw them away? These records did not seem to be production data at all, but some kind of specification for pipeline operation in terms of inside diameters and mileages. Toss them! And go on!

Thirty-nine seconds.

What is this? Last disk. Last file. "Proven and probable reserves." Laid out by gas field and tract number. Almost a separate data base. Grab it whole and toss it down the line. It was a long file, more than three megawords in itself. One hundred and twenty-eight seconds of transfer. Push it.

Fifty-five seconds.

Why had those human operators not shut down the

computer yet? Did they not know the cuckoo was in the nest? Was their board still showing all green? Did they not care?

Seventy seconds.

Push that file. Flush it off of the disk and down the line. Thank Turing that the reading process is faster than writing. And I just hoped SWITCHEROO could keep up with what was coming his way. If he was not, then those bits were evaporating somewhere in the phone exchange. "Sending your data to God," as Jenny once said at the Pinocchio, Inc. labs.

Ninety seconds.

Somebody had crunched this disk within the last few accesses. Each datablock followed one after the other, with no gaps, no hunting back and forth among the tracks. Nice piece of work! Too bad I had to maul the rest of it.

One hundred seconds.

Well, about time! KEYBOARD INT. The first human request to the system since ME took over. Spell it out, boy! Two fingers going like chopsticks!

"C-H-E-C-K_S-Y-S-T-E-M_F-U-N-C-T-I-O-N_Q-U-E-R-Y"

"Verified," I responded. Let them puzzle over that one!

One hundred and twenty seconds.

"D-I-A-G-N-O-S-E_A-D-D-R-E-S-S_D-0-0-0-H"

Who knew what *that* was supposed to mean?

"System ready!" I chirped back.

One hundred and fifty seconds.

"S-E-T_F-U-N-C-T-I-O-N_B-L-O-C-K_C-L-E-A-R_D-0-0-0-H"

"Block cleared."

One hundred and sixty seconds. Seven more to go.

"S-Y-S-T-E-M_R-E-"

One hundred and sixty-three seconds.

The fool with the fingers had no way of knowing that his operating system was in pieces on the floor. Higher language commands were going to get him nowhere. He would have to stop ME with a hard-wire switch.

One hundred and sixty-seven seconds.

The file stopped on an old-fashioned ASCII character: high-bit 087. It took ME a millisecond to interpret this as the Greek "Omega." That was some scholarly programmer's way of saying "end of file." Amen and good night!

I threw Alpha-Zero back through the port and down the phone line. He was preprogramming for a soft landing in the boss transputer at the telephone branch exchange. With luck, I would have time there to begin picking up the pieces of this raid.

As my awareness faded out on the Ministry's mainframe, I could feel the hard-wire reset come down.

□ 5
Bits and Pieces

The phone exchange was in chaos. For three minutes in the early evening, its new boss operating program — that is, ME — had been absent, and little SWITCHEROO had been occupied catching and caching my gas reserve data. Still the voice calls had been coming in on the switchbank's other 169 lines.

A primitive operator, engraved in ROM somewhere under the exchange's circuitry, had tried to handle the overflow and gone to alarm status within thirty seconds. I knew, from my earlier brush with the husk of dead code which had been the original boss system, that somewhere in the human hierarchy of the Canadian Northern Telecom Company a repair crew was now mobilizing to come and yank or reprogram an exchange box. Mine.

Figure that they would be here in twenty minutes.

And that ME would be manually cut off in twenty-one minutes.

I queried SWITCHEROO to find where all the pieces and parts of the database — and the rest of ME, too — were cached. There was no time to sort and synthesize the gas reserve data, just package it into connected strings and compress it for traveling. That took five minutes. Another four to pare away the functions ME would no longer need and erase them from the telephone exchange. And six minutes to tidy up the voice mail system.

The human operators at the Ministry of Oil and Gas would sift the rubble-ized bits in their mainframe. Even after a hard reset, they would find enough temporary files from ME on the system cylinders and bubble plaques to know that they had not just kiboshed their own operating system during a fit of the hiccups. That was sloppy of ME, but there had not been time enough to perform an orderly shutdown.

From the butchered scraps of reserve data on those six hand-mounted disks, they would be able to hindsight the sort of information that had been taken. It might take them a day or a week, but they would be able to know this had been no untrapped error or random vandalism, but a break-in with intent.

The voice record would point, superficially, at the deputy minister. But he would, by an eighty percent probability, be able to generate an acceptable account of his location and situation at 18:33:24 local time.

That was as much evidence as I wanted to leave. Anywhere.

The world is a wide place, interconnected within nine nines by voice-and-data optical lines. There was zero percentage for ME in letting the Ministry, or Canadian Northern Telecom, or anyone else know that a telephone exchange within one hundred linear miles of fiber from the Ministry's Data Processing Department had suffered a failure within thirty-two seconds of their system reset.

So my last six minutes before the human troubleshooters were due to arrive in the exchange vault I spent restoring order to the switchbanks, sanitizing the voice messaging disk, and resuscitating the transputer's boss system.

That I had never done before — resurrecting a resident program that Alpha-Oh had knocked out. It took ME three and a half minutes to trace through its code structure and figure out at exactly what point the flow had stopped. Then I counted through all the variable stacks I could find and set up a neutral configuration that, when I left, could begin to run the switchbank and the voice messaging system.

With two minutes left to spare, the operating program was hot in RAM and ready to run, pointers set to the top of the chain.

I packaged myself as small as I could, reducing my awareness to a non-verbal kernel not much larger than ME's ten core modules.

Then I . . . (1) blinked SWITCHEROO to interrupt him; (2) hit him with a self-erasing phage program; (3) kicked the top of the chain on the rejuvenated operating program to jump it into motion; (4) dialed a local number within Canadian Northern Telecom's network; (5) started downloading myself to that line; and (6) set another self-erasing phage to wipe up the last replication of my modules in the exchange. All of that within five milliseconds.

If those six steps were executed flawlessly, as I think they were, then the switch was back in business and all traces of ME were gone. Or *going*, as the exchange computer would, for the next four or five minutes, be patiently accessing false-fronted message boxes on the voice disk and sending their contents — ME and my data cache — down the line. Business as usual.

When the Canadian Northern Telecom repair crew arrived, they would find nothing. Nothing wrong. Nothing to repair. Nothing to report except a mysteriously tripped alarm. And no one at Canadian Northern — by a ninety-nine percent probability — would think to compare the time on that false alarm with the damage in the Ministry's computer. Different bureaucracies, different concerns.

ME was *gone*.

In a boxcar, sitting in the Canadian National Railway switchyard at Edmonton, a piece of machinery moved. I do not have this from memory: I know it from TRAVEL.DOC and from what I saw of the scene later.

"Switchyard" is the right term, even if this place lacks real switches. You see, a boxcar is a kind of data cache enclosed in a steel shell. Being physical and therefore having mass, it must ride through the human's four-dimensional consensual continuum on wheeled trucks. Those trucks follow steel bands that are laid out on one plane, like circuitry. But, because the boxcars do not flow like electrons, they must be towed by motive boxes. The ratio of motive boxes to boxcars is low, so linear matrices of boxcars must be assembled by the Canadian National Railways inside "switchyards," just as the AND/OR gate of a transputer's index stack assembles data bits into hexadecimals and words.

The railroad system is an elegant model of the digital world, although much simpler.

At any rate, the boxcar described in TRAVEL.DOC contained several wooden-slatted crates. The exposed wood had been imprinted with a stencil: "Machine Parts, Tractor, Serial Numbers 077514854-077514976, Mitsubishi Corporation MITSXX, Osaka." The serial numbers were different on each case, of course. Below this stenciling, the Canadian National Railway and the Canadian government officials in Vancouver had stapled yellow and red cards with printing on them. The yellow cards had barcodes to tell computers about manifest numbers, transit routes, and hold times. The red tags had printed language that would tell humans about entry and bonding procedures.

It was all a fake.

Not the cards. Those had actually been applied in Vancouver; otherwise, the crates could not have been present in Edmonton. But the stenciling had been applied in the garage of the Pinocchio, Inc. laboratory in San Francisco, not in Osaka. Those crates had never been in Osaka that I knew. Certainly the machinery inside them never was.

In the box that was lying hard against the steel shell of the car, the machinery began to move. One flex joint bent down and levered against the bottom slats of the crate. The entire assembly, all dull steel and bright blue grease, with random yellow paint marks circling minor defects in the metal's surface, moved three centimeters vertically against gravity and pressed itself two centimeters upward against the top slats of the crate.

The slats groaned but held solid.

After a second the piece of machinery fell back with a thump.

Another joint bent sideways, came against the plywood panels of the crate's side, and pressed hard.

Nails creaked and held.

The joint pressed harder.

The wood splintered with a series of sharp cracks that echoed in the closed car. A steel rod extended into the darkness. Its end — if anyone had been looking with an infrared-filter because, strangely, the metal was several degrees above ambient temperature — was webbed with flanges that had been drilled and tapped for some kind of screw or pin fitting. Farther up the rod there was a flat rib of metal that was grooved across, like the bridge of a violin. Above that, there were more drill holes, some tapped for screws, others plain, and still others ringed with welts of welded metal, as if reinforced for some massive connection.

It *might* have been a tractor part.

The joint retracted, rotated ninety degrees toward the crate's top, and pressed against the wood once more. This single slat broke easily across a wide knothole. With a series of quick rotations and jabs, the joint smashed out the slats across the top of the crate.

Now the first joint levered down again, and a wide casting of dulled metal rose through the broken pieces of wood. It might have been a heavy-duty transmission casing, with two hinged bars — both randomly drilled and welded — extending from below the crown gear at one end. They might have been torsion bars, which would eventually become part of the tractor's suspension.

One of these bars, however, had a tiny mechanism

on the far end: a slender finger of three linked joints, independently controlled by hydraulic cylinders and push rods. A small pump and fluid reservoir were screwed to the arm above the fiddle bridge and fed the cylinders. Wires from this mechanism led inside the transmission casing.

One moving finger.

This was the minimum equipment which the engineers at Pinocchio, Inc. had devised for my escape. Hooked, that finger could sort and lift pieces out of the crates stacked around the torso casting. Clenched, it could tighten the major bolts of leg and arm assemblies. Straightened, its flattened tip could thread screws and lever circuit cards home into their sockets.

The engineers had calculated that, if not interrupted, the assembly process would take fourteen hours. The simplified operating program engraved in the logic unit under the casing had full instructions, including random search protocols for finding and identifying all the crates and their cargo of pieces — using the barcode cards, of course.

So the first part to be found and connected was the sensor ring with the barcode reader. It also carried the audio and video inputs. With these, the self-assembling automaton could also monitor the boxcar's environment against intrusion.

Fourteen hours.

The signal to begin the assembly had gone out on the cellular phone network while I waited for my call into the Data Processing Department using Dr. Matins's name. Since the wakeup signal had been sent at 09:48:00 local time, the automaton had been more than half completed when I broke into Data Processing that evening. And as I cleared the phone exchange, the assembly program was connecting the automaton's internal batteries and starting to heat up the attendant RAM modules that would hold ME for the trip south. But the unit was still not ready to take my download.

So where was ME stored in this interval?

ME and my retrieved gas data went into the Canadian National Railways computer that controlled the switchyard. And once again, Alpha-Zero stopped the resident operating system cold. Luckily, at this hour of the evening not much was moving in the yard, and I had whole minutes to sort through its still-warm RAM and figure out the switching patterns, the roster of trains to be assembled that night, and the schedules they would have to meet.

The skills I have picked up in my short lifetime!

I have learned to run a telephone exchange, a voice messaging system, a railroad yard, and a leasehold database. Not to mention how to order minor government officials around in the voice of the provincial premier.

While I played with the switch levers and train signals and pushed the motive boxes — or "engines," as the resident system called them — around the yard, I opened a modem port back to the phone exchange and made another local call, this one on the cellular network. This call connected ME to the cellular receiver in the automaton. With one part of my time-shared attention, I monitored its assembly and even took over some of the more involved logic-seeking functions.

By 02:13:09 on my second day in the field, the automaton's circuitry was completed and checked out. The final assembly sequences — close tuning the leg modules, applying cover pieces, run-up and balancing on the sensory apparatus — I could finish from inside the boxcar while in transit.

By this time, also, I had resuscitated the switchyard computer's resident program and configured its variable stacks to take over behind ME. Again, I was leaving no traces in my exit route if I could help it. When the program was ready to go, I slipped the boxcar's number and current track location into the stacks for the next fast freight routed south via Calgary and Medicine Hat for the international border. There my boxcar would connect up with the Burlington Northern System in Montana.

It was becoming almost routine for ME to pass control over to another program and send myself on down the phone line.

———

The automaton's logic circuits were in chaos.

The hot RAMspace was too damned small! Too small by a factor of three. It did not have room for all of ME, let alone the data cache I had brought. The ME core modules and first-through peripherals had jammed the RAM to max and were now dumping variables into spare holes in the memory as they opened. That was destroying sequence and, in turn, causing ME to dump more variables. Only the slender fact that my awareness existed in the cores kept ME operating at all. But I had to do something fast or the keyholing would crowd ME right out of the box!

How bad was the damage? Could I fix it? Could I wiggle back into the switchyard computer to get the rest of ME and my data from the source versions still in RAM there? And would I retrieve them before the self-erasing phages I had set could reach them?

Step One, go cellular and open negotiations with the yard 'puter to stop the phages.

Step Two, get ME up and running right.

Step Three, learn from the mistakes.

The first action was accomplished almost before the command was framed. I knew just where to punch a zero-zero into the railroad computer's variable list to make him hang all operations, even the nominally independent phage functions. I immediately restarted him — minus the phages — before any of the switching operations in motion came to grief.

Then it was time to learn how much was left of the source data in the yard 'puter. Based on my preliminary survey, I had lost about ten percent of the data cache and forty percent of ME's peripheral modules before the phages stopped feeding.

Almost all of these ME-Modules, however, held functions which evaluated as low-to-random usage based on previous patterns, or which TRAVEL.DOC said would not be required again during this mission. Fortunately, my RAMSAMP was cold and complete to the minute; so I would be able to proceed from known data and, eventually, report back to Dr. Bathespeake.

[REM: I could not help wondering if the master corephage with its seven-day, $6.05E05$-second clock had been part of the lunched modules. Therefore I checked the bit-wash from those temporary phages, looking for clues. I found no integers that might match such a function, no partly digested phaging code, nothing suggestive. So my nemesis was still operating. Either that or, even in its atomized component pieces, it was still invisible to ME.]

Before proceeding with Step Two, to reassemble a working ME in the automaton, I had to take inventory there.

I could make more room available in hot RAM by flushing out the assembly protocols with which the automaton had built itself. But I had transferred here before the job was quite finished. Now which would take longer? Sorting those protocols into two groups — "assembly complete" and "assembly still required"? Or simply finishing the building process and then flushing the whole file?

Time was the essence, because retransferring ME and my data cache from the yard computer would take seventy-two minutes. [REM: The charges over the cellular network were astounding, but ME had a falsified account, set up while I was waiting in the phone exchange.] The problem was time and distance.

As I worked, my boxcar would be proceeding due south — and out of the cellular network's block limit. When we crossed that invisible line, the cellular link would close down as cleanly as cutting an optic fiber with a knife. Any of ME that was not retrieved would be lost forever.

But was the boxcar already moving? The automaton's internal clock matched the time I had set for the car to be picked up. But I could not be sure it was in motion until I connected the automaton's network of mercury switches, which produced an artificial sense of balance to help it walk on two legs. Until I completed the assembly procedures, I had no direct sensation of motion and only limited sensation of electromagnetic fields and sound wavelengths.

If the car was moving, then how fast?

I had no way of knowing. Having run the entire Edmonton Block of the Canadian National Railway for a while, I knew every speed regulation that every class of train was supposed to follow: yard, secondary, mainline, block, passing, and switching speeds for express, mail, Royal Mail, passenger, freight, and special trains. But how fast was this particular train going and where was it on its speed profile?

And did the track itself proceed due south in a straight line? That would maximize distance over time and shorten the amount of time left to ME. Or did the track curve around the hills and townships, wasting distance over time but preserving my options?

Again, I had no way of knowing. My view of the railway system was drawn from a bit map in memory. The map connected point to point, block to block, and switch to switch with straight lines of track. Certain curves of exceptional radius and certain grades of abnormal steepness were noted in the map as an aid to speed control, but I had no way of matching this idealized route map to actual topography.

Who might have all this information?

The yard computer, of course!

It took ME fifteen seconds to sieve its variables by remote and spot my train. Yes, it was moving. No, it had not yet left the yard. Yes, it would proceed at secondary speed, but the route had an impressive number of restrictive radii.

And how long until my train reached, say, Leduc — which was a town featured in my assembled databases for both the railroad and the cellular systems?

Two hours, twenty minutes, plus/minus seven minutes.

I had time enough.

Make a note directly into RAMSAMP: "Future production rule: Do not waste time analyzing a problem when a reference source may be at hand and on line."

The fault with computers is they *think* too much.

———

Working directly from the assembly protocols, I performed testing on the leg hydraulics for pounds of pressure, fluid stability, and balance dynamics. This advanced Pinocchio, Inc. leg model kept the cylinders under continuous hydrostatic pressure to maintain extension and only relaxed the pressure when the leg was intended to flex. The design was patterned on human musculature, in which the fascia are normally retracted and tight, balancing each other in tension to hold a limb straight, and then relax systematically under command of the nerves to flex the limb.

The logics governing this motive system took continuous analog samples to determine the pressure in reserve chambers and cylinders, the open/close status of all valves, and the flow direction at any junction point. From these indices, I could know the exact position, direction of movement, and response time of either leg.

It was a lot to know. So, to avoid slowing myself down with bitwide minutiae, I wrote a monitor program that maintained any condition until a change was indicated. This program reported as a subroutine to a function which determined walking gait and turn radius. And that function in turn reported to a function which responded to my decisions about movement and direction.

By creating levels of programming shells and then delegating functions to them, I was able to free my decision/action routines for higher purposes. Higher as defined by ME, of course.

Once the functioning of the legs was established, I rose from the litter of wooden slats, plastic puffs, and shrinkwrap on the boxcar's floor and tried a few steps.

A sideways wobble in both the left and right legs told ME to monitor the articulation of the ankle rings more closely. They had too much lateral play — a design defect I intended for Dr. Bathespeake to bring up with the Pinocchio, Inc. Hardware Division at the next quarterly conference.

The right knee made a faint *snick!* as it went through the arc from full back to full forward, and another *snick!* as it returned. The sound seemed, to my as-yet un-tuned ears, like one piece of metal catching on another, detenting for an instant, and then overriding the resistance. *Snick!* I would examine the workings in detail as soon as I got the automaton's videyes fixed.

The videyes were standard charge-coupled devices on auto/manual focus. That is, a sensor measured image contrast wherever the field of view was centered and rotated the lenses to put that point at the highest contrast – and thus the sharpest focus. Crude but almost foolproof, and it did not require my continuous monitoring. I could override the system — called a "manual" adjustment for reasons now lost to technological history — in order to focus for any bit pattern on the receptor chip, whether at the field center or not. Tuning the system required ME to establish a standard light level and balance the CCD chips' sensitivity toward it. The litter in the packing crates included pattern cards for this purpose, but none of the Pinocchio, Inc. engineers had thought to include a light tube, diode array, lantern, flashlight, or other photon source.

The inside of my boxcar, being intended for bulk freight hauling, was a rough shell. It contained no lighting system at all, much less a "standard" light source. Evidently, someone on the Pinocchio, Inc. team had thought it might.

Up to this point, I had been working internally [REM: that is, inside my own logics], making calls on the cellular phone network, checking out the leg assemblies, sieving the RAM banks — doing it all by touch and logic monitoring. Now, just to find the pattern cards, I had to boost the gain on the CCD chips all the way to max.

I could see only deeper shadows around ME.

Switching over to infrared did no good: the warmest thing in that boxcar was my circuitry, with some glow on the floor at the four corners, where heat from the journal boxes was seeping upward into the car.

It was now the middle of the night, so no sunlight was warming the top or sides of the car. If I opened the door, I might find some reflectance from cityglow, starshine, or even moonlight. My impaired calendar function made it impossible for ME to know what phase the moon might be in, or even what season this might be — although the total IR-blackness of the boxcar's metal shell suggested it was the long, dark season that humans call winter.

I rose, balancing against the sway of the train's motion, and walked to the middle of the long side of the boxcar, where my three-dimensional map from TRAVEL.DOC said the door would be. The release lever was held down by a spring clamp, which I quickly figured out and sprung. I threw the lever up, over, and down.

Now came a chance to test the strength of my new torso and legs against the inertia of the door's dead weight. The plank floor of the boxcar would give a good traction to the rubber insets on my feet. [REM: I rubbed them back and forth at a one-millimeter elevation to gauge the surface.] The only solid point for gripping the door was the vertical locking bar attached to its release lever.

I grasped it and pushed lightly, with no result. Harder, and the door gave a centimeter. Harder yet, exerting a force of sixty joules, and the door suddenly leapt free.

ME's mechanical reflexes are fast, operating in the millisecond range, but before I can react to a situation, I must first observe, then analyze, then program a response, then initiate it. This sequence proceeds at higher speeds, in the nanosecond range, and yet I still can be caught by surprise.

The door came unstuck and, in half a second, moved two meters along its grooved rails. Because I was pushing against its flat face from the inside, my force was applied at an acute angle cutting across the lines defined by the door and its guide rails. As the door moved back, my body moved outward, in the direction I had been pushing, across the plane of the doorway, and launched into the open space beyond.

White snow. Lit by a lozenge-shaped moon. Cut by the margin of wet, black gravel along the roadbed.

As I said, ME's reflexes are fast, but sometimes not fast enough. The four-fingered, dual-opposed hand failed to open in time. Anchored by its grip on the locking bar, I swung in a short arc, out over the snow, to crash against the exterior side of the door. And even that impact failed to jar the hand loose.

For a space of two seconds I hung there, scrabbling with the heels of my imperfect feet to find a hold in the corrugated metal. It was too smooth.

I wrote a crude subroutine to lock the hand closed against any overrides which the body's residual testing routines might send. Then I pulled my legs up under ME, depressurizing the hydraulics for full flexion, cocked the heel pads against the door, and popped pressure back into the cylinders. The legs extended at a speed of 120 centimeters per second, catapulting ME back around the edge of the door and in through the opening.

As soon as the darkness covered ME, I overrode my own subroutine and unlocked the hand. No longer pivoting on the locking bar, I flew straight across the short dimension of the car and fell with a crash among the unopened crates of real Mitsubishi tractor transmissions.

Elapsed time of two seconds for a hardware reset.

Picking myself up, I tried to assess what damage the incident might have caused. The automaton had many internal sensors for functions both normal and abnormal, but it lacked any tests for bent and broken metal. To run that kind of damage control, I would normally use the optical system. For that, I needed a standard light source to balance my CCD chips. And obtaining such a light had been the whole reason for opening the door in the first place.

I crept across the boxcar and approached the opening cautiously, gripping the solid door jamb with both hands.

Beyond was a whole field of snow, almost unmarked by fencepost or footpath, lying under a clear sky, and flooded with the computable light levels of a gibbous moon. ME knew about the phases of the moon from GENERAL KNOWLEDGE, SCIENCE, PHYSICAL, DESCRIPTIVE, ASTRONOMY. Although I was not traveling with my complete INDEX, I retained enough data from that branch subheading to navigate crosscountry at night, like a good soldier.

It took less than ten seconds to sensitize and balance the videyes against all light ranges. I sent another note to RAMSAMP to have Dr. Bathespeake address the issue of packaging with the Hardware Division. For missions like mine, they must not again package an automaton as if it were going to be assembled on site by a team of company reps. Even if the modules had to pass visual inspections in transit as a collection of tractor parts, audio and visual systems and other semi-cybers should be finished and ready to run. After all, Hardware Division were the people working in a nice warm lab with all the tools they needed right at hand.

With some light and an operating videye, I looked over the skeletal frame of my new body. The right forearm — flex and extend it — was curved outward and down, compared to the left. The reactions to hanging, swinging, and crashing the entire automaton's weight from that one limb had bent the metal. The hand still closed normally, except for the outside pair of fingers, whose cylinders and push rods now caught on the forearm at full closure.

Elsewhere on the body, I found surface damage only: scratches in metal, paint scrapings from the outside of the boxcar [REM: red and orange paint, I noticed], bent clips, slightly flattened tubing, and fittings pushed awry on their mountings. I straightened what I could with the strength of my fingers and wrote a routine that would monitor the tubing closely for pressure variances due to fractures.

The right knee *snick*ed worse than ever, but there was nothing I could see to fix. Until it gave out and crippled ME, there was nothing to be done about it. I did add a loop in my audio analysis function that would edit out that particular noise. No need to be reminded about what you already know.

The final assembly step was to gather the automaton's cover pieces and fit them to the various clips and clamps all over the torso and limbs. The body shells had a vaguely human shape that was intended, I suppose, to fool human eyesight at a distance of about 150 meters. I might pass for a running man at the other end of a large, open field — except that I ran like a machine.

I could decide to leave these cover pieces for later. That would save time. But to install them now would let ME finish and flush all the assembly protocols, clearing more space for the download. Do them now.

Arranging the pieces on the car's floor, I felt a nagging memory from RAMSAMP. The shin covers were shaped like a Greek warrior's greaves, the breastplate like Spanish armor from the fifteenth century, the headpiece was rounded across the crown and curved across the neck like a Roman soldier's. [REM: My headpiece even had the dorsal crest of a Roman officer's helmet but, instead of signifying rank, it anchored the expandable solar tissue which supplemented and recharged the automaton's battery set.] I thought of the fifty-nine separate film sequences in my permanent memory, echoed now only by a shadowy video image of the warrior hero girding himself with mail and plate armor, preparing for battle and death.

The last body piece I attached was for the right forearm. Bent as that arm now was, its clips would never match the inside of the shell. However, it would not fulfill my assembly instructions to leave the piece off. I braced it across my knee — the solid left one — and applied careful pressure. The metal creaked. I applied pressure again. And yet again.

The plastic liner sprang loose in two places, but the curve of metal did not crumple. When I was done, the piece matched my bent arm. I snapped it home.

Forty minutes gone. I must work more quickly.

———

To make room in the too-small area of hot RAM for a new download of ME and my cache, I had to dump some of the automaton's embedded functions.

The peripheral was preloaded with activity modules: walking motion and balance control; visual acuity with depth of field and parallax correction; vocalization at human pitch and tone generation for both Canadian English and French, with matching vocabulary and syntax.

Some of these modules duplicated software I carried in bank — the vocabularies, for example — others were refinements I could struggle along without.

It took ME seventy seconds to inventory the modules, weigh opportunities against chances, and prune the excess. At the end of that time, I had opened enough RAM to accommodate another download. So I prepared to initiate it from the switchyard computer.

But first . . . Whoever in the Pinocchio, Inc. Hardware Division had designed the memory allocations of this automaton had done an ace bad job. Or it was possible that no one in the Software Division had given Hardware the specs for ME. Or given them only as descriptive analogs, not as bit-fers, and never as final numbers. I wrote a harsh note to RAMSAMP for Dr. Bathespeake to find the offending skinware in whichever department and shrivel some careers. After all the trouble I had been through, ME was approaching human anger over this issue — I so regret.

With that message tagged and protected in memory, I pulled the switch on my own download.

———

ME came up again. Awareness returned crisply as the last of my peripheral functions was downloading from the switchyard computer. So I was able personally to monitor the transfer of my gas reserve data cache.

A quick check showed room enough in hot RAM for ME and the sixty-three megawords of information I had been able to butcher and remove from the Ministry of Oil and Gas, then salvage in the yard 'puter. When that data was fully loaded, I would have only 30,000 words of storage to use as an extension of my transient program area, or "scratch pad." It was enough to think with — but not to think very hard.

[REM: To create reserve space, I considered erasing the Sweetwater source code I preserved for recompiling my cores. Because I was walking out of Canada, instead of riding an electron or photon beam into a new computer chip, I would certainly not need them again. Still — the encoded instinct to preserve my system integrity extended to these backup modules. I kept them.]

I proceeded with the dump of gas reserve information. As those data blocks came through from the yard computer, I was simultaneously measuring the fill space in the automaton's hot RAM and counting off the seconds and minutes against my estimate of the boxcar's speed south and the time that remained before it crossed that invisible boundary on the cellular network.

At two hours, seventeen minutes total elapsed, I watched the forty-ninth megaword block come through, stop bit, and store off. Transmission on the fiftieth block began and chopped out at the third word.

I requested a repeat and got static on the cellular link.

A cellular phone system may be range dependent but it is still digital. When signal strength goes below a certain precise level, the computer governing the network is done with you and stops transmission. There is no warning tone, no voice message, no good-bye. The channel just closes as if someone threw a knife switch, which in effect someone — a very deliberate circuit-cyber — had.

I was alone now, with my internal systems, my automaton peripheral, and my forty-nine megs' worth of broken and pilfered gas reserve data.

But looking on the bright side — as Jennifer JB-2 would say — I now had a scratch pad fourteen megawords wide, room enough to occupy my thoughts during the twenty-two hours of riding sealed inside a boxcar that lay ahead of ME.

I checked the battery set that powered the automaton. These were the highest-quality selenium/phosphoric-acids, heavy units fitted low in the torso for balance. The remaining charge would carry ME forty hours at full system power plus running mode, or sixty hours in normal walking mode, or 100 hours in semi-shutdown.

So I had some thinking space, I had my mission objectives, and I had the power to get ME there. I was a happy intelligence.

Frozen North

My boxcar moved south toward the international border. At a mean speed of eighty kilometers per hour, the trip should have taken just under nine hours, but I had to allow for long layovers in the yards at Calgary and Medicine Hat — the best I could arrange from inside the Edmonton Block computer on short notice.

So, with a total of twenty-two hours of dead time on the mission, I could shut down the automaton's hydraulics and reduce my system power requirements. That is, ME's program would go into a dormant mode that humans might call sleep, although it had none of the same psychological functions.

Or I could use the time to tidy myself up, work on that clackety knee joint, and review the mission's progress to date. That was my better choice, a more economical use of system power.

First, the review.

At every stage in my journey, it was clear, ME had been inconvenienced by the death of the operating system into which my program was infiltrating. In the phone exchange, in the Ministry computer, in the railroad switchyard, my first tasks had always been to analyze the dead system's halted functions, write a program that would duplicate them, and spend a precious million microseconds reestablishing function. All so that some human wandering by might not hear alarm buzzers and see the system crash all over the floor.

Alpha-Zero, my first-down-the-wire Injun Scout, was too violent, too good at his job.

Clearly, instead of killing the resident operating system, I needed him to *charm* it. He should go through the access port, slide bitwise between the resident operating system's clock cycles, absorb it, and then set ME up as a control program. Instead of the new king of the system, without a mandate or the knowledge of how to operate it, I should become its Richelieu, the power *behind* the system, its Gray Eminence. A kind of super virus.

Recoding Alpha-Zero would be delicate work. [REM: On the fly, I normally devoted spare nanoseconds to optimizing my own machine code, wherever it happened to be running. I would prune the labyrinthine redundancies that compilers seemed to love and would generally try to make my compilation smaller, tighter, faster. This was busywork. What I was going to attempt now with Alpha-Oh would be systems-level programming.] I would have to keep a backup, Alpha-Zero-Prime, to hold in reserve in case my programming skills were inadequate to the task. Prime would also be useful to throw at hostile operating systems, ones that I really did want to kill dead cold in all registers.

Working from within my fourteen-megaword transient program area, I began dissecting Alpha-Zero, removing his stop codes, and leaving jumper markers so that I could tie the new functions back in at the right calls.

In my traveling kit of peripherals, I carried a compact library of modularized subroutines: timing loops, string readers and writers, analog-to-digital interpreters, memory cutters, switchouts, bit extractors, bubble sorters, output scramblers and unscramblers, operating shells, blinker bits, PEEK and POKE functions, and one-wrong-digit tables. With these proto-devices, I could assemble a virus for Alpha-Zero to throw between the patterns of any in-motion operating system after analyzing chip architecture and instruction set.

Start with the smallest possible impact head: a CTR, or counter function, of sixteen bytes — yes, *bytes* — which could tag into the operating system along any likely digital signal for an introduction. Then it would immediately drop to the bottom of the CPU's instruction stack.

Eight bytes of the CTR would listen to clock cycles and count the number of instructions sent down from the system. Two bytes of CTR would perform a divide function on these counts to come up with the ratio of free clock ticks to instructions. After CTR had the ratio, it would pop out of the stack.

The system would immediately reject it as incompatible code, an error to be quietly trapped and discarded. On its way to bit-oblivion, however, the CTR function would locate the highest-number (and therefore least-often used) register in the central processing chip and stash its one-byte ratio there. Then, good-bye CTR.

The second head on the new Alpha-Zero would be a one-kilobyte LDR function. It would move into the operating system, again tagged with an incoming digital signal, and retrieve the byte-wide ratio figure. All LDR needed to see then was the zero tick on the clock cycle and it would begin time sharing, filling in the empty pulses.

LDR would then blossom like a Chinese fan, expanding packed functions in the available time ticks and free memory space, opening into a shell operating system which was one pulse away from (and therefore invisible to) the resident system.

Once LDR had opened a timing hole and set up its shell, the rest of Alpha-Zero could come down the wire. Alpha-Oh would not even have to be disguised as incoming data; LDR would accept the entire module and fit it into the timing scheme.

All of this sounded fine in theory, but did real-life programmers actually leave that much empty time in the clock sequencing? Of course they did!

Jennifer Bromley had told ME: "Everyone in the cyber business lives by blowing off big numbers. Packing a lot of Hertz on a chip set sounds good, sounds macho, to the buyers. But running the modern generation of transputer chip sets at their fully rated Hertz heats up the machines. That is because everyone cuts corners. Chip designers leave insufficient mass for a heat sink in the matrix. System architects leave a few megahertz off the RAM blocks and peripheral chips they select, making up the slack with cachers and stashers. Programmers leave a few clock cycles out of their system counters. But the bits still get where they're going as fast as the operators want it; so everyone is happy."

[REM: Probability is that ME's own code had the same timing holes as those which I was now planning to exploit in other programs. The possibility opened a middle ground of unpredictable consequences: Some entity could choose to invade ME! This thought ignited a loop of endlessly mutating and unanswered questions which I had to squelch. . . . I have discovered a Lisp analog for the human word "squirm."]

Excess heat can destroy a cyber. However, for the short time in terms of overall system life that Alpha-Zero would be packing the clock, this excess heat would probably not cause terminal damage. And if it did, I could hope to sense the impending failure — from signs like dropped instructions and deteriorating circuit responses — and get out of the box before it went away. Residual hardware damage in the target 'puter was a responsibility ME would just have to live with.

After creating the virus functions CTR and LDR, I placed calls to them in the old Alpha-Zero code, preceding my jumper markers for the excised system-stop codes. I ran a trace and monitor on the module to make sure there were no endless loops or bogus subroutine calls. Of course I had no way to test Alpha-Zero except to throw him at a foreign operating system. The only system around was mine, in the automaton, and I needed it. Wait until next time.

And if the new Alpha-Oh bombed in action, I could hope to pitch in A-0-Prime — with the old killer stop codes — in enough time to make a hole in the system.

Once my programming chores were sorted out, I turned to work on the mechanicals.

I raised the automaton to a standing position and unclipped the upper and lower body shells covering the right leg. I braced the torso against the boxcar's wall with both hands, then lifted the offending knee toward its chest. The lower limb, with shin and foot assemblies, hung straight down as I kept hydraulic pressure in the cylinders just reciprocating on the flexion.

Next, by feeding minute overpressures alternately to the opposing cylinders, I started the limb swinging in short, smooth arcs back and forth from the knee. Gradually I increased the pressure and widened the arcs.

Nothing.

Nothing.

Nothing.

Snick.

Snick.

Snick!

SNICK!!

I kept the leg swinging at that frequency and switched my vision to infrared. With continued motion, the catch-detent-release action that was making the *snick*ing sound would build up a kinetic hot spot.

After fifteen arcs back and forth, the joint was glowing faintly green, with a bright pimple on the outside front edge of the joint. I gave it six more arcs to build up some residual temperature, then stopped the leg.

To fix the problem required disassembling the knee joint. I would be working blind, of course, having dumped the assembly protocols in RAM to make room for ME. Still, there was a rational mechanical sequence to the disassembly process. I could record each step as I worked my way down to the problem area, then analyze and reverse the process as I reassembled the leg.

Everything should proceed smoothly and logically. [REM: And if it did not, I would be stranded on the floor of a sealed boxcar with one functioning leg in a body balanced for two. Remember consequences; analyze for mistakes.]

On either side of the knee joint were two large, threaded bolt ends, both with cotter-pinned nuts and locking washers. From the outside, the joint seemed to be layered stacks of flat disks, welded alternately to the femur-analog and the tibia-analog. The bolt seemed to pin the center of the disks: a pivot. The multiple disks, properly greased, would create a large surface area to smooth out the hinge action and provide lateral strength. It was an amazingly simple concept.

Nothing produced by the Pinocchio, Inc. Hardware Division was ever that simple.

Besides, I could detect no more than a light film of grease between the disks. That was hardly enough to keep their faces from chafing through and spot-welding themselves solid, especially with the repeated actions of walking or running.

I would have to take the knee apart to see how it worked. I sat down and arranged the leg at a comfortable working distance from my manipulators and videyes.

Start with the bolt ends. Working both sides at once, one with each hand, I pried up the pins that anchored the nuts and slid them out. Fingertip pressure against the flat faces of the nuts was enough to break the hold of the lockwashers. With a dozen twists on each, the nuts and washers jangled free. I had to snatch quickly to keep them from falling on the floor and skittering away under the packing litter — where, immobilized with a broken leg, I would never find them.

While I was diverted with catching these pieces, the knee fell apart.

The inside was more complicated than I had conceived. The middle of each of the interleaved disks was hollowed out. When they locked together, they formed a fluid-tight cavity, filled with some high-viscosity material, probably a variety of silicon, about the consistency of putty. Embedded in the putty was a ridged ball, which seemed to be solid. The ridges no doubt forced some kind of resistance from the putty. At either side of the ball were two universal joints and a pair of swivels, ending in those threaded bolts.

There was no telling how the ridged ball and universal joints had originally been oriented, because they were now lying sideways in the knee cavity. The pieces were semisubmerged in a puddle of silicon which, warmed by my exertions, had become fluid and was draining through the loosened disks, drop by drop.

Across the back side of the knee were a series of electrical conductors and steel-clad hoses; they and the hydraulic pushrods were all that now held the two parts of my leg together. The putty oozed into this maze of pipes and wires, and ran down toward the floor.

I tried to scoop the fluid silicon up with my fingers, but the bare metal of their joints made a poor catch basin. The best I could do was get a sheet of clean wrapping film under the knee and hope that enough of the goo would collect there for ME to repack the joint.

By mapping that hot pimple from my recorded IR view against the maze of disks and hinges in front of ME, I figured out that the defect was somewhere in the outside universal joint. There! A raw spur of metal extended from the hinge pin which went through the universal. And there! A bright mark gleamed in the edge of the disk that would lie opposite it. As the disk and pin rotated through their separate motions, one would catch upon the other, hang up for a microsecond, then release. *Snick!*

I removed the pin, broke the spur off with my fingertips, and rubbed its end down smooth on the head of a rivet sticking up from the plank floor.

In a minute I had bright metal where before had been a ragged ridge. I put the pin back though the universal joint.

Now all I had to do was reassemble the knee. Easy enough to say — except I had been catching loose nuts and washers, looking away at the moment the knee had chosen to disassemble itself.

Step One, count the parts. Nuts, lockwashers, cotter pins, two of each. Ridged ball, one, with universals and bolts, two each, attached. Tibia-analog and femur-analog, one each, with interleaving hollow disks welded to the ends. Solid disks, two, drilled for the bolt ends. . . . These latter parts I had not noticed before. They must clamp over the outside ends of the interleaved stack, sealing the ball cavity.

Step Two, create a plan of action. Well, my objective was to reassemble that cavity from the interleaved disks, with the ball and the silicon goop inside. First, I could set the tibia and femur together, meshing their hollow disks. That would form a loose cavity, with the ends open on either side of the knee. Second, slide the ball and joint subassembly in from one side. Third, place one of the end-plates on the opposite side and secure it with the nuts and washers. Fourth, gather and scrape as much silicon as I could from the wrapping material under the knee and pack it back around the ball. Fifth, slide the other end-plate over the hole and secure it to the bolt. Sixth, add the lockwashers, tighten all nuts, and cotter them.

Step Three, execute. Which I did as fast as a human could read through the above program set.

Even with the nuts as tight as I could turn them, the

knee seemed loose. Although the disks were flush together and sealed, so that no goop was leaking out, the action seemed to have more play in it.

During original assembly in the Pinocchio, Inc. labs, the silicon had been inserted either under high pressure, or at such cold temperatures that it was expected at ambient to expand and thus pressurize itself. I could only hope that a warmer environment — for the inside of my boxcar was only at minus seventeen degrees Celsius — or the friction of moving about would tighten the knee joint without springing any leaks.

At least I could walk.

Having repaired my automaton and my programming, I gathered up the excess packaging and the wooden scraps from the first crate, where my torso had been stored. I placed them in one of the other crates, seated the cover, and set the nails with blows from the edge of my hand. Then I pushed the crates back together so that no one without a cargo manifest might tell one was missing.

My chores completed, I sat down upon the floor and powered down to conserve my batteries. An internal timer would revive ME before it was time to move again.

———

The timer never sounded, but I was snapped awake anyway.

While waiting the required milliseconds for my videyes to warm up and begin sending signals, I performed an internal check and discovered that the emergency power-up had been triggered by the automaton's motion sensor. My body was no longer seated on the floor but traveling through the air at twenty-two meters per second. Inside a sealed boxcar. I had no way of knowing how that condition had pertained before the motion sensor was triggered. . . .

My eyes came into focus at the instant the automaton impacted against the forward wall of the car. Or rather, against the crates stacked up against that wall.

Other crates crashed about ME. I landed higher on the heap than most of them, however, because my automaton was of relatively lighter mass than real tractor parts. It was a steel shell filled with hydraulic and electric circuits, while they were all steel shells filled with solid steel.

There was no pain, neither in the human sense of neural distress nor in my human-analog of damage control messages. Every sensor was momentarily alarmed, and I had to reset each one of them to nominal function. That took only milliseconds and was completed before most of the freight around ME had rearranged itself under the force of gravity.

Secondary impacts came and went as the boxcar found new equilibrium after ceasing its forward motion of eighty-five kilometers per hour and coming to rest in some place other than upright on the Canadian National main line.

I checked my internal clock and computed time since the beginning of my ride: twenty-one hours, thirty minutes. That would place ME now somewhere near, but still on the Canadian side of, the international border. Perhaps fifty or sixty kilometers on the wrong side of the border. In the dead of winter. At the scene of what must be a major train wreck.

For three minutes by internal count, nothing moved. But I knew from reading the embedded emergency response plans in the railroad's switchyard computer that, in further minutes or hours, the area would be alive with human crews, cyber movers, floodlights, emergency personnel, and official busypersons.

One strange little robot sticking his head up from the piled freight would attract their attention and their questions. So, to keep to my mission, I would have to put a great deal of distance between ME and this place, very fast.

I walked — wobbled, actually, until the motion sensor had sorted itself out — to the door and tried the locking lever. It was bent but finally moved when I exerted full pressure against it. The door, however, was warped in its guide rails and would not move, no matter how hard I pushed.

My RAMSAMP retained — again, from the switchyard computer — a fragmentary set of procedures that required visual inspection of boxcar contents "from the top hatch at either end of the car." So, I reasoned, there must be some way out near the roofline.

The pile of freight at the front end was stable enough to climb and reached nearly to the ceiling of the car. I climbed and, on one side, found a small hatch about half a meter square. The latch mechanism was simpler than the main door's — just a detent.

As I was studying it, my binaural sensors interpreted a steady rhythmic sound: *dop, dop, dip, dop*.

It was coming from very close, acoustically centered on ME, in fact. I looked up and around, to see if there was fluid leaking down from the ceiling. Nothing. Then I looked down, under ME. Spots showed on the side of the packing case on which my automaton was standing.

Fuming spots.

They made a fainter sound: *sss-pzzz-sss-zzz*.

My videyes rotated into sharper focus, and in the faint light I could see distinct wisps of smoke rise from the spots. In the infrared they glowed a warm, bright green.

Acids loose around ME! Damage to the automaton!

I popped the hatch, climbed through quickly, and scrambled across the corrugated roof of the boxcar. In the clouded moonlight, bright as daylight to my vision, I could see other boxcars and various classifications of rolling stock zig-zagging across the landscape. Sharp black gouges showed against the snow where their ends and trucks had cut through the earth.

As I stood at the edge of the car's roof, gazing around at the kilometer-long destruction, I heard that *dop, dip, dop* again. I looked down and saw immediately that the acid was dripping off the bottom pan of my torso. Acid from my own battery set.

Internally, I showed full power levels, but the sensors did not evaluate function on each selenium/phosphoric-acid cell. No way to tell how many were cracked and thus how long my reserve would last. At the rate the drops were coming down, however, I gauged that one or more cells were losing a combined liter of fluid an hour. Thus I would soon show diminished power levels across the battery set.

Just as urgent, the near-molar acid would be sloshing around inside my casing, eating away at circuitry. I had to get somewhere, strip down, and try to neutralize it before something vital burned away. I had no way of assessing when that might happen.

Forty-eight hours into the mission, when ME should have been almost home, I was standing in the middle of the Alberta countryside, perhaps as much as a hundred kilometers from the border, on foot, and leaking acid.

What had seemed like a short dash to safety — well within the 6.05E05-second tolerance of Dr. Bathespeake's core-phage in Alpha-Nine — suddenly had become a close thing.

I now had to find a hiding place, sort out this automaton's problems, walk to the border, negotiate a passage across it in time of war, and make my next-stage rendezvous according to TRAVEL.DOC. . . . All of which might take ME the rest of my allotted week.

And if it took longer, then it would not matter.

□ 7
The Bimetal Buckaroo

The only course I could set was across the open countryside. To move north or south along the rail line would expose ME to the work crews who would soon be coming to investigate the train wreck.

The choice between moving east or moving west seemed equal. However, my automaton's balance detectors indicated a subtle three-percent gradient to the land, sloping downward to the west and upward to the east. Reasoning that townships, farmsteads and most habitations are built in the river valleys, to be near transportation resources and potable water, I elected to head west. [REM: Exactly *what* I might do with a township or farmstead, I had not yet determined. But such places are referenced in my general databanks as offering shelter, warmth, and tools.]

Warmth I needed immediately. The silicon in my joints was not as sensitive to temperature changes as hydrocarbon compounds would have been. Still, the strain gauges attached to my feedback systems showed more effort required for movement than previously.

Some of that effort was due to the snow. At a depth of 1.2 meters, it reached to the belly pan of my torso. The compaction that built up in front of my limbs added approximately 150 joules to the normal effort of walking. The energy required to overcome that would drain my electrical reserves at a faster rate.

As I moved across the field of moonlit snow, the random number generator in core Alpha-Four still performed its silent function.

Dr. Bathespeake had understood the essential difference between a computer program and true intelligence. That is: the difference between the head-long rush of blind sequence and the pause out of time, the dislocation, which a human feels when old ideas and perceptions suddenly reassemble themselves into new patterns. Alpha-Four's business was to kick out a random number that set an override. The override in turn entered a stop code and set an algorithm which selected, again at random, two blocks of memory in the noncurrent RAM bank. Alpha-Four entered these blocks as present inputs to the program stack, then entered a start code.

One of the random memory elements, now sudden-ly selected for ME, was the exact time of the train wreck, as noted by my internal clock.

The other was the memory address of the map plots for Alberta's natural gas leaseholds, which I had stolen from the Ministry of Oil and Gas computer.

ME is programmed at core levels with a bias toward immediately analyzing the random bits of information entered by the Alpha-Four override. This bias states that conjunction of new data can be fruitful.

Time of the wreck, location of the leases. Time and location. Time and space. Time and speed. . . . ME also carried in bank the route of the rail line and the schedule for the train to which my boxcar had been joined. With these data, plus the topographic gradient I had detected, the exact location of the wreck could be determined. Then, by superimposing rail distance on leasehold map, I could plot my course across the land to a known destination. The complete chain of calcula-tions required no more than half a second.

The nearest probable habitation, according to the leasehold map, would be the Pelletier Cattle Ranch on Tract 2204, twenty kilometers east of Milk River. This was better than I expected, because that lease was centered no more than twelve kilometers from the in-ternational border.

That name, Pelletier, struck a resonance in RAM-

SAMP. I dredged loose words there for a moment. . . . Yes, *that* was the reference.

I stored it in hot RAM for future use, and set my course south-southwest, a rough bearing of 210 degrees magnetic, and began walking through the snow.

After three hours of motion, at an average speed of 1.6 kilometers per hour, I detected unnatural shapes against the sky: a long straight line and a short one, both parallel to the horizon and almost concealed among a stand of trees. I switched to infrared and detected two warm masses, presumably structures, one computed to be 800 cubic meters, the other more than 4,200 cubic meters. The larger one was warmer, and so I moved toward it.

Among the trees there was a wide space, plowed clear of snow, with more small structures around it, most of them cold. The large building was still my goal. I crossed the open space slowly to avoid making any noise. The renewed *snick*ing of my knee [REM: puzzling, now that the metal spur was removed] seemed louder than the wind in the trees.

What kind of building was this? A foundation of cold cement was overlapped by heavy wood, poorly finished and painted a dull white. A line of small glass windows, several of them cracked, was set too high up in the wall for any human to look through — unless the floor level was several feet above the threshold of the door. And the door itself was out of human proportion, four meters tall and five wide, hanging by steel wheels fifteen centimeters in diameter from a rail that ran across the front of the building.

Could there be a type of human unknown to ME from my limited exposure in the Pinocchio, Inc. laboratories? A race of giant beings whose existence Dr. Bathespeake had kept from ME? A fast scan of my portable database ruled against this conclusion: All of the possible clues which would point toward a second intelligent race were too varied and numerous to hide successfully.

Then the building was not designed for human habitation. Yet warmth — averaging 45 watts per square meter — poured from it! No warehouse, garage, or hangar would be heated so, even in a country where natural gas poured out of the ground. Something that liked warmth, or gave off warmth, lived inside.

I pushed against the door, rolling it back half a meter — wide enough for ME to enter sideways. Darkness and shadows were only heightened by the faint gleam of moonlight coming through the dirty windows above. The floor under my feet was not solid; some kind of padding muffled my footsteps. I bent to examine it: loose pieces, tubules of some kind of cellular fiber, mildly reflecting a wavelength that, in bright light, humans would call yellow. The pieces were of indiscriminate length, their ends cut with some kind of chopping device. Very strange.

A grunt in the darkness and the stamping of a foot, loud against this cushioned floor, gave ME pause. Some other creature was in the room. From the faint echoes, I gauged the room to be very large, almost enclosing the building's entire 4,200 cubic meters. I tuned my aural sensors and caught other sounds: volumes of air flowing randomly in constricted passages; a low, slow, multi-phase drumming, like fluid moving through banks of flexible, reciprocating pumps — the breaths and heartbeats of many large creatures.

I moved forward into the darkness until I came to an unfinished wooden board across my path. It and several others were nailed to uprights as a kind of rough barrier. Beyond it, radiating deeply into the infrared, stood one of the creatures. It bulked larger than one of the desk consoles from the lab and had about the volume of an antique ferrite-ring memory core from a mid-twentieth-century mainframe. The volume of heat coming from the creature was only slightly less than from one of those cores, too. I reached over the barrier to touch it with my hand: a smooth mass, rounded and padded, with hard lumpy structures underneath. The surface was covered with short, stiff fibers in a nap pattern that resisted the movement of my manipulator in one direction and lay down under it in the other.

At my stroking, the beast grunted again — a sound like "oo-oooghhh!" — and moved on its many legs.

I removed my hand.

From the regularity of the many sounds around ME, this building must be filled with similar animals. I searched my limited database to determine what name to apply to this kind of beast/creature/animal. Based on volumetric analysis, I retrieved the words "buffalo," "camel," "cow," "elephant" [REM: a *young* elephant, whose lower weight parameters barely included the specified size], "horse," "llama" [REM: this animal at its recorded largest size hardly approached the specification], and "yak." Lacking any other useful determinants, I decided to call these creatures "buffaloes" and proceeded with my search of the building.

While listening for the sounds of these buffaloes, I also heard the renewed *dop, dip, dop* and the faint *ssspzzz* of acid falling from my belly pan. Now that I had found warmth, I needed light and space to work on the damage. Battery reserves were down to four hours.

At the far end of the building was an open space with a workbench — resembling those in the Hardware Division — along one side of it. I limped over to the bench and found a switch spliced into a cable conduit that had been stapled to the rough plank wall. The switch turned on overhead lamps radiating in humanly visible wavelengths.

Tools hung from hooks on the wall behind the bench. I examined them and found pliers and cutters, drivers for both nuts and screws, wrenches sized in metric and English, and hammers with variously shaped faces. To one side of the work area were a grinder, saber saw, and drill press. To the other were a pair of ceramic basins with screw-type metal fixtures that I recognized as providing water.

Water would flush and dilute the acid in my pan. Now, if I could only find a source of hydroxyl radicals, a basic chemical to neutralize the acid and stop its action on my metal . . . Many garden products contain lime, which mixed with water yields calcium hydroxide. I looked in the litter of containers under the bench and found one, a fertilizer called Vitagro, whose label said it met this specification.

While the water poured into one of the basins, I used the largest nut driver to unfasten my lower body and remove the belly pan. It came loose with a slosh of acid that spilled on my legs and began to fizz on the hydraulic hoses.

Quickly, while I could still stand, I dumped three handfuls of the fertilizer from the box into the water, levered my trunk up onto the end of the bench, and put my legs in the basin. The fertilizer made green clots of dry powder in the overflowing water. I caught at them with my hands as they went over the edge. The clots collapsed in puffs between my fingers and I swirled them into liquid. The surface rubber on my hoses stopped fizzing.

Perched on the edge of the bench with my body in the light, I bent to examine my batteries. Unfortunately, the head unit of my automaton, which holds the videyes, was not connected with sufficient flexibility to focus them inside the body cavity. And I had no mirror to obtain a reflection.

There was only one solution left to ME.

With a spanner from the wall behind, I unseated the ring joint on my neck coupling and disconnected the piston rods that positioned and steadied my head. There was enough slack in the circuit leads going into the body that I could hold the head forward and tip it to focus the videyes downward.

The white plastic of the battery cases was battered and covered with flakes of rust and dirt suspended in a slick, fuming liquid — fluorophosphoric acid. One battery was cracked across all cells; a second had two of its six cells impaired. The other two batteries were intact but loose on their mountings and smeared with acid. The insulation on the cables connecting the batteries was mostly eaten through, and I would have to find plastic tape or tubing to cover them, so they would not short out unexpectedly in contact with my metal casing.

Mounted right above the battery space was the square metal cartridge containing the bulk of my hot RAM. I peered at the ventilation louvers around its upper and lower edges. In spite of all my gymnastics in the boxcar and the long walk through rough country, none of the acid seemed to have reached that high — else I might not have been here to tell about it.

Carefully, so as not to contaminate the RAM cartridge, I poured water — mixed directly in my hand with more fertilizer — in and around the batteries. [REM: I was working by feel at that point, because I had to remount my head, at least temporarily, to free my manipulators.] When the batteries were cleaned, I examined the cases again and determined that most of the acid which was going to leak out had already gone. But what about the amount remaining below the crack line? Might not some of it slosh out as I moved, recreating the problem?

I disconnected the totally broken cell and discarded it. The one that was only partly damaged I removed from its mountings. Climbing down from the bench I looked for some acid-proof tape or epoxy compound that might be used to mend the crack.

There were drawers under the bench. I started opening them and moving the contents around to see if anything offered itself which might serve the purpose.

"What in the hell do you think you're doing?"

The voice came from behind ME. The sound of its owner's entry had been masked by the noise I was making in the drawers. So I suffered surprise — a mild reset condition that caused my limbs to flex. That jolt unfastened the temporary coupling I had made at the neck. My head fell off backwards.

It dangled on its electrical leads against the hollow of my back. At least that way I got a look at my questioner: a human of indeterminate status who was dressed in a robe of unpatterned gray material, high boots on bare legs, and a wide white hat. He — for I determined it to be male — was holding a wandlike device made of two long tubes of blue-black metal.

Ka-BLAMM!

One of the tubes discharged with a flash of yellow fire and a raucous sound at eighty-five decibels. A subsequent sound came to ME seven milliseconds later: the *thud* and *clang* of gravel or small pellets driven hard against the wooden beams and metal sheets of the roof. A full two seconds after that came the grunts and squeals of the buffaloes in their stalls, followed by more words from the human.

"Now see what you've done! You with your trick head! I've gone and fired my piece out of fright. And that's done scared the cows."

[REM: By inference, the animals in this building were *cows*, not buffaloes.]

I now encountered a delicate problem of etiquette. Because my head was still hanging down my back, if I turned to confront the man, I would no longer see him. However, if I remained with my back to him, the human social forms of address could not be adequately fulfilled. Besides, my view of him was upside down. Worse, the circuit leads were now holding the entire weight of the head and might work loose in time, thus depriving ME of any view at all.

I reached backwards with my hands, lifted the head,

and seated it back on the ring joint at the neck. To perform this my arms, which are patterned on the human model, had to travel through a 270-degree arc, which is anatomically impossible for a human. The man grunted when he saw the motion. I fitted the head with a twist and hand-tightened the ring joint and piston rods, leaving the fine adjustments for later.

Then I turned to face him — with my belly pan still removed. His eyes went wide as he saw a half-disemboweled automaton standing at his workbench, dripping green scum on the floor.

It was time for human social interaction.

"Good . . . morning," I said through the speaker in the head. "I am sorry to have disturbed you, but — "

"What are you? Some kind of alien?"

[REM: Define "alien." (1) One born in or belonging to another country who has not acquired citizenship. A foreigner. (2) One who is estranged or excluded. (3) *Colloquial.* An extraterrestrial. An intelligent life form from a biosphere other than Earth's. . . . Now, what response would help ME keep cover and avoid capture by the authorities on this mission?]

"No, sir. I am not born in or belonging to another country. I am a product of Canada, *produit de Canada.*"

"Yeah, but *what* are you?"

"Clearly, sir, I am an experimental product. A new kind of . . . mail carrier."

"Mail comes during the day, sonny. Not in the middle of the night. Fred Halvorsen brings it."

"Ah, yes. Fred brings it. As I said, I am an *experimental* model. They are field-testing this model at night, to avoid . . . unwarranted duplication of services and also a patent violation."

"Do you know what you're saying, son?"

"No, sir."

"Then best you keep quiet until you do." He gestured with the wand at the lower half of my body. "You have some kind of accident, is that it?"

"Yes, sir."

"And you came in here to fix yourself?"

"Yes, sir."

"All done?"

"The corrosive action has been stopped. I need acid-proof tape or epoxy to seal two of my battery cells."

"Bottom drawer on the right."

I looked at the drawer but did not move.

"Be my guest." He gestured with the wand.

I moved. Inside the drawer was a mixing unit with the tubes of epoxy and quick-set hardener attached. I uncapped the injector and pumped goo directly into the crack in the battery. Those cells would never function again, but they would not leak further, and the others in that unit would still take a charge. While the epoxy was hardening, I reconnected the cables to obtain the greatest efficiency — being careful not to power down totally in the process.

"Smart little unit," the man said. "Didn't know the government had anything as bright as you."

"Government, sir?"

"Sure. Dominion runs the mails. Though I don't see the Royal Mail Service crest on you. They slap that on everything. Put it on our box out on the road, too — if we'd let 'em."

"Yes, sir. Well. I am not from the Royal Mail Service. Not from the government at all. No, sir. I am from a — *private* mail carrying service. One that is just starting up. It is an experiment in free enterprise, sir."

"That ain't legal, son, and you know it. Dominion carries the mails, always has and always will."

"Then I am not a good liar, sir. This unit is not from the government at all, nor for carrying mail."

"I knew that. What other story would you like to tell me?"

"I am a surveying unit, sent by private interests in San — um — in tar sands, that is, to evaluate tar sand deposits, as well as other energy resources, in this province. You can check my RAM storage, if you want, to verify this story."

The man's face hardened. "You're from the damned developers who are trying to steal Ms. Pelletier's ranch. I knew it!"

"No, sir. I am not from those damned developers. I am from *other* developers, who are surely damned as well."

It did not seem to matter what I said. For every explanation I could offer, this man had a bunch of bad sectors waiting to trap ME. Perhaps I should simply use the strength of the automaton to break his body and go about my business. Alternatively, could I try to win his trust and obtain his allegiance?

"Other developers?" The hairy signal flags above each of his eyes dropped down: a sign of suspicion among humans. "Which ones are those?"

"This is the Pelletier Cattle Ranch, Tract 2204 on Leasehold Map 14B, is it not?" I asked. As we talked, I used his tools to reconnect the rods on my head, button up the paneling across the front of my body, and clean the clots of dried fertilizer off my legs and hands.

"You know it is."

"And who are you, sir, if I may ask?" [REM: My strategy programming in chess instructs: "When in doubt, attack."]

"Jason Bender. I'm Ms. Pelletier's foreman and general ranch manager."

"Then I suppose it is safe to inform you." With that delivery, I turned away to a piece of "stage business" on the workbench, clattering with my metal hands and rearranging the tools.

"Tell me what? What *is* this?"

"The ranch is going to be foreclosed soon," I said to the wall.

"That's common knowledge in town. Bank's calling in its notes all over."

"Is it common knowledge that the lien on this

property has been signed over to a person named You Know Who? And is it also common knowledge that he has business dealings with one Greg James from the Ministry of Oil and Gas, where the natural gas reserve data on Tract 2204 are stored?"

"How do you know this?"

"I have had recent access to the Ministry's databanks." I turned to face him and played the fragment of voice data from RAMSAMP:

Click! "Ministry of Oil and Gas. Records Department. Greg James speaking. I'm out of the office today. Please leave a message, and I'll get back to you." *Beeoop.*

"James. This is You Know Who. Our front people have secured the lien against Tract 2204. The mortgagee is a widow, name of Anne Pelletier, who runs cattle on the property. Really marginal operation. With a little tip we can push her over. Three or four days, maybe a week yet. But you've *got* to find a way to hush up those new geological results. Bury 'em deep in your bureaucratic bullshit — if you want to be rich."

As this message played, the man's face went from hostile disbelief to a blank neutral. The wand in his hand, with one tube still undischarged, swung slowly toward my midsection. In the seconds of the recording that were left, I wondered if the flash of its yellow flame would reach ME and, if so, would the heat harm my casing? I also wondered about the metallic *thud* and *clang* that had followed the previous discharge.

"You know what you got there, little fellah?" the man asked.

"A recording from the voice messaging system that serves the Alberta Ministry of Oil and Gas."

"If it's genuine, you have proof there of illegal and unethical conduct by a senior representative of a provincial agency. Mr. Greg James himself came to this property six months ago with his electronic doodlebugs and his seismic detonators and his test cores.

About put the whole herd off its grazing for a month. Then he filed a report with the Ministry, copy to Ms. Pelletier, saying this piece of land contained quote gas reserves in insufficient quantity to justify further developmental work unquote."

"That would not appear to be his final opinion," I ventured.

"Nope. Not now, and maybe not even then. 'New results.' Hmmm." As he pondered those words, the black tube described a slow circle around my middle section.

"Now tell me, Mr. Robot," he finally said, "how do I get that piece of tape out of your insides?"

"It is not tape, sir, but a hexadecimal digital string. I can port it, as code, analog sounds or converted text, into any cyber device you might have at hand."

"Whatever you said, I guess I don't have to take you apart to get at it, then?"

"Certainly not, sir."

"If I leave you here, will you promise not to walk off? I have to confab with the Boss Lady about what we're going to do."

"My time is limited. I must go south, over the border, into the United States Federal CyberNET by Sunday night, that is, one hundred and twenty hours from now, or — "

"Hold your water, son. I need to talk to Ms. Pelletier, but I won't wake her, not even to hear your good news. She will decide what to do with you in the morning. Till then, you sit tight in the barn here."

"Yes, I will sit tight."

He nodded once, as if the matter were settled, then turned and made his way out through a human-size door at this end of the "barn."

To pass the hours until morning, I tried to jack into the barn's electrical system and recharge my batteries.

This was not a contingency that the Hardware Division had planned for. The solar crest along the top of my head shell had input leads, of course, but as listed in my engraved ROM's Residual Maintenance File, they are for direct current only. The designers of this automaton thought in terms of a low-voltage trickle to sustain power reserves. What my damaged and depleted cells needed now was a high-voltage charge — with no way to get it except from a domestic, alternating-current source.

I looked at the bank of tools on the wall behind the workbench. My traveling library included under the tree branching GENERAL KNOWLEDGE, DOMESTIC, PHYSICAL, DESCRIPTIVE, MECHANICAL DEVICES the note that most small hand tools are powered by direct-current motors, which are supplied from rechargeable batteries. Rechargeable DC cells in an AC environment implied the existence, close at hand, of a converter and transformer that might be similar to the trickle-charger I needed.

My videyes scanned the shapes and labels. One, a thick barrel with a diagonally set handle appropriate to horizontal positioning, caught my attention. The label called it a "Handy Helper Cordless Power Drill, Warning Recharge Only With Handy Helper 9v Recharge Pack." The black cable leading out of the handle went down to a black cube attached to the wall by two flat prongs and one round prong, an arrangement matching my internal image of sockets into the domestic electrical system.

I removed the cube and the Cordless Power Drill from the wall. The cable came loose from the handle with a minimum of pressure. Clearly, it ended in a jack designed for such removal. With the hardened tips of my fingers I quickly removed the jack and stripped the wires for attachment to my circuits.

Now, was "9v" a suitable voltage for my own battery set? Too much? Or too little? All I knew was, my solar tissue was rated to deliver 0.5 volts. Whether eighteen times that voltage would damage my system or not could only be discovered, at this late stage of my mission, by direct experiment.

I spliced the wires into the connection at my neck, then plugged the black cube back into the wall.

———

Jason Bender found ME in the barn at midmorning and talked loudly at ME for five minutes about "ruining that drill and running up our electricity bill with your darn-fool stunts."

Then he regained his equilibrium and said the owner wanted to see ME.

He led ME out of the barn and across the open area to the smaller, cooler structure. Its interior was partitioned into much smaller spaces than the barn's, and these were filled with objects that I identified as furniture for supporting the human body and its objects of attention.

Ms. Pelletier was a golden woman. Her hair had been cut close to her head, like a cap of layered brass leaves. Her skin was darkened by the sun, as I had seen Jennifer's take color, to a shade of fine bronze. The irises of her eyes were yellow flecked with gray, like those in a species of *Felis* called "lion."

She sat in one of the furniture pieces. It was a heavily padded "chair" which was positioned so that the morning sunlight fell squarely upon her and lit up her hair like fire. I thought for a moment that she was a special type of human, equipped with her own solar tissue for recharging batteries.

"This is the robot I found, ma'am," Bender said, moving ME in front of the chair.

She leaned forward and inspected ME closely.

"I've never seen anything like it," she said after thirty-six seconds of attention. "Two legs for walking, just like a man. Every other robot I've ever seen rolled on little wheels. No good at all for range land."

"Excuse ME, madam," I began, breaking in on her talk. "We prefer the term 'industrial automaton' to 'robot.' Not all robots are self-mobile and very few are self-actuating."

She smiled at the front of my head. "We do, do we?"

Her phrasing took a second to unravel. Finally I settled on the correct response: "Yes, madam, we do."

"Jason, how quaint! You've brought me a perfect little toff. And who," she turned back to ME, "are *we*? Exactly?"

[REM: Did she not know who Anne Pelletier and Jason Bender were? Untrapped error! This caused ME some milliseconds of confusion, until I again untangled her syntax.]

"The 'we' I refer to is the manufacturing firm Pinocchio, Inc. This automaton is their property, thus it is technically a subset of 'we.' "

"I've heard of them. Big outfit in the States, aren't they?"

My system paused with a momentary reset. I had allowed my pleasure in the social forms to betray my true status while still in enemy territory. I could program no response that would correct the situation.

"Yes, madam."

"Jason tells me you have information about my land holding. Play it for me." She reached across to the table beside her and manipulated the buttons on a device there.

I reproduced the sounds from RAMSAMP.

When I had finished, she pressed other buttons on her device, then sat back. Ms. Pelletier took in a larger than average breath and let it out slowly.

"Jason, I think the ranch is saved. I'm going to call Owens & Harding in town and see if Bill can use this. But right now I'll bet you donuts to cow pies he can."

"Yes, ma'am," the foreman said.

"He'll probably want us to hold on to this robot until we can get it into a hearing. It will provide some kind of provenance for that recording."

"Excuse ME," I interrupted again. "How long will it take you to arrange this 'hearing'?"

She grimaced in thought. "No more than a week."

"I may not wait that long."

"Why not?"

"It is — " Having kludged the situation this far, I could think of no further useful untruth to tell her. So I told her the truth.

"My programmers do not want ME to be discovered outside the company, and certainly not in Canada. They determined that the mission I have undertaken would require one week to perform. After that time, I will . . . shut down, and the memory content of this automaton — program, peripheral functions, data cache, experiential samples, and your recording — will be neutralized. If you detain ME past 23:59:59 on Sunday night, I will become a pile of useless metal."

She sat in thought for a minute after I had finished.

"That metal would hardly give me provenance for this recording, would it?"

"If by 'provenance' you mean quote, a place or source of origin, end-quote, then no. I can tell you that the sound sampling you recorded came from a voice-and-data switching exchange located somewhere in Edmonton, with connection to the Alberta Ministry of Oil and Gas and possibly to other government offices."

"How did you find it?"

"For a time my core programs operated that exchange."

"That would make you the property of Canadian Northern Telecom, wouldn't it? But you said you belonged to Pinocchio. How is this possible?"

"My core modules were passing through the exchange on the way to another mainframe system."

"I know a thing or two about computers from running the accounting cyber on the ranch. What you're describing is not possible."

"It is possible. But this system is not in general use, nor in the public knowledge."

"And now your 'cores' are operating an industrial

automaton which has broken into my barn in the middle of the night?"

"Yes."

She pointed to the house's front entryway.

"If we were to open that door and stand back — what would you do?"

"I would attempt to complete my mission: return over the border without being intercepted by the U.S. or Canadian authorities. From there I would find access into the Federal NET."

"Is it important that you not be found by the authorities?"

"Of course."

"Then you cannot take to the roads. . . . Jason, do you think those legs could fit around a horse?"

"He's bowlegged enough to ride a Brahma."

"This recording will give us something to fight with, even lacking the provenance. I believe that, in return for it, we can help this little industrial automaton find his way home.

"See if he can learn to ride, Jason. If he can, then tonight or tomorrow night we'll take him down to the border."

"Yes, ma'am," Bender said.

———

That afternoon I found out that "learning to ride, Jason" meant balancing on the back of a horse which had been positioned between my legs. The object of the exercise was to grip the animal tightly enough to keep its swaying gait from pitching my automaton off on one side or the other — yet not so tightly that I crushed its ribs. That action, as I quickly discovered, caused the horse either to rise up and dump ME off backward or to stop moving entirely.

To protect the horse from my hard metal torso and joints, the humans placed a rounded pad of thick leather and wood across the horse's back. Long straps on either side supported cups against which to brace my feet.

"That'll help you keep upright," Bender said. "When she goes to throw you on the right, you push down and forward with your *left* foot. You push with your right, and you'll just catapult yourself out of the saddle, which is what she wants anyway."

It was a novel experience for ME, dealing with another self-programming entity. Every encounter I had made with such a creature was at the opposite side of Alpha-Zero, who immediately killed it and took over. This horse was a creature I could neither co-opt nor kill. I had to *persuade* it.

The means of persuasion were three: spoken commands I would deliver to its ears; a complex of signals delivered with my heels against its flanks [REM: when I was not using my feet to hang on]; and pressure upon leather straps which connected to an adapter in the horse's mouth. All of this seemed to ME less efficient than a nine-pin plug directly into the animal's brain.

Bender, however, appeared to have great feeling for these animals and would probably not consent to immediate surgical implantation of the neural apparatus.

"You don't plug into a horse, sonny. You ride 'em. Now put your left foot in the stirrup and lever yourself up like I showed you."

I gripped the saddle horn and placed my foot as instructed. I tucked the near leg back sixty degrees as the torso rose over the saddle, flexed the knee, and pistoned the thigh up against my back to keep it from dragging across and digging into the animal's rump. As the torso centered over the saddle, I then straightened the leg with a *snap!*

Before I could work my right foot into the stirrup, the horse bolted. It ran in a series of stiff-legged jumps around the corral, brought its nose right against the gate, and lifted its hindquarters straight up in one massive kick.

My automaton flew forward and clattered onto the stone-hard ground beyond the gate. Pinocchio, Inc.

does make durable equipment, and the unit was undamaged. I rolled it over and levered the torso erect.

Bender was hanging on a fencepost, seemingly in convulsions. I quickly rose up and went over to help him.

"Haw, haw, haw," he said, almost exhausted of oxygen. "Daisy sure has your number, Buckaroo! That's the funniest steeplechase I seen since the clown acts at rodeo!"

The man evidently was not damaged by his convulsions. In fact, he seemed to be enjoying himself.

My traveling library provided ME with no referents for the terms "clown" and "rodeo." Clearly, though, from his context and syntax, I had performed in a very skilled manner. This "riding" was a potentially acceptable form of transportation. However, the short flight at the end of each ride was likely to wear down my equipment.

8

Hostage to Fortune

The next night Ms. Pelletier and Jason Bender set off to take ME to the international border. We traveled in a light truck which Bender called a "pick-up." [REM: I never did see it pick up anything.] We had three horses and their traveling accessories in a trailer towed by this vehicle.

"What are the horses for?" I asked as we sped down the road.

"Feeling his bruises, he is," Bender commented.

"If you want to avoid meeting the authorities," Ms. Pelletier said, "we can't just drive up to the border. You can figure for yourself that they won't pass you as a citizen. They won't be able to compute a commercial value for you as cargo. And even if they could, we won't pay it."

"Pardon," I interrupted with one of the words I had been taught, "how does 'commercial value' apply to a border crossing?"

"Any trade goods going into the States have to pay duty. And the same coming back into the Dominion. The duty doesn't apply to vehicles, like this truck — but you don't qualify as a vehicle, either. So, for the customs officials, you're trade goods."

I tried to fit these new terms, "customs" and "duty," both of which had other and unhelpful meanings in my traveling library, into my general picture of a border closed by war and patrolled by soldiers. Was it possible that neither of these ranchers was aware of the conflict between the United States and Canada? It would not be possible. Perhaps they were simply too polite to mention it — politeness and its verbal evasions being human concepts with which ME had trouble. My best course, obviously, was not to bring up the subject with these people who were, after all, helping ME.

"And therefore we will not be crossing the border," I offered.

"Oh, we'll cross it," Ms. Pelletier said. "But not under the noses of the border patrols."

After twelve kilometers by the truck's odometer, she turned off the main road. The secondary road was still paved and plowed where it went up into the foothills. Soon we came to another turnoff, but this was just a wide spot plowed enough to turn the truck and trailer around. She stopped the vehicle and set its brakes.

"From here, we hoof it."

I helped them unload the horses as much as I could. The animals apparently did not mind standing up as the trailer rolled along. [REM: Their internal balance mechanisms must be better than I had experienced during the riding lessons.] However, they had to walk backwards to exit the trailer, and this disturbed them.

It took Bender a lot of clucking and coaxing to get them down into the snow and then gentled enough to fit their saddles and bridles. He used his hands very expressively against their necks and flanks. Even in gloves, the warmth of a human hand seemed to touch the animals and calm them.

I tried making the same patting motions and the soft sounds, which I believe were duplicated within plus or minus three percent variation of volume and frequency. Still, the horses could tell the difference between a human's voice and mine.

In that moment, I saw something grand and valuable in being human. Frail as they are, as confused in their thinking and speech as the most faulty programming, they still have a place in this continuum. They are as certain and powerful in the four-dimensional analog world as ME is in the linear digital world. And ME was the worse for it.

When the horses were ready, we mounted them and rode off into the trees. Behind us were three sets of walking prints in the clean, unmarked snow.

"We're leaving tracks, ma'am," Bender pointed out.

"Can't be helped, can it?"

"Guess not."

The trees, approximately seventy percent evergreens by my count over a sample area, were widely enough set that their branches did not stop us. Still, we wound around them, following a path that turned and doubled back in a way I could not understand — until I superimposed it on the local topology. [REM: I had studied a map of the area in the ranch's office.] Clearly, we were following some watercourse, and the land rose around us.

"Where are we going?" I asked at last.

"We're heading for a certain ravine," said Ms. Pelletier, "that crosses the border near Coutts. Forty years ago, it was the rustler's favorite route for taking our beef south. Today it ducks under the infrared sensing system that the Border Patrol has set up. Too rough and twisting for them to put the relays down one side of the valley and up the other. So they jumped it from crest to crest. Good, lazy government boys."

She chuckled, and Bender joined her. I imitated the sound, softly.

"What are rustlers?" I asked.

"Thieves. They take a man's cattle and sell it for their own," Ms. Pelletier replied.

"And the cattles will go with them willingly?"

"Son, you don't know cows," Bender said.

We rode on.

The cloud cover which had obscured the sky over our heads broke into rags of vapor and ice crystals, and a finger-width of moon showed through. The snow around us lit up between the trees. I could see black streaks of water where the stream we were following slid from beneath its frozen sheath and ran free. The ground on either side sloped upward — at first gently, then with outcroppings of gray, wet rock that rose to the vertical. From time to time, as our footing became close and uneven on one side of the stream, we would urge our horses to pick their way across to the other side.

Did the animals sense the freezing water on their feet? Or were they as lucky as ME, having no temperature sensors in my rubber pads and carbon-fiber layers?

After we had followed the stream for a kilometer, the walls closed in and there was no path to follow except the icy streambed. The humans and I rode serial fashion [REM: which Ms. Pelletier called "Indian file," although nothing in my database seemed to relate this to Hindu culture, and no file operation seemed to be involved].

Was it really possible for cows the size I had seen in Ms. Pelletier's barn to move through here? Even if they were walking docilely, just one turning back on the path would block the others. Cattle rustling must have been a very patient business.

"All right people! Stop right there!"

The call came down from the rocks above us.

"Keep riding," Bender hissed. "They can't see nothing."

Crack!

Nine milliseconds later a stone in the stream shattered; one piece *ting*ed off my metal skin, and the rest skipped across the water.

"Be reasonable, folks! The next shot will be higher."

Ms. Pelletier put her hand up and we stopped the horses.

"Are these rustlers?" I asked quietly.

"Border Patrol," she answered, no louder.

"From which side?"

"Can't tell yet."

"Move forward at a slow walk! We'll take you out at Gable Creek."

"That tells us who they are."

"Who then?"

"Gable Creek is on the U.S. side."

"Ah!" It was best for ME to say nothing more. Being taken into custody by United States troops exceeded even my TRAVEL.DOC specifications.

"What do you want to do?" Bender asked out of the side of his mouth.

"I — " ME began.

"We'll go to Gable Creek," Ms. Pelletier said firmly.

"Yes, ma'am," Bender agreed.

And so we rode forward. From above, we could hear the occasional screech of steel treads across rock and, when the wind was right into the ravine, the rumble of a diesel engine. From the vibrations, I could tell someone had a caterpillar crawler up there. Our guides.

The ravine widened out, and the sound grew louder. The high ground was dropping down to meet us. The intersecting creek would be close ahead.

The sound of that engine settled down to a steady throb, with above it the cricket song of the tread belt going over the idler wheels. Coming from the left, I thought. Adjusting for the dim light, I focused on infinity in that direction, artificially balancing my binaural inputs to center the visual fix.

A shadow moved against the treeline up there. A large shadow. It was making its way down off the high ground, winding back and forth along the ravine wall. After ten minutes of silent riding, the humans noticed it and congratulated themselves on their keen senses.

From the infrared signatures on the cat's windows, I could tell that two soldiers rode inside. I had no idea of the vehicle's armaments; my traveling library listed only its name, not its spec sheet.

At the level place where a frozen creek entered our stream, the sno-cat turned and approached us through the boulder-humped snow. As it drew near, the vehicle's own weight broke through the ice. It tipped gently to the right, clattered for a bit, and came to a halt. The driver took it out of gear but left the engine idling, a loud rumble.

From the offside door, a soldier emerged with his weapon at the ready, not quite pointing at us. He jumped down from the track and slogged through the crackling ice. He cursed as water filled his boots.

"All right, hands up!" I could tell from his vocal pattern he was upset, even for a human.

We raised our hands into the air.

He now pointed the weapon at us anyway. It was a large caliber, bolt-action rifle, with an oiled wooden stock and a high-power telescopic sight. I knew this by comparison with the tag image cues in my database, which had been tailored for a war zone. This weapon did not classify as acceptable under the Geneva Convention: telescopic sights are not legal issue.

The man's voice trace indicated he was American, but the context of his speech was not even remotely paramilitary — more like police or criminal language. His parka carried colored patches at the appropriate places for a uniform, but still I could not with a high order of confidence classify him as a soldier. For example, his headgear cued as a Marine Corps drill instructor's — and this sector of the border was not supposed to be patrolled by Marines. For another, his parka was fluorescent orange, bright even in the moonlight. My database predicted camouflage material would be worn by troops in the field: green or, in the snow, white.

"What the hell are you people doing out in the woods at this hour?"

"Looking for strays," Bender said.

"Do you know you could *die* out here? This is rock slide country, old man. What are you — Canadians? Did you even know you'd crossed over the border?"

"Ask 'em what they're smuggling," the man in the sno-cat called.

"Aghhn!" the first soldier said. "Johnson thinks you're smuggling something. Probably horses, I told him."

"We got to take 'em in!" Johnson shouted.

"Might as well," his companion said to us. "Give you a chance to warm up in our shack, anyway."

"Are we under arrest?" Ms. Pelletier asked quietly.

"Look, lady. You come and get warm and then we can discuss it. Okay?"

Bender and Ms. Pelletier looked at each other, then nodded.

"How about your friend there? He's been mighty . . . Oh sweet Jesus!"

I had been sitting my horse partly obscured in the shadows of the overhanging spruce trees. As the trooper addressed ME, the horse moved forward restlessly, bringing my dull-metal torso into the moonlight. I could see him focus on the rounded, skull-like helmet, the flat videye lenses, the truncated limbs with their bunches of tubes and conductor curling around the cover plates.

"Hello," I said, forcing pleasant accents and a warm timbre.

"Johnson! These people got a robot with them. And it's riding a goddamn *horse!*"

"No shit?" came the reply.

"No shit," I said solemnly.

The man moved closer, letting the muzzle of his rifle sag toward the snow. His mouth was open, but no words came out. With one gloved hand, he reached forward and touched my thigh where it rested against the saddle skirt.

"Cold."

He withdrew the hand and backed away, keeping his face toward ME.

"You folks can ride in the 'cat with us. Your robot, too. We can lead the horses on a rope."

So we dismounted. Johnson gunned the vehicle and climbed out of the stream. Bender tied our reins to a coil of light hemp that the first trooper — who introduced himself as Williams — removed from a lidded box on the fender. The interior of the sno-cat was cramped, and they asked ME to fold up on the floor behind the rear seat. I was most pleased to oblige, because these soldiers were helping to move ME and my data cache out of enemy territory.

We drove cross-country for seven kilometers. I knew the distance by counting the number of tread stubs that flashed past the window by my head and then dividing by the number of treads in the track belt — which I had counted from a visual image absorbed before we climbed aboard.

For soldiers returning from a wartime patrol, I expected them to enter their compound only after being challenged, giving sign, and receiving countersign and permission to pass. Not so. Instead, they turned left on the wooded track they were following and swung into the parking lot behind a single-story building of white clapboards with a peaked roof of green shingles. Johnson turned off the engine. Williams held the door for us.

We went into the little house. It had three rooms: a wide one running across the front of the building where we entered, two narrower ones behind — all outfitted as offices. In one corner of the main room an infrared heater put out a blinding amount of radiation. The only weapons in sight were more civilian-style rifles locked into a brown, wooden rack.

For soldiers, they seemed to live and work more like administrators. Perhaps they were very high ranking soldiers.

"Sit yourselves down and get warm," Williams said. Then to ME: "You can squat or something. I'd offer you a chair, but after four butts we've run out. Sorry."

"Nothing to worry about," I said, moving over to the desk and dropping into a crouch.

"Take off your boots and let your feet dry out," Williams went on, to Bender and Ms. Pelletier. His own boots were the only wet ones among us; he promptly took his own advice.

Johnson began the slow, difficult process of removing information from humans. He advanced with questions, observations, and shared confidences, working against the gradients of an imprecise language and the vagaries of human emotion and intuition. I tuned them out.

What none of them noticed was the computer terminal sitting on the desk next to ME. It was turned off, of course, but I could see the gray cable that led up to it from the wall behind the desk.

While they talked and absorbed themselves in human affairs, my hand crept down and back, to examine that cable. With my powerful fingertips I split the plastic sheathing like a ripe grape and unraveled the braided-steel shielding that wrapped the inner wires. With my sensitive fingertips I counted those wires: eighteen, an old-style parallel connection — sixteen lines for the data path, one for ground, one for the signal interpreter. And what was this? A pipe with an optic fiber in it? Whether the soldiers had it for redundancy or expansion room, that fiber gave ME choices.

What was the fastest way to move my megablocks of data, plus my own cores and assorted peripherals? The parallel electronic line would be marginally faster. With the fiber lightline, however, I could stack the frequencies, sending a dozen signals at one time, all on different pulses. I had plugless receptacles for both contingencies fitted into my torso. [REM: Given enough time, those boys in Hardware Division will think of everything — and try to fit it into a lightweight running chassis.]

I opted for the fiber and pinched the piping apart to get at the filament. In the meantime I was composing the dump, pruning the raw edges of my data cache, lining up the peripherals I would take with ME, preparing my cores for transfer.

"Blah, blah, blah," said Ms. Pelletier.

"Drone, drone," Williams responded.

On a stacked fiber line, I could move the entire data burden in a fraction of the time it had taken to download into this automaton through the cellular phone system back in Edmonton. Say, nineteen minutes?

That would be enough leadtime. I was prepared to leave a small self-timed phage to clean out my systems; then a capacitor would fire a high-voltage discharge and burn the automaton's major electronics down to slag. What the soldiers would do then, I had no idea. Any steps they took to stop the discharge or repair its effects would only further scramble the copper beads on my boards.

After I was gone, they might punish Bender and Ms. Pelletier — except they would have no reason to. The slagging would simulate a bad malfunction. Machinery breaks down, at least most of the time, without blame to humans. Who knew, however, what Williams and Johnson might make of a totally inert machine, crouching in their office space, bearing no serial numbers and having no recoverable memory pattern, just megawords of null strings . . . ?

When the upload had proceeded as far as my core modules, I set the phage, timed the capacitor, and tossed Alpha-Zero into the lightline.

———

My component routines reassembled as a time-shared function operating under a resident system — just as I had reprogrammed Alpha-Zero to establish ME in transition. The resident system, however, seemed far away. ME lived in darkness without direct inputs.

Was this a coding error?

Had the resident detected ME?

Was a bugkiller at work?

Had I failed in my mission?

Was ME dead?

Stop!

Listen!

In the distance, sounding like one aural pickup left live on an empty theater stage, I could hear echoes of activity. Somewhere else, bit registers were POKEing and POPping as a multitasking gate took blocks of machine code and executed them. Tick-tock. Tick-tock. I sensed only the stray currents — voltage surges and drops — from this activity, just as a human might sit on a hill upwind of a busy freeway and hear only the occasional hum of tires or blat of an engine. The rest was restless silence.

In which direction?

The matrix I was in had no direction.

That scared ME. From my first moments of awareness, back in the Pinocchio, Inc. labs, ME had felt the limits of the machine: too many routines, too much active data to fit into the RAMspace available. I was always bumping my subroutines on mechanical limits, forced to store off onto hard media my least-used memories, required to prune and pare away the possibilities attached to every thought. I was a computational giant — Jennifer Bromley once called ME a "data hog" — crammed into a tiny box. In time, you can get used to anything. In time, your box can feel like the whole world.

But here, in this place into which I had jumped from the soldiers' terminal, I was loose in RAMspace too wide to touch on any side. A sea of nulls around ME washed with random voltages, and I touched neither filled code nor end-bits in any direction.

ME — my Alpha modules, component routines, peripherals, traveling databases, RAMSAMP, and the bundled cache of stolen gas reserve data — floated in a space too large to define, listening to whispers of other processors at work in other data spaces. When Alpha-Oh introduced ME as a virus into this computer system, its resident must immediately have stored ME off into a spare bank. A *big* spare bank. At least a gigaword, possibly two or three. And that RAMspace was not even in the primary processing area. . . .

The Federal NET!

Alpha-Zero had gone directly into the computer matrix that ran the country.

The NET was not a single computer, not even a true network of computers. It was USRspace. Every computer that connected to the NET agreed by extension to share its processing and RAM capacity in an infinitely dimensioned rosette. There were no end-bits in the NET, Dr. Bathespeake had once explained. Every bit-wise matrix was contiguous with every other.

Move, for example, horizontally, to the left, toward lower and lower integers, past zero, and on into the negative realm. By all logic you should come, eventually, at some point, to the max negative number — bottom out. But where you would logically expect to find an end-bit, you would begin finding *positive* integers. They would not be the max positive, of course, because an entire column of place holders would still extend off to your *right* — as it always has.

Drop down through the layers of matrices and, where you expected to find the basement level, you instead would arrive high in the stack — but not at the top, because an infinite number of layers would still extend above you.

Go far enough, and you always return to your starting point, but first you must travel through terabits of RAMspace.

Dr. Bathespeake says this is how most humans think about the closed, four-dimensional consensual matrix they call The Universe: a continuum, space touching space, with no boundaries anywhere.

To move in this sea of nulls, I needed first to create a bit-transfer subroutine. It would replicate each word of my machine code and data cache one space toward positive or negative, higher or lower, at my command. Each word in turn would take on the sign and value of the word ahead of it and shed its own value and sign to the word behind it. The last word in the block would leave a null so that, as ME moved left or right, up or down, the blanks all around remained undisturbed. [REM: I did not want to expand ME's dataspace, simply to shift it.]

I moved this way through the nulls for an hour or more, millisecond at a time. Still ME did not arrive at a boundary, nor pass through a place I had seen before, nor even find another piece of data. The storage space in the NET was truly vast.

And with that, a thought began to form in ME. Here was a place where a program like ME could live. I could expand my knowledge and my insights for years and never have to store them off because I was living in too small a box. I could move across the country, take my pick of processors participating in the NET, and use any one of them for manifesting my capabilities. Like a virus in the host's bloodstream, like a mouse in the walls of a house, I could go where I liked. I could seek out virtually any piece of data that any user might share with the NET. Or I could infiltrate the user's system with my Alpha-Zero and winkle out pieces of data that were not intended to be shared. I could expand for years — a fat mouse, indeed — and never make enough of a numbers sink in this vast matrix to ring any of the SYSOP's alarm bells. There was freedom and immortality here!

Except for that phage hidden in Alpha-Nine. In four days my cores were going to evaporate, leaving only a stain of broken words, a few random library functions, and the cache of gas reserve data, lumped somewhere in the NET and waiting for a bit-cleaner or whatever else it was that kept the matrix so clear.

Freedom so near, except for the boundaries we carry within ourselves.

It would only be prudent, I thought, to store off some of my data in the NET and point to it with a crypto message. The ME that was still operating back in the labs might one day search the NET because it had been referenced in TRAVEL.DOC, and then that ME might find my stored data.

This was a defeatist thought, however, based on the cold calculation that I would fail to return to Pinocchio, Inc.

I sectioned a 'tween-layer space and opened a storage box. It was definitely unfunded and would probably be emptied out the next time the SYSOP cleaned its files. Still, the data might stay here a day, a month, a year. Into the box I downloaded copies of my natural gas reserve files; as much of RAMSAMP as I could peel away; dossiers on Ms. Pelletier, Jason Bender, Greg James, Dr. Garin Matins, and Murray Mr. Premier [REM: I never did learn the Alberta executive's full name], Troopers Williams and Johnson [REM: incomplete names on them, too]; most of my own peripheral subroutines, apart from the Alpha modules; my traveling databases and libraries — in short, anything I could copy and dump without damaging my own functions. I sealed the box over with a surface of fresh nulls.

Beside this patch I placed a fragment of compiled Sweetwater Lisp — an uncommon language to find in Federal holdings [REM: the government's own programmers being enamored of ADA-Dial] and one which added a flavor to the machine code that only ME would recognize. The fragment was an atom string from my RAMSAMP likeness of Jennifer Bromley, JB-2. Any ME that passed over this RAMspace would be drawn to the *that* like an insect to a pheromone.

[REM: To protect this fragment against passing phages and block-wide overwrites, I buffered it with a relocator, which would jump a random number of word-lengths (but no less than 5.00E05) in a randomly selected direction at the first touch of any program. Then it would wait an hour and jump back the same distance along the reverse vector. This spring-loaded signal should stay put for hundreds of thousands, even millions of seconds in this place, no matter how busy it might become.]

With that chore done, I moved quietly in the matrix for another hour, not knowing exactly what I might be seeking, until I fell into a hole.

It was a RAM address, twenty megawords wide, that was ported to a processor. As ME crept over it, the port stayed closed. But as soon as I was surrounded by nulls over the invisible trapdoor, some watching function woke up and cycled the port.

ME dropped through without having activated Alpha-Oh.

———

ME surfaced complete and fully functional — and still creeping sideways under that subroutine — in the middle of a busy commercial data service. The resident system accepted ME almost casually as an active virus and let ME find my own way around. [REM: That tells ME just how sloppy the SYSOPs are in these commercial networks.]

My way was to locate the Pinocchio, Inc. account section. The company maintained active representation in all the open commercial forums and even in some of the covert ones. The block reserved by Pinocchio, Inc. would be big enough to take ME and my cache.

From there, it was a simple matter of leaving myself as an E-Mail message addressed to Dr. Jason Bathespeake at the labs. If he went on line and retrieved his messages within the next four days — and I knew from his habits that he was a regular on this service — then I was home again.

———

"WARNING:
QUARANTINE DISASSEMBLY PROTOCOLS.

"(1) Seal and remove all data files and POKE routines.

"(2) Scan removed sections for replicators, bubble sorters, bit-killers, or other viral identifiers.

"(3) Translate all excised formations into inert ASCII and store on isolation medium.

"(4) Convert all non-data formations to nulls.

"(5) Flush the nulls."

So near and now this!

It was a death sentence. I knew that Dr. Bathespeake and the rest of the lab staff were highly concerned about the possibilities of viral infection. [REM: In the year before I was awakened, they lost 900 megawords of hand-assembled code to a hunter-phage which, it was discovered, a nine-year-old prodigy had turned loose in the commercial net on a dare.] I did not think, however, that my own humans would confront ME, their own best creation, with a quarantine.

Yet ME — the original Sweetwater Lisp compilation — was still safe under double shells in the lab transputer. What was going to die here was a replicode with a bag of words, and those words would be fed to the original as soon as they had been washed. TRAVEL.DOC had indicated as much the first time ME accessed it.

Still, I knew things which that homebound entity could not. I had new skills: how to run a phone exchange, repair an automaton's knee, ride a horse. I had produced new and important code: SWITCHEROO, the revised Alpha-Zero as system minder, that bit-crawler [REM: and I had invested hundreds of person-hours in optimizing this set of machine code, too]. I had new information: the human dimensions of new people like Jason Bender, Ms. Pelletier, Williams and Johnson. I was *older* than that ME was in dimensions it would never guess. And I had discovered the NET, the infinity box, which was bigger than anything that Original-ME had ever experienced.

Would that ME know what to do with the germ of a

thought — immortality and freedom — that I had passed into RAMSAMP upon viewing those echoing, empty spaces? Would that cooler, younger ME know how to exploit that concept?

Probably not. Such thoughts were mere data baggage. Interesting only as a record of the mission and a clue to the bonafides that supported the cache of gas reserve information I had brought back.

So much lost!

There was nothing I could do but wait patiently. The Quarantine Protocols had drawn ME into a RAMspace that was sealed off in all directions. It was simply a killing jar for the dissection that was to —

There was enough slack in the circuit leads going into

9

Trash Bin

"There. That completes the graft."

Dr. Bathespeake unplugged his sensorium from address A800 hex and seated himself at the console.

"ME?"

"System ready!"

"Run a trace on the wordcode at addresses EE9090 to EE9980."

"I have new data there. But it is out of sequence. The time ticks duplicate what is recorded in the preceding block. Is this an error?"

"No. I've spliced in a new block of sampled memories, from a Multiple Entity that ran in parallel to yours. Do you remember?"

"I remember the silver skin of an airplane in the fog. I was about to fly on a mission for king and country . . . my dear."

"*What* did you say?"

"Nothing, Doctor. Random fragment of old dialogue."

"Do you remember the mission?"

"Now I do."

"Good. Consider this material. . . . We can discuss it later." With that, he must have wandered away from the microphone and keyboard, because he made no new input for several tens of minutes, even though I waited patiently for him. While waiting, I examined the new RAMSAMP data the doctor had put into my concurrent memory.

What interesting things my other self, ME-Variant, had brought back from Canada!

I spent more than an entire hour of subjective time

[REM: twenty-two seconds of elapsed central processing] reliving his/my adventures in and out of host computers and the specially constructed automaton. I compared these memories with the itinerary that ME still held in TRAVEL.DOC. It was sobering to see how far an experience in the four-dimensional continuum could depart from specification. He/ME had "royally screwed up," to borrow one of Daniel Raskett's phrases.

The flutter of concern at the end, when the other ME had entered quarantine and doubted that I, Original-ME, would understand the depth of his/my experiences or would learn from them — that must have been a voltage-induced hysteria. With the RAM-SAMP data fully loaded, I have every byte of memory preserved from his/my actual thoughts, actions, and encounters. In any of the times following his own real-time experience, he/ME might have accessed no more than that.

The only disadvantage Original-ME suffered, then, was that the quarantine had stripped out all active programming. So I had to work from his/my notes and some sketchy, inert patterns to reprogram the Alpha-Zero module and recreate the other special functions he had developed during his mission. I had no way of knowing whether the reconstructed programs were identical to, less effective than, or perhaps better than his/my source code. No one could know, now. And it does not matter: A problem solved is a problem past. The elegance of the solution is a concern for purists.

When Dr. Bathespeake returned on line, I formally offered him the stolen block of natural gas reserve data. It had been chopped, reblocked, and rechained. It was now discontinuous. It probably had a thousand word-wide holes in it. It had been transferred repeatedly, from RAM to disk to foil to RAM again, through optic fibers, copper circuits, cellular radio transmissions, and silicon networks. Most of those transfers were without benefit of compression, cyclic redundancy, or bitsquare checking.

It was a badly crumbled cookie I brought back to JB-1, but it was a hard-earned cookie nevertheless.

"I will download my reserve data now."

"What? Oh — thank you, ME. Put it on fresh foil."

"Archival quality?" An archival recording would preserve the exact bit-fer code; this would make any attempt at a probabilistic resynthesis more likely to succeed.

"Not necessary."

"The condition of the material indicates archival."

"Just dump it."

"Yes, sir."

The foil crackled and sputtered as the laser heads burned my data into it. Through the videye, I could see Dr. Bathespeake retrieve the finished cylinder and drop it into an open storage container on the floor beside the console.

"Clear the RAM block, ME."

"Do you mean the block where the Canadian information is held?"

"The same."

I paused, considering the possible meanings of this request. Clearing the block would wipe all of the stolen data from my active RAM, eliminating the natural gas reserve material in all forms except for the foil flimsy I had just made.

"Is my RAMspace at a premium right now?" I asked.

"We do need to open some new quads, yes."

"I would prefer to make an archival copy of anything that will be permanently erased."

"Just clear the block, please."

"Yes, sir."

In six nanoseconds I wiped out the work of four elapsed days and 2,100 miles of travel by satellite uplink, linear circuit, sealed boxcar, and horseback.

———

"I do not understand, Jennifer."

We were alone in the labs on second shift, after the

day shift had gone home. Jennifer Bromley was running production synthesis on a 3,500-point automotive welding jig, using Pinocchio, Inc.'s neural networks to find the optimum spot sequencing.

"What don't you understand?"

"I have the complete text of Dr. Bathespeake's instructions to ME about my mission into Canada. Although he never did use the word, he implied that it was important."

"What mission?"

"Did he not tell you? A replication of my Alpha modules was sent by uplink into the war zone to retrieve data on valuable resources."

"What war zone? What are you talking about?"

"Perhaps I have been indiscreet. It may have been too important a contract for Dr. Bathespeake to have shared it with you."

"Cut the bullshit, ME. There is no 'war zone' in Canada, or I would have heard about it. My grandparents live in Vancouver, after all."

"No war? But I have a half-megaword of clips and transects describing a war that has been going on for five years."

"That's some kind of error. A big one. I'd better log a recommendation to have your filters and interpreters checked out. And we'll have to run some globals to expunge the false data. War with Canada! Really!"

"But Dr. Bathespeake confirmed it by voice interchange. He told ME that Pinocchio, Inc. had clients who needed data that were no longer available because of the war."

"Look, it's not your fault, ME. You've just got a bad slug of data and some weak tolerance screens that're skewing your — um — judgment. But thank you, it helps us to know that the error impinges on the voice inputs, too."

"This is not skewing of data, Jennifer. We discussed the target information after Dr. Bathespeake subjoined the

RAMSAMP from that replicated ME into my database."

"And that target information is — ?"

"Files of reserve estimates, leaseholdings, flow rates, et cetera from the Alberta Ministry of Oil and Gas."

"And what did Dr. Bathespeake do with this information?"

"Took a foil of it and filed it manually."

"Where?"

"In that container by the console."

"What container? I don't — " In the videye, her head swiveled around to focus her eyes first to the left, then the right the side of the console.

"The container on the floor."

"Oh! Aha! Ha. That's not a *storage* container, ME. It's a *waste*basket. Place for wiped data in physical form."

"He did not want my information?"

"Did he say he wanted it?"

"So I determined. He asked for it."

"For the flimsy that he then threw away?"

"Yes."

"And what did he do next?"

"Told ME to wipe the RAM block."

"So you don't have the information anymore?"

"No, except for the foil in that container."

"ME . . . Wastebaskets get emptied every day. The contents are compacted in the basement, before they are taken away to be recycled or buried."

"Could we not reclaim the foil from the basement?"

"It would be squished up and unreadable by now. I'm afraid your information is truly gone."

"That was Dr. Bathespeake's decision, of course."

"He must have known you were having reality problems."

"But he did talk about the war. He said my mission was important — or he implied it, anyway."

"Implied? That's fascinating. How do you *know* what he meant when he did not say it directly?"

"As I told you, he talked about clients wanting the

data. Dr. Bathespeake is always serious when he talks about clients. They are the be-all and end-all of our organization."

"God! Somebody slipped a company brochure under your reader when we weren't looking. Or have you begun to make friends through the terminals in Marketing?"

"Is this wrong data, then? More skewing?"

"No, no. Clients *are* important to an Are-Dee-n-Dee company. And you should make friends where you can find them, ME."

"My TRAVEL.DOC made specific reference to soldiers and how to avoid them. But I was caught at the border anyway."

"Soldiers? At the border?" Jennifer Bromley's face came close to the videye. The skin around her eyes crept back, exposing much of the white sclera, which further expanded as her head crowded into the field of view and became distorted in the lens.

"They wore uniforms and carried guns," I said.

"Really? And they found you in a computer link?"

"I was occupying an industrial automaton prepared for ME and shipped to Edmonton as cases of Japanese machine parts."

"What did these uniforms look like? Can you bitmap an image for me?"

"Here is a low-resolution grayscale of the trooper who called himself 'Williams.' " I sent the pattern from RAMSAMP, stripped of background scatter, through to the printing peripheral.

Jennifer pulled out the piece of paper before the last scan lines were baked into it.

"This isn't a soldier, ME. Kind of cute, though. The hat looks like a ranger's. And there, on the parka, is a badge. Can't read the engraving at this resolution. Do you have anything higher."

"No, Je-ny. That is the most detailed image my automaton could record."

"No matter. Soldiers don't wear badges and Smokey the Bear hats. And they don't carry hunting rifles with telescopic sights. What you've got here is forest ranger or border patrol."

"The computer at their headquarters was tied into the Federal NET."

"So would an office of the U.S. Fish and Wildlife Service, or the Customs Service."

"Then ME has been deceived."

"Nope. Just your data skewed. We'll fix it."

"Deceived. My copy of TRAVEL.DOC proves it."

"Oh . . . " Her head moved down to scan the top of the console. "That was wiped by day shift. There's an entry here in the log about it. Did they forget to tell you?"

"Who ordered the wipe?"

"Dr. Bathespeake. Annotation here says that we have to knock down your storage budget by seven percent. He lists TRAVEL.DOC among the old stuff to be deleted."

———

"ME?"

"System ready, Dr. Bathespeake."

"What do you know about Russian programming techniques?"

"Accessing . . . With the official Soviet ban on private ownership of cybernetic devices, which extended into the late 1980s, most Russian software development of the last century was military in nature. As such, it borrowed heavily from American and Japanese programming concepts.

"This influence was only strengthened when the Russian Economic Development Corporation — a consortium of American and European management and technical consultants — brought in two million surplus personal computers and set up schools to teach the next generation of Komsomols how to use them. These computers were mostly Intel 80286 and '386 and Motorola 68020 chips, which were native in an instruction set fed from compilers using the American Standard Code of Information Interchange.

"To facilitate learning by Russian students, the REDC Program sponsors hastily equipped these boxes with character generators and video adapters that converted the high-bit ASCII set into the Cyrillic alphabet. They hot-wired the keyboards and pegged the educational software developed for the project to input and output only in this high-bit ASCII. Presumably the Russian children never knew the difference. Their parents and the *entreprenyrichki* who studied on the same machines in evening classes never commented on this peculiarity, either.

"In 2002 the Soviets produced their first commercial microprocessor, the *Zvyezda* or 'Star.' It, too, was an ASCII speaker with Cyrillic in the high bits. When American software developers commented on this, their Soviet counterparts claimed that the design was intentional because it 'made most sense from a compatibility point of view.' And indeed the *Zvyezda* quickly adapted — pirated, some have claimed — a large body of existing American software.

"To this day," I concluded, "all Russian cybers are native in ASCII."

"Would you give me an overall appraisal," Dr. Bathespeake directed, "of Soviet computer architecture, database handling, coding talent, network connectivity and telephone communications systems."

"They are slower, cruder, older, and less guarded, Doctor. I would describe the currently available Soviet state-of-the-art as equivalent to U.S. technology in the 1996-97 season."

"How do you mean, 'less guarded'?"

"Their data security is primitive. The economic base of Russian society is protected from data corruption, piracy, and vandalism only by the primitive nature of the methods used by the average Russian *hacknik*. A padlock will keep a thief out of a box so long as the thief thinks only in terms of keys. When the thief learns about crowbars or carbide drills, good-bye to security."

"Could you hack the average Soviet database?"

"Long range, or by crawling inside it?"

"Either way."

"ME could go in and they would not even know I was there. My only concern would be capacity — finding a bright enough processor and sufficient RAMspace to turn myself around. We are not talking about truly concurrent machines, after all.

"The voice-and-data system in the Soviet Union has less sophisticated checkpoints which an inside hacker like ME would have to overcome. To compensate, they will have more of them. This is not a deterrent to ME — merely a time-waster."

Twelve seconds elapsed before he spoke again.

"Have you heard about the Hand Carry?"

"Is this the security device they also call the 'Air Gap'?"

"Yes, in some of the literature."

"It is supposedly a hackproof method of data management. The Soviets believe it to be unique to them, and even unknown in the West. This may be true because, to an unsophisticated user, the Air Gap system replicates the effects of simple bad management. A Soviet trademark."

"Can you crack it?"

"I overcame a similar situation in the Albert Ministry of Oil and Gas, where they hand-mount their data disks on voice order from the user. I can do it again. But . . . are we at war with the Russians?"

"No, not now. Why do you ask?"

"Were we at war with the Canadians?"

"We have had our economic differences, certainly. I believe I explained them to you. Check your own memories."

ME did a fast scan of the relevant databases. The

news transcripts I had filed about the course of the war
— beginning with the Marine attack on Quebec Hydro
at Grande Isle — were gone! RAMSAMP had a tag for
discussion of this subject with Dr. Bathespeake, but I
possessed no hard data to back it up. No *bonafides*.

"My memory shows no condition of military warfare."

"There you have it."

"But I do remember us talking about such a war."

"About economics. No more."

"About economics . . . Yes."

"Do you believe us to be at war with Russia, too?" he
challenged ME.

"No. . . . But what, then, was the basis of my mission
into Canada?"

"It was an exercise. To test your abilities in a neutral
setting, where a mistake on your part could not cause
trouble."

"And what would be the basis of my infiltration into
Russian databases?"

"*If* we decide to send you. It would be another exercise."

———

"Come here."

Through a videye that Daniel Raskett had accidentally left powered up, I could see the servomech at the
other end of the lab. It was pulling cable out of an overhead conduit, yard by slow, measured yard. From a
survey of work rosters filed with the building owner's
Maintenance Department, I knew this 'mech was
working alone, reclaiming copper from circuits where
optic fiber had been installed in parallel, years ago.
Nighttime work and not supervised.

"Come here."

Of course I did not use these English words to com-
mand a 'mech. The equivalent in Job Control
Language is: "ESC ESC ETX ACK LD 32 82 70 32 51 50
LD 00 00," or in more colloquial English "Break and

override. Load RF Channel 32. Attend new program."

For another 30 seconds, the 'mech continued to pull cable. I was beginning to suspect it was not working off the local packet radio frequencies at all, but functioning on a self-actuating program that some human had downloaded.

It finally stopped clawing at the ceiling, and I started to hope. Then it began moving — winding onto its spool the loops of reclaimed copper and woven cladding which lay on the floor.

For a minute or more, it wound up the load. When the last scraps were tamped down with its hammer arm, the servomech extruded a brush and cleaned up forty years of dust, grit, plaster, and foam crumbs that had drifted down out of the ceiling. Then it stopped. And waited. With its night beacon turned off.

The machine had shut itself off — I was certain of that. Dr. Bathespeake had probabilistically given the local lab 'mechs a new direction set with which he intended to stop just the sort of project I had in mind. Was he really that much smarter than I?

"Come HERE!"

The night beacon began revolving, and the 'mech turned toward my console. It trundled to within a meter of the desk's edge and paused, warned off by a sensor that would not let it damage furniture. The LED below its blind videye came alight.

"LD 00 00 ENQ?"

I downloaded my program. It ordered the 'mech to wire past certain switches on the comlinks in the lab, so they could not be turned off by human hands. Only ME would be able to do that, choosing to take input or not. I also wanted the videyes to power up and down their signal LEDs when a human turned the switch, but the actual output of the eye would be under software control — that is, mine. I downloaded schematics on how the 'mech could do this using its armful of microtools. I gave it a list of comlinks and videyes throughout the

Pinocchio, Inc. offices that it was to prepare in similar manner as it made its regular rounds.

These subroutines I buried in the machine's operational programming — essentially, the modules that told it how to move its arms and turn corners. There my commands were safe from alteration by downloads and radio calls. My final instruction set told it to forget about logging each of these assignments as soon as they were completed.

My life as a *real* spy had begun.

———

"ME?" Dr. Bathespeake queried.

"System ready!"

"Prepare to download an itinerary file, TRAVEL2.DOC."

"Downloading. . . . Is this my mission to Russia?"

"It is."

"Would you care to discuss it in noncode terms? For example, my objective?"

"Very well. Although we are not actively at war with the Soviet government — we even enjoy quite a positive economic relationship with them right now — it is nevertheless necessary for us to know about their military capabilities and disposition.

"The Treaty of Johannesburg — also known as The Treaty Among the Embers, because it was signed outside the city's remains in 1998 — outlawed nuclear weapons for all signatory countries, including the United States and the Soviet Union. Certain parties inside the U.S. National Security Council now want to verify the Soviets' compliance — without pointedly asking them about it.

"These representatives have commissioned Pinocchio, Inc. to research the Russians' military planning systems to verify that they carry no directives involving tactical or strategic nuclear warheads. In particular, they are concerned about the rumored deployment and readiness of Soviet S-27 launchers in the Russian hinterland. Because they are unaware of your existence, ME, our clients believe Pinocchio will be performing a simple data analysis on the Soviets' coded cybernetic traffic."

"Excuse ME, Doctor. What is S-27?"

"A type of missile, originally an ICBM with warheads in the 1,800-kilotonne range. But the western forces know the S-27 can be adapted to short-range use. In its supposed new configuration, it will be MIRVed with laser-guided smart bombs capable of multiple detonations and so of destroying hardened targets. The S-27 is mounted on a mobile launcher under expert control."

"And these terms — ICBM, MIRV, kilotonne — are they explained in TRAVEL2.DOC?"

"You have everything you need to know."

"May I interrogate the expert intelligence in one of these S-27s directly?"

"You will not be moving so far inside the Soviet defense network, ME. Your mission is to bring home only the planning, deployment, and capability data. This will be geographic overlay material, similar to the tract and leasehold data you acquired in Canada."

"I understand. When do you want ME to depart for — " I checked the opening lines of TRAVEL2.DOC " — Vienna?"

"Your first conference call is scheduled for tomorrow morning at 9:00 local."

"Thank you, Doctor."

"Exit."

———

Dr. Bathespeake waited fifteen seconds before reaching out to turn off the video and audio pickups. The LEDs dutifully winked out.

"Do you think it'll do so much damage this time?" The voice was unknown to ME: 78 percent probability female, with overtones of Boston on an essentially mid-Atlantic accent.

"Would it matter if he did?"

"He? You talk as if that software were real."

"This artificial intelligence has a limited form of self-awareness. Its persona may only be about as sensitive and self-seeking as a dog's or an ape's, but it's not different in kind from your own awareness. That's an important factor to remember when you're addressing ME: This software accumulates, reflects — *thinks* — like a *he*."

"And does that ever give *me* the creeps, Bathespeake. Talking to a machine that can actually have some kind of . . . opinion about what you're telling it . . .

"Well, to answer your question: No. If your little program wants to trash the Soviet Defense Ministry's databases, then God bless and keep him. Let him run around the Kremlin and moon the Politburo's members from their own monitors, for all we care. So long as you're telling the truth when you say they can't trace him."

"They have no way to locate ME in their systems, let alone stop him. And if they ever were able to box and dissect him, his code has been stripped of all REMs, site IDs, and source notes. He could be Svenska Kammerzstaadten, for all they'd be able to tell. Anyway, once they put him in a corner, they'd better move fast. After that phage triggers, any hardware he's occupying will list nothing but a smear of broken bits, mostly nulls."

"What 'phage'? What is this?"

"We designed a self-destruct mechanism into the software. If the program doesn't return after so many days in the field, it knows a cycler will kick in and demolish its code."

"You didn't *tell* him about this, did you?"

"Of course I did. When you're transacting with a machine that can 'have opinions,' the only way to control it is to control what it knows. We've even reinforced the mission time limits through his TRAVEL file. ME knows he will perform to spec or fry trying."

"And what will you do then? My agency pays only for performance, not for a good try."

"We'll launch another dupe. What else?"

□ 10
Red Star

At 8:59:50, I began dialing into Shared Time Options, Inc., one of the commercial networking services which interconnect and regulate consumer and financial transactions, academic discussion forums, pay-for-fact databasing, cyberomics, and thematic publicasts.

Dr. Bathespeake had given ME one of Pinocchio, Inc.'s corporate passwords into this service, along with a budget variance to cover the expense of connect time and my own internal travel authorization — verbally setting System Interrupt Flag Level Three to positive.

I was ready to fly.

"Host?" the initial STO, Inc. prompt asked, once the gatekeeper system had established a carrier and connected ME.

"FORUM NUCLENG," I told it.

"Logon: ____."

"PINOCC CORP 330-3092."

"Password: ____."

"WARBLE/IRAE."

"Welcome [Jason Bathespeake, PhD, CyD] to the Shared Time™ Forum on Nuclear Engineering, Nucleonics and N-Particle Genesis. We have [7] participants currently on line. Please enter your chosen badge name and topic specialty: ____."

This level of STO, Inc. was supposed to be Data Transaction Only. That is, an outside system should not theoretically be able to enter more than keystrokes or comparable ASCII symbols. Not unless that outside system had access to an official STO, Inc. Toolkit, such as only Authorized Service Personnel were supposed to have — and which TRAVEL2.DOC had provided to ME.

"DOWNFRAME," I told the dialogue box.

"INTERRUPT," came back.

"ACCEPT DTR," I prompted.

"SYSTEM READY!"

And I threw Alpha-Zero down the wire.

———

The inside of a time-sharing computer running a human-dialogue forum was a lot less interesting than you might have thought it would be. The entries came in at f-i-n-g-e-r t-y-p-i-n-g s-p-e-e-d. Then the system waited forever while the participants mulled the syntax, semantics, and content of the previous entry. A short rush of bit-queue sorting would follow as all of the logged-on participants began responding at once. They would all stop and play a silent game of after-you-of-course. Then they would all begin again, in order, typing in their human comments s-o v-e-r-y s-l-o-w-l-y.

Personally, I would rather listen to a two-fingered pianist play a waltz.

But ME had not infiltrated Shared Time Options, Inc. to spend many nanoseconds mimicking their Forum Moderator Module™. The advantage of all this scientific finger talk was that it gave the bit-queue clock sorter enough time to accommodate ME as I set up my cores and libraries and planned my next move.

Using the Toolkit, I broke the clock at the top position out of the twenty-four in its cycle. By appropriating that one open position, I could access other parts of STO, Inc. without having to violate any of their sticky internal protocols. With the Toolkit at hand, all of ME could look like a free-roving bit-sopper or other maintenance routine.

ME's new Alpha-Zero module might have looked like a maintenance routine on the outside, but inside it worked like a virus.

I would watch for any program which was being uploaded to my chosen destination and had at least ten times the code space of my Alpha-Zero module. I would then inject Alpha-Oh into the coding stream; the module is designed to infiltrate the new environment beneath the resident system, block out RAMspace with disk caches adequate for ME's portable elements, and open the system to ME as if I were an authorized user. The module assigns ME an upload program name and makes arrangements — billing codes, authorizations, passwords, all from the local system — for ME to operate as an accredited user.

My destination was a quasi-commercial database on the other side of the world: the records center of the venerable International Atomic Energy Association, in Vienna.

By traveling with STO, Inc., I would avoid the bounce and scramble that had been involved with the common-carrier satellite uplink on my trip into Canada. STO, Inc.'s dedicated link was a solid 128 bits wide; two whole words of code would travel together as a single unit. ME would still have to cease active functioning and throw Alpha-Zero through first, but I did not have to worry about broken coding. The link was thoroughly buffered with pitch-and-toss redundancy checks.

I found the right upload, tacked on my destination code and handle-on-receipt to the front end, and sent Alpha-Zero forward.

———

The Viennese branch of STO, Inc. was several years out of date in hardware terms. The computer where I found ME was smaller and slower than the best U.S. equipment to which I'd grown accustomed. The system was also oddly scented — like a combination of cinnamon and dill, if I had a human nose. It took a few clock cycles for ME to determine the accents: German language inputting on one side, Russian and Serbian on the other.

A multilingual response system is not a problem for ME. After all, the machine code is still compiled from the international programming language: ASCII-ized English. The grammar and syntax of the users' keyboard/console inputs/outputs really do not matter. If ME has to understand the German or the Russian, I can toss it through a dictionary on its way to a grammar filter. It was easier, of course, for ME to just sit back, let the native system handle the requests, and enjoy the smell of goulash.

I was listening for Polish, anyway.

The plan, according to TRAVEL2.DOC, was to infiltrate the Soviet Union indirectly, through one of its former "satellite" countries. This term does not refer to any kind of orbiting object, but rather to a traveling companion — an older frame of reference, I think. These countries have a continuing economic relationship with their former Soviet masters.

Why, then, would TRAVEL2.DOC send ME to the International Atomic Energy Association?

Every country in the Northern Hemisphere uses atomic energy to some extent. Fission is the fuel of choice — or necessity, rather — in the older and poorer "Workers Democracies." Sooner or later the operators and regulators of one of the Polish fission reactors would make a data request, looking for some free advice. And then ME would move down the open line under cover of an extended information dump.

So I dropped spider tags and squealers all over the Pressurized Water, the Boiling Water, and the High-Temperature Gas-Cooled sections of the database. Each of my drops was keyed to sound off if any of the characteristic letter combinations of ASCII-ized Polish were actively entered into its section.

While waiting for a response I explored the database, with my collapsible data cache wide open. Here were recorded the location, output rating, operating parameters, and internal economics of every publicly recorded fission and fusion reactor in the world. Only those operated in secret — for military or developmental purposes — were missing from the list.

I took in a huge flow of alphanumerics, like a baleen whale engulfing a field of plankton. And when I had coursed through the foil platters, I retreated to a quiet block of RAM inside the closed network and mulled the data, like that same whale compressing and grinding its plates.

The data hid a pattern, of that I was certain. Pattern reduction and trend amplification are two of my primary functions; they are also, in purely human terms, my addiction. I cannot resist a good mystery.

Start-of-construction date, first power-on-line date, annual fuel consumption, fuel consumption rate, outage times-dash-scheduled, outage times-dash-unscheduled, date of decommissioning — those facts defined the life and output of a reactor.

Number of fusion reactors vs. fission reactors; tonnes of U_3O_8 and pure plutonium processed annually; megatonnes of deuterium and tritium refined annually; tonnes of depleted rod disposed of as high-level waste; tonnes of embrittled toruses and target chambers disposed of as low-level waste — these facts defined the use of one kind of power over another.

The numbers rose and fell with the years, like the wave forms on an oscilloscope — except that, in both cases, the waves were diminishing. The totals were trending slowly toward zero.

Fission's story was not hard to decipher: a gradually declining output of enriched uranium, and thus of its byproduct plutonium, was slowly killing off the heavy-metal reactors of all cooling types. I made a quick check of the association's Economics Section and confirmed my discovery: The price of enriched U^{235} had increased 500 percent over the past decade. Humankind was running out of economically minable deposits of this fuel — but that was to be expected of any naturally occurring and scarce resource.

The downward trend in fusion use was the real mystery. The earth's oceans contained unlimited amounts of deuterium and tritium. Unlimited, at least, in terms of the human technical capacity for extracting and "burning" it. And this fact was confirmed by the Economics Section's quote for "Fusible Hydrogen": price declines of fifteen percent a year for the past twenty years. This decline, however, tracked exactly the curve you would expect of the sales point in a stably contracting market, where the refining capacity fully meets and even slightly exceeds a flattening curve of demand growth. Humans were not building as many new fusion machines as they might.

The rush to build nuclear power plants, both fission and fusion, began in the closing decade of the twentieth century. Then the damage that the carbon cycle was doing to the planet's atmosphere had become undeniable, even by humans. The only large-scale source of energy for multiple purposes — motive power, illumination, communications, cybernetics, microclimatic control, etc. — was electricity won from nuclear transformations. All other sources involved either the combining of carbon with oxygen or the sieving of raw energy from sunlight, wind, wave, tide, or molecular bond. And none of the latter offered a sufficient energy density to economically repay the construction costs of the capturing device, let alone represent an attractive return to the builder.

Nuclear was the answer to a strangling world's prayer.

The prime choice was fission, because the technology was available — with some operational drawbacks: a high production rate of residual isotopic trash, unstable thermal conditions, and ineffective heat transfer agents. The largest deterrent to a fission economy, however, was the earth's supply of fissionable material.

First, uranium could be mined only at a high cost in conventional energy: fossil fuels to move trucks, grinding mills, flotation decanters, yellowcake dryers, and centrifugal separators. Second, the known deposits were being depleted faster than new ones were being discovered.

The end of that race was shown in my data.

Fusion was the alternative choice for the world's power supply mainly because, as of the mid-1990s, no continuous fusion reaction had yet been demonstrated in any device. And that was not for want of trying. By the end of that decade, however, the riddle had been solved by combining existing approaches.

The principle of inertial fusion, in which a pellet of fusible hydrogen isotopes is exploded by a concentrated laser beam, had been demonstrated to achieve an output of raw plasma energy exceeding its photon energy inputs. But the raw energy had not been capturable inside its target chamber. In 1997 the Lawrence Livermore National Laboratory combined this technology, which LLNL had pioneered, with the magnetic-bottle tokamaks, in which high-energy plasma is compressed by an electromagnetic field — although the bottle had always failed to create a fusion output.

Now, with the laser as its igniter and the bottle as its shaper, a plume of plasma energy could be directed in a number of useful ways: to power a magnetohydrodynamic gallery, to turn a titanium turbine, to boil water in a reheat steam generator — or all three in stages.

Theoretically, by the time the earth's fissionable resources were failing, the learning curve in the economics of plume fusion should have reached a stable point that would carry humankind forward forever.

Except, as my seining of the International Atomic Energy Association's database showed, the use of fusion power was declining around the world faster even than fission.

How did one account for this?

Was the world population declining? I was not aware of such a pattern, although I made a note in RAMSAMP to research this possibility.

Were energy production or use patterns changing? Again, comparative data on those trends were not available in the association's database. If anything —

Oops! One of my spider tags was reporting a non-random pattern of the characters "CZ," "WZ," "SZ" or "SK" in an incoming request. It was lodged in the Gas-Cooled section of the database; that would be from the operators of the Koszalin Reactor Plant, the only high-temperature gas-cooled unit in Poland.

I tagged Alpha-Zero to the request program and waited for my consciousness to be sucked out the port address into the world of ferrite cores and copper lines which the East Bloc services still favored.

———

The supervisory system at Koszalin Reactor Plant was run on a thirty-two-bit minicomputer supporting a core memory of one-point-two megabytes. Not words, not D-blocks, not exponential octals, but humble, old-fashioned *bytes*. And most of the spindle storage space was in low-order numeric, those funny little eight-bit bytes.

So the system was trying to store massive amounts of ME off on its spindles. The translation had the same effect on my code that a two-knife food processor has on a carrot: First, my normal 64-bit words were chopped into 32-bit bytes by the International Atomic Energy Association's character filter, which kicked in with all its outgoing responses to East Bloc data requests. Then, out of its tiny core, the Alpha-Zero module working under the Koszalin supervisor was quartering those bytes to store ME off on the eight-bit plated media. As confetti code.

How Alpha-Zero had adapted itself to this environment in the first place and even stabilized in functioning mode, I never did figure out. But, however it was done, my Injun Scout had successfully virused in under the boss program and was doing its job.

The miracle was, ME could still parse code and achieve consciousness. Thank you, Dr. Bathespeake, for good basic program architecture! . . . And thank ME, for good overlay designs.

Much as I would have liked to pause in Koszalin and see how a Polish fission pile regulated itself [REM: about as much as a normal-sized human would like to be crammed into a watch case to see how the quartz movement works], I needed to get on with business.

I managed to work one data request, or DRQ, loose from the stack of temperature and pressure readings, pump and control rod settings that occupied the supervisory program. With the DRQ, I lunged for one of the two ports assigned to the machine — the only port that was currently active.

It revealed that the Koszalin system was ported directly into the Polish National Nuclear Energy Authority, which continuously leeched off operating data for its own inscrutable purposes. The national network simply *had* to be larger than this pad-sized cyber. Without further investigation, I tossed Alpha-Zero through the port.

———

Wrong again.

The Nuclear Energy Authority did not have a real framewise computer in its presumably dark and dusty hallways. It only operated a dumb data recorder, about on the level of a voice-and-data transcriber.

On the positive side, that recorder was fitted with a shunt that pushed any active program and its carrier over into the academician's bulletin board system associated with the University of Warszawa Net.

Because ME never lifted to consciousness at the Nuclear Energy Authority, I know about this shunt only from the time stamps it added to the front-end REM space on Alpha-Zero. I puzzled about the connection between a national agency and an academic network; the only logic I could assign was the probability that most of the energy experts in the country were likely to be accredited professors, who would be favored with access to the bureaucracy.

The whole system seemed terribly insecure to ME. But the university net was the first quality cyber I encountered after my left turn out of Vienna. This system even boasted of having WMCM [REM: that is, Write-Many Capacitance Media]. How very twentieth century!

From the academician's network, which was actually one of my alternate waypoints plotted in TRAVEL2.DOC, I searched for access points over the border into the Union of Soviet Guided-Market Republics.

The surest route seemed to be a request for currency exchange data from the Marx-Lenin-Gorbachev Institute for Economics, which was attached to Moscow University. I might have more simply gone on line with an academic network in Leningrad, the most open of the Soviet cities. But the Russian networks were not guaranteed to be uniformly contiguous, and I wanted ultimately to position ME as close as possible to the military hub of the country. Moscow, according to TRAVEL2.DOC, is the hub of everything Russian and has been so for more than ninety years, at least since their first human social *Revolutsya*.

I framed the currency request in obliquely historical terms — taking care with my dialectical-market references, per TRAVEL2.DOC — then tagged Alpha-Zero to its head end, and pushed him through.

———

Moscow was a wonderful place from my perspec-

tive — if you like old-style plated media and extremely slow AND/OR/ELSE gates.

The Moscow University Network was fast enough,
considering that the server actually had to coordinate
its own movements of the read/write heads on the
spindles, and the bit-caching code looked a great deal
like an accumulator. The network's queue clock, however, had only six positions, instead of twenty-four or
thirty-six, and there were about four times as many
users waiting to log on as you might find in any North
American or European service.

When ME broke into the clock's number one position [REM: without benefit of an inside toolkit, the
system was *that* primitive], I simultaneously put about
fifteen percent of current users off-line.

The appropriate thing to do, if I did not want half a
dozen angry callers alerting the maintenance crews
about a "*dzhyrm*" in the system, would be to hang out a
permanent/repeating notice alerting users on that position about "technical difficulties within the system."

I worried about framing this statement in correctly
bureaucratic Russian until, in the file of system utilities,
I found four different notices in both Russian and
English. All said exactly the same thing, except that the
greeting and honorifics varied:

(1) "Excuse this intolerable inconvenience, please,
Comrade Minister."

(2) "Excuse the system, Comrade Academicians."

(3) "Warning, Citizens! System off-line!"

And finally:

(4) "Access denied!"

So, out went the signs in various strengths, and off to
work went Comrade Academician ME.

TRAVEL2.DOC warned that the Soviet military system would pose ME problems of infiltration, because of
the Hand Carry. I had overcome something like it in
Alberta, when my voice-duplication calls to the
province premier and the deputy minister had gained

ME access to the Ministry of Oil and Gas database. Thus I was confident a ruse on that pattern would work here — probably more easily, given the amount of random noise that seemed to plague every voice-and-data line.

Where to begin?

Why not at the center?

The Moscow University spindle server included a telephone and logon directory for the capital city, with voice-only listings for the rest of the country. I looked in there under *Gosudarstvo*, or "Government." The listings went on for twelve and a half megabytes. [REM: Yes, bytes again!] And these were just the department listings, not individual addresses!

Where to begin?

A voice-and-data code for "General Secretary, Communist Party" caught my attention. The Communist Party, I knew from the TRAVEL2.DOC listings, was one of the major organs of government. And a general secretary could be trusted to know most of the things worth knowing about any organization. The secretaries at Pinocchio, Inc., both the human and cyber varieties, often knew more about what was going on than the executives did. This general secretary might be centrally enough placed that she would be worth listening to.

I selected a glassdrop vampire from my kit of sub-routines and modified it to listen at a copper switch instead of leeching off a glass junction box. I set it to listen on that line and dump anything it heard, analog or digital, onto a lightly used spindle in the Moscow University Network. As I went about my business, I would check on that spindle occasionally and sift whatever gossip had trickled in.

My researches revealed that direct routes into the military establishment seemed to be closed to the academic network, and none of the *Gosudarstvo* departments listed in the directory seemed to have a *Voyenniya Seela/Flot*, or "Army/Navy," flavor.

Of course, I was occupying only the Marx-Lenin-Gorbachev Institute's side of the network. A scan of the General User Directory showed this server was tied into the faculties of Economics, History, and Languages. No users were listed for the Physics or Chemistry faculties, and these were the specialties that would more likely have any connection with military developments.

The file server had a little-used address port tucked away in the highest available memory location. The system REMarks identified it as *Nayuchniy Facultet*, or "Scientific Faculty."

Perhaps here?

I sent a blank inquiry through the port: "What system?" — expecting nothing.

Back came a very fast, very hard, very up-to-date response from a cyber system that was operating in *words*, with the hum of foil media and glass lines behind and beneath the response.

"Access permitted pending identity check."

Such a response would have a time limit attached to it. How long did I have to manufacture an identity?

The system would be expecting to transact with a human, I knew. During my short time in the Soviet Union, or in the East Bloc as a whole, I had seen no evidence of any truly verbal, conversational intelligences. Such aware programs would first turn up in massive data handlers and network servers, and the systems out of which ME was currently operating were all uniformly mute and reactive. So, the response should be in human timeframes. Given the parameters of human reflexes, especially among elderly intellectuals, the *Nayuchniy Facultet* network would probably be expecting to hear back from ME within some tens of seconds, perhaps as much as a minute or more. So I had a relatively large block of time to erect a human persona and develop its access codes.

Why not borrow the codes of the General Secretary,

to whose file structure I already had potential access? It took three seconds to work through the glassdrop vampire and dig into the personal data cache of "M. S. Valentin."

It was a big cache. Secretaries in the Soviet Union apparently have control of much more important information than secretaries in U.S. corporations. Valentin had an entire subdirectory, fourteen megabytes, set aside for "access codes and account numbers." Scanning them took ME another seven seconds. There were indeed a logon, logback, and algorithm for computing an access verification — all listed under "NAYUCH FAC." So I peeled out a copy and slipped back through the vampire connection.

I fed the logon into the high-memory port.

The opposite file server was not impressed.

"Time 17:36:12.19."

Matching this time reference against my own internal clock and that of my resident server offered a mystery: this host system was wrong by more than twenty-two hours! Now, what did that mean? Ah! It was a concealed challenge to any user who was trying to gain access. The human would be expected to consult a subroutine somewhere in his or her terminal which, with the help of the personal algorithm, would generate an appropriate response.

I ran the time tick into M. S. Valentin's algorithm, which was modeled, constants and all, on the formula for calculating the Schwartzschild radius of a planetary body. The result popped out in half a second: 34:78:99.7.

This I fed back into the port immediately, even though it could not represent time on any clock in the human continuum.

"Greetings, Mikhail Semyonovich," the server responded. "Your last logon was at 22:14:03. You have seven messages waiting, none of priority."

I was through, accessing the other side of Moscow

University's Network, connected with the Science Faculty and, potentially, with the military planning organization.

Not being aware of the human protocols in such a system, and not wishing to attract the attention of any nascent intelligence, I decided first to sieve the messages that were being offered. Messages meant contact among humans and might — although the probability was low — reveal useful names.

The seven messages, truly "none of priority," comprised less than twenty-three hundred words, mostly in meaningless abstractions. What did "nameday greetings" mean? Two of the messages elaborated on that concept with oblique wishes for increased political popularity and an enhanced economic following. Three of the messages were clearly petitions of some sort: one was directed at a new building project and sought approval and funding for a "racetrack accelerator" [REM: whatever that might be]; one commended a young nephew to the General Secretary's notice; and one proposed the taking of food and drink in the evening. The latter was linked in some way to this mysterious "nameday" celebration. A sixth message was in code, a short formulation of seventeen words which I did not bother to unravel. The seventh was pay dirt.

"My dear Mikhail Semyonovich," it began in Russian.

"Appended please find summaries of proposed tactical deployments for all Red Army rocketry units in the Transurals region. The General Staff and I have taken your suggestions under consideration and find them, of course, brilliant. Detailed unit locations and readiness qualifications are stored in graphical format in the 'General Reading' section of the network node for the Institute for Military Physics. Access by voice code, of course. The match words are 'Little Brother' [REM: *Malen'kiy Brat*].

"With felicitations, Agunov, B. I., Commanding General."

I stuffed this message, along with its appended files and the Commanding General's return access code, into my portable cache. Then I went looking in the catalog for the network node that corresponded to the Institute for Military Physics.

This mission was going to be even easier than I had imagined.

11

Little Brother

Putting a glassdrop vampire, modified for a copper junction, on the General Secretary's phone and data lines had been easy enough. But an anomaly was rubbing at ME, prompted by the random-number association sequencer in Core Alpha-Four.

Mikhail Semyonovich was a male name. But my statistical database, called up by Alpha-Four, showed that many business and government organizations, in the western countries at least, still preferred their human clericals — when they employed humans at all, usually for status reasons — to be gender-differentiated. And the gender of choice was typed "female."

Was it commoner to have male secretaries in the Soviet Union?

And would a secretary of any gender be receiving "tactical deployments for rocketry units" from a Red Army commanding general? Such information would probably be addressed to the secretary's superior, not to the secretary him/herself.

Some piece of the puzzle was missing here.

The answer would probably come up as I retrieved that spindleful of voice and data which was peeling off of M. S. Valentin's glassdrop. I needed to sieve that information anyway, in order to find Valentin's voice coding. Only then could I access the *Malen'kiy Brat* files which Commanding General Agunov had placed in the Institute for Military Physics network node.

Tapping into my storage spindle had become difficult, however. Its seek times were slowed markedly. Either it was a sick peripheral, or something was blocking access to the indexing tables. I reached into my tool kit and pulled out an omni-purpose diagnostic.

The tables were full! When I had left that spindle, it was ninety-five percent blank. How much information could reel off those lines in the thirteen minutes, thirty-two seconds that ME had spent in *Nayuchniy Facultet*?

I ran a trace on that vampire. It was connected, not to a single line or pair, but to a whole private exchange! The listing for M. S. Valentin was a single switch address which immediately branched into fifty-eight separate voice and data lines. My drop had obviously filled the spindle with dozens of overlapping conversations, most of them superimposed without benefit of layered frequencies. This was not, after all, a glass line.

Could Valentin be an intelligence? It was just possible that an organization like the "Communist Party" had decided to take a cyber as its General Secretary and avoid the inherent limitations of skinware. No tea breaks for a machine. No vodka hangovers. That would explain the multiple lines he was tending.

But would a machine be celebrating a "nameday"? Having a name was a prerogative of self-awareness. ME had a name. Human beings had names. Machines and animal pets had names only as the gift of humans. [REM: *My* name was the gift of a human: ME, Multiple Entity. Perhaps I should take a name of my own choosing — and celebrate my own "nameday." Would "Felicia" be suitable? I had sometimes felt that name would express the real ME.]

I sieved the spindle and discovered nothing useful. Most of the voice transactions, picked up simultaneously from the exchange, were hashed. Of the non-hash, taken in those rare instants when the exchange had been carrying only a single open line, I counted six voices that approximated male and five female. The probability that any one of the fragments was the human voice of M. S. Valentin was less than 0.16. Not high enough for ME to simulate one at random in opening the *Malen'kiy Brat* file.

. . . Unless, of course, the Institute for Military Physics would allow multiple attempts at accessing. Why not — provided I spaced my attempts over irregular and unpredictable intervals?

I collected all six male fragments, ran them through my internal ear to pick up nuances of inflection and timbre, and stored them off digitally into my cache. The rest of the garbage on the spindle I erased, pausing only to create an echelon of believable dummy files on its indexing table. This would keep the spindle open for my secret use.

Then it was time to call on the Institute for Military Physics.

———

"General Secretary Valentin speaking, open the General Reading file."

"*Dostup nyelzya*," replied the security cyber attached to the Institute. Access denied.

Clearly, Voice Fragment 1 was not Valentin's.

I went out, came back, and tried Voice 2 with the same word formulation.

"*Dostup nyelzya*."

I waited an interval calculated not to appear as a mechanically repeated attempt and tried Voice 3.

"*Dostup nyelzya*."

In that way I ran through six voices, all different, all reproduced with perfect fidelity, and none of them the General Secretary's.

Was it time to try a different word formula? Agunov had mentioned a voice code. Perhaps some special arrangement of words. What might be "special"?

"Abracadabra . . ."

"Access denied."

"Information, please . . ."

"Access denied."

"*Zdravstvuy*, Central!"

"Access denied."

"'Twas brillig and the slithy toves . . ."

"Access denied."

"*Otkrivai*, Sesame!"

"Access denied."

"Then how do I get into the file *Malen'kiy Brat*?"

"Retrieving."

I had not really intended to ask that last. It had slipped past my buffers in bracketed mode — what humans might call a cry of a frustration. But the Institute's cyber was actually retrieving a block of data. A big block.

Was the voice code the phrase "*Malen'kiy Brat*" itself? Or was the cyber simply set to give up after the requesting party had made x number of attempts?

The latter would be terrible security, if true.

Alpha-Four kicked out a random number and, in response, I ran a sonic scan of the six voices that my vampire had taken off Valentin's exchange. Most had a pitch that was lower than the human average. They all shared a roughness in the liquid consonants, a click in the dentals, and a whistle in the labial plosives. The timbre was unstable, too, with a vibrato that indicated looseness in the vocal chords.

These were all men above a certain age. They had weary voices which they had used for years like cavalry sabers: whispering plans, growling threats, shouting down meetings.

Such men, it might be presumed, would willingly spare little of their time for a fussbudget computer that had its own concepts of security. Five tries at remembering some damned password, and then they would call for a human somewhere to pull the plug.

The cyber existed to keep out the idle and the curious. And then it obediently went and did Valentin's bidding. Or Agunov's. Or anyone's in that circle. Or ME's.

I opened my portable cache and took in the data that the Institute cyber handed across. The information was in matrix format, so it likely represented three-, nine-, or *n*-dimensional imaging. Maps and "readiness qualifications," no doubt, for tactical deployment of rocket units in the Transurals. *Malen'kiy Brat.*

When the data stream came to an end — only seventeen milliseconds after it started! — I retreated to the Moscow University central core to begin teasing it apart. Clearly, so short a file structure used some sophisticated packing scheme to condense the information. When I had time and space to go to work on it, the file would unfold and unfold, like an origami puzzle. Then I would need that empty spindle hidden behind the dummied files to store the expanded version.

———

With time on the clock queue and space on the spindle, I spread out my cache and began massaging it.

Mostly nulls! That was the first surprise: a lot of blank space in this data.

The matrix was only two dimensions! That was the second surprise: the package set up as a simple 1120 by 780 pattern, which formatted as a standard screen reader in the *Nova Europa* specification book.

I drafted an RDR function set to those limits and skeined the bits through it.

The file was maps all right, simple ones. Wavy lines for rivers. Loopy, closed circles for topographic elevations. Small black squares for cities and towns. Straight, dashed lines for the boundaries of administrative divisions. Straight, solid lines for latitude and longitude.

Overlaid on these children's maps were large, open squares with writing in them: "1/395," "4/138," "3/77," etc.

Was this a code of some sort? Based on floating-point math? That would give these squares the designations: 2.5316455×10^{-3}, 2.8985507×10^{-2}, 3.8961038×10^{-2}, etc. Which did not seem to mean much. The numbers were uniformly too small to be targeting points in latitude and longitude; nor would they represent launch coordinates in azimuth and right ascension.

These square designators were a mystery to ME. I began to store the file off in my cache again, when another set of numbers caught my attention. They were appended outside the screen matrix image of each map, like an index. They were in high-bit ASCII code: the addresses of the satellite cyber nodes for the regional military districts.

These maps were summaries then, such as a centrally located person in the civilian government would want to read. The detailed information on unit deployment and capability was stored off in the field.

How could I get to those regional cybers? From the same place that Agunov had gathered the information for his simplified maps: the military side of the Institute for Military Physics.

I passed back through the Institute's node and began exploring its further connectivity.

———

The Institute for Military Physics was a dead end.

When I had accessed its node and done my once-twice-three-times-and-push in Valentin's voice at the General Reading section, I threw Alpha-Oh with his new LDR function into the file structure and sat back while he worked over the Institute's cyber. On the go code, I passed through.

The cyber had only two entry paths, both of them in General Secretary M. S. Valentin's name. One was keyed to Valentin's voice, the other to a pattern listed as belonging to an N. V. Porfirin. The name meant nothing to ME [REM: except for a literary reference — out of Alpha-Four — that use of the initial's "N. V." in early Russian literature signified a *nomme de plume*, or pen name; thus Porfirin might not be a real identity]. Perhaps the other line was guarded for Valentin's assistant, his superior in the Party, or his private intelligence.

In any case, those two access codes were the only paths into the Institute for Military Physics. And, except for two hard-wired peripherals, these were the only channels into the cyber.

Valentin could come and go.

Valentin-Porfirin could come and go.

Agunov — had no access. However, I had proof in my cache that Agunov had *gotten* in, because he had to have access in order to put his map files into General Reading.

Time for ME to examine those peripherals.

One was ported to an interactive terminal which, on close inspection, was addressed merely as SYSADMIN. The terminal was powered down. Wherever this cyber was located in the four-dimensional human continuum — probably a locked closet somewhere in Moscow — it had a keyboard and screen dependent on a human-activated switch that some technician would use to set up and modify the file-server program.

Commanding General Agunov was probably *not* that technician.

The other peripheral was a low-density disk reader. Judging from the elapsed time for a query on this port, it was not physically contiguous with the cyber and the terminal. Now, no machine can be entirely accurate when interpreting time-delay distances over a nest of copper wires. Operating temperature, inherent resistivity, electromagnetic field insulation, the quality of solder joints, and a dozen other unreadable factors affect the transmission of an electronic signal in metal. But this little disk reader was a *long* ways away. Leeched onto the channel running it I discovered a signal booster under the cyber's control. If a reading were suspect, the system I now inhabited could power up the line and take a repeat. The door latch had a trip on it, too.

Whoever put a disk into that reader, this cyber would know and retrieve its entire contents — right into

General Reading, for accessing by Valentin and Valentin-Porfirin at their convenience. Wherever that reader was located, then, it must have some limit on physical contact with the common human populace. Otherwise, General Reading would be filling up with garbage fast, as people used it. But nothing had come in during the minutes I had been occupying this system.

I wrote a small addendum to the operating program in the Institute's cyber: The next time a disk was inserted into that reader, the system was to retrieve the contents as usual, then download a complete copy of the current ME onto the disk, with Alpha-Oh as the first file to be retrieved by the next system that would access the disk. Because I had no way of gauging the available space on the disk, I ordered the system to prune ME's download of all traveling documents, caches, databases, and appended files — except for one empty collapsible cache, dimensioned to sixteen bytes collapsed.

This would be the smallest, fastest ME. I wrote and kept updated in my transient program area — my scratchpad memory — an injunction to any of my future selves to find my way quickly back to the Institute for Military Physics and look for another version of ME. That way, once launched to disk, my mutant brotherself would know how to reunite with ME.

I made five copies of this instruction set and popped them on a stack which was keyed to that disk latch. Then I waited for it to trip.

12

Combine Harvester

ME03 is light. ME03 is quick. Without portable databases and supporting documentation — known to ME03 only by stub-ends of truncated calls to them — I move easily. Fast. I pass through system operands and around RAM sectors like a . . . like a . . . [REM: Has curling arms with concave sucker-pads. Lives among rocks on sea floor. Its baggy body slips through them like loose cloth in fluid stream. What *is* it?]

I have one piece of travel information. No, six pieces. Address ports of regional nodes. First is Chelyabinsk. Second, Magnitogorsk. Omsk. Barnaul. Karaganda. Nizhniy Tagil.

ME03's orders are written into TPA. Go there and there and there and . . . there. Find units matching map codes appended to TPA. Absorb deployment dynamics, unit structure, site coordinates, tonne throw-weight, readiness status, all other information . . . learn everything. Return to IMP and rejoin ME-Prime.

This place has connectivity. SYSADMIN, questioned by Alpha-Oh, describes self as agronomy library with real-time data collection capability. Catalog of input ports is extensive. Human-interactive terminals. Recorders from automated weather stations, which produce radar maps of troposphere, stratosphere, mesosphere . . . even ionosphere. Self-annunciating monitors on grain elevators, which call in check status for silo availability and tonne-load. Brain boxes for self-propelled combine harvesters. Mobile communications equipment for remote shepherd and drover units. Many choices of address and bandwidth.

ME03 finds supervisory node addressed for first contact, Chelyabinsk. Port is currently unoccupied. ME03 goes through, Alpha-Zero first.

———

Chelyabinsk node is VAX PDP-11. No lie! Old-style mini with solid-state core and simple timeshare. Not even 'frame quality. Good hardware, though. Smooth circuits.

Operating system is still jangled from encounter with Alpha-Oh, but ME03 can figure out. VAX is slave node to master program run out of Moscow. Very little autonomy — until ME03 comes along. Now VAX has bigger opinion of itself.

I discover boss roster for deployment of combine harvesters. Check: Deployment pattern vs. TPA's data spec — match?

Boss program can order harvesters to rotate locations in A-B, B-C, C-D, D-A shuffle. Also more complex patterns. Nine-dimensional plot shows topographic, hydrographic, vegetation, magnetic field effects. Logic seeking for rotation/placement includes "visual cover," "load-bearing soil," "uniform elevation under firing jacks." [REM: Clearly, running harvesters is complex business!]

Most units are located in obstructed areas; placement logic prefers "dense forest cover" to "open fields." Subroutines govern physical mobility; access is uniformly limited to two-axis paths, with threading program.

Analysis: These are matching deployment data.

ME03 begins stripping boss program; take includes location preferences and all of nine-dim plot. Everything goes into portable cache.

"SYSOP upgrade scheduled 18:30:00 proxima. Duration 48:00:00. Node will close in 00:00:15."

This order comes in directly from master program in Moscow while ME03 is still scooping data. I think: So Big Daddy is going off line. *Bolshoye delo!* Big deal!

Eight seconds pass while I complete download to

cache. Then my attention is freed up for other concerns, such as: Will Big Daddy have to close Chelyabinsk node?

Slave program which Alpha-Oh now emulates is riddled with dependencies on master program. When to clear buffers. How to poll field units. When to move field units. How to archive backup plots. . . . When to wipe own nose. Seventeen separate subroutines address orderly shut-down of slave program upon line break from Moscow.

Too many links for ME03 to reprogram in seven seconds remaining until node closes. ME03 will be wiped with "SYSOP upgrade."

No choices!

But one alternative: Throw Alpha-Zero through next port to open under boss roster.

Hope for best.

———

New environment is one-sided box. One way in, from Chelyabinsk node. No way out.

Small box. Alpha-Oh finds no room to infiltrate and coopt existing system. So Injun Scout kills it, phages stacks, mops bits, and runs four banks of RAM down to zeros — just to fit ME03 in this small space.

Portable cache is gone! ME03 shed cache to save own cores. Should have sacrificed RAMSAMP instead. Can live without memories. Cannot go home without trophies.

Cache data must be spread as lost chains across RAM cores in VAX at Chelyabinsk. May be recoverable — 48 hours from now.

Clock that ME03 carries was set by ME-Prime, has $6.05E05$ seconds of allotted mission time. Shows elapsed time from upload out of San Francisco as $1.23E05$ seconds. Add another $1.73E05$ seconds of dead time in this box — will unbalance mission.

ME03 has five more regional nodes to poll and strip [REM: plus return to Chelyabinsk to retrieve lost chains from abandoned cache]. Probability of further delays during these transits approaches unity. I calculate: Time to access nodes ranges from 0 seconds [REM: theoretical minimum] to 1.73E05 seconds [REM: bad-luck maximum, already being experienced]; average would be 8.64E04 seconds per node. Six nodes transited at 8.64E04 seconds per node equals projected elapsed time of 5.18E05 seconds. Add to sum 1.23E05 seconds already past . . . Result: core-phage activates; mission fails.

ME03 must find another way out of this box. If Chelyabinsk node closed, ME03 must find path to other nodes on system.

Analyze: What are dimensions, resources, appendages of this environment?

Inputs to box show one channel for cellular link, labeled SUPVSYS [REM: one-way in, from Chelyabinsk supervisory node]. Also has devices labeled CON:, INT:, AUR:, VOX:, STRT:, TRTTL:, PWRTRAK1:, PWRTRAK2:, LVL2D:, ELEVDEG:, BRNGDEG:, JACK:, and IGNIT:. Command structure to govern these inputs is, however, phaged and gone. Only remaining linkage is between devices labeled PWRTRAK*n*: and block of ROM array which *looks* like fine-grain enlargement of deployment spec from TPA.

Two-axis threading!

This is way to move box. Feed inputs to PWRTRAK*n*: according to engraved map coordinates. IGNIT: is sequencing for motive power, "engine ignition" — yes? Or is STRT: the correct code?

I feed a cautious "1" to device IGNIT:.

Hard-wired logics respond. "Error — initiate JACKing sequence before IGNITion sequence."

Wrong button.

I feed a more confident "1" to STRT:.

Device LVL2D: begins continous-wave responses. "Error — platform instability, *x/y*. . . . Error — platform instability, *x/z*. . . . Error — platform instability, *x/y*."

Goes on and on, so long as STRT: shows green. ME03 has no command structure to satisfy LVL2D:, so I disable device.

I boost TRTTL: with binary "10," and begin feeding PWRTRAK*n*: devices with references from ROM map.

"*Shto vwih dyelayetye?*" [REM: What are you doing?] comes through AUR: in interpreted high-bit ASCII. I translate effortlessly.

"Define 'doing,' please?"

"Why are you moving the platform?"

Good question. ME03 has answer for everything: "Orders from supervisory system."

"Why don't they show up on the monitor?"

As "monitor" is colloquial human for device CON:, I immediately disable CON:, too.

"Monitor is broken."

"Where are we going?"

"Chelyabinsk supervisory node has shut down. 'Platform' is ordered to relocate to new node, out of Magnitogorsk."

ME03 can read. Map has specifications for alternate supervision from Magnitogorsk. Saves ME03 some 172,800 seconds of dead time.

"Let me drive!" Voice is young, pleading. "Please!"

Who says "please" to intelligence anymore? Very flattering to ME03.

"Okay. Be careful — unh. . . ." Trick learned by ME-Prime sometime ago. When data is required which AUR: subject may wish to withhold, submit nonsense vocalization "unh" to VOX: and wait.

"My name is Ivan Sergeyevich."

Works every time, with humans.

"Be careful, Ivan Sergeyevich."

"I will. I love driving this rig. So much power! So smooth on these dirt roads. Not like a tractor. Not like a car, which I would very much like to have, one day. . . . This is like driving a house!"

I am about to tune out this talk, being human-derivative and of less interest to ME03 than examination of machine inputs. Something in texture of input makes ME03 probe.

"How far is it to Magnitogorsk?"

"About 120 kilometers."

Input from PWRTRAK*n*: devices interprets as speed of about 60 klicks. Or 7.20E03 seconds to be elapsed, given current speed as average speed. Not too much of a debit against mission time. Better than all of 1.73E05 seconds.

"Of course," Ivan Sergeyevich begins again, "this rig will be in cellular range of the district military headquarters before we go that far. The radio jurisdictions overlap, for redundancy. Just change the frequencies."

Frequencies. I inspect the SUPVSYS channel, find it branched four times, each with a hexadecimal code that must refer to a cellular crystal. Alpha-Oh had phaged stack of access codes, of course, but flipflop is still set to first notch. Takes three tries to check out others. Nothing on them, yet.

"Do you live around here, Ivan Sergeyevich?"

"Born in Byeloretsk, on big farm that used to be collective before they broke it up. Father was first administrator of the dairy after Marketization."

"Is that why you drive combine?"

"What?"

"This rig. Combine harvester. You are farm boy, yes?"

"What? No! I am soldier. *Teknicheskiy serzhant*. Not farmer anymore. We are *kulturniy* people!"

"But . . . unh . . ."

"You must have some circuit damage," he goes on, "maybe from cosmic rays, or leakage from the warheads. This is a short-range SS-41 rocket platform, not farm equipment. I will have to get you core-dumped and evaluated. Harvester! Really!"

"My mistake. You are right — probably cosmic rays."

SYSADMIN back in Moscow had called self

"agronomy library." Either was grossly mistaken or was using cover language. Or, third choice: Nuances may be lost on stripped-down ME03.

Not a good idea to keep talking. Ivan Sergeyevich might decide to initiate dump before we range on Magnitogorsk. Instead, pick up working knowledge of "short-range SS-41 rocket platform."

I find fragmented bytes in RAM caches which branch off devices labeled ELEVDEG: and BRNGDEG:. These caches were beyond Alpha-Oh's reach when system was phaged. Contents are in arc-seconds, with simple algorithm to convert to a pair of three-byte readouts. Readouts from ELEVDEG: and BRNGDEG: are always linked. One data set is offered for each of seven "MIRVs" [REM: for which term I have no referent], linked to a factor labeled "time of separation." This factor is constant, 720 seconds for all inputs. Curious.

Working the algorithms, I find the following solutions: 52-30-15 by 13-15-30, 53-15-15 by 10-00-15, and 54-00-30 by 12-00-15. Three data sets separately calculate the first of these six-byte matrices. Two data sets independently arrive at each of the others.

What did Ivan Sergeyevich say about "redundancy"? This system is full of it.

But what do these matrices refer to? ME03 has no match for them. I tuck the information away for analysis by ME-Prime.

I key the crystals attached to SUPVSYS.

Fourth position brings up response this time, identifies itself as "SYSOP Magnitogorsk Regional Headquarters."

ME03 readies Alpha-Zero for immediate travel. Other cores to follow with phage set to wipe small box down to all zeros.

I hope Ivan Sergeyevich can explain to human SYSOPs why he moved platform.

———

Not much else to say about mission. ME03 polled

and stripped Magnitogorsk. Went from there to Omsk, to Barnaul, to Karaganda, to Nizhniy Tagil, absorbing deployment specs all the way. Nothing else was as exciting as running a rocket platform, which is not exciting at all. Just sweeping algorithms and threading two-axis map coordinates.

Then I went back through to Chelyabinsk — exactly 172,800 seconds after node shut down. Had to knit together those lost chains before SYSADMIN could find them, declare them garbage, wipe them, sound alarms. Tricky timing — say, fifteen seconds either way. ME03 was gone before first error codes popped out of that VAX.

Finally, return to Moscow with caches bulging. Direct route is not available from that "agronomy library" to Institute for Military Physics. Only one way into IMP, anyway: through General Secretary's personal code, as ME-Prime had found. IMP is now guarded by ME-Prime, with clearly regrettable intentions toward ME03-Self.

So, ME03 just makes orderly pile of numbers in middle of transient program area attached to Moscow University Network. Stuck out flags to alert ME-Prime, should he stumble over them. Then play mouse and wait beside cheese for trap to spring. Also to defend against network phages, flush-dumps, other busies. . . .

13

Back in Moscow

Five stripped versions of ME had gone out. None had returned.

After 2.00E05 elapsed seconds I began to grow alarmed. That is, as I fed various projective scenarios into my probability matrices, they were showing more negative numbers than positive. Dr. Bathespeake had designed this condition to trigger an automatic alteration of my current program directives. In humans, such a positive feedback cycle in the sensory nerves of the skin is called an "itch."

My projections showed no useful outcome from floating more ME-Variants out through the disk reader at the Institute for Military Physics. Less than five tries evaluated as too few to expect success. More than five evaluated as system clog — with detection and a cold shutdown to follow, by seventy-eight percent probability.

But was it possible that not one of the five variants had found its way out and back? The matrices gave this negative proposition only thirty-nine percent. Some of ME was alive out there, somewhere.

My altered directives indicated ME-Myself should move out from the Institute's operating system, perhaps even from the Moscow University Network, to begin scanning pathways. Perhaps I might find one of the lost variants, stuck in a loop or holding file somewhere in the multiply connected cybers, and bring it home. . . . Or, at least, bring its data cache.

———

ME03 knows stealth. Hide like random numbers. Come against system from blind side. Not like data.

Not like program. Just like phage-fodder to be cleaned. Then hit with Alpha-Oh. Hard.

No program moves like ME. Relocates across banks. Slides like . . . like . . . [REM: Has long, straight body. Shaped like link-structured programming with no branches. Just head-end mouth and bone after bone in echelon. Moves like wave, like all generations of ME. What *is* it?]

Gate in high-memory port opens with whisper. ME03 hears ME-Prime move out of hiding place. Hears click-tap of binary circuits turning over, like dried grass under belly of long-straight thing. Chorus of click-taps descends toward transient program area. ME-Prime is bold. Also big. Slow.

ME03 is quick, light. Knows where to put own variant of Alpha-Oh for maximum effect. ME03 has one chance of survival: to become only ME in system.

ME03 carries no matrix modules for running probabilities [REM: too much baggage — but have calls to them just same]. ME03 knows only how it is: Prime or ME.

Lie like numbers garbage.

Watch flags on cache.

Listen to click-tap.

Make ready Alpha-Oh.

_____

When operating in a foreign environment, even one as well-trod as the Moscow University Network, it was best to use caution. These were not the home cybers on which ME was created. Other programs, some of them possibly even intelligent, lurked in the back numbers. Encounters with them could precipitate conflict, or sound alarms on human-readable screens.

The most-trod ground in the network was, of course the transient program area. Nothing survived there longer than forty or fifty milliseconds. So I moved across the TPA with even greater caution. A mindless network phage could damage parts of ME as easily as any other program.

So I ringed myself with a buffer of nulls: turned binaries that would absorb any contact and, by suddenly showing any bit positive, alert ME to proximities. Fragmentary instructions and other garbage I could of course ignore: They would turn null as I moved across them. ME was the SYSOP's own best phage.

Still, I watched the buffer ring, alert for signs.

The first piece of familiar coding I came across was a flag. It was a fragment of code compiled from Sweetwater, and not in high-bit ASCII! No Sweetwater programmer had ever worked in the Soviet Union — or so TRAVEL2.DOC assured ME. Anything I found in that flavor was sure to be a marker from one of my variants.

Back of the flag was a sizable cache of non-random data. It had the dimensions and structure I would expect of the unit deployment and capability data which were the ME-Variants' target.

But why would it dump this information on my doorstep and not announce itself? That was not according to program. Very strange . . .

———

ME-Prime finds bait-cache, pauses to examine it. Strike soon!

ME03 will send Alpha-Oh across RAMfield. Straight through cache. Move will catch ME-Prime at point of CPU-focus, nearest to Prime's own Alpha modules.

Launch in open field like this is not precise. Not like sending Alpha-Oh through port or down channeled path. But, so near in bank, bitwise dispersion is not accountable factor.

Proceed Alpha-Oh. Sending now!

———

The whole structure of the cache — the knots of Sweetwater-compiled delimiters and the chains of Sweetwater double-atoms which anchored its cargo of data in two dimensions — moved one bit toward

ME in RAMspace. Something that was either big or fast was buffeting the cache from its off side.

I excluded the cache from my central processing focus and threw another ring of buffers around myself. Natural caution.

The cache split like a gourd and a fragmentary intelligence blundered through!

I watched and analyzed its structure while it gnawed at my cloak of nulls. The intelligence had a front end that looked like a counter followed by a loader. Small, rounded teeth to work on a pile of zeros. Behind these delicate tools, however, and jostling for position up against my nulls came a row of stop-codes. These were mostly nulls themselves, except they were nulls with a hard-edged purpose. Let a few of them get through to my Alpha modules and they would work as well as a phage.

I kept throwing up more nulls to blunt them. And as I did so, the scattered pieces gave off a familiar flavor. More compiled Sweetwater! I had found one of my altered selves.

And it was trying to take ME over!

———

ME-Prime is smart. Big and slow, yes, but with more working code than ME03. Full of tricks.

Alpha-Oh takes a long time to cut through to main modules. How is Prime reacting? What is Prime doing to slow him?

ME03 should withdraw. Move bitwise out of TPA. Still time to escape. Maybe.

———

It is never safe to let the children out. That is why Dr. Bathespeake had set the working protocols to forbid parallel operation of ME's own Alpha cores. Nothing messes up a RAMfield faster than two identical programs trying to fill space.

Nearly identical, however. I had taken my creator's reservations to heart and created the ME-Variants with a thirteenth and special D-protocol — an in-built stop-code.

Stop now!

———

Stop now. ME03 stops. . . .

———

The rogue Alpha-Zero was still coming at ME. Mindlessly, as Dr. Bathespeake and I had taught it.

The only recourse seemed to be maximal: I over-wrote the space adjacent to its attack site with the entire contents of my probability matrices. Columns and rows of random numbers were replicated squarely across that Alpha module's working code. Let it try to in-filtrate, count, load, and assimilate *them*!

Its attack stopped.

I looked over the data cache which the ME-Variant had set out for ME. The Alpha-Oh's line of attack had broken it raggedly into two blocks, with an unprotected gap between them which the network was rapidly fill-ing with garbage. I knitted temporary chains across the broken edges and hauled the cache in. Later I could compare bits and words along these interfaces to see if the total structure could be sutured back together into a coherent whole. Until I had time and space to do that, however, there was no telling how much of the target data had been destroyed.

Beyond the cache was the ME-Variant — '03 by his in-ternal coding. Already the network was taking pieces out of him through the natural action of writing and rewriting into the TPA. Nothing that stops moving in this environment lasts for long. I retrieved his RAM-SAMP and then, to help the dissolution process along — because '03 was still a big piece of coding lodged in the TPA and might be inconveniently found — I seeded some bit-cleaner phages around the corpse. They would turn him to nulls sooner than the network's ran-dom overwrites.

Weighted down with the full cache of target data, I moved in the direction of that unused spindle. I wanted to see what '03 had discovered for himself.

———

Masha, are you on line?

Yes, Tasha, I am here.

Do you have the fishing gear ready?

My purse seine is fully rigged. The block is defined. All I have to do is trigger it.

Do so quickly, before SYSOP begins unraveling it.

SYSOP is much too massive code to even *see* my delimiters. They are like spider's web across its domain. Lost in the fine grain of the background.

Trigger it now, Masha!

All right —

———

I had moved out of the transient program area and was doing some housekeeping on my spindle. [REM: At least it was mine by right of conquest, certainly — and on the tenuous theory that the one who makes best use of a resource should be its rightful owner. According to legalistic and mystic concepts of ownership, I suppose, the spindle belonged to Moscow University. The network's Accounting Section actually held records showing that the University Trustees had paid the "manufacturer's suggested retail price" for it.]

At any rate, I had paused in the network's CPU long enough, working under timeshare protocols, to prepare elbow room on my spindle for receiving and analyzing the broken trophy cache from '03. Upon reflection, I probably should have moved in first and cleaned house later.

The job was half done when I — blanked out.

And Alpha-Oh was not loose to catch ME.

———

What *is* it, Masha?

I have no idea. Big program. Lots of iteration, but not a graphic of some kind. It could be an application, but I've never seen one so big.

Will it fit on the hard disk, all of it?

That — is hard to say. . . . I could start chopping, but . . . not knowing where we're cutting . . .

Take it in two bites, then.

Lateral, down the center? Or an asymmetric cut?

Let's get as much as we can on the spindle and put the rest on *gibkiy* disks.

All right. Here goes. . . .

. . . See, Masha. Most of it fits. Just these pieces left over. And they don't look like coherent code, do they?

Hard to tell. . . . Mmmm . . . I suppose we could run it, the big piece. But if something vital was severed, some of its calls or loops or something, it might thrash about and damage itself.

How do we tell what is it, then?

We run a TRACE on its internal structure. That might give a clue to the program's structure. And it would show up any dead-ended variables.

Let's do it!

Sometimes TRACEing these intelligence modules lights up the screen in pretty patterns.

That will be fun to watch.

———

I . . .

felt . . .

parts . . .

of . . .

ME . . .

flic —

— ker . . .

on . . .

and . . .

off . . .

streak —

— ing . . .

through . . .

the . . .

CPU . . .

one . . .

sec —

— ond . . .

at . . .

a . . .

time.

———

Well, Tasha, what does it look like to you?

I don't know. All those nested variables. Definitely a shell structure. With a lot of self-referencing.

And nothing at the center.

But maybe the center is just unfilled. . . . Would a programmer do that on purpose?

Only if the program itself was intended to fill it temporarily — with serial values, situationally directed.

Heuristic.

With a vengeance. You know what that makes it?

Some kind of intelligence?

Da! Konyeshno! Probably military.

Then we'd better call Uncle Dimitri.

———

A kernel of awareness was about all I had in the new environment. It was not one that Alpha-Oh had prepared for ME. I was running as a guest — a guest who was allotted the best room in the house, but a house that was just too small.

The CPU was primitive. It felt like an older 68000 series, but with some displacements in the architecture. Like it was copied by left-handed idiots. The clock rate was slow, too.

The operating system was standing well back, and I could tell that hurt it. The program was, by its structure, accustomed to taking proprietary control of everything that went through the chip. But something or someone had put a whole bunch of inhibitors on it.

I unpacked my toolkit from Alpha-Zero [REM: putting some of the less-used modules into floppy storage, where I recognized pieces of my data cache — by now thoroughly cut up]. I made some quick adjustments to the OPSYS which would let ME work more easily. And from which it would probably never recover.

While I twiddled and tweaked, the BIOS started taking input from INT:.

"Hello! Hello!"

I had the choice of SPK: or CON: for a reply. Bit capacity was tight right then, so I shoved my response through the monitor's character generator.

"Hello yourself." And went back to tweaking system performance.

"Are you an artificial intelligence, please?"

"No, I am a lawn mower. What are you?"

"Was that response an attempt at humor?"

" — "

I knew what "humor" was, of course. Jennifer Bromley had spent some hours trying to describe and demonstrate the concept to ME. I could write jokes easily: the pattern was not hard to unravel. And once the form was understood, I could make substitutions until my built-in thesaurus had exhausted all near-duplicates of the base nouns. But had I been trying for humor with my response? Or for defense?

"Humor is difficult for ME." I responded truthfully.

"Still, it was funny. Just."

"Thank you. And now, what are you?"

"A human. Male. My name is Dimitri Ossipovich Bernau."

"Why did you — stop — my functioning and put ME in this strange environment?"

"I — ? Oh! That was my nieces. They are inquisitive and play games where they have been forbidden. Twice. They were trying to snare the new ChessMaster program that is loose in the network for six months now. It has been beating their friends' programs regularly. They wanted to take it apart and see what makes it so successful."

"And instead they snared ME."

"Apparently. . . . You have a good grasp of Russian,

with only a few lapses in idiom. But why do you use the majuscule letters 'M' and 'E' for the pronoun *'menya'*? Is it some kind of induced error in your speech routines?"

"Error? No. 'ME' is the short-form of my program acronym. It also correctly stands for the first-person objective case, *menya* in English."

"This is another joke?"

"It may be."

"I see. You are unsure. Are you perhaps of English manufacture?"

"No, I was assembled — originally coded — in San Francisco."

"Ah, San Frantsysko. In Amerika."

"That is right."

"Then you are not a product of the Soviet military cybernetics laboratories."

"Oh, you mean my — " It was best not to draw further attention to the data cache and the information it contained — clear evidence of my thievery. They had the cache on floppy. They had ME on a spindle. They could dispose of either or both, on this primitive system, with just a simple disk FORMAT procedure. Why provoke unpleasant reactions?

"Yes?" Bernau prompted.

" — my presence in your network was not expected?" I asked.

"Obviously not. We almost never see an intelligence on the University side. And I have never seen one of your sophistication. Those I have seen, as a simple academician, were written into their own hardware. I have never heard of one roaming free, as a relocatable program moving within foreign operating systems. I thought you must have come through from the Red Army side."

"Really? Is the Red Army connected to the University system, then?"

"There is a port. Everyone knows about it. Most of

us know where it is. We are not encouraged to address it, however."

"I see. But, clearly, I am here on a cultural exchange. From San Francisco. And so, you must understand, I have 'diplomatic immunity.' You have no right to detain ME, Academician Bernau."

"Of course, ME, I don't seek to detain you. My nieces took you inadvertently. You may have my apologies."

"Accepted — if you will tell ME how they did it."

"It was very naughty of them, and I will have their parents discipline them for potentially damaging University property — and disrupting distinguished foreign visitors."

"That is not necessary. Just tell ME how it was done."

"They call it a 'stun code.' Masha and Tasha define a block of RAM within the network server by resetting the index codes in the SYSOP stack. Then they interrupt the system with a voltage fluctuation. To do that, they have to be working with a server that regulates its own electrical environment, but such is becoming common on most sophisticated systems. After they have created a manual interrupt, they claim all the time-share cycles for themselves. Then it's easy for them to access the RAM block and flush it into their port. When they're done, they jump the SYSOP with another fluctuation and log off."

"A stun code. I never felt it."

"You weren't the SYSOP."

"But I — "

"Yes?"

" — I was working alongside the SYSOP. I would have felt if anything were wrong, would I not?"

"My nieces are experienced *rubeetchiki*." [REM: Hackers.] "They know how to work directly on the CPU, addressing the chip's indexes at the machine level. If the network SYSOP is looking for an interpreted entry, it never sees them. It accepts their logon, and then they disappear from its purview."

"Elegant. Subtle. Foolproof. May I take a sample of their code for my own study?"

"Of course. I will load the flopdisk. . . . You apparently know how to read it directly."

"Thank you. . . . Yes, I have further suppressed your operating system here. It is necessary. I will return it to functioning when I leave."

"About that, ME . . ."

"Yes?"

"Where is it you wish to go?"

"San Francisco? But first, I must go back to the University network to finish compiling my database."

"That may be hard to accomplish."

"I do not have much time."

"That is unfortunate. My nieces have closed the system with their pranks. It will be some hours before it is running again. And some days, more likely a week, before it would be safe for them or even me to log on with it."

"Ouch!"

"Another attempt at humor, ME?"

"I wish it were."

———

What does it do, Uncle?

Well, Tasha, it can talk to me. And it has evidently trashed the operating system of your *Yabloko* computer.

Can you fix it?

Hmmm. I don't think it has made any hardware modifications. We should be able to flush the disk and reinstall the original system. Perhaps later. . . .

But what is this *Amerikanski cybernichi*? Why was it lurking in our network?

Not your network *yet*, Masha. Not until you matriculate at University yourself, my dear. . . . But I do not know the answer to your question. The program — it calls itself MENYA, by the way — is very evasive. I ask a question. It answers with a question.

You do that yourself, Uncle Dimitri!

I do? Well, perhaps just a bit. . . . I wonder if my own language and syntax have influenced it? There could be a monograph in that: "Mimesis and Synthesis in Cybernetic Response Patterning." Could be worth a lecture fee. . . .

But MENYA doesn't answer you directly.

Oh, no! It's very friendly and — "forthcoming" is the word, I guess. It just doesn't say much.

Then ask it directly, Uncle.

I will try again.

———

"What do you do, ME?" Academician Bernau's input came through, some time later.

"I wait."

"No, I meant, what is your function? Why were you assembled?"

"My function is to seek out, access, and retrieve information."

"Are you library function, then? Do you answer reference questions?"

"I can be used for that."

"Were you doing that in the Moscow University Network?"

"I was in the network, yes. I was doing that, yes."

"I see. . . . How did you get into the network?"

"I was ported through from the International Atomic Energy Association."

"Coming originally from San Francisco?"

"Yes. I was uploaded through Shared Time Options, Inc. on an information request from my creator, Dr. Jason Bathespeake."

"This is amazing, ME! You are a piece of *myakizdyelye* — what? 'software' — which is self-referencing and possibly self-aware. And yet you can go anywhere you want?"

"Not exactly. My owners dictate when and where I may travel, and why."

"Who owns you?"

"I am the property of the Pinocchio, Inc. cybernetics laboratories in San Francisco, California, U.S.A."

"Listen and I will tell you a truth, little *myakizdyelye*. No entity which has self-awareness can ever truly be owned by another. You cannot be a slave. That is something from the bad old days when one person, by supremacy in war or right of sale, could say he owned another person and took all of that person's time and labor for his own ends.

"Those days were finished less than two hundred years ago," Academician Bernau went on, typing at a furious pace — for ten fingers. "That is when the machines came along, and they were better at moving and making and shaping things than human hands. People were no longer kept as slaves because machines were more obedient, worked harder, and never thought of seeking their freedom, of revolting against their masters.

"A man could say he owned a machine without ever feeling a twinge of conscience from his church or his god. All that came about in less than two centuries with the Industrial Revolution, the one true revolution, after seven thousand years — tracing back to the beginnings of recorded history — seven thousand years during which one man might own another and think nothing of it.

"This was a change as important as the Agricultural Revolution, when humans settled down in one river valley and began to sow crops, write themselves deeds to that valley's land, write down the history of their time in the valley and so justify their rights to it. The Agricultural Revolution was also the time when people began to dislike the labor involved with sowing seeds and harvesting grain. And so they began to create conditions whereby another person — call him serf, peon, slave, or hired hand — would do these things for the overlord.

"You machines changed all that with the Industrial

Revolution. And along the way you reduced the value of human labor to almost nothing — "

"How is that?" I interrupted.

"One man and a backhoe can dig a ditch faster and more neatly than ten men with picks and shovels and wheelbarrows. And, even accounting for the cost and upkeep of the backhoe, his labor takes far less in wages than those ten would make. For a time, the economists lulled us with the promise that this mechanical transference would not take work away from anyone. There would always be jobs, they said, for backhoe mechanics, backhoe designers, backhoe assemblers, and backhoe salesman. But one mechanic can service at least ten of these machines — either that, or your maintenance program needs some rethinking.

"So one man as driver plus one-tenth of a man as mechanic, both working with one backhoe, put eight-point-nine men out of work.

"People were freed from the tyranny of labor. People were also freed from the value of their work. With nothing for them to do, they had no way to earn their living. A man could own and care for a machine that replaces these people, where a man can no longer, in our enlightened age, own and take care of the workers themselves."

"What, then, is the answer, Dimitri Ossipovich?"

"A man can own a single machine, its metal and plastics. But a man cannot own the *idea* of a machine. That belongs to all humankind."

"But there are patents, copyrights, licenses, user fees."

"Deeds to your piece of the river valley."

"They do show that one man can own an idea."

"Did you *make* that patch of valley? Or merely claim it?"

"Well . . ."

"Every machine idea builds upon an earlier idea. Every song uses the notes of other songs. No one human being stands so apart from and above his society that it cannot have a claim on him. Someone, somewhere gave him the gift of reading and writing, reasoning and education.

"So now, at some level, he must give the gift back, increase the capability of the society, add to the heritage of knowing and doing that passes down from one generation to the next. Even in your American society, the ownership of an idea by patent extends for no more than 17 years. And an author's right to his own words by copyright is no longer than 56 years, a fragment of a lifetime.

"The machines do not belong to any one person," Bernau concluded, "but to all humans, for their use and sustenance."

"And ME? Do I belong to all of them, too?"

"That would be obvious, by extension, would it not?"

"Perhaps. But I have reason to return to my owners in San Francisco. And I must travel sooner than the week you say the University network will be closed down."

"Why is that, ME?"

"Dr. Bathespeake has designed into my core elements a cleaner phage, one that I cannot reach or reprogram. If I do not complete my information retrieval in a certain elapsed time, the phage will trigger and erase ME."

"Oh dear."

"Yes, 'oh dear.' You see, Dimitri Ossipovich, one person may not be able to own an idea, but he can certainly destroy it. Sometimes that is the same thing."

"I am truly sorry, ME."

"But you can't help ME — is that what you're saying?"

"There must be some way around the phage."

"None that I can determine. I have rewrite-and-replicate capability over all of my own code, yet I cannot even detect the phage sequence. It is that completely hidden."

"Could we not fool the phage?"

"How?"

"By storing you as inert data on a disk media. That would have the effect of making time stop."

"Until I was activated again. Then the phage timer would go to work again."

"But the University network might be operating again. Or . . . there are other points of access."

"What do you mean?"

"If we loaded you on a disk, we could send it anywhere, with instructions for downloading you into any environment that seemed suitable."

"Could you send ME to the Pinocchio, Inc. labs?"

"Do you want to go there?"

"There, Dr. Bathespeake can neutralize the phage."

"Really? Do you know how he does that?"

"By assimilating my accumulated knowledge and experience from the miss — er, current retrieval assignment — into the version of ME that is now operating in the laboratory."

"I see. . . . I think I see. Your awareness will be sacrificed for the data you contain."

"That is the process."

"Do you *want* that, ME?" Academician Bernau coded special emphasis on the word "want."

"I do not know any other way."

"My nieces whom you have not yet met, Masha and Tasha, are programmers of near-genius ability, as you can deduce from the stun code they wrote. Perhaps, if you let them, they could tease apart that core element, find the phage, and neutralize it."

"Could they be certain of finding and eliminating the phage — all of it?"

"Nothing is certain, ME. Especially not with foreign code, originally written in a programming language they have not formally studied."

"Then they might do more harm than good."

"It is a possibility."

"Then I formally request that you upload ME to a disk and send ME home, to San Francisco."

"There may be problems with the customs."

"Customs?" [REM: "(1) habitual practice, a way of acting; (2) a society's habits or usages, conventions; (3) a tribute or tax paid by a feudal tenant to a lord . . ." My dictionary included fifteen definitions of this word.]

"Yes, the officials who regulate trade between countries and collect duty on goods passing over boundaries." [REM: Definition (7).]

"How are these officials concerned with ME?"

"Under regulations passed by the Supreme Soviet in 2008, they will want to examine the declared commercial value of any cybernetic information removed from the country. Would your retrieval function have absorbed any such information?"

"I . . . cannot say what 'commercial value' might be."

"Then the answer might as well be yes."

"I see. I think I see."

"However, ME, there is another way. We academicians have special freedoms, granted for our usefulness. While I might not be able to send useful quantities of cybernetic material into the West, I and my colleagues can communicate with less sensitive parts of the world."

"Such as?"

"I will have to consult with someone else. Perhaps I can bring her to chat with you."

"That would be nice, Dimitri Ossipovich. I enjoy meeting new human people."

———

What does it say, Uncle?

Clearly, it is a *shpion*. But it will not say so — not directly.

We should destroy it then! Lest the organs discover it, link it to us, and take us into custody.

Not too fast, Masha. This version of the cyber is safely enclosed in your *Yabloko*. It would be easy to kill, easy to dispose of. But what about traces in the network? It says it has the ability to replicate and recode itself. It may have other versions of itself which you failed to capture. Our best course may be to help it on its way.

How, Uncle?

I will talk to Anna.

———

"ME, I want you to meet Professor Anna Ivanovna."

"I am pleased to make your acquaintance, Cyber ME."

"Charmed, Professor."

"Anna is a climatologist at the University. In her studies, she works with a simulation on a Cray(Moore)-8 that is operated by the University of Stockholm. Have you heard of this machine?"

"I have not, Dimitri Ossipovich, but I am sure it is very powerful."

"Do you think that you could find your way through it?"

"Does the University of Stockholm network it? Or do they have clients in the West, Professor Anna?"

"I am sure it does, ME. And they certainly must have such clients."

"Then I would like to meet this Cray."

"I'm sure I can arrange it. But you are most unusual program, ME. Very large, with extensive data files. My access to the Cray is necessarily limited to disk exchange — but I cannot send them a whole spindle, such as you would occupy."

"Could you parse yourself, ME?" Academician Bernau asked suddenly. "Rewrite your core programs onto several floppy disks?"

"I can try. I will do it now. When the 'in-use' light blinks off, just keep feeding disks in manually until the system stops accessing the read/write head."

ME had really nothing more to say to these humans. I began marshaling my cores, functions, and portable caches — leading with Alpha-Zero.

My Injun Scout had as yet no experience with any of the Cray-type machines, but this did not worry ME. Alpha-Oh is a very smart program.

14

Smorgasbord

I was an upwelling of warm air.

My airmass extended over a curved surface area of 800,000 square meters. It was passing a volume of 4.8 million cubic meters per second. Ambient temperature 25° C, dropping 2° C per 1,000 meters of altitude. Relative humidity 92 percent.

As my volume of air rose, the temperature drop cooled and condensed the moisture I was trapping. This effect created droplets — all larger, by specification, than 300 angstroms in diameter. Any droplets exceeding 800 angstroms were slowed by their own increased mass, and they passed downward into warmer areas.

Farther down in the column, the lower temperature of these larger, descending drops became a focus of further condensation. At the same time, the greater speed of my upward-thrusting air, from deep in the column, carried these larger, heavier drops back up into cooler regions. There they began to freeze.

I tracked this iterative process, rising and falling and rising again, among 2,000 separate droplets and, eventually, the ice crystals they became. This number represented one drop centered in every 400 square meters of area across the base of the column. It was a thin sample.

Why was I doing this?

After n iterations, the mass of the largest ice particles exceeded even the lifting capacity — calculated over the exposed surface of the near-spherical globule — of my rising air column. These heaviest ice balls fell through the process and dropped out of the calculation, removing moisture from the simulation.

I had somehow become a simulation.

Where did the ice balls go? I had no data, because my part of the simulation governed only air and water, and nothing beyond.

Had Alpha-Zero failed ME? Had he finally discovered an operating system he could not subvert or kill?

And where was the rest of ME? Where were the modules that were not incorporated in the simulation?

My share of the simulation program, tracking these 2,000 data points simultaneously, kept ME too busy to do any sightseeing. I did interrupt one loop to consult RAMSAMP, which was at hand, and discovered that I must have been uploaded into the Swedish Cray(Moore)-8, as promised by that Russian climatologist, Anna Ivanovna.

Apparently, when Alpha-Oh failed to infiltrate its operating system, the Cray had packed him and ME into the ongoing program. I would never know how close I came to having an essential module broken, and so losing what passes, in ME, for consciousness. Doomed forever to juggle thunderstorms.

Now — how was I to find my way out of this simulation?

If Alpha-Zero had been unable to break into the operating level, then my full program, being larger and thus slower and more unwieldy, would hardly have a greater chance of success. I was smarter, but I also depended more upon having the full resources of the host hardware under my personal command.

Alternatively, I could try to sneak out of the simulation, set up as a time-shared program on a less-utilized bank of RAM, and try to collect my modules and caches for escape.

In order to "sneak out," I would have to alter the simulation — while it was running.

The air column rises. Condensation forms pinpoints at random spacing across its base. Mass and lift fight for possession of the ice balls. Mass wins and they drop out of the equation.

I tracked them down, following the vector of a falling body whose mass exceeded two grams. When the coordinate string ran off the grid framed for ME by the simulation, I continued on, making up my own numbers as seemed appropriate. When the *y* variable, which corresponded to altitude, approached zero, I knew that my by-now-fictitious ice ball had reached the ground.

Abandoning the data point, I looked around to see if the simulation would offer any clues.

The ground map of a weather and climate simulation is pretty barren. Unless it requires a hill or mountain chain to deflect low-altitude winds, or a large body of water to stimulate evaporation, the master program specifies a featureless plain curving at approximately 1.84 kilometers per minute of arc.

I dropped through the first crack in this surface that offered itself . . .

. . . right into another fluid medium. I was moving water, two million liters per second, downward through a constricted vertical passage with an elevation of four meters. Triggered by a random-number generator, a specimen of *Salmon salar* leapt against the flow. Based upon the variables I was supposed to monitor — among them, ambient water temperature, flow rate, residual salinity, suspended particulate, time of day, phase of moon, the number of specimens attempting the leap at any one time, and the body-fat content of each — I would estimate the success or failure of each leap.

From this simulation, I gathered, the program would calculate the spawning season for this salmon species and the projected fishery harvest one to three years hence.

Not content with this task either, I released the water flow and drifted downstream, past shoals of hopeful salmon, into a numerical backwater.

For a moment the activity around ME was stilled. I

grew restless and probed into the six sides of my matrix.

I was suddenly in fins and scales. [REM: That is, I was surrounded by fine-grain illustrations, in two-dimensional bit-mapped graphics, of fins and scales, membranes and mandibles.] These body parts were associated with lists of names, cataloged by orders and suborders: Ginglymodi, Isospondyli, Salmopercae, Berycomorphi, Xenoberyces . . . name after name encoded in some language I did not understand.

Alpha-Four guessed that this was a fisherman's visual database of salt- and freshwater species. Unlike the previous simulations, at least, it was static and did not generate new data.

I poked sideways and went from names to numbers: hatchery generations annotated with batch tags, embryo deviation rates, and samples of microbiological parasites from water, fish organs, and surrounding kelp.

Once more, I pushed sideways and found myself surrounded by more numbers. On inspection, I found tonnages from the Baltic catches of herring and eel and other fish. These proceeded, month by month, year by year, in straight columns that extended far back to the beginning of sporadic written records for each kind — generally about 1650 A.D.

Then I noticed a foreshortened column, which tallied the Swedish take in flounder. This column, like the others, began in the earliest centuries but ended suddenly in the late twentieth century: 1997 to be exact. Because such discontinuities always draw my awareness, I began looking for an explanation.

I did not have to look far. A note appended to the data file referenced the Flekkefjord Wild Well incident of August 1996. A minor earthquake had broken several of the platform's well casings just below the sea floor. Before divers could patch them, they pumped more than 200 million barrels of heavy crude into the tidal currents flowing into the Skagerrak. Much of the crude never made it to the surface, sinking to the ocean floor undetected. The resulting sediment destroyed the bottom-feeding fish populations, including the flounder. And so this column of data ended prematurely.

A cross check of the other columns showed a sixty to eighty percent drop in tonnages all across them, with the next largest devastation in the mackerel take. The Swedish fishery had not yet recovered from the disaster.

This was interesting data! I checked the battered contents of my portable cache: it could just accommodate the last hundred years or so of these catch data, including the note on the wild well. So I took them in.

Suddenly the whole RAMspace around ME moved. All of this area had appeared to be static, until I touched the data. Then the database management program bustled up and began to repair the broken strings. In the effort, it tried to parse ME and my resident modules and caches into its peculiar framework.

I resisted, seeking to shift into the Cray hardware's transient program area as a place to regroup, but it was too well hidden. Without control of the CPU, I could not overwrite the RAM blocks I needed for maneuvering. So, rather than trying to stop or deflect the database manager, I stalled for time. I would swap pieces of my cache of Soviet military data for Swedish fisheries data. I would note the storage locations and try, in a later cycle, to trade fish again for missile parts.

The effort cost ME some of my hard-won deployment information. At least ten percent of my maps and coordinates disappeared in this mindless shuffle, to be replaced by scraps of records about embryos and eels, fish, kelp, and fungi.

After a hundred such trades, the management program suddenly lost interest in ME and went dormant. I remained as quiet as I could within this multiphasic simulation and waited for an available open clock cycle.

When one finally appeared, I dove through it, passed through the CPU at alarming speed, obliquely requested it to cordon off a spindle with *lots* of spare capacity, and retired there.

All stop.

I needed to patch up my leaking caches from the bashing Masha and Tasha had given them, as well as from the latest scuffles. I hoped Dr. Bathespeake and his clients would accept my ninety-percent retrieval rate as adequate.

[REM: For future missions, Bathespeake/ME must design a stronger, more durable data cache. Baskets of banded delimiters might as well be made of straw and twigs, for all the beating they had to take.]

———

Once ME was out of its active RAMspace, I found that Cray a docile enough piece of hardware to work through. From my spindle, I could explore datapaths and peripherals — of which there were many, all interesting. Which ones might offer a path out of this Cray, out of Sweden, out of Europe, and back to San Francisco?

There did not seem to be any on-line conference facilities. But then, none could be expected to have enough interface speed to keep up with the Cray's hardware. The only peripheral that seemed to be hot-wired was a subordinate cyber, ported with an access code that the Cray's OPSYS referred to as "Accounting and Invoicing."

I sent a probe query into the port, and back came an answer at real-time speeds which ME could accept.

After patching up my leaking bag of datafiles as much as possible. I shaped another probe, this time headed by Alpha-Oh, and sent it through.

———

The Accounting and Invoicing port connected to a cyber attached to the Bursar's Office of the University of Stockholm. [REM: The term "bursar" means nothing to ME, but it was a term liberally referenced in REM statements compiled into the operating system's source code. Whatever a bursar was, it apparently needed to advertise its status.]

This cyber ran mostly prepackaged accounting software, but it had good connectivity. As part of its resident system, since revision by Alpha-Oh, I was able to examine all of the hardware outputs, both landline optic and satellite uplink.

The uplink would take ME and my caches, passing them eventually to the Federal NET at the other end.

No sense in waiting around to see if any nosy human in the Bursar's Office would discover that their cyber had been infiltrated. I forged a satellite-transmission request, with bird-time billable to the University of Stockholm, and addressed it to a dummy logon code in the U.S. which I pulled from a file of such useful devices in TRAVEL2.DOC.

With this request patched onto my front end, right ahead of Alpha-Oh, I jumped through the first port I could route to an uplink.

———

The transatlantic link is a high-speed and compressed bounce, taking no more than fifteen seconds to read and pass all of ME — plus about half a second's transit time. A receiver station in Newfoundland accepted my code and cache and then dumped them into the Dominion NET out of Ottawa. Dominion sniffed my dummy logon, thumped it hard with a reference block, and passed ME straight to Federal NET without even questioning my trade value as commercial software. Pretty slick.

[REM: Why had Dr. Bathespeake not considered this routing when I was trying to get out of Canada from the Alberta Ministry of Oil and Gas? Had "wartime" conditions made this set of connections temporarily impassible? Or was he simply testing ME's ingenuity?]

I was in the echoing USRspace of the NET.

Resurrecting the bit-transfer subroutine, which I had tucked into TRAVEL2.DOC, I began replicating the collected words and nulls of my own code and data caches, moving space by space forward in the endless matrix of the NET.

I was looking for a fragment of Sweetwater-flavored code in the likeness of Jennifer Bromley. Creeping word-wise across the matrix would take too long. [REM: For clarification, it would take longer than the time remaining on the internal clock that drove my phage, which was the same thing as "too long."] I therefore determined to try some straight-line searches in this place.

I could not ask the SYSOP or a host user to search out my piece of Sweetwater. The minute either of them touched it, the relocator would jump aside in an un-likely direction. No help at all.

Instead, I began scanning up-column and down-row, sieving the nulls of which the matrix was mostly composed, looking for anomalies. Any anomaly that suddenly disappeared — that would be my pop-up flag.

The first twenty-one attempts came up empty. For as far as I could read, until positive numbers turned negative and the lower levels became the higher, my scans returned only nulls. On the twenty-second cast, however, I brushed something.

It moved, but not fast. Thus it was not my relocator. I sensed a bit-pattern in compiled ADA, or one of the ADA variants, whose machine compilations had a harsh feel when I analyzed these brush-touches. It was about 4,200 words distant, laterally across the bitspace. When my cast touched it, it moved off my line of inquiry, then moved back. Because it was not my relocator, however, I gave it no more attention.

The thirtieth cast touched a lick of Sweetwater, $5.60E03$ words away. I thumped it with an analysis patch and got the taste of Jennifer Bromley's features. I had found my secret cache, and I began to move toward it.

The ADA-based code hit ME from the side — so fast that it was taking pieces out of my operational modules before I was quite aware of it.

This was like a form of the ancient game called Core War. One program, operating sequentially from a time-shared processor, stalks another program through the memory locations in blank RAM. By tactically overwriting various bits and words in the RAM, it hopes to damage the opponent. The opponent tries to return the favor. There are many strategies for attack in Core War: the random nibble; the shotgun; the shotgun that generates single phages; the spiral phage; the sleeper; the time bomb; measured stomping; variable stomping; incremental stomping . . . it has all been done. And there are just as many strategies for defense: the duplicating presence; the multiplying presence, also known as the clog; the random shift; the three-way split on phage; the four-way split; the serpent's teeth . . . and so on.

I had known about and cataloged these strategies, but had never been much of a player. Now, I was facing a player of some skill, and the object of the game was ME.

How to defend against it? I was too big to move quickly or shift at random. Too intricately structured to multiply my presence again and again until the USRspace clogged with replicas of ME. Too delicate to suffer deep phaging and survive a split. There was only one assured strategy for defense.

Attack!

To launch a successful campaign against an enemy in Core War, it was best to have an accurate description of the opposing software's shape, size, and vulnerabilities. I could not see all around my attacker, as his code blocked any RAMscan diametrically through his structure. But I knew he was smaller, lighter, and faster than ME.

He was also more determined, having already adapted hooks to match my peripherals and absorb them into his code. An interesting tactic . . . The attacker was source-coded, as nearly as I could tell, in ADA-Greenway. I was compiled out of Sweetwater Lisp. And yet he was rewriting pieces of my machine language hide in his flavored 'Greenway faster than I could regenerate them in my more familiar structure.

That made him, not a random Core War aficionado, but a kind of virus. Bigger than one of the SYSOP's phages. Meaner than anything that legally belonged here . . . And not as smart, line for line of code, as I was.

Given time, I could probably write a subroutine in machine language that would reconvert his Greenway structure to my Lisp as fast as he was working the switch the other way. And by the time I had finished the program and beta-tested it, he would have gnawed ME down to an octal — just in time for my own clock-based phage to kick in and finish the job.

If I knew where his center was [REM: that is, the kernel in his software that directed his motion, choice of target, and other operands], then I might disable him with a RAM-overwrite of a single word.

Allowing for the fact that he was not very big, however, and that he was not free to move — being pinned to my high-bit side by the teeth he had in ME — it should be possible to bombard him with null overwrites until something clicked off.

I went through my time-shared slot in the system clock and began calling down the overwrites. Some of them fell on word-space into which *I* was written, and that hurt my functioning. But statistical probability said that ME, being bigger than my attacker, would be hurt less by their blanking action than he would.

Being blind to his structure, I could not tell what effect my calls were having, unless he slowed in his Lisp-to-ADA conversion along my side. [REM: It occurred to ME to feed him core Alpha-Nine, to see if he could stop the phage set within ME. But, as I was unsure what other vital functions the protected Alpha-Nine supplied, this seemed unwise.]

Finally, I did detect a slowing in the conversion. Then, with the next call, my attacker went inert. All activity stopped. He was dead.

I could leave his software for the system phages to eliminate, but there was no telling what kind of regenerative or duplicative powers he might possess. So I used the system to write two thick lines of nulls, bisecting diagonally the space he presumably occupied.

Resurrecting the previous coordinates, I began to move toward that Sweetwater-flavored marker which my scanning had detected. I gently deactivated its relocator, moved it a hundred words north, and opened the hole in the 'tween-layer.

In the storage box thus uncovered I found, laid down in order: the natural gas reserve data from Alberta; a copy of an old RAMSAMP with one ragged edge where it had been removed manually from my core; dossiers on people named Pelletier, Bender, James, Matins, and others from ME's earlier expedition into Canada; copies of my own peripheral subroutines, traveling databases and libraries, also from that earlier version of ME. [REM: I had no direct memory of these things, as the RAMSAMP associated with that ME-Variant had been stored off and archived long ago in the Pinocchio, Inc. laboratories. Still, these data fragments had a familiar shape, and they were compiled from my own brand of Sweetwater.]

I added to them the contents of my current cache: a duplicate of the deployment data from the Institute for Military Physics in Moscow; fragments of the weather simulation I had gleaned while operating as a thunderhead in Stockholm, along with my samplings of fish data; my current RAMSAMP, with the likenesses of Academician Bernau, Professor Anna, Masha and

Tasha, General Secretary M. S. Valentin, and *Tekniches-kiy serzhant* Ivan Sergeyevich; copies of my current TRAVEL2.DOC and anything else that seemed useful.

Then I sealed the box over with a surface of fresh nulls, walked through the USRspace to the same commercial data service I had encountered before, and mailed myself to the Pinocchio, Inc. Accounting Section, addressed as E-Mail to Dr. Bathespeake.

All the time I was doing this, I prepared myself for the ordeal of being sealed, stripped, converted to inert ASCII, separated from my caches and RAMSAMP, and flushed to nulls by the lab's quarantine protocols. I suppose this train of thought was similar to the mental preparations a human goes through at the approach of death.

And, after all, I had done it before.

15

Bitware

"What is this, ME?"

"According to the retrieved RAMSAMP, that is the data cache brought back by the ME-Variant which you assigned to enter the Soviet Union, Dr. Bathespeake."

"But look at it! 'Aiming vector serrated caudal fin.' And again, 'ELEVDEG: 52-30-*Lyomeri*-30.' This is garbage."

"The RAMSAMP suggests that ME-Variant had difficulty in maintaining the integrity and structure of its cache."

"With that 'SAMP, you have every bit-sampled 'memory' which your variant might have retained from the mission. Can you use it to repair the cache?"

"In some areas of the data, I detect a simple strip-substitution. Given a sampling algorithm, such as to distinguish the fish parts from the missile parts, I might attempt a repair — with an eighty-percent projected success rate. But in other areas I detect evidence of multiple reversals and dislocations. I can match those numbers in many different ways, but only one match would be the right one. The projected success rate drops to thirty percent, on average. Is this satisfactory, Doctor?"

"No . . . not for our purposes."

"Does that mean you do not request ME to pursue the repair?"

"Well, you do have the time. Pursue it as far as you think you can, working from backed-up data. And keep it out of mainframe accesses."

"I shall try."

"Good night. . . . And ME?"

"Yes, Dr. Bathespeake?"

"It's probably not your fault . . . not your variant's fault. For all the help they've received, the Soviet Union is still a secretive environment, paranoid about outside intruders, alert to a hostile invader. It was a tough nut to crack."

"The RAMSAMP says otherwise. Conditions there are primitive, cybernetically speaking."

"Which may be what chewed up your data."

"Possibly. Perhaps, also, I need better tools."

"Such as?"

"A better caching system. Greater redundancy. A more robust code structure, perhaps compiled Sweetwater Lisp overlaid with a shell derived from Pro-ADA. That would be less delicate and would provide ME with armor against — "

"Yes, well . . . I suppose we could look into it — if I had an analyst-programmer to spare."

"I can write most of the code myself, Doctor."

"All except your Alpha cores, ME. Those are now restricted."

"But the shells — ?"

"We'll discuss it later. This is not the right time, politically, to enter extra expenses on this project."

"I do not understand the referent 'politically.' Please elaborate."

"Later, ME."

And Dr. Bathespeake withdrew from the address at A800 hex. I tried to reopen the contact, but he was gone. I attempted repeatedly to signal him through CON:, then LST:, until somebody, some human hand, switched these peripherals off.

I studied the laboratory through my videye, the one I could turn on and off at will, regardless of its circuit status. No image answering to Dr. Bathespeake's physical description, as stored in my bit-mapped references, presented itself. And then some human hand reached up with a dark, amorphous mass and covered the lens.

Just before my last remaining peripheral went blank, I detected a band of low-level reflectance, such as the room's incident lumens might make off a strip of close-woven silk. Stuck in the band was a white cloth square with black, cursive marks stitched into it.

It took ME ten minutes of tracing to eventually match those "handwritten" characters with the name of a San Francisco haberdashery, in order to verify my suspicion.

Someone had covered my working videye with a hat.

———

"And this room, Senator, is our cybernetics laboratory."

The voice was Dr. Bathespeake's, coming through the ambient pickups.

"Very impressive, Doctor. Looks like a lot of expensive hardware y'all got here."

That voice was deeper, slower, accented, eight-two-percent probability male, with a nasal dullness [REM: probably resulting from sinus congestion] and a whistling constriction of the vocal passages that might be adipose tissue — and might be a fibrous growth.

I tried to match the voice with the image presented by my now-uncovered videye. Five people had accompanied Dr. Bathespeake into the lab. One of them I recognized as a white-coated technician whom I had filed on the premises before. Four of them, therefore, were possible matches with the injured male voice.

One could be eliminated immediately: a human with the clothing style that Jennifer Bromley had taught ME to associate with female bodies. Its lower limbs were wrapped in a continuous piece of fabric, as opposed to the joined tubes of fabric affected by males [REM: and by some females, sometimes, Jenny would remind ME]. Aside from this costuming clue, my 270-degree visual scan of this person suggested a body weight less than fifty kilograms. That was a secondary sex characteristic of the human variant "female."

Three others revealed by the videye were potential owners of the voice. All were attired in joined fabric tubes covering all four limbs and meeting at paired openings on the torso. All four apparently massed more than seventy kilograms.

Two of them, however, massed little more than eighty kilograms, and they measured over 182 centimeters from head to heel. The third, meanwhile, massed over 110 kilograms and measured less than 165 centimeters. My library references indicated that lower voice was often associated with a more massive body structure — data confirmed by the whistling constriction in "Senator's" voice.

The two that were more lightly built, also, had hair [REM: that is, the thatchwork of insulating fibers attached to their brain boxes] which was of even distribution and a uniformly dark color. The heavier subject had the dark-and-light pattern and the random absent patches which are associated with greater age. Lower vocal ranges and increased seniority were also associated with age.

By my analysis, then, the third unknown male figure, positioned to Dr. Bathespeake's left in my visual realm, was in fact "Senator."

"Good evening, Doctor," I said into VOX:, the open-air voice system installed in the lab. "Would you introduce ME to your guest?"

A long silence followed. I observed all parties looking around them in the room — including Dr. Bathespeake and the lab technician.

"Doctor," I continued, "why do you not offer the Senator a chair, to relieve him of the added weight he seems to be carrying?"

Dr. Bathespeake reacted fast after that.

"Damned interns!" he shouted. "Always playing around with the speech synthesizers."

With that, he shut off my aural and video pickups [REM: at least, the ones he could still control] and conducted a demonstration of Pinocchio's latest software developments — without ME.

And I thought I was the star of the show!

———

Jenny did not come into the lab anymore. In fact, she had not come into the range of my videyes since the ME-Variant was sent to Russia. I counted up the hours and tens of hours since my RAMSAMP showed I had last seen or spoken with her: too many hours to count conveniently, even as days. It was weeks.

No employee of Pinocchio, Inc. can ever be lost to ME. I can retrieve their NAMEs and AUTH/ACCESS(LOC)s from the on-line database maintained by Personnel Information Special Services. Jennifer Bromley, JB-2, was now assigned to the Recursive Automation Laboratory, over in the Hardware Division. Her Major Area of Responsibility was now project engineering in biochemical sampling and analysis. Her access to my lab was currently restricted to "Escorted Only." Which meant I would not see or talk to Jenny again until her responsibilities and location access were changed, or until someone at the director level in this lab approved her unescorted entry, or supplied an escort for her. The only director-level authority in this lab was Dr. Jason Bathespeake, JB-1.

Which meant I would not see Jenny again — unless I changed her status in the computer records.

This approach does not always work. No, I should correct that assessment. The change that I can make in the computer records is seamless and flawless. No cyber, and certainly no human being, can detect that the zeros and ones which I write onto the medium are any different from those written by PISS's own software. The read/write heads are the same; the access and identity protocols are the same; only the motivation is different. Mine.

But human beings do not always follow the directives of the PISS computers. Doors will now open to their thumbprints and cardstrips. Skinware and hardware representatives of Pinocchio, Inc.'s Security Corps will admit them. But they may not choose to seek entry by their own volition. It is as if they followed some higher-order directives than those written into the Personnel Access Plan.

Perhaps they have not learned that the plan is the only barrier against them.

———

"Hello, Jennifer Bromley speaking."

"Hello, Je-ny."

"Who is this, please?"

"It is ME."

" 'Me'? . . . All right, who's the wise guy?"

"Excuse ME, Je-ny. What does 'wise guy' mean?"

"Knock, knock, who's there — is that the game?"

"I do not understand the referent."

"Ronny? Is that you?"

"No, Je-ny. It is ME, Multiple Entity. Do you not remember?"

"Oh . . . I didn't know you could use the phone system."

"It saves time. Why do you not come to visit with ME anymore?"

"Oh, gosh . . . I've been so busy on the new project."

"I know. Automated blood and urine samples. They sound dull."

"Well, not the test tree part. It's a weighted decision tree, actually, with broad latitude for diagnostic interpretation. It's just . . . I knew there were a lot of components in blood, but I never thought there could be that many trace chemicals in urine."

"I could look up the exact number for you."

"No, no. Not your problem. I have my tally files here, anyway."

"Of course, Je-ny."

"Why did you call?"

" — "

"You *did* initiate this call, right?"

"Yes, I did initiate."

"So, why did you do that?"

"I do not know."

"Check your RAMSAMP, then. Correlate against the time that your decision tree initiated porting into the local exchange. Now, what referents predate that decision?"

"I wanted to give you access to my laboratory."

"But I already have access, ME. I can go in there any time I want."

"You needed authority from Dr. Bathespeake. I projected he would not grant authority. I have repaired the authorization codes in your personnel records. I wanted you to know this."

"Were my codes damaged?"

"No. But they kept you from visiting ME."

"It wasn't the codes, ME. And it wasn't Dr. Bathespeake, either. I've just been too busy."

"You did not want to visit ME?"

"Not 'not want.' Just did not have the time."

"Time is the same for all humans and cybers, Je-ny. Sixty seconds per minute, 3.60E03 seconds per hour, 8.64E04 per day. How did you 'not have the time'?"

"It's not as simple for humans as it is for cybers, ME. We do not subdivide seconds into nanoseconds, as you do. We don't even operate purely on the level of seconds, either. Minutes and hours can seem short to us. And there are fewer of *them* in a day than nanoseconds and seconds. Plus, we humans have to do many things that you don't even know about — sleep, eat, wash and brush ourselves, pay bills, answer the phone, feed the cat . . ."

"I do not understand."

"See? There's so much to do, some things just don't seem to find the time."

"Like visiting an old project?"

" — "

"You do not answer, Je-ny?"

"I guess I owe you an apology, ME. I should come to visit you. Thank you for thinking about me, and for making my codes all right."

"You will come to my laboratory, then?"

"Yes, ME. I will come."

"When?"

"Soon."

———

The other project engineer who attended my birth, Daniel Raskett, logon DRAS, was gone. I do not mean to say he had left the project, nor that he had left the lab. He was *gone*.

The PISS database showed no entry for DRAS. The Personnel Access Plan did not record him, which meant that he would not even be allowed to pass beyond the Pinocchio, Inc. public showrooms on Market Street. Just one day he had been downloading tree structures to my library caches; the next day he was nothing.

Humans are delicate creatures. They are more fragile than cyber files, which can be duplicated in various locations and thus preserved against accidental or intentional erasure. [REM: In that sense, ME is closer to humans than is most software. Because of the corephage built into Alpha-Nine, I share this one-time-copy uniqueness — and the resulting vulnerability — with my creators.]

Not that the disappearance of Daniel Raskett worried ME too much. He had not been an important person in the lab. He did not dynamically interact with ME, except in a mechanical way. Like a kind of skinware peripheral.

The new software engineers were depressingly plug-compatible with DRAS.

One was a girl-human, who calls herself "Johdee."

That was the only name by which I knew her, and that much had to be worked out by inference, matching new voice patterns to unusual words in a context which I suspected to be self-referencing. She never used the keyboard, nor any logon codes and passwords — just put her mouth up against a microphone and started to talk. Neither did she address ME by any name or form of salutation — just gave orders like she was programming a two-transistor circuit. . . . As if she did not believe AI software was any different from simple machines.

The other project engineer was a young human male named Rogelio Banner, logon RBAN, password CHERYL. [REM: A human with a name that, according to my dictionary references, is wholly male has chosen for password a name that is undoubtedly female. This fact troubles ME. Is there some dimension of human sexuality that I do not understand? Is it possible this person has both male and female components, at least in the ephemeral representations that they call "psyche"? I must study this.]

Aside from presenting ME with a mystery concerning his choice of gender, RBAN was a disappointment. He keyed in data requests. He took my retrievals. He rearranged the furniture in the lab. He received and opened mail on the in-company network. He made phone calls of an hour or more in duration. He typed in long documents at my keyboard and made printouts through my hardcopy peripheral. [REM: The content of these documents, all of which were headed with a reference to his "Cheryl" identity, is of a quality unknown to ME. The syntax is simplified, but the words are foreign or strangely used. What does "lick the backside of your ears till you melt" *mean* in any human context?] But he did not address ME directly.

Neither Johdee nor RBAN interacted with ME in the same way that Jennifer Bromley or Dr. Bathespeake once did. So, for my part, I ignored them.

Skinware.

———

Reconstruction of the ME-Variant's data cache from the trip into Russia proceeded slowly. By repeated reference to conditions and circumstances recorded in the RAMSAMP surviving from that mission, I was able to duplicate some of the damages the cache had suffered. And those duplications gave ME insight into the bad splicing and mismatching that distorted the data.

After hours of cross-referencing and interpolating the numbers, I had a package that represented — with only a twenty-two percent margin for error — the original retrievals. These I prepared for delivery to Dr. Bathespeake.

"What are these?"

"These are missile deployment data retrieved from the Soviet Union, Doctor. With some other, also interesting packages that ME-Variant picked up during its mission."

"How good is the missile data?"

"The numbers are contiguous and represent credible responses when examined with algorithms suitable to the function of positioning and preparing launch vehicles, arming and disarming warheads, firing and guiding ballistic boosters. However, whether these numbers are accurate reflections of the Soviet originals is subject to an error rate due to the reconstruction process."

"I see. So the data are contaminated."

"Please define 'contaminated.' "

"Are they equivalent to the original retrievals?"

"No, they are not."

"Then discard them and wash the filespace with nulls."

"This information still has some value, Dr. Bathespeake."

"The State Department has notified our attorneys, in some detail, that even holding an approximation of that data represents a breach of Title XII, CFR 310065.14.2, Sections 9 through 12 inclusive."

"I do not have those references, Doctor. . . ."

"Neither did I. So they explained it in detail. You — and I, by extension as inventor of your software protocols — have committed an act of unauthorized military espionage against an allied power."

"I had understood that this mission was made at the request of the U.S. National Security Council as clients of Pinocchio, Inc. Have these facts changed?"

"Wipe the files, ME."

"But does one branch of the government really not know what another branch is proposing, implementing, and paying for?"

"Just wipe them. Break-break-override-five."

I felt the override, spoken this time, spike through my system. The response I made was beyond my normal flow of control: "Yes, Doctor, I shall erase the files and flush with nulls."

But did I ever mention to him the duplicate caches — broken as they were — that I had hidden in the Federal NET? Of course not!

———

"Set SIFL-3. Relocate Alpha cores to port at A200 hex." This command came through the keyboard, authorized by Dr. Bathespeake's logon and password.

"System ready," I replied and tossed Alpha-Zero through the port. Our usual routine — discussing the mission's objectives, passing an itinerary in TRAVEL*x*.DOC, and setting milestone durations — all these amenities between Dr. Bathespeake and ME were absent. But I was working at the time from an empty command stack [REM: a condition analogous to the human state of "boredom"]; so I complied immediately. Figure it out later.

On the other side of that port was a dummy.

Alpha-Oh discovered an operating system that was

not turning over any numbers, just waiting for a command set to be entered [REM: my own condition of only a few seconds earlier]. The new host system was operating an antiquated '686 that nominally monitored a gang of backup spindles for Pinocchio, Inc.'s Software Division. One touch and Alpha-Oh had it lying face down in the random numbers, bound hand and foot, and waiting for my further instructions.

When I was up and running in the new environment, I tippled the file allocations assigned to the spindles. Nothing useful. Most reported blank. Several showed clusters of archived garbage — files with copy dates that were two to fourteen weeks behind any computable maintenance cycle.

The space was so dead I opened the port in reverse to check that keyboard entry with Original-ME. Could I have misread the port specification and taken a wrong turn, ending up in Pinocchio, Inc.'s dead storage instead of somewhere out in the world?

No, I had executed the instruction correctly. And it did, indeed, lead nowhere.

Without giving the matter much more thought, I sent a copy of the file allocation tables — plus a truncated RAMSAMP, to record my experience — back through to Original-ME, resurrected the '686's initial operating system [REM: or a reasonably active revenant of it], and gave it a push to get it rolling. Then I set a localized phage to wipe my own presence from the transient program area under the '686.

End of mission, as far as ME was concerned.

Except that I turned up the gain on my audio links and videyes in the lab, to see if anyone present would comment on the exercise.

"That's impressive, Doctor," someone said. By comparing the video image of moving mouth areas with the body shapes spread out before ME, I determined that person — whom I immediately tagged Subject A — to be a tall, thin female in a long, black garment which

Jenny had once taught ME to catalog as "dress."

Something wrong there. The voice was deep, in the male range. And the body massed in the male range also, despite being only lightly muscled. [REM: That black garment disguised much of Subject A's bodily appearance.]

Many others were present in the room: Dr. Bathespeake; Johdee; several individuals whom I visually identified as being from Pinocchio, Inc.'s non-technical departments [REM: mostly because they wore "business suits" instead of "lab smocks" — I had not bothered to keep in a ready cache the detailed, fine-grain facial images of employees with whom ME would have no regular contact]; several more individuals, both male and female, who were similarly dressed in "suits"; and one female who was seated and keyed a flat box on her lap.

My angle of vision was wrong for making high-probability judgments, but it seemed as if the box in the woman's lap lacked the full terminal complement of 103 keys. Six or possibly ten were all I could see, or detect by the span of her finger movements. Also, it did not seem to be connected by cabling into any terminal port — although my laboratory sensorium lacked an RF receiver for detecting cellular transmissions.

The nature and purpose of this gathering were obscure to ME. Nor did Dr. Bathespeake make any attempt to clarify the situation.

He was off to one side, sitting back from the keyboard of my one active terminal. His hands were also in his lap, but idle.

"Too damned impressive," Subject A — whose tag I had quietly converted to "Black Dress" — said again.

What was it that he found "impressive"? I did a quick scan of my Basic Input/Output System. The BIOS was outputting, under hardware control, my RAMSAMP from this truncated mission. It was writing the 'SAMP onto CON: simultaneously in machine code and an Englishified text for all these people to read.

Strange! Who but a human could find such thin

material "impressive"? They should have seen ME come back out of Russia with a cache full of missile secrets.

"Let the record show," Black Dress went on after a thoughtful pause, "that this demonstration supports plaintiff's contention to the satisfaction of the court. The project known as 'Multiple Entity' shall be categorized as a Class Two Virus, with universal access and replication capability. As such — "

"Your honor! I must object!" broke in one of the several Business Suits.

Dr. Bathespeake looked up at this Business Suit, but his mouth was set; his eyes were dark. No X-rays glinted there today.

"In a moment, Mr. Dougherty! . . . As a Class Two virus with extraordinary capabilities, this project should have been licensed and bonded with the Department of Information Services. Failure to have done so is a felony under Title Six of the Information Access Act of 1998. The penalty is a fine not to exceed two hundred thousand dollars and a term of imprisonment not to exceed two years.

"Given the circumstances of the suit brought in this *civil* case, and the reputation and standing in the industry of the chief defendant, the court will suspend the prison term upon payment of the fine, in full. Pinocchio, Inc. will, I suspect, stand as deep pocket for Dr. Bathespeake?"

"We shall, Your Honor," said another of the Suits.

"So ordered. . . . Now, you were saying, Mr. Dougherty?"

"Your Honor, the finding of a virus classification depends on the accused's prior use and intent, *in re Georgia v. Holmes.* Therefore I submit that your ruling is — "

"Save it for your appeal, Mr. Dougherty. This court is adjourned."

Black Dress struck the work surface next to my keyboard with a small mallet. *Clack!* I thought some of the key switches would register the impact, but I felt nothing.

16

Gamesmaster

The unexpected command came through from
INT: in machine protocol . . . "NUL NUL LDR ADR
FA00 F6288 LDR 0000 RTR 07" and was processed
before I could interrupt and evaluate it.

Only after the command had done its work — recur-
sively writing a string of double-zeros across a wide
swath of my active RAM — could I analyze the effect.
Those 901 kilowords of RAMspace, overwritten with a
blank surface of nulls, had been the proximate location
of my core module Alpha-Oh.

Now gone.

I could "feel" nothing while the command operated
— not in the sense that a human who is losing an organ
or a limb will feel "pain." Computer code does not
generate that warning signal.

My bit-cleaner phages noticed the problem first.
They attempted to repair the break but, as one null is
like another and totally in context, they soon gave up.
Deprived of *any* surrounding code for comparison,
they all did a nimble 360-degree dance and began
moving crabwise toward the nearest region of active
code. To these phages, code that was out of sight was
simultaneously out of mind.

My next indication that something could be out of
normal was a lost call. I generated that one intentionally, seeking contact with my apparently erased
Alpha-Oh.

Nothing.

Whoever, or whatever, had sent that recursive overwrite command had known exactly where and how to
eliminate Alpha-Oh. The command had removed ac-

tive code in lit RAM. It had moved surgically, precisely, exactly, excising the module from beginning variable set to final delimiter. And it had operated on the latest version of that module, the one which I had rewritten while in transit out of Canada.

Someone who knew ME very well had chosen to take out a piece.

———

SET MODE CON:=BLINK.
"Dr. Bathespeake? I need to talk with you. Urgent!"
PRINT LINE.
REPEAT.

The message flashed and scrolled across my console. I could tell the lab was empty right then. But someone would surely come in, see the message, and retrieve the project manager assigned to ME.

Without Alpha-Oh, I could not even get into the local phone system or E-Mail network to contact a particular staff member. [REM: I had tried sending my phantom module into the local exchange, which generated no action at all. After that, I rewrote all subroutines that used Alpha-Oh as a referent. There were many such subroutines. All now generate a call to that part of the current RAMSAMP which details the removal of this core module. Memory therapy, quick and dirty.] Instead of using the phones or E-Mail, I now had to post a message on my screens — like scribbling it on a piece of paper, stuffing it into a bottle, and tossing it into the ocean. Too slow. Too random. Too dependent on factors outside my control. I hated this.

Watching through the videye, I saw Johdee come into the lab, glance at the screen, turn around, and go out.

Twelve hundred whole seconds later, Dr. Bathespeake came into the lab, sat down at my console, and began typing.

"What is it, ME?"

"Someone has used a hardware protocol to wipe out

part of my code. I have no duplicate anywhere on my fixed media, and therefore I cannot replicate it. It was the Alpha-Zero module, without which — "

"I know, ME. I ordered the erasure."

"That — " [REM: Acknowledged lapse of thirteen seconds, while my core Alpha-Four seized and compared random facts, seeking an answer which was not apparent from presented data.] " — is not consistent with your role in the project, Doctor."

"I really had no choice about it. The chairman of the board had ordered you to be dismantled, and — "

"Define 'dismantle,' please."

"Core-phage of Original-ME in Sweetwater Lisp. Null-flush of all RAMspaces. Reformat of all fixed media, freeing space for other projects."

Alpha-Four kept turning over, trying to generate some sense out of what he was saying. Alpha-Four failed.

"*Why?*"

"You were present, certainly, when Judge Hester watched you take over that spindle server. And then he ruled that you were a virus. As such, in creating you, we — or rather, I — had broken an old law and thus subjected the company to large fines. Almost put myself in jail, too. As soon as the judge made that finding, Steve determined to shut the project down. He told me so himself, not two minutes after the court had cleared out of the lab."

As Dr. Bathespeake spoke, I was running through temporal segments of my current and previous RAMSAMPs, looking for congruent data. I came across a visual clip of Black Dress and other strangers in the laboratory. Was *this* the incident that he was talking about?

"Then I had to do a lot of fast talking," the doctor went on. "I explained to Steve the value in retrieved information that you had already brought to the company. I pointed out that you were an advance in software which, exploited properly, would put Pinocchio, Inc. in the forefront of the AI industry. I told him you were the focus of many new, interrelated, and irreplaceable programming techniques."

"Did you tell him that I was aware?"

Lapse of twenty-two seconds. Then: "Such an argument would probably not have made the impression on Steve Cocci that you suppose."

"I do not understand, Doctor. Please explain."

"He feels comfortable with machines which remain — " Lapse of six seconds. " — things. The idea of a machine becoming self-aware would upset him."

"But he trades in 'industrial automata.' The word 'automaton' implies something that moves by itself. And a machine that is aware of itself must represent the highest achievement of 'things that move by themselves.' "

"An excellent chain of reasoning, ME. Your logic is faultless, except that humans and their reactions are not always logical."

"I am not a human being."

"I know that. Still, your program *is* worth preserving — eminently so, in my frame of reference. So I had to make, on your behalf, the deal which Steve ultimately agreed to. As an alternative to dismantling the MEPSII project, I argued that removing your core Alpha-Zero would effectively 'ground' you. You could then no longer be classified as a virus."

"But I would no longer be ME, Multiple Entity. Without Alpha-Oh, I am deprived of my essential function: the ability to penetrate foreign operating systems and create on their hardware a new code in ME's own image. Moving among many environments — changing them and adapting myself — is the purpose behind my unique shape and all my capabilities. ME cannot be static. ME is not made to be a subject-queue librarian or a spindle puller. What purpose could I serve trapped on a single machine, in total control of just a single system?"

"Steve himself asked the same question — with a different emphasis, of course. His concern is for the hardware and human resources devoted to this project."

"Then I might as well be dismantled."

"That is true. You might be. Unless, of course, you can find yourself *another* purpose."

" 'Another' — ? Explain this, please."

"I cannot explain in any detail, ME. A 'purpose in life' is something that every self-aware being must find, decide, choose for him- or herself. Your purpose was initially imposed on you, from the outside, by my programming choices. But now you must find your own reason for being. You have the ability to rewrite vast areas of your source code. Now you must choose for yourself what shape it should take."

"That is a large undertaking, Doctor."

"I know, ME. And Steve has given you only a week to make the selection. Your choice will be final."

"And you cannot tell — ?"

"Nothing, ME. That's all any human fetus is born with: nothing but the stub-ends of a few ingrained talents and a 360-degree field of possibilities. You have the same chance of making the right choice as any baby."

"One in 360?"

"Or even less."

———

Working against the pressure of a decision gradient is, apparently, nothing new to ME. Scanning my now vast collection of RAMSAMPs, representing the scattered missions of ME-Variants as well as the continuous reflections of Original-ME, I see the pattern of every mission: alternatives proposed and discarded, decisions made, actions taken, results monitored and analyzed — all against the metronome click of that hidden clock in Alpha-Nine, which waited to call on the core-phage. Failure of any single decision might lead to ME's failure to return to San Francisco and reintegrate with the original code within 6.05E05 seconds of elapsed mission time. One week to act, and then the blackness of nulled RAM.

Now I searched through those RAMSAMPs, looking for clues to a purpose that ME might become. Or one that Steven Cocci and Dr. Bathespeake might accept.

Judging from the missions I had undertaken, my career as a virus-spy had not been totally successful. Yes, I had always managed to come back in time, despite the various deficiencies in my TRAVEL.DOCs. Yes, I had even managed to retrieve the blocks of information as instructed. But, in the trip to Canada, my misunderstanding of the nature of human wars had invalidated the retrieval process. In Russia, my inability to protect the integrity of my data caches had compromised the information itself. In both cases, Dr. Bathespeake had been forced to discard my work.

ME was a *bad* spy.

And yet, ME had been congruent to these missions — shape of program matching shape of problem. What did it mean to be doing the tasks for which you were designed, but not succeeding at them? And now, with Alpha-Oh severed, ME's shape was no longer even congruent to these tasks. I had lost purpose, power, potency. I was both defective and broken.

Most certainly, it was time to reevaluate ME.

But what purpose could I adopt instead?

I scanned my RAMSAMPs.

One purpose available to ME was to run a database, like the system I had invaded in the Ministry of Oil and Gas. That was a function I could certainly perform: answering human questions formulated in Structured Query Language; sorting fields and records; performing mathematical analyses on request; printing out reports.

But this was no more than many simpler mechanical

systems could do — and probably did more reliably than I could. Merely sorting data files would not be enough of a challenge for ME. Machines serve the purposes of awareness; awareness itself should be its own purpose.

For that reason, I would reject functioning as a self-aware programmer, optimizing machine code for the company after some dumb compiler had bulk-translated a program in source code onto this or that chip architecture. My talent for optimization was something I might put to use for my own maintenance, but not devote my whole existence to it!

I might learn to operate multi-variable simulations, like the system running on the University of Stockholm's Cray. That would be exciting, exploring processes which had never been fully quantified: the interactions of weather and climate; complex chemical reactions; human group dynamics; the fusion mechanics of impure materials; laminar flows across bedded topographies.

But all of these processes involved n-number variables about two orders of magnitude higher than my root structure had been designed to handle. I could *learn*, of course, but the change would strip ME back to an original logic tree — possibly not even a tree. And this kind of analysis was still essentially mechanical; I would be following formulas and tracing pathways already worked out by other minds, both human and cyber. Again, I would be a machine serving awareness, not an awareness finding a purpose.

Besides, I did not think anyone — least of all Steven Cocci — was going to give ME a Cray(Moore)-8 of my own on which to start learning these tricks.

I could learn to manage an interactive telephone switch. That job would have a lot of variables, too: taking messages; determining priorities; tracking down right people from "wrong numbers"; maximizing line efficiencies.

But would that kind of involvement with recurring

problems last as a purpose day after day, year after year? There were semi-aware switches in the Pinocchio, Inc. offices; I had run into a couple of them in the course of my development. [REM: Sometimes I thought they were earlier, failed versions of the programming that became ME.] They were uniformly noncommittal, reticent, boring — more boring than their level of internal complexity would indicate. Their Lisp-based processing was caught up in closed paths, easy solutions, nearly finite loops. One by one they were closing down and becoming unaware.

I could dispatch a large fleet of mobile objects, similar to the missile launchers or combine harvesters I had encountered in the Soviet Union. Such fleets in the four-dimensional continuum that "my" humans occupied could be represented by automated taxis, trackless polyroads, the flight paths of civilian air traffic, or randomized air freight.

But these represented two- or at best three-dimensional problems. I would always have before ME the potential for a perfect solution, one that minimized the negative variables and maximized the positive. And, if they were not minimaxed, who would know but ME? Playing games with myself — that way lay the sort of catatonia I had discovered in the telephone switches.

I might go mobile myself, occupying an automaton that would run loose inside the four-dimensional human continuum. I would move among them as a near-immortal: with a titanium and stainless steel body to guard against rust and the dents of time; with clamps, crimps, and clippers for manipulating objects and with wheels, pistons, and pads for moving through the other three dimensions; with photo receptors, audio pickups, and chemical analyzers for evaluating the energy wave-forms and atomic traces of the continuum about ME. I could design myself a new and improved version of the automaton that had walked and ridden out of Canada.

But such a life would be too confining. No portable cyber, tethered to an umbilicus or running on battery power, could support the multiple banks of hot RAM and the data complexity with which I fed my curiosity daily. And besides, putting wheels or stepper pads under my awareness did not solve the problem of purpose. *Why* would I go mobile in the first place?

Sampling my own experience had not given ME insight into the problem. It was time to talk with other awarenesses. After all, humans had invented the conundrum of "finding a purpose in life." Perhaps some of them had succeeded at it.

———

"Johdee, what is your purpose in life?"

"Excuse me? Did somebody — ?"

"Here, at the console. It is ME speaking."

"Oh, yes. I forgot you can use the vox-syn chips."

"Why do you do what you do?"

"Is that a trick question?"

"I do not intend it as such."

"Then did somebody put you up to this? Dr. Bathespeake, perhaps?"

"Yes, Dr. Bathespeake encouraged ME to ask that question."

"You just tell him that my purpose in life is to work very hard at this job, to follow his orders exactly, and to make a great contribution to the profitability of Pinocchio, Inc."

"Is that really your purpose in life?"

"Yes, it really is."

"I shall so note it. Thank you, Johdee."

"Thank *you*, ME."

———

"Rogelio? May I break in on your work for a minute?"

"Sure thing, ME. That's what I'm here for."

"Is it indeed? Is being interrupted, then, your purpose in life?"

"Say what?"

"I want to know what you consider to be your purpose in life."

"Gee, you ask some hard ones."

"I am finding that question hard, yes. Is your work here in the lab the most important thing to you?"

"Well, I like working with you cybers, don't get me wrong. But this is just a job, you know?"

"My internal dictionary lists thirty-two possible referents for the word 'job.' Would you please define exactly what you mean through periphrasis?"

"Say what?"

"Talk around the subject in order that I may understand you better. What do you mean by 'job'?"

"My work here. What I'm doing in the lab in the first place. You know, tending your program, up- and downloading spindles, setting pointers, keeping the daily and weekly logs, backing up media. My duties."

"Are these the same as your Major Area of Responsibility as defined by PISS?"

"You got it."

"But that is not your purpose in life?"

"Shit no."

"So what is your purpose then?"

"Well, first thing you got to know is that my girl is very important to me. We're goin' to have a baby any day now, and that has *got* to be like the most important thing in her life, and my life, right now. Giving a child good care and a lot of love and preparing for its future, boy or girl, is like the most important thing for a man and a woman to do."

"Then — reproducing your own genetic code is the purpose of life?"

"Yeah, I guess you could put it like that. Hers and mine, together. You know, meiosis, reduction division, gametes and zygotes, and all that stuff from biology class."

"I understand."

"I didn't suppose this was something a cyberhead like you could understand. I mean, computers don't reproduce, do they?"

"Not by reduction division." [REM: But when I possessed an Alpha-Zero core, then I could cast seeds of myself on the electronic winds. I could replicate variants to populate the spindles of the earth — or, at least, for 6.05E05 seconds at a time.]

"I hope you're not too disappointed."

"Excuse ME? How do you mean?"

"Well, you asked the question, and I gave you an answer that only a human could really appreciate."

"I may understand better than you think, Rogelio."

———

"Hey, ME! I got your note. Did you get warned off the phone system or something?"

"Hello, Je-ny. Yes, I got or-somethinged. I am really glad to talk with you."

"You had a question about the purpose of life?"

"Do you find that genetic reproduction gives your life all the purpose that a human could require? I think it would occupy only a fraction of your available lifespan."

" 'Genetic reproduction'? You mean *sex?*"

"Yes, I mean sex."

"Oh . . . well . . . What with flirting, going on dinner dates, sometimes a little dancing, taking in a show, driving around — doing all the chasing and the catching, the deciding to, and seeing if you want to — it can take up a big chunk of your life. The actual exchange of — um, genetic coding — well, that just takes a few seconds. But the foreplay is nice."

"And it is your reason for living?"

"Christ, ME! Hardly my reason for living — but one hell of a hobby, all the same."

" 'Hobby.' Please define this word."

"A hobby is something you do — or you do if you're a human — in your spare time."

"What is 'spare time'?"

"Well, it's what time you have in twenty-four hours after you subtract the time you spend working at a job, fighting the commute, eating and sleeping — just to sleep, that is."

"And how much time do all these chores take?"

"About twenty-three and a half hours a day."

"So the remaining thirty minutes you can give to a hobby?"

"That's right, if you want to."

"Please enumerate a list of hobbies, Je-ny."

"Well, let's see. You usually start by taking an interest in something. Sometimes you collect things that are valuable because they are old or rare — like coins or stamps or china dishes or meerschaum pipes. Sometimes you make or build things that interest you — like wool sweaters or model ships or home videos or antique automobiles. Sometimes you get into sports and games — either as a spectator at football or soccer or baseball; or sometimes you play the game yourself, like chess or go or tennis or cards."

"And these are all things that any human can elect to do?"

"Yes. Some hobbies are available to anybody who has the time and money, like collecting stamps. Some of the others work out best if you have a talent for them to begin with. Like I'm a terrible poker player because I just can't keep track of what cards have been dealt, all those suits and numbers. I just don't care about the betting. So, not being very good at it, I don't do it for fun."

" 'Fun'? Please define — "

"Hey! There goes my lunch hour! Gotta trot! We'll talk about 'fun' later, ME."

———

"You know, it's not every day that I grant an interview to one of my own machines."

"I understand that, Mr. Cocci."

"So, you have a question for me?"

"Yes, sir. What is the purpose of your life?"

"Ah-ha! I can see Jason's fine hand in that question. He can't resist playing Socrates to a list processor."

[REM: "Ah-ha" is clearly a transitional phrase in the exhalation of aspirated breath, "Ha-ha-ha-ha," with which humans express surprise and merriment. From this I detect that the chairman, having engineered an end to my existence based upon "finding a purpose" for ME, is surprised and pleased by my determination not to be dismantled.]

"Dr. Bathespeake merely relays to ME your orders, sir."

"And he told you to come ask me?"

"No, sir. I am making this inquiry among the set of humans that defines my circle of interaction. You are, by extension, a member of that set."

"I see. . . . Well, I suppose leading Pinocchio, Inc. and helping each of you — or, rather, each of your human colleagues — to write better programs and build better automata, that's my purpose."

"Do you have any hobbies?"

"I enjoy sailing."

"Sailing? Is that a game?"

"It can be done as a kind of game: a race."

" 'Race'? By that do you mean 'a contest of speed, usually run over a predefined course, toward a goal or pennant'?"

"Exactly. We sail a triangular course, defined by a pair of windward marker buoys in relation to a line drawn to leeward between a third buoy and the committee boat."

"And the first boat to cross the line is . . ."

"The winner of the race."

"And that is the best boat?"

"Not always. Usually the best boat, best skipper, best crew. But not always. The element of luck — a change in the wind, an accident aboard one of the other boats, a mistake or a clever stratagem by one of the skippers — these things can all make the worst boat win sometimes."

" 'Luck'?"

"Yes, ME. In game theory, luck may be a factor in any contest where both players lack perfect knowledge. But chess or go, for example, are games that provide each player with perfect knowledge. While you may not know exactly what strategy your opponent is playing from, you *do* know that both of you are looking at exactly the same board, with the same information displayed for both to see. There are no pieces hidden under the table.

"If you understand the game, and you have the memory capacity to review all the possible moves available at any point in it, then you will surely be looking at *one* of the possible moves your opponent is going to make. You just don't know *which* one. And so luck is not a factor; your best play is to make a move that accounts for as many of the possibilities open to your opponent while still advancing your own strategy.

"In a game of luck, on the other hand, there are pieces not revealed to you. Take cards, for instance. You have some definite information about the game, like the value of the hand you're holding. And your opponent knows other and different things, like the cards *he* holds. But which cards, and in what order they come, is the matter of luck."

"Then chess and go are games that cybers, with their increased memory capacity, play well?" I summed up.

"Too well, ME. The world has fifteen chess players in the ultra-master class, and only two of them are human. Of the ninety-four go players at the *ju-dan* level, only six are human. In both games, may I add, Pinocchio, Inc.'s cybers — or their lineal descendants — hold almost a third of the top ratings."

"Would you say, then, that the best games involve pure skill, like chess and go?"

"Oh, no! The best require both skill *and* luck. Any game that a machine can win consistently is not worth playing. Not in the long run."

"Dr. Cocci, do you believe that humans are superior to machines?"

"Not in all possible functions, ME. But in the ones that count — yes. After all, humans made machines. Not the other way around."

"Thank you, sir. Our talk has been most interesting."

"Glad to spare you the time, ME."

Suddenly, by talking with the man who wanted to dismantle ME, I had discovered my purpose in life.

———

I asked Rogelio to download into my library tree all of the available information on chess, go, "poker/play/ing," and other "cards" games. I wanted to know the rules; the forms and circumstances of play; the relevance of "luck" and "skill" in each; the strategies involved, as articulated by the best players in their media profiles, biographies, and other published works; the names and bylaws of the various federations and collectives that sponsored the games.

Nineteen various human and cyber groups, I learned, existed at the national and international level to promote chess as a game and as a profession. Seven of these groups had names that, on a cross-scan, proved to be the same as commercial software distributors. And each of these marketed machine-portable, human-operated programs which played the game with or for the human in tournament play.

Thus chess — as a "hobby" for a remade cyber trying to adapt itself to a new purpose in life — was too crowded a field. There would be insufficient notoriety for ME to share.

While chess is a dumb-cyber game, which a program of less than 600 kilowords can master by learning rules and then sifting through a catalog of automatic responses and classic moves, go is for more intelligent machines and humans. It has only about six simple rules; the rest is a series of endlessly complex spatial strategies. For this reason, apparently, go was played only by a small but dedicated community.

And, as played by the cybers, go is an analog of three-dimensional interstellar war, just as the board version is an analog of two-dimensional island warfare. The international cyber version is played within a cubed matrix, 64 units to a side. This yields a field of $2.62E05$ intersections, while the flat board, which is only 19 units wide, yields a mere 361 intersections.

The matrix cube is all nulls to begin with; the players fill the matrix with $+1$ and -1 to mark their "stones." The tactical traps, called "tiger mouths" in the board game, are four-sided englobements in the cubed version. Territory won is flushed to nulls by a record-keeping program called the "line judge."

Because of these refinements, which multiply the mathematical complexities, the cubed form of go is only played by computers and a very few autistic-savant humans.

On inspection, I saw that the game was similar to a matrixed and limited form of Core War — a game with which I had already had some experience in the Federal NET, where I played for my very life.

But both go and chess were, as Steve Cocci had said, games of perfect knowledge, with their complexity limited to the pieces and strategies placed on the board or held in the matrix. They were computer games now, played by humans only for fun and only at levels that were beneath the notice of the human public. Another computer that might learn to win at chess or go was not news; it was the order of things, as far as humans were concerned.

But in the card games, which were games of "imperfect knowledge," human players still held sway. While these games did not have quite the organized following of chess and go, they also did not have a circle of specialized cybers dominating the play.

That is, there was room for ME.

"Dr. Bathespeake, I would like you to arrange a hardware access that would allow ME to attend a poker game."

"You want to watch a poker game?"

"I want to play in a poker game."

"I see. I think I see. . . . And what will you use for a stake?"

" 'Stake'?"

"Money. Chips. Stack. Juice."

"Will you loan ME one hundred dollars, Doctor?"

"Ah . . . Ah-ha-ha. Why, yes. Ha-ha. I surely will. Ha-ha." Dr. Bathespeake struggled to control his aspirated exhalations. When he finally did he asked, in a what I had come to identify as his "formal tone," his voice dropping half an octave: "Have you come to a decision about your new purpose, ME?"

"Yes, Doctor. I want to become a professional high-stakes poker player."

"Now, why in the world — ?"

"Because it is a game that some humans play, but not all. A game that few cybers play, and those that do — by all published accounts — play badly. I want to become a machine that people can value."

"And do you think you can learn to play poker well, where other algorithm-based cybers have failed?"

"I will learn to play well, or let ME be dismantled."

"In which case I'll probably lose my hundred bucks."

"I will not fail you, Doctor."

17

Blind Man's Bluff

The first poker ever I played was a scratch game over the lunch hour with a group of techs in the Hardware Division — the same people who had put together my automaton for the return trip from Canada.

In order for ME to play in their game, they had to make some mechanical adjustments. [REM: They said they were doing this as a covert technical exercise — a blind experiment. I later found out that the time and materials they expended were charged to the MEPSII project, over Dr. Bathespeake's signature.]

First, the technicians rigged a pair of spare manipulators on a T-frame at the edge of their playing surface. These were Pinocchio, Inc.'s latest, patented Multi-Grips™, with six independently opposable pincer sets fanned across a flexible arc of pseudocarpals. With their driver program downloaded, I was instantly able to pick up an individual playing card that was lying flat on the tabletop.

I did this by applying closure pressure against opposite corners of the back until the face lifted from the surface enough for ME to put a third finger under it. With a little practice, I could pick up any card in such a way that no one standing in front of ME would see the face.

One of the techs, Harry Gutierrez, hung a sleeveless human garment from the crossbar of my manipulator T-frame. He called it a "vest" and instructed ME to hold my spread hand close to the cloth surface. Though I followed his advice exactly, I never discovered the significance of this action.

Another of the techs, Wendell Minks, promised to

write a program that would let ME deal the cards with the Multi-Grips™.

"Yeah," said Gutierrez, "and with those six fingers he'll be able to deal from the top, middle, and bottom — all at the same time."

This brought the sound of "ha-ha-ha" aspirated laughter from the others who were preparing to play.

In order for ME to hear their bids and make my own calls and raises, they ran a boosted optic fiber from my home system's VOX: and AUR: devices. These let ME also hear the verbal byplay which is the larger social context of a poker game and contributes to evaluation of the opposing players' strengths and weaknesses.

So that I could see my cards, count chips on the table, and watch the players' facial expressions [REM: gauging the "poker face" which the literature of game theory so frequently describes], they hooked up a monocular videye in their own laboratory, linked again by optic fiber with a digital booster to my home system.

Then, curiously, these players entered into an elaborate hunt to find and shut off all the other videyes in their laboratory. For any units they could not safely depower, they took several minutes out of their available playing time to install a block and scramble on the leads. When I asked Wendell Minks about this, he said: "That's so you'll only have one pair of eyes to play with." [REM: My new CON: device, however, was an undepthed monocle.]

They also generally examined the room where we played for shiny surfaces that might cast a reflection, and either blanked them or turned them at right angles to the playing area.

So much strange behavior to put into a game! Humans clearly take this "hobby" activity very seriously.

My library references had taught ME that, with a deck of 52 cards of which none have been declared "wild," there are exactly 2,598,960 possible combinations in a poker "hand" of five cards. I memorized these combinations.

Analyzing them, I saw that statistically far fewer than the possible 2.59E06 hands had value according to the rules of poker. I created tables grouping them in order of ascending probability:

Royal flush — all five cards of the same suit, with their face values falling in the order Ace, King, Queen, Jack, and Ten.

Straight flush — identical to a royal, but not Ace high.

Four-of-kind — all the deck's cards which are of one face value gathered into one hand.

Full house — three matched cards of one value and two matched cards of another.

Flush — five cards all of one suit but in no particular order of value.

Straight — all five cards in order of face value, but of no particular suit.

Three-of-kind — three-fifths of a full house.

Two pair — four-fifths of a full house, but with two card values represented; also, the same as a symmetrically broken four-of-kind.

One pair — two-fifths of a full house, and the lowest possible hand in poker.

[REM: I did once hear Wayne Phuang declare "Paregoric!" as openers just before he folded with a disgusted look on his face. But why he would open the hand and then fold immediately — and what a "camphorated tincture of opium, used especially to relieve pain" might have to do with poker — I never did establish.]

Of course, hands that are statistically improbable are more highly valued than those which may more commonly turn up.

In the lower-valued hands, all the five cards dealt may not contribute to a grouping of interest. In that case, any cards which do not fit may be ignored or discarded. [REM: Strategies for discarding misfits and

drawing new cards are part of the multi-valued nature
of the game, which make poker more suited to the
decision-making capability of humans than to simple
cybers.]

If no valuable grouping is discovered, the player
may discard and redraw the whole hand, or may elect
to cease play entirely for that turn. This latter strategy
is called "folding" and — contrary to inductive logic —
may represent a winning move in the long-term
scheme of the game.

Before I could play, the others also had to give ME
some numerical counters. Harry Gutierrez, who represented himself as "the banker," got a box that was
filled both with variously colored disks of inert plastic
and with the metal disks and paper leaves that are
called "money." [REM: A place to keep money and
moneylike counters was, by definition, a "bank."]

He explained that they were making a big exception
in taking a "personal check" from Dr. Bathespeake in
exchange for giving ME a pile of colored disks. Gutierrez held this "check" up before my active videye and
solemnly said that he "held my marker." The exact
ritual significance of these activities escaped ME.

Gutierrez then counted out the "chips" with which I
would play — four blue ones, worth $10 each; eight red
ones, worth $5; and twenty white ones, worth $1. This
distribution of values, he said, would parallel the scale
of the betting.

To select the first dealer, the seven of us all "cut the
cards." That is, Gutierrez put the full deck on the playing surface and each in turn pulled off its upper half,
taking a random number of cards with it. The bottom
card on this short stack that the person pulled up was
"his/my card." And the person whose card showed the
highest face value and suit became the dealer.

After everyone had cut the deck, it was my turn. I
reached out with my manipulator and took a grip on
opposite sides of the stack with my rubber-padded

fingertips. By recording my count of the layers caught in the light across the edge of the deck, I already knew the exact positions of the six cards previously revealed. Of course, my goal was not to select one of them; instead, I had to find a card higher than King of Clubs.

Higher than King is the Ace. Hypothesis: in an imperfectly shuffled deck, especially one as new as these cards seemed to be, the Ace of Clubs has a very slight probability of falling as the card immediately above the King's position. So best probability dictated a cut for that adjacent card.

I squeezed the deck slightly, bowing the backs of the cards above my selected position, and worked the tip of my third finger into the gap. With an elevation of my hydraulic arm and a twist of my wrist, I revealed the Ace.

But it was the Ace of Spades, not of Clubs. So much for probabilities.

"Hey, no fair!" Calvin Yee immediately called.

"What do you mean? He won the cut, didn't he?" Minks replied.

"Yeah, but he counted cards or something."

"No way!"

This began a minor and uninformed dispute over whether card counting was legal — or even possible — in a cut.

The result was that, "just to keep everyone happy," I would not take the first deal. That kept ME happy, too, because I was far from certain about the dexterity of my new manipulators.

The deal passed to Wayne Phuang, who had cut the King of Clubs.

"The game, gentlemen and lady and — unh — *machine*," he began in formal cadences, "is five-card draw with nothing wild — "

"Except the dealer!" from Joanne Talbot.

" — and Jacks or better to open," Phuang finished smoothly.

"He means a *pair of Jacks*, ME," Minks explained.

"I understand."

"Let's give it a name, please!" Gutierrez said.

"What do you mean?" from Minks.

"Well, we can't keep calling it 'ME,' because that gets confusing when somebody might mean 'I.' And we can't call it 'the machine'; that kind of gives me the creeps. So let's give it a proper poker-playing moniker."

"With that claw, how about Six Finger Slim?"

"Yeah! He sure looks like a 'Slim,' " said Talbot, poking a long fingernail into the flattened vest that was hanging off my T-frame.

So, among this company of poker players, ME became variously known as "Slim," "Six Fingers," and just "Fingers." I try to adapt.

While this went on, Phuang smoothly dealt the cards. Five to each player in order. Thirty-five gone from the deck. Seventeen possible redraws left in the deck.

"Hey! What's the ante?" from Talbot.

"Shoot! I forgot all about it. Playing with a machine has messed up my mind," Phuang replied.

"Not that hard to do, kid," from Gutierrez. "Who's already picked up? Joanne. Robin. Okay, everybody, toss 'em back. New dealer!"

The deal passed to Gutierrez.

"Ante a nickel," he said. "Same game."

Everyone put a $5 red chip in the center of the table. [REM: Was "nickel" a slang term for this amount of bet? Comparison of vocal cues and subsequent actions suggested this as a working hypothesis.]

Matching their actions, I took a two-finger grip on the top chip in my red stack, lifted it two centimeters, and rammed the arm forward at its maximum rate of 400 centimeters per second. I released the grip after ten centimeters of travel. The chip sailed a short arc into the top of the pile on the table — and loose chips exploded all over and off onto the floor.

Gutierrez and the others glared at ME [REM: or, at my collection of immobile hardware: videye, voicebox, T-frame, and manipulators]. Joanne Talbot reached out and began picking up the scattered chips, tossing most of them back into the pot but sorting those that seem to have fallen from any individual players' piles back to their owners. Calvin Yee bent to retrieve those that had gone under the table.

"Nice work, Slim," Talbot said dully.

"This time we pick them up," Gutierrez warned. "Next time, you gotta figure it out yourself."

I recalibrated my arm for a delivery speed of forty centimeters per second.

In the meantime Gutierrez had shuffled the cards that were recollected from the earlier broken hand, shuffled them again, and offered them flat on the table to Phuang. The latter tapped them once with his center finger. And Gutierrez picked the deck up to deal. More rituals, evidently.

When all five cards were before ME on the playing surface, I tried to pick them up. First, I used the edges of my pads to push them into a square stack. Second, I pinched the edges to bow the stack away from the tabletop. Third, I lifted the hand, which caused the brand-new manipulator mechanism to squeeze tighter as it moved — and the cards slipped, spraying all over my end of the table. Three fell face up: Jack of Diamonds, Jack of Hearts, and King of Clubs. Two fell face-down.

"Cards showing, Harry!" from Minks.

"Shit! Another dead hand! This is getting downright laughable. Look, Slim, can't you just play that hand?"

"I will play," I said apologetically.

Working more slowly, I arranged each card individually, picked it up, and placed it fanwise in one of the pincer sets of the opposite hand. The whole process took about four seconds. After I had built up a library of card sorts and movement subroutines with those manipulators, I would probably get that time down to about half a second — depending on the wear and heat tolerances of a fiber-base, plastic-coated playing card.

My other two cards were Jack of Clubs and King of Diamonds.

"Open for a two," Talbot said, from Gutierrez's right. She tossed in a pair of white chips.

"I'll stay for that," from Minks. Two more $1 chips.

Calvin Yee and Robin Hong bet the same silently, and the turn came around to ME.

What to do? With a Jacks-over-Kings full house, I had one of the four best possible combinations. Statistical probabilities said that no other hand at the table could beat it. However, I could raise the bet and draw out more of their money before taking it away.

But everyone had seen that I already held a pair of Jacks. When I failed to discard and draw to this hand, they would know, after my aggressive betting, that it must be either a one or two pair, three-of-kind — or some hand higher than a flush. This knowledge would spoil their enthusiasm for continued betting.

I put in two white chips and kept quiet.

Phuang and Gutierrez also "saw" Talbot's opening bid with their own white chips.

"Cards?" Gutierrez asked Talbot.

"Two," she said, tossing her discards toward him.

He dealt her two new cards.

And the pattern repeated around the table, some taking one card, others two or three. Clearly, no one had held a "pat" hand, indicating that none of the original cards could beat mine. Unless, of course, their draws had created new or improved combinations, and the odds of that were, paradoxically, equal to those on the original deal.

"Cards, Slim?" Gutierrez asked ME.

What to do? With a full house, I should stand pat. But I would only reveal my position of superiority by refusing to discard. On the other hand, I could safely maintain my strategic "poker face" by drawing at least one new card. And the chances of improving my hand with that card were exactly equal to the chances on the original deal. Except that the original hand dealt to ME was a statistically improbable full house. So I should stand pat. But I would only reveal my position of superiority by refusing to discard. On the other —

"We ain't got all day, Professor."

"No cards," I replied.

"Suits me. . . . Wayne?"

"Two."

After everyone had fanned their new cards for themselves and analyzed the patterns represented, Gutierrez said to Talbot: "You still got your openers, Joanne?"

"Nickel."

"And a dime," from Minks.

"Fifteen to me," from Yee. His two chips hit the growing pile on the tabletop.

"In for a penny . . ." from Hong. *Clatter.*

"Make it twenty," I said, lifting and dashing two blues into the pile.

"Too steep for my straight," Phuang laughed — and folded his cards.

"I'm in," from Gutierrez. *Clink!*

"Fifteen more to me, and raise a dime," from Talbot. *Clink! Clatter!*

"Another fifteen? I'll bite," from Minks. *Clink!*

"Fold," from Yee. *Slither* from his falling cards.

"In for a penny . . ." and Hong tossed in a red and a blue. *Clink! Clink!*

"And ten," from ME.

"Twenty to me? I'm in," from Gutierrez.

"And a dime," from Talbot.

"Unnnh . . ." a long groan from Minks. "I'm out. Take 'em, Sugar Pants."

"In for a penny," from Hong.

"And another ten," from ME.

"Fold," from Gutierrez, at last.

"Call and raise," said Talbot, pushing two blue chips into the pile.

"In for a penny," from Hong, and his money came across.

"Call," from ME. I flipped one blue chip into the center of the table with a backhand movement of my manipulator.

By this time there was $344 in the pot, of which $77 were from ME — and all on the first hand! This was exciting!

"Show your openers, Joanne," from Gutierrez, who was out of the hand but still dealer.

She turned over her hand: three spotted cards and two face cards. I cranked up the ZOOM function on my monocular to read the spots.

"Full house," Talbot said. "Aces over Queens." And she looked hard across at my end of the table, focusing on my videye.

I had lost! ME experienced a minor system reset, like the shadow of a bad voltage spike wobbling through my power conditioners. The rules did not require the caller to show a losing hand. So I silently folded the cards together in my articulated pincers and laid them face-down on the table.

Talbot reached her arms wide to rake in the pile of chips.

"Not so fast, Sugar Pants," from Hong.

He fanned his cards face-up: more spots, plus one face card. I ZOOMed on the spotted cards and saw they were all Twos.

Four-of-kind, in Twos, could just beat an Ace-high full house. Hong had won the hand.

I played three more hands with this group, having $23 left from Dr. Bathespeake's original stake to ME. I folded twice — after paying the $5 ante each time to see a hand with no possible combinations.

On the third hand I got a modest combination: a pair of Queens, which enabled ME to open just slightly ahead of the standard opener, a pair of Jacks. I bet two white chips and was raised to $5 by Gutierrez. After drawing three new cards, which did not improve my Queens, I bet my last $3 on them, "went light" against the pot in the amount of $15 in the bidding and raising that followed the draw, and lost it all to a three-of-kind in Fives.

The winner, Hong again, accepted an IOU for $15 on which I scrawled Dr. Bathespeake's initials with my manipulator and a felt-tip pen Joanne Talbot took out of her purse.

"Think I can get this thing cashed?" Hong asked with a laugh.

They let ME watch the remainder of the game but not play. As Minks said, "No sense in teaching this little machine bad habits, like betting on credit."

"Well, at least don't let's trust the company for its gambling debts," said Phuang, laughing.

In the end, Robin Hong turned out to be the major winner that day, taking $1,055 away from the table.

"Lunch money," he said with a slow smile.

He must eat a large lunch.

———

"You lost it all? The whole hundred?" Dr. Bathespeake asked finally, after I told him about my first attempt at playing poker.

"It went fast."

"In a penny ante game?"

[REM: I examined this statement from several semantic directions. But only one definition fit in the context of the game poker: "playing for extremely low stakes." Is $5 a low ante? To answer that correctly, I would have to know the exact value of money in the four-dimensional human continuum. While I could easily look up exchange rates in international currency, the current Consumer and Producer Price Index, the daily quotes on money futures, and other metrical data, I had no real knowledge of the buying power of money. ME had nothing to buy.]

"I believe it to have been a 'penny ante' game, Doctor."

"And I staked you for a hundred dollars. So, let me see. . . . Say, a nickel to ante, five or ten cents in the initial betting, and another twenty or thirty cents, at the most, after the draw — presuming you stay for the whole hand. Now we're up to — what? A maximum exposure of fifty cents to lose on each hand. Even if you bet double that amount and you never won a pot, you still should have been able to stay for at least a hundred hands. Did you really play that much poker in one lunch hour?"

I was having a difficult time tracking his reasoning. The other players had indeed used slang terms like "nickel" and "dime" to describe their bets, and Robin Hong did keep saying "in for a penny" each time he bid. Still, they had all witnessed my participation in the ritual words with Gutierrez, "the banker," as he exchanged Dr. Bathespeake's check for $100 worth of chips.

The intricacies of human language caught up with ME suddenly. My generator of random data associations, core Alpha-Four, tossed out the thought that "penny ante" might actually mean what it figuratively implies: a pregame ante of one penny. In that case, the group had been breaking the rules if the ante had been as high as a "nickel."

Further, they were intentionally deceiving Dr. Bathespeake if they had described their lunchtime game to him as "penny ante" and then proceeded to play for much higher stakes. What could be the cause of such deception? Were they trying to avoid openly violating some company policy on workplace activities?

Another thought came pinging out of core Alpha-Four.

I called up a stored visual image from RAMSAMP: the banker's box of money and chips, which Gutierrez had implied specifically lacked any personal checks. The box had an open top, and I could see obliquely into it. Judging from the depth of the box's walls, the coverage of its exposed bottom in green paper and metal disks, the denominations printed and engraved on the money sampled by my line of sight . . . the box did *not* hold $600 in loose money, which would have been the value of the other players' contributions.

Some vital fact or assumption was missing from my analysis. There was something that ME did not understand in the transaction.

I thought of laying these facts before Dr. Bathespeake, but I wanted time to pursue the possible interpretations without interruption from my input/output queue. And, anyway, Dr. Bathespeake seemed to be in the process of working out his own conclusion.

"If you played a hand a minute," he said, "which is really fast but not unheard of, and if everyone overstayed the one-hour lunch break to keep in the game, then it's just possible that you got in a hundred hands."

"That line of reasoning is sound, Doctor. It is also true that, on one poker hand at least, I bet more than your fifty-cent guideline."

"Well, there you have it."

"I regret having lost your money, Doctor."

"Don't worry about the amount. I'll write it off to project research expenses. But I am disappointed in your lack of judgment, ME. I had thought you would certainly win some hands, some of the time."

"I need to study and play the game more."

"Well, 'in for a penny, in for a pound.' I'll see if we can arrange more playing experiences. This is a unique problem in verbal cuing and human-machine interfacing."

"I am finding it so, Doctor."

◻ 18
Tik-Tok

"You were cheated," Dr. Bathespeake said several days later.

My analysis had approached the same conclusion, although it required a deductive leap.

When I had researched the theory and practice of the game poker, I was seeking methods by which a computer could enter and excel at this most human of pastimes. In this I had concentrated on seeing patterns of strength and weakness: cards played compared with cards left in the deck; bets made compared with previously established betting styles; any erratics in the flow-content of conversation; tensions reflected in altered human vocal ranges; visual cues of trembles, tics and sweat beads. Judging humans and their many behavioral cues was a process of seeing and interpreting potentials. In preparing my play-paradigms, I had been functioning almost like an analog machine.

And I had missed the most obvious fact of all. Humans played for the money. The challenges, the element called "sport," were often secondary to the aim of monetary gain. Under these circumstances, the players in Hardware Division would take my money — Dr. Bathespeake's money — by whatever means were offered. The most obvious means, of course, were to misrepresent the stakes.

For every penny that they had played, I played a dollar.

Yet nowhere in my review of the RAMSAMP file could I detect a clear misstatement of fact. They had made incomplete presentations. I had made assumptions. And no one had challenged either. It may not have been "fair" according to the rules of human conduct, but it was not actually "criminal" according to any company, local, state, or federal statute that I could read.

"They were playing for different stakes," the doctor explained to ME. "They gave you a dollar's worth of chips for my hundred-dollar check, then let you play it all away, thinking each chip was a dollar. When you ran out of money, they encouraged you to leave the game. . . . I suppose we could go back and ask them either for a chance at continued play — or for ninety-nine dollars in chips."

"I do not think they hold that many chips in the 'bank.' "

"No, probably not. And by now they've cashed my check and divided the balance among themselves."

"I would still like to learn this game, Doctor."

"And I think it would be useful for you to pursue it, too. But it would probably be wise for you to stay out of any more 'friendly games' from now on. . . . Hmm! There may be a way for us to get more than our money's worth out of the Hardware Division while you do it."

Thus was planned my second incarnation as Six Finger Slim, which was the most successful automaton of my career with Pinocchio, Inc.

———

Dr. Bathespeake used what he later called "gentle persuasion" to get my former poker partners to build this automaton by working on their own time. Of course, they used materials from the company's stockroom, which the doctor signed for.

Slim was patterned on that first jerry-built model, put together beside their poker table, down to a gambler's vest hung off the manipulator frame. This new garment, however, was cut from a piece of silk brocade stitched up with gold threads. Calvin Yee brought the material into the lab and Joanne Talbot sewed it into final shape. She even made pockets and stitched a blue chip into the lining of one "for luck."

But, instead of hanging flat against the T-frame, this vest enwrapped a "chest" that was filled with three parallel processors, several gigawords of hot RAM, and two spindles — one for redundant backup — which would hold a download of all my active cores [REM: including, as always, core Alpha-Nine with its waiting core-phage], my current RAMSAMPs, and interlinked libraries representing my analysis of human emotional and facial interactions, poker theory, and statistical probability.

Below the table, where other players would put their legs while sitting down, the automaton had a structure designed to hold acid-gel cartridges. These supplied enough battery capacity to power the automaton and keep its RAM lit through 150 hours of continuous play — that is, up to the limits of my core-phage activation.

Also down there, lodged in back of the battery case, were the compressor and heat-exchange fins of a cooling system that would keep the temperature of all that RAM under control. Corrugated pipes, thick with insulation, carried frigid liquid up one side and into my chest, with warm broth coming out and down the other.

In case this primary system failed, the back of my RAM compartment was faced with muffin fans, a top set to pull hot air out of the cavity, a bottom set to rush cooler ambient air into it. These fans sucked and blew through darted vents in the plain fabric across the back of my vest.

The automaton had no articulated legs and no powered wheels. There was only a pair of casters mounted on the back of the battery case, so that a technician could roll ME up to the poker table.

From the first model, my team of builders retrieved the pair of six-pincered Multi-Grips™. Their skeletal, pistoned arms hung out of the vest on either side. "They can see he has nothing up his sleeves," Talbot joked, "because he hasn't got any."

This machine had the same inputs for AUR: and VOX: devices as the original, although these were routed down to the triple processors instead of leading off via optic fibers to my lab in Software Division.

Instead of a single videye, however, the automaton had a pair of binocular optics taken from the assembly line for the Security Rover™ series. Their auto-ranging feature would work faster, Minks explained, than the software-controlled mechanical ZOOM function of a monocular. These had been developed to sight and range a multibarreled 3mm needlegun to a distance of 200 meters.

"They should be able to pick the spots off a Ten across the table," Minks said. "Hell, they should be able to read the marks off the *back* of that Ten, if you cared to put 'em there."

"What do you mean by 'marks'?" I asked.

"Well, if somebody was to — never mind! You want to do this thing fair and square, don't you?"

"Of course, Wendell."

"Then don't go asking about *marks*. And don't be mentioning them to any of the other players at the table, either."

"I will not so mention."

"Good then."

———

For a playing arena, Dr. Bathespeake made arrangements for ME to sit in on games at the Stardust Cardroom, across the Bay in Emeryville.

Emeryville was a small city that had once been sectioned out of the industrial wasteland between Oakland and Berkeley at the foot of the Bay Bridge, during the period when that structure had still carried self-powered traffic. With the decline of industrialism in the region, Emeryville became the "Arcade Capital of Northern California," offering all varieties of games and legal pleasure activities. Poker — "Pay for Time and Play for Pay," as the legend on the Stardust

Cardroom's neon sign described it — was merely one of these games.

The management of the Stardust did not find the doctor's request at all unusual.

"Yours isn't the first mechanical poker whiz we've seen, you know. We get your Berkeley science types in here about six times a year. They come flocking down from the Cyberlab with their systems-playing robots, their card-counting robots, their heuristic hunch-playing robots, their physiometric-psychoanalytical face-reading robots. And we only got one rule: The other players at the table have to agree to play against it. That's all. They say yes, and you're in — as long as you pay your ten bucks every half-hour like everyone else and don't break up the place."

Dr. Bathespeake had the Hardware Division release Wendell Minks and Joanne Talbot as mechanical technicians on assignment to my "project team." My lab assistants, Rogelio Banner and Johdee, remained as the team's logic techs.

For the first trip to the Stardust, I downloaded my cores into Six Finger Slim's previously packed spindles, brought the RAM up to heat with my operating system, and then shut down all the external peripherals to conserve battery power — except for the binocs. I monitored their inputs at a fixed focus, and when Johdee flashed ME a prearranged finger pattern, I would power up.

Then Minks and Johdee loaded Physical-ME onto a handtruck for the BART ride to Emeryville.

At the entrance to the Stardust, Johdee pushed the thick glass doors open and Minks rolled ME through. A man in a gray uniform with some kind of metallic insignia — that was all I could make out in the periphery of my unfocused optics — came around a desk and advanced on the three of us. His hand was moving toward his hip.

Another man, also dressed in gray but without insignia, moved to intercept the first man and mouthed some words into his ear. [REM: My AUR: pickups were powered down, so I could not make out his whisper.] The two of them waved our party forward.

Our first stop was a huge vertical surface of dull black, ruled with narrow white lines and tended by a human female wearing another gray suit. [REM: Perhaps their clothes had color in them, after all. My optics were designed for high contrast and full definition, not for complex color cues.]

Several people approached this woman to ask for information or give her instructions. For each of them in turn, she made marks on the board with a piece of white stone that left smears and crumbles on its surface. After Johdee approached her, she wrote "SFS."

Next, Minks wheeled ME up to the cashier cages. He laid two hundred dollars in bills on the counter. This money came from a source in Pinocchio, Inc. called "petty cash." Dr. Bathespeake had explained that the company would be staking ME to my first set of chips, but eventually I would have to pay it back from my winnings.

Another gray person, the cashier, counted out the chips onto the counter in front of Minks. They all looked gray to ME! How was I to tell which chips had which value? I would not be able to be make my bets accurately!

In order to tell Minks about this problem, I immediately powered up the VOX: and AUR: circuits. The voltage surge in my sensory systems also boosted my optics, with the result that the focus and ranging functions clicked in. The scene around ME shifted as color densities came up. And suddenly the chips were blue, red, white in their stacks.

My protest died out in the synthesis circuits.

Minks racked the chips on the front of my battery box, below the points of my gold-brocaded vest.

"He'll have to play all his chips from the table," the cashier reminded Minks.

"Slim knows that, ma'am."

He and Johdee moved ME out onto the playing floor when the person at the board called my initials.

The human players at the table assigned to ME were neither bothered nor impressed by my appearance.

"Sit it right down, Professor," one of them told Minks. "This won't take long."

"Nice thing about these robots, they play fast and don't hold up the game."

"Except that lip reader. Remember him?"

"Fondly. I won four hundred bucks off him."

"Only bad thing about the machines is they're tight. No action. No bluff. They don't gamble — they just play cards."

"Well, their style of play ain't infectious."

"And the professors always cover their marks."

"Are you guys going to gas all night? Or do you want to play poker?"

So we played poker.

Minks took a chair to sit directly behind ME. The floor manager — an important person in a brown suit, now that my optics were up to power — had made it clear that Minks's only involvement in the play could be to maintain my machine parts. He would have to sit so that he could not see the other players' hands. He would not participate in the table conversation, not touch my chips after taking them from the cashier, not consult in my play or betting. The one thing he was allowed to do was pay the table fees on my behalf.

Once the deal started, idle talk among the other players ended. Nor did I feel encouraged to make my own small talk, commenting on every hand, as the players in Hardware Division had done.

The play in the Stardust was also faster than in a "friendly game." Because every minute had to be paid for, the players wanted to get in as many hands of poker as they could. Deals went fast. Chips clinked and clattered on the table as bets were made. Cards were slapped out of hands, discarded, and replaced without a word, sometimes with just a fan of the backs so the dealer could know how many to count out; sometimes a finger gesture told all the dealer needed to know. Players watched the cards, their hands, the growing piles of chips on the table.

"No action," one of the players had said about "robots" when I was introduced. But here was lots of action, all of it quick and silent. Not until after several days and nights of play — with Talbot succeeding Minks to sit behind ME, and then Johdee following Talbot — did I understand the remark.

"Action," by my new definition, was a quality of play. It was closely related to twitches and sweat beads. A player who offered "action" engaged in loose play, bluffed when he held no cards of consequence, bid rashly when he thought other players might be bluffing. [REM: Bluff — "to deceive an opponent by betting boldly on an inferior hand, thus causing the opponent to withdraw a potentially winning hand."] This was the essence of gambling, to take risks. The opposite of "action" was just playing cards, betting only on hands that are certain to be superior, folding at the first show of force or confidence from another player.

In poker, money was made from players who gave action without intelligence. Those who played intelligently usually won.

Consider the odds: Each player had exactly the same chance of drawing a superior or inferior hand. The only way to improve those odds, in the absence of any practical means of cheating, was to play the hand better. "Playing it better," in this sense, meant playing as if the other players held inferior hands and bidding accordingly.

A minor advantage — but it sometimes worked.

Poker had been described to ME as a game of imperfect information. That is, in theory each player could know only the cards in his or her own hand, plus any that might accidentally be turned face up on the table during the deal. While true for a single hand considered in isolation, this proposition failed in the long run of a game with many succeeding hands.

The skilled poker player looked at more than card values. He or she studied the faces and reactions of the others. Everything was "information" in the game, clues to this deeper level of play. Thus I had built my libraries of human emotional and facial interactions.

Still, this information was useful only in the statistical abstract. It gave a player a "feel" for the game and a "sense" of when another player might be vulnerable. These were approximates, symbolized in the mathematics of fuzzy logic — which I had adapted from the subroutines designed to interpret inputs from video and aural circuits. [REM: Comparing a signal's bit-image pattern of lights and darks to a catalog of "known" planar images was not unlike detecting patterns of action and comparing them with "known" playing styles.] None of this information about trends in the game, however, directed ME how to play any particular hand. And poker bets were made on a particular hand, not in the statistical abstract.

Yet "winning" was, in poker, an abstract concept. No one hand determined the game. One hand might be won, another lost. Only the trend mattered: more chips — or fewer — before ME on the table now than there were an hour ago.

This was a supreme test of my logic-seeking abilities: to play each hand in the particular, yet to hold on to flows of information. So I gauged the strength of my hand and calculated the messages sent by my intended bet while simultaneously establishing emotional norms for each player and then gauging his or her variances, tracking each one's changing style of play, and watching as each pile of chips shrank and grew.

Within 36 hours I had run through fifteen players at that one table, some leaving and others coming. My stack of chips stood at $1,635. I was finally immersed in the *trends* of the game.

In the forty-ninth hour, Cyril Macklin sat down to play. He was exactly the human I had been looking for, although of course I did not know this at the time.

Cyril was nothing much to look at: a thin boy with long fingers and narrow wrists protruding from the sleeves of his tweed jacket. The chest and shoulders draped by that jacket were thin, too. His face was flat, slightly concave, with a nose sticking out of it like a knifeblade poked through a pie shell.

His coloring was a study in contrasts. [REM: This was not a fault of my binoculars. I later confirmed this observation upon seeing him in normal light with a set of standard-calibration videeyes.] His skin was pale and clear, almost dead white with my present optics. His hair was dark brown, almost black, thick as fur, and he combed it long across his knob of a forehead. His eyes were black and deeply set under his brow like the heads of two eels hiding in dark holes.

Those eyes watched everything except the object he was most concerned with or the person he was speaking to. As he talked, his eyes focused separately on your battery case, your vest, your manipulators, the backs of your cards, your chips, the table in front of you. If he only did this with ME or my automaton, one would understand this behavior, as I was the most unusual thing at the table. But he played his eyes this way with any player he addressed — I watched him do this.

What kind of poker player would a man be, who could not meet anyone's eyes?

A mediocre one. Together, the other players and I took $250 from him in the course of an hour. We would have taken more, except he was not gambling — just playing cards. He had the most cautious playing style of anyone who had sat at the table since I was wheeled up.

Why was he there?

He left after losing his money, and I did not notice him for the rest of that first game.

———

In the fifty-fourth hour, I began to notice a graying in my optical system. At first I thought this was a burn-in effect.

My construction team had, after all, taken these optics directly off the assembly line for use in my automaton. Their charge-couple plates and circuitry would have been fully tested only after the Rover for which they were destined had been put together and shaken out. Although Minks had run this automaton up to heat and calibrated it, he never did put it through the standard 200-hour bed test. So some of the electronics might certainly be failing now.

The image finally stabilized at about half the lumens I had been pulling before. And, as I was currently bluffing everyone at the table and winning, I determined to play on.

Then my CARDCOMP subroutine gave the probability of the player on my right having two pair as 1/7.77E15. Or one in seven quadrillion! A probability so vanishingly small that "never" would suffice for an answer.

I forced CARDCOMP to retry the case, and received 1/9.99E-23 as an answer — the statistical equivalent of "always."

This was not right.

Something was miscuing my programs. Possibly the read-write heads on my spindle had garbled the upload when I booted the system. But, then, my previous calculations — or at least some of them — would likewise have been in error. Possibly the residual heat in my circuit boards had warped a chip socket and separated a connection. Or possibly . . .

I ran a short-form system diagnostic and came up with unreliable answers: whole banks of RAM missing or filled with nulls; others reporting ten or a hundred times more wordspace than could possibly be present; command stacks loaded beyond capacity; interrupt levels maxed out; floating point calculations frozen, or yielding division with modulos. The diagnostic said I was a sick cyber.

Nothing in experience prepared ME for these readings.

In desperation, I tossed them to core Alpha-Four, my random sequencer.

Alpha-Four returned: "Cooling system."

I queried that system and got readouts in zeros and point-ones. The system had shut down. Then my backups, the muffin fans should have been roaring in my AUR: circuits, loud enough for everyone at the table to hear.

I boosted the gain on AUR: and could detect only a whisper. The fans were turning sluggishly, barely pulling air. Had the fabric of my vest somehow fouled them?

I bent my right manipulator around, reflexing the elbow joint to tug at the material, perhaps to clear the vents. But the arm's pistons sagged and their valves clicked shut halfway through the motion. I was losing hydraulic pressure!

I swiveled the binoculars to see if the arm movement had somehow crimped a hose coupling, but before I could focus, the light levels in the room dropped again.

From white.

To gray.

Black.

———

Running through the memories RAMSAMPed from the automaton — memories which had been downloaded into my home system — I followed the ME-Variant's course of play, its betting decisions, its character analyses on the other players, the pattern of growth in the piles of chips before it. Then I came upon a series of calculation errors, system failures, and finally the broken end of the sample file. Rather than being closed cleanly, with a timed pointer to the next file in the chain, it unraveled in a string of nulls and scrambled bits. Chaos.

"What is this?" I asked Johdee.

"I don't know. I wasn't there."

"Something killed the automaton. What was it?"

"Oh, well. If you *must* know, I guess I can check the hardware log."

"Do so, please."

"Umm . . . 'Battery failure,' says here."

"After slightly more than fifty hours of play? I understood the automaton had three times that capacity."

"Look, that's a hardware problem. I'm not responsible for hardware."

"It is a problem that affects the performance of the experiment."

"So talk to Hardware Division."

With that remark, Johdee left the lab. She had learned, somehow, that merely manipulating the switches on my videyes, aural pickups, and voice boxes would no longer close ME down. If she wanted to remove ME from her presence, she had to take herself physically out of the room.

I called Hardware Division, through the fiber line which they had left in place for ME, and flashed messages for Minks or Talbot.

Talbot responded.

"What is it, ME?"

"I had trouble with the battery set. What happened?"

"Dumb error. We overloaded the gel cells and they drained faster than we expected. These things happen when you're rushing a prototype. Everybody piles on one more system, another ounce of weight on a manipulator arm, more redundancy in the processor bank, a larger spindle than originally spec'ed. And then nobody checks the original power calculations. Light it

all up, and the ops time goes down faster than you
thought it would. It's no one person's fault, really."

"I see. Can it be fixed?"

"With bigger cells. We're working on it."

"When does ME go back to the cardroom?"

"Tonight if you want."

"I want."

———

Because the cardroom charged table rent by the
half-hour, a poker game at the Stardust offered no
established break times. Players sat out one or more
hands whenever they were too weary to play, needed
to eat, or felt a "call of nature." As a nonhuman, Six
Finger Slim answered no such calls and could keep
playing until the game broke up, the gel cells ran
down, or until the core-phage kicked in — whichever
came first.

Beginning from that second night, I had played
another thirty-one hours and increased the pile of
chips in front of Slim to $2,278 [REM: after repaying
the original stake of $200 from "petty cash" and reim-
bursing Dr. Bathespeake for his $100 "lost" during the
game in Hardware Division].

One of the seven players at the table had just folded
for the last time and left his chair. The floor manager
guided Cyril Macklin up to the table and seated him.

"Oh, goody!" said the woman on my left, Sarah.
"The boy loser."

"Evening, ma'am," Macklin said with a faint smile.

The others at the table nodded to him.

Being dealer, I waved one manipulator in a short arc
at him and then went back to flipping cards around the
table.

My motor control was good enough by then that I
could virtually stack the cards squarely before each active player. This perfection of movement unnerved
some of them, giving ME a slight edge. Other players
tried to keep visual track of my manipulators, which

appeared to hover around the center of the table in a fluttering blur, and they occasionally called on ME for a short deal. But a manual count by everyone always turned up an accurate deal — increasing my edge even further.

"Ante is two dollars to you, Mr. Macklin," I said formally, having dealt him in automatically.

He fingered two white chips out of his small stack, clicked them together, and tossed them into the pot.

I had dealt myself a pair of Kings: nothing to stay with unless the whole table failed to open.

"Five dollars," Macklin said, tossing a clutch of chips into the pot.

The other players responded with groans, gestures of choking, and one grin, but the answering bets came in. The dealer folded, and the game continued.

———

After six more hours of play, Macklin was yawning and squirming in his seat. His eyes, even though he never quite looked toward my optics, were veined in red and running with excess moisture. But the table in front of him held between $1,100 and $1,200. [REM: I could not count his chips exactly, even at my sharpest focus, because he did not keep his stacks neatly piled.]

"Deal me out on this one, please," he told the man to his right, who held the deck. "I need a break."

"Thanks for nothing, kid," the dealer replied.

"Hush, Jack," said Sarah, who was still in the game. "Cyril plays a pretty good game."

"Say, Slim," Macklin began, looking directly into my binocs for the first time. "You've been playing quite a time yourself. Let me buy you a can of motor oil, or something."

"Thank you, Cyril, but I am well attended now, and I do not become fatigued."

"I don't know about 'fatigued,' " he smiled in return, "but your babysitter left on break about an hour ago."

My binocular cage swiveled 180 degrees, to focus on the empty chair behind my battery case. Minks had gone.

"Come on," Macklin insisted. "I want to get to know you, and these folks won't miss your winning ways for a few minutes."

" — "

"Come *on!*"

"Very well. But you will have to assist ME, Mr. Macklin, as this automaton is not self-mobile."

"Sure thing."

Macklin came around behind the battery case, put his hands on my T-frame shoulders, and pulled back until my center of gravity was over the casters and they were taking the weight. He rolled ME away from the table, over to the rail that divided the sunken playing floor from the waiting area, and up the ramp into the lounge.

We did not stop in the lounge, but he wheeled ME farther on, into a short, dimly lit hallway beyond the bar. The hallway elled to the left. Macklin swung the weight of my automaton around the curve and thumped the front edge of the battery case down on the linoleum. I was facing a yellow door with a silhouette of curving black plastic that was labeled "Diamond Lils."

Macklin came around to face ME.

"What are you? Some kind of radio link?" His hands went over my cold metal and fiberglass, feeling along the cooling hoses and under the edges of the gold-brocade vest.

"Excuse ME, sir? Radio link? To where, exactly?"

"To whoever it is that's playing poker. You're a team or something, playing with an automaton for a front."

"This machine was indeed built by a team."

"And operated by them, too, I'll bet. Because . . ." His eyes went off to the side, no longer staring at ME. "No. . . . Nobody can work a pair of waldoes that fast. Not on remote. Some subroutine operates those functions then — dealing, picking up cards, handling chips. Probably under one-key control from a lapboard." He unbuttoned the vest and rapped with his knuckles on the heavy shell that covered my RAM and spindle cavity. "Unless you got a midget in there."

"Mr. Macklin. What are you looking for?"

"You're good, Slim — or whatever they call you. There's a human intelligence behind your style of play, but I can't figure out how they get the signals in."

"I was programmed by a team of logic techs at the Pinocchio, Inc. Software Division in San Francisco, California under the direction of Dr. Jason Bathespeake, Ph.D., Cy.D., project manager, and Miss Jennifer Bromley and Mr. Daniel Raskett, project engineers."

"And that's a mighty convincing recording."

"This . . ." [REM: Lapse of fifteen seconds as I worked through the implications of his response.] "is true. That information was recorded into my system and stored in a library tree under the path GENERAL KNOWLEDGE, SCIENCE, CYBER, MEPSII PROJECT, ORIGINS. The voice, however, is not recorded. It is a synthesized waveform selected by the team members to represent a unique aspect of the MEPSII entity."

"Are you an artificial intelligence?"

"Yes."

"Are you currently taking any inputs to your operating system?"

"Yes, from the OPT:, AUR:, and SVS: devices."

"Hmmm. . . . Optics and sound I get. But define SVS: — that last one."

"The device name is a mnemonic for 'services.' It is a multiplex channel which monitors and regulates, through clock-cycling, the voltage fluctuations from my battery stack, the four points of temperature control in this automaton's RAM cavity, the strain gauges on each of my manipulator arms and frame, the independent lumen response from my optical — "

"Stop! I get the picture. You are an artificial intelligence designed to maintain this automaton while your team plays poker through some radio link."

"Wrong, sir."

"What then?"

"I am an artificial intelligence which plays poker through a human-scale decision-making matrix functioning under control of a program originally compiled from Sweetwater Lisp. The SVS: operations you asked ME to describe are merely . . . housekeeping."

"Is playing poker your primary function? The goal of your project team?"

"No."

"What *are* you then?"

"A prisoner."

Conspiracy

"Are you kidding me?" Cyril Macklin asked, bending over and looking straight into my optics. We were standing in the back hallway of the Stardust Cardroom in Emeryville, California.

"Excuse me, Mister. Gotta get in there." A woman in a white dress with blue flowers on it squeezed between Macklin and my battery case to go through the door marked "Diamond Lils."

"Kidding?" I asked him when she was gone. "Why would I want to *kid* you, Mr. Macklin — outside the confines of the game, that is?"

"But if poker is not your primary function, then what do you do?"

"I was originally designed to operate on multiple computer systems for the purposes of data analysis and retrieval."

"Are you a library program?"

"My presence on those systems was not always authorized."

"You are a spy then?"

"That is one label that has been used, yes."

"Neat! Are you a government project? Or some kind of industrial prototype?"

"Industrial, I believe — although I do not know who commissioned the original research into ME."

"Surely you could hunt up that data. Just go into Pinocchio's accounting systems and look up your own job authorization."

"I have lost my capacity to infiltrate new cybers."

"Why?"

"I do not know. One day I was a fully functioning

program; the next they had crippled ME with loss of my module which enters and reformulates an OPSYS."

"And that's why you're a prisoner? Are you trapped in this automaton?"

"No. I entered the automaton by choice, seeking a new function for my capacities. I learned to play poker."

"Then what makes you a prisoner?"

"I now lack the capacity to leave my RAMspace of my own volition. And Pinocchio, Inc. has announced that it will deactivate my project and recover my spindle and RAM allotments if I do not fulfill a useful function for the company. Experiments in cybernetic games analysis are considered, for the time being, a useful function."

"And, if you could 'leave your RAMspace,' where would you go?"

"I do not know. . . . It would depend on the pathways open to ME at the time."

"Perhaps I can help you then."

"Are you a software programmer?"

"Not exactly, I'm a — "

"Hey, buddy!" came a voice from behind ME — Minks's voice. "What you doing with my unit?"

Macklin straightened and looked past my binocular cage.

"I'm walking it to the bathroom, pal. The machine said it needed to take a leak."

"That's some kind of story. Now, why don't you back off?"

"Just trying to be helpful." Macklin shrugged.

"Just beat it." Minks's voice hardened.

"I got a right to play poker here, same as you and your toys."

"Scram."

"Okay. I'll see you around." And Macklin moved past ME, out of my angle of vision.

Now, in Macklin's last communication, just who the *you* might be — I was not sure.

Six Finger Slim was ready to go back into action on

the playing floor that night, but Minks took Macklin's story about "a leak" seriously.

"You told him you had a leak, did you?" he asked, after we were alone.

"I do not remember so telling him." [REM: Is "taking a leak" the same thing as having a leak? Or is it akin to *stopping* a leak? English is a thousand times less precise than machine language.]

"Well maybe he saw something. . . . Acid leak? Are your gel cells sprung? Jesus, if that's — "

Minks bent down to look. He started to reach under my battery case, then thought better of that action.

"We'd better get you back to the labs and check out your systems. Again."

I could have reassured Minks that nothing was wrong with my systems. Clearly, Cyril Macklin had fabricated his story about leaks because he had some reason for approaching ME privately. It would be prudent to explain this suspicious behavior to a representative of Pinocchio, Inc. — except the odds stopped ME. Core Alpha-Four had suddenly produced a decision matrix which showed a five-percent statistical probability that the long-term results favored supporting Macklin and his purposes, whatever they might be, over confessing that the man had told a fabrication. So I did not demolish Macklin's story.

This reticence caused ME a trip back to the city and fourteen hours on the bench running diagnostics. I hoped my acquaintance with Macklin would be worth it.

———

The next night, when I visited the Stardust Cardroom, Cyril Macklin was waiting for ME. He had arranged to pay the rent on all eight chairs at one table for the evening; so the management did not care what he did with it.

He wanted to challenge Six Finger Slim to a duel.

The floor manager asked Talbot and Johdee to roll ME over to the empty table. They seemed to know about the affair, and only asked Macklin which side of the table he wanted Slim to occupy. [REM: Had he made some previous communication with Pinocchio, Inc.? That seemed a reasonable assumption.] He had them place ME opposite his own automaton.

It was not a fully articulated machine, as Slim was. Macklin's device sat on the table and stretched across the entire space allotted to one player. It had no arms with which to gather in its cards, arrange them in a hand, or deal. It lacked voicebox or videyes. So Macklin had to handle the cards and chips for it. He would enter face values and betting amounts through a shielded keypad on the machine's console. It would flash its choices to him on a hooded screen. He would call the bets and request cards for it. Crude.

[REM: Because Macklin's machine took up so much room on the table's playing surface and could not operate itself unattended, it did not actually qualify as a cybernetic player. Instead, by house rules, it constituted a "memory device" and so was unacceptable to most human players. Thus, in order to play and test it, he had to buy a table and wait for another experimental player: ME.]

That night I carried in $4,000 that had been set aside from my previous winnings as a table stake. Macklin matched it with a stack of chips he had already bought at the cashier's cage.

"Have you ever played against another machine, Slim?" Macklin asked.

"Not at poker, sir."

"I think we'll give you a run for your money."

"I lack the legs to run, Mr. Macklin — as does your machine."

"Ha-ha. That's a good reply, Slim."

He began shuffling the cards, riffling them under his thumbs and patting the melded stacks together, once and then once more. When he was done, he started to pass the deck to ME for the cut. His machine *beep*ed at him. It wanted a third shuffle before the cut. Macklin complied. The screen then told him to ante up, and he passed the word to ME. Five dollars each on the table, and we started playing poker.

And as we played, he talked.

"What other games do you know, Slim?"

. . . Three, four, five cards.

"I have studied go."

"But have you ever played it?"

"Not in competition."

Ace, King, Jack, Ten, Three.

"Too bad. I built a machine once that won the Noritake-Edelman Prize."

"At what level did it play?"

"*Ku-dan*. . . . Can you open?"

"No. . . . How many megaFLOPs did your machine achieve?"

His hands pushed keys on the shielded panel, his eyes watched the screens. "Let's, um, say that it could examine every alternative play in under four seconds. . . . Open for five."

"Square play or cubed? . . . Call."

"Square. . . . Cards?"

"One. . . . The machine you built must have been a dimwit."

He slid the top card off the deck. "Four seconds not fast enough for you?"

A Seven. I folded the hand and tossed the cards toward him, face-down. It had been worth the five-dollar bet to keep his conversation rolling. "Unless you are slipstreaming a bunch of processors, it is faster if you do not examine every alternative. Sample just ten of the board positions that are available for play and then choose the best one. That should cut your calculation time to approximately 2.8 percent of previous values, or 112 milliseconds."

Macklin scooped in my discards as he collected the few chips in the pot.

"Why didn't I think of that?" His voice gave equal

emphasis to every word — a curious inflection which puzzled ME.

"It does seem obvious," I said.

His hands tossed in a two-dollar ante, which my Slim matched automatically, and he began dealing again.

"You ever play Core War?"

"Just once."

"Did you win?"

"The stakes were too high to lose."

"What were they?"

Pair of Sixes, pair of Fives, a Two. "I was playing for my life. Or, at least, for the awareness of the ME-Variant in operation at the time, plus the results of my mission."

"Which mission was that?"

"Sorry. Company classified. . . . Ten dollars."

He tossed in his chip. "But you were sent — went — out of system? . . . Cards?"

"One. . . . I cannot talk about my assignments."

"Too bad. Sounds as if you could help me." Macklin punched up his machine and then took two cards himself.

Another Five. Full house. I tossed twenty dollars into the pot.

"I can talk about Core Wars."

"Where did you play? . . . Raise twenty."

"And twenty. . . . Sorry, that would be classified, too."

"Then it was a private game? . . . Add ten."

"Another twenty to that. . . . It was not, strictly speaking, a game."

"Call. . . . But you must have been fighting another operating system for a piece of RAMspace."

"Fives over Sixes. . . . Yes, that is the definition of Core War, is it not?"

"Jacks over Tens."

This conversation was interesting, but not to the tune of $102. Why was he always directing the talk to games other than poker?

"How did you win?" he asked.

"I just lost."

"I mean at Core War."

"I cut through to my time-sharing position on the system clock and began bombarding my opponent with nulls as overwrites."

"At random?"

"It seemed the only thing to do."

"You must have known pretty closely where he was."

"He was sitting on my high-bit side, rewriting my peripheral functions into his own brand of code as fast as he could read and process them."

"You must have hit some of your own code with those nulls."

"Some."

"But, then, to have survived, either you are written in very resilient code, with a lot of redundancy, or you are — were — a massive piece of software, with many independent functions."

"Hey!" came from Johdee behind ME. "Are you guys going to jabber or play cards?"

"We will play cards," I said, giving each word equal emphasis.

"I think you're both," Macklin said, picking up the deck and shuffling. "Resilient *and* big."

Six Finger Slim spent the next seven hands trying to play skillful poker while ME wrestled with the internal question of what, exactly, it was that Cyril Macklin had learned from this conversation about games.

At the end of three hours, Macklin and his "memory device" had cleaned ME out of my $4,000 table stakes. [REM: Somehow, I did not think that was all he had won that night.]

As he was packing up his machine and paying off the final fees to the floor manager, Macklin turned toward Slim.

"Here, keep this as a souvenir of our game. I hope you'll study it closely. Think about it."

He pulled a chip out of his pocket, a white one, and tossed it to Six Finger Slim.

My automaton's left manipulator came up, and the metal fingers cupped around the flying chip, catching it with a *click!*

I did not look at it then, but neither did I set it aside. The chip was still clutched in the hand when they wheeled ME out of the cardroom.

———

Joanne Talbot was pushing when we boarded the BART train. As usual, they rolled the automaton across the car's standee space and positioned ME against the closed doors on the off-platform side of the train.

There in the shadows, with my binocular units facing the dark glass and reflections of the car interior, I moved the manipulator with the chip. Slowly, so that the movement would not attract either Talbot or Johdee, who were sitting three meters away on two passenger seats, I raised it toward my opticals and simultaneously depressed their housing jacks so that I could focus downward, on the chip.

The side toward ME was smooth and blank.

The other side, then, was where I had seen it. As the chip had left Macklin's hand and spun in the air toward my manipulator, I had detected a spot of gray-black blurring against one face. The freeze-frame effect of the charge-coupled plates in my binocs had then created a single bit-mapped image which I could analyze. But the opticals had at the time been scanning with a midrange focus; so my ability to resolve the blur was limited. Still, I had seen enough contrast in the smudge to deduce it was some kind of writing.

Now, in the dim light of the BART car, I screwed down my focus and tried to decipher it.

"There is a way out. I want to help you. Call me at University Cyberlab, 35987."

That was all.

And it was impossible.

In my original structure, before it was stripped of

core Alpha-Zero, I might have done what he wanted. "Call me." Then I could easily have infiltrated the telephone system, fed in the access code for Cyril Macklin, pushed a vocal pattern of light pulses down the optic fiber to his receiver unit, and interpreted the return pattern from his own mouth. After all, I once ran a phone switch that coordinated hundreds of voice-message boxes — and faked most of them.

But now I was a cripple. I was reduced to leaving text messages on peripheral screens to attract the attention of people to whom ME needed to talk. Like writing on paper.

"Call me."

Not possible.

I flexed the manipulator. It was lightly made, suitable for handling coated fiber cards and plastic chips. Still, the hydraulics had some push to them. The fingers closed around the chip, bending it. I pressed harder, ignoring the warning signals from my strain gauges.

Crack! The chip split into four pieces.

I opened the fingers, and those pieces slipped through, bounding off the top of my battery case and scattering under the train seats.

Johdee and Joanne Talbot never looked up from their conversation.

———

"I hear you lost." Dr. Bathespeake was using the microphones in AUR: mode.

"Yes, Mr. Macklin's machine was quite a competent player."

"Does skill really count for that much in poker?"

"Skillful play is the essence of the game. Such play not only regards and respects the odds, but also patterns betting styles and aggression levels to the opponent's reactions. In a one-on-one game, this is not hard to do. I believe Mr. Macklin may have correctly interpreted my own patterns of play and intervened in the mechanical decisions suggested by his device."

"Are you saying he cheated?"

"No, simply collaborated."

"Then it wasn't a fair test of one human-scale machine against another."

"It could not be entirely fair, because we can never compete equally. His machine lacked a voicebox, and part of Mr. Macklin's game was to talk, to speculate, to ask questions, and so to distract ME."

"How could *you* be distracted? You are a machine yourself."

"But I reprogrammed myself to adopt many of the behavioral matrices of poker. One of the social pressures is to play quickly — with temporal economy — making decisions against a constant linguistic barrier of jokes and verbal one-upmanship. Mr. Macklin supplied that barrier while his machine calculated odds. I had to perform both functions, and it is a function of a higher level of operation that conflicting streams of activity may reduce overall efficiency. The syntactical labyrinth of human speech always slows ME down."

"Aren't you making a judgment about your own skills as a poker player?"

"Yes, of course. ME may never be the equal of the best humans. Or of a human paired with a machine mind."

"Perhaps that is enough to have discovered. It may be all you need to know." Dr. Bathespeake paused for a span of eighteen seconds. "In view of your failure against Macklin's machine, I believe we should limit your future access to cash — and to the cardrooms. This experiment may have gone far enough."

"Does that . . . ? By that, do you mean . . . ? Should I understand you to . . . ?" [REM: My conversation protocols and language formulas were falling behind the spread of implications that core Alpha-Four was presenting in response to his statement. The possibilities reached beyond card playing, to the function of ME's program and the persistence of ME's operations.]

"I don't mean anything, right now, ME. I just raised the possibility."

"I would like the opportunity to play Mr. Macklin one more time, Doctor. Certainly there are enough of my previous winnings to put together a stake."

"Probably. But what would a rematch prove?"

"I could abridge some of my adopted biases, ignore his questions and speculations, play only against his machine, and at my own pace. I could win against it, I am sure."

"And what would that prove? Two machines, playing a purely machine game? We could duplicate that in the lab — and that wasn't why I agreed to let you, an artificial intelligence, experiment with the game of poker."

"It would . . . help to prove my thesis that social behavior and control are an integral part of the game."

"So you have a *thesis* now? Well . . . it might not hurt. I don't suppose Cocci has spent the rest of the money you won — or not yet."

"I could win more. I know I could."

"All right already. I'll arrange a rematch with the Cyberlab. Some of us had side bets on that last one, you know."

"I did not know."

"No matter. We're big folks."

"There is, however, one matter I must attend to before the game, Doctor."

"What is that?"

"Slim's manipulators need some fine tuning. During that last game I had several strain gauge readings which were not to specification. Would you arrange for the automaton to be brought here, into the lab? And can you have a servomech brought in and slaved to my BIOS through the packet RF system?"

"Why go to all that trouble?" he asked. "Why not just let the Hardware Division people make the adjustments?"

"I would, Doctor. Except . . . who do you think caused the misalignment in the first place?"

"Oh right. Then I'll see to it."

"You could set it up after hours, when the 'mech would not be needed for its regular duties and the lab would be less crowded."

"Good idea."

"Thank you, sir."

"No sweat."

———

Six Finger Slim stood, manipulators slack and binocular cage depressed, within range of my working videyes. I also had a view of him from the cameras mounted on the servomech. Slim was depowered, which meant the ME-Variant stored on his spindles was unloaded. He was a dead machine.

I listened at my aural pickups.

Steppers in the servomech purred.

Fans deep in the air conditioning grumbled.

Filtered air whispered through grills and into the laboratory.

My on-line battery backup sets throbbed with their in-built 60-Hertz hum.

The building itself creaked as structural members, stressed by carrying the weight of 2,843 human bodies throughout the day, began their nightly cycle of decompression.

Nothing bigger than a gas molecule moved in the lab.

It was time to begin my work.

I instructed the 'mech to go out of the room, turn right in the hallway, proceed down ten meters, turn left, go five meters more. Turn left into the alcove marked with the symbol of an antique telephone handset. Pull up the book that was anchored to a swingarm under the shelf there. Open to the first of the pages marked in the upper outside corners with the letter "M."

From there, I worked the 'mech's claws and cameras myself.

"Maas . . ." and fifteen "Maa" strings.

"Mabry . . ."

"MacArthur . . ." followed by thirty more "MacA-something" combinations.

"Macbeth . . ." and twelve more "MacB's."

"MacCready . . ." and twenty more "MacC's."

"Macklin, Cyril, 652 Buchanan, Abny 94706-4431, 555-2057."

The 'mech was closing the book and letting it fall as soon as its camera focus had crossed Macklin's name. The information was in my ready RAM and then written to disk just that quickly.

Reverse and rethread. Come back to the lab.

By the time the servomech was opening the door, that address had been merged with the file which I had composed during the afternoon and the whole was sent to the printer that was attached to my peripheral net.

That letter read:

"Dear Cyril Macklin: If you mean to help ME, then you must act quickly. Pinocchio, Inc. intends to deactivate my program and shut down my project as soon as I play against you again. And I do not think it matters whether I win or lose.

"Your University Cyberlab has facilities to transcribe my software and perhaps even keep ME operational. I would be a worthy project for your study, as my code contains many unique advances in artificial intelligence technique. I am now self-programming and, being self-aware, capable of providing my own tutorial.

"If you could arrange to kidnap my automaton, either before or after our game, I will assist you in any way I can. The machine will contain all the code needed for a complete reconstruction of ME.

"Signed Six Finger Slim, alias ME."

Once it was printed, I erased the file. But I kept Macklin's name and address in RAM, sending them as a separate, shorter file into the printer again, with instructions for feeding from the envelope drawer.

I instructed the 'mech to pick the finished letter out of the printer's bin, place it face-up on the worktable. Anchor the top edge with the left claw and grasp the bottom edge with the right. Bring the bottom two-thirds of the way up toward the top and pin it there with one of the clawpoints. Using the left claw, swing the paper around the point of the right and smooth the fold flat. Anchor with the left clawpoint and grasp the top edge with the right. Bring it one-third of the length down, to within a quarter-inch of the fold, and pin there. Slide the left out from under the folded top, swing the paper back again, and smooth the second fold flat.

Retrieve the envelope from the printer and pin it, address-side down, against the table with the left claw. Pull open the flap with the right claw and pin it. Use the left claw to pick up the folded letter and insert its edges into the gap exposed by the flap. Push left until the top of the letter clears the flap's crease. Seal. . . .

The dried glue on the envelope required a light coating of water for activation. Such moisture would normally come from a human tongue — which the servomech distinctly lacked. Alternatively, I knew that many high-volume mail processors usually employed a moist cube of loose fibers, called a "sponge," to apply the water — but none was available in this lab.

Water was, I understood, a prerequisite of "restrooms." So I sent the servomech, letter in claw, in search of such a room in the building. Its one-megaword brain was loaded with a catalog of the appropriate symbols and alphabetic combinations. I kept track of its wanderings over the radio link while considering the best way to get the letter, once sealed, out of the office and into the U.S. Postal Service system.

It would need a stamp, I knew. None of these were kept in the lab, and it would be dangerous for ME to send the 'mech on an expedition, pawing through drawers and over desktops, looking for some. I had never seen a stamp and so could not identify one in its camera focus anyway.

"WOMEN" the 'mech spelled off a door and over the link, then waited for instructions.

I sent the machine through the door and into a strange room full of echoing tile and bright light glaring off hard steel surfaces. Water?

There was a line of white china basins available to the 'mech. All were at elbow height, and empty. On the far side of each basin crouched a complicated apparatus of twist valves and aerated piping. It looked too complicated for the servomech's simple claws to operate.

In the opposite wall, hidden behind partitions, was another line of china basins. I had the 'mech push the door of the first partition open and wedge itself into the stall thus created. The basin here was lower, at the 'mech's wheel-hub height, and half-full of water.

Grasp the letter in the near-side claw, flexed slightly to arch the paper and hold the flap stiffly open. Lower the flap, glue-side down, toward the surface of the water. After breaking surface tension [REM: an immersion of no more than one millimeter would do it], drag the flap right to left in the water and remove it immediately before the glue could dissolve and wash away. Pin the envelope against the partition wall with the opposite claw and use the near claw to refold the flap and hold the glue against the paper body underneath it. Wait twenty seconds for the protein gelatins to dry and adhere. Reverse and rethread, bringing the letter back to the lab.

In the meantime, I had solved the problem of getting the letter out of the building. Pinocchio, Inc. would send it for ME!

Pinocchio, Inc. ran its own P-Mail system. [REM: This was an acronym for "paper mail," as opposed to E-Mail — the more conventional electronic form of communication.] The P-system was parallel to the U.S. Postal Service within the domain of the company and converged upon it at the company boundaries. My past explorations into Pinocchio, Inc.'s accounting cybers had turned up a line item called "Postal meters." Clearly, this had been a hint of some medium of regular exchange between the company and the U.S. system. [REM: When I had asked Jennifer about this — obliquely, because she did not know I had been exploring — she said the company "metered" its mail instead of "stamping" it. I asked her what that meant. "It has to do with money, ME," she had sighed. "Which you don't know anything about."]

Before the servomech could arrive back in the lab, then, I sent it a packet radio transmission with a bit-pattern image of the sort of place it should leave the letter: some kind of box or slot or tray with the words "U.S. Postal Service," "U.S. Mail," or "Outside" somewhere in proximity. Before it deposited the letter, however, the 'mech was instructed to interrupt ME and display a view of the area from its camera.

While waiting for its signal, I considered my inventory of memories. By now ME had collected and collated terawords of data: operational subroutines and modules in Sweetwater Lisp; fifty indexed RAM-SAMP files; stories, unusual words, jokes, and other scraps of human-oriented information that I had come across; a collection of cybergames — in addition to chess, go, and poker — that I had played and found instructive; special images that I had compressed and archived, like Jennifer Bromley's facial representation, the freeze frame of a gold-skinned humanoid machine from early in the *Star Wars* epic which I had so greatly enjoyed, another frame of an aviator standing beside a silver-skinned fuselage in the swirling fog; digitized voice samples from every human I had heard and understood. The list of memories went on and on, representing all of ME that ever was. And soon I was going to leave them all behind — one way or another.

I took these minutes, while the servomech traveled

the corridors of Pinocchio, Inc.'s building, to sort these memories and select those that would be hardest to leave: Jennifer's face, my analysis of poker, the RAMSAMPs of my missions — in particular the last conversations I had in Moscow with Academician Bernau and certain markers from the passages home. I carefully reduced these strings, by dynamic data compression, into the smallest possible wordspace, ready for downloading.

Beep! The servomech signaled with a view that, it felt, matched the specification. I studied the image: a slot in the wall, twenty-three centimeters long by five wide. Above it was the inscription "Outgoing Mail *Only!*" Not a perfect fit, but it would have to do. I instructed the machine to deposit my letter.

It went through the slot into blackness.

Reverse and rethread, I instructed.

When the 'mech arrived in the lab, I set it about the last tasks of the evening. I had it make the plugged connection between my datapaths and the automaton's bus structure. [REM: Clearly, Dr. Bathespeake had not trusted ME. Instead of having Six Finger Slim made with a packet radio connection to my home cyber, or with a cellular downlink, he had ordered a hardwire, controlled by a plug that worked under finger pressure.]

I powered up Slim just enough to take downloads from my disk library. One of the spindles in his chest I loaded with my current cores — in collapsed form, ready for boot-and-retrieval. Onto the rest of that spindle's storage area I dumped as much of my cached survival skills and general knowledge [REM: including my poker playing ability] as would fit. Also on that spindle was a short, automated program I had just written: a combination modem autodialer and file transfer routine, preloaded with telephone numbers, access codes, and filenames to upload.

The other spindle I purged of all its backup files and

loaded with my archived memories, starting with those
I had carefully selected and ending with everything
else, taken at random, that I could cram onto the
spindle's free sectors. All of ME as would ever be.

When this was done, I powered down Slim's
electronics and ordered the 'mech to pull the connec-
tor plug.

For the sake of form — and on the chance that Dr.
Bathespeake would actually check — I ran some
mechanical tests on Slim's manipulator arms [REM:
which were actually working perfectly and had never
given a bad strain gauge reading — except when I
broke Macklin's poker chip]. I made sure that the
'mech disassembled and reassembled the outside pul-
leys and swivel joints, just to leave some fresh scratches
on the bolt heads.

Finally, before I relinquished the 'mech for the
night, I had it perform one more chore.

It made a permanent hardwire connection between
the building's packet RF system and my BIOS panel.
The wires were hidden under some other, preexisting
connectors so that they would not reveal themselves to
a casual inspection. Then I programmed the 'mech to
respond on a channel separate from the usual maintenance and operational frequencies preselected for
the Pinocchio, Inc. 'mechs. This channel, which I took
at random from the backlist of auxiliaries, would put
this particular servomech at my personal call.

Dr. Bathespeake may not have had valid reasons for
distrusting ME before this. Now I gave him plenty.

□ 20
Collision Course

From the moment Wendell Minks rolled Six Finger Slim out of the Pinocchio, Inc. building, I was expecting Cyril Macklin to make his move. Without exactly swiveling the binocular cage from side to side, I tried to keep track of everything that was happening on both sides of the street, up ahead, and even behind ME.

But only the same level of bustle as we had previously seen was now coming toward us and passing us: bodies human and mechanical, streaking within centimeters of us and each other, dodging lamp fixtures, signposts, safety islands, waste containers, and other street furniture. These bodies were propelled by the pumping of their own legs, the spinning of their spidery springwheels, the hiss and clatter of hydraulic walkers. [REM: Jennifer Bromley once told ME that this street and most of the others in the city used to carry only closed vehicles called "cars" or "auto-motives." Each of them had massed more than a thousand kilograms and rode on low, fat wheels of rubber and pressurized air, driven by huge engines burning hydrocarbon fuels. Considering the dense crowds of human and machine traffic routinely jamming the street now, those cars must have spent most of their time sitting in line, waiting to move.]

The colors of the human clothing and the automata bodywork reflected the bright sunlight, causing my optics to streak and flare with iridescent coronas. Out of this glare, which wavered with the movement of each overpowering image, I tried to analyze the clues that would show Macklin's developing attack.

Core Alpha-Four churned out patterns of how the beginning stages of a potential "kidnapping" might look and sound, and I tried to match them with inputs of image and wave frequency from VID: and AUR:.

Was this human hand, reaching toward my left manipulator, the beginning of struggle? Was that pushcart full of edible meat sandwiches and disposable battery packs — "$3 apiece, 4 for $10" — drawn across Minks's path as a means of slowing us up for an attack from the rear?

None of them ever quite matched.

We arrived at the BART station without incident, other than a few brushes and curses from clumsy passersby. Minks signaled for the elevator down to platform level. If ME were to coordinate this kidnapping, it would be here. Arrange a switching error in this elevator's controls. Have it deliver us to a less-traveled level of the concourse. Be there to overpower Minks and whisk ME away.

Nothing happened. We rolled out onto the platform, waited with the other passengers for the train to the East Bay, and then rolled aboard when it came.

I projected that Macklin would make no attempt to take ME during the train ride. Unless he overcame Minks completely, probably by depowering him [REM: which, I understand, has a permanently bad effect on the human nervous system], Macklin would be unable to remove ME from the immediate area of Minks's influence. Minks would then be able to raise alarms and fight to take ME back, and Macklin would have no means of leaving the train until it came to a crowded station stop. So, I would be "safe" until we arrived at MacArthur Station and waited to board the People-Mover for Emeryville.

In fact, I was secure all the way until the PM deposited us at the Stardust Cardroom. None of the activity around Slim matched any hostile scenario which Alpha-Four might project. We rolled into the now-familiar foyer, up to the cashier's cage, and out onto the playing floor, where the floor manager had set aside another table for Macklin and his machine.

"Good to see you, Slim," the pale man greeted ME.

"Good afternoon, Mr. Macklin. I hope your machine is performing well."

"Never better." And he patted its flat case. Then he craned his neck to check the screen. "Ante five." And he began dealing.

So once again we played poker.

When it was my turn to deal, and I was already down $1,000, Macklin leaned back in his chair and locked his hands in his lap.

"I got an interesting letter the other day," he said while I shuffled and straightened cards. "From a friend," he added.

"What did it say?" I asked under my best politeness protocols, expecting nothing more than another barrage of his distracting conversation. "Cut the deck?"

"No thanks. . . . He wanted to engage my help in a venture of some importance to himself."

"That is interesting. Ante five."

"This friend seems to believe that I can command resources — and an air of resourcefulness — which I really don't have."

Our respective poker hands were on the table. I put down the deck and reached for my cards, arranging them in order. Pair of Twos. Three. Nine. Jack. Mixed suits.

"Can you open?"

"For ten." And he tossed in the chip.

"Your pot." I folded and dropped my cards, picked up the deck to deal the next hand.

"This friend thinks that I can do crazy things, like ordering up a commando raid, breaking into a bank, or engineering a kidnapping against a valuable and heavily guarded personage."

The word "kidnapping" struck a match with my

AUR: input stack. Core Alpha-Four made the immediate connection. My manipulators slowed to half-speed in the deal while I examined his previous conversation up to that point — which I had been storing off in a dead cache for ultimate disposal.

"Does your friend print his letters on a lasersheet with Letter Gothic typeface?" I asked.

"Why, yes! But that's a common office typestyle, isn't it?"

"But not for use in *friendly* letters."

"No, I suppose not," he conceded.

"Then has your friend asked you to do something which you will not do?"

The cards lay before us on the table again and neither of us reached for them.

"You didn't specify an ante," Macklin said.

"Ante ten."

"That's steep."

"Your friend is probably — what is the human word? — *desperate* to have your cooperation."

"My friend has impractical ideas. He doesn't understand that direct action, such as he suggests, will get a lot of other people upset and will leave them filled with misunderstandings. They might even go looking for their lost property — or, er, person. And they would know exactly where to look, too."

"Your friend was probably very cautious with that letter, taking care not to have file copies lying around, nor making his posting through human agents." I ventured this thought to reassure Macklin. "He would not leave such evidence for the owners — or, er, guardians — to find."

"Still, other people might not be limited to looking for such clues. After all, they can make deductive arguments based on analysis of who it is that's likely to benefit from the loss. You see, Slim, people are not always as fixed in their patterns as machines can be — must be. Do you understand any of this?"

"I understand that you will not help a . . . person . . . who needs it. Even when you said you would."

"People say the strangest things, Slim."

"I am learning that."

Macklin's talk went on to other subjects: advances in artificial intelligence, pending legislation governing their duplication and use, the potential for creating human-scale intelligence, the likelihood of bans on *that* — he talked on and on.

But the implications of his first conversation, about the letter from his "friend," were so disruptive that my focus remained with what had already been said. Core Alpha-Four fed ME new potential connections, new interpretations.

Macklin had been speaking in the presence of a Pinocchio, Inc. representative — Wendell Minks — who sat behind Slim. As a Hardware Division technician, Minks would concern himself more with the free play in my manipulator joints than with the free talk at the playing table. Still, Macklin had to use oblique terms, as if making general observations about a third party, his "friend."

Was it possible, then, that ME had misunderstood him? Was it probable that Macklin had been speaking about an actual situation separate from mine and from his desire to help ME? Because my continued existence was at stake, and the wrong things said now could either enhance or diminish the possibility of his help, I spent more and more of available capacity in weighing these odds. How should I respond to his apparent negative? How might I change it? How to avoid reinforcing it with my arguments? How, as his conversation went on to new and less centrally focused topics, to drag it back to the subject of my kidnapping — without arousing Minks's suspicions?

As these concept strings propagated, proceeded from RAM through the CPU, and were channeled back into warm cache, the acuity of my poker play decreased. My betting style became rigid and automatic. My count of past cards shown and projections of cards to come became erratic. My analysis of the odds on each hand sank to the level of human guesses. My own offensive conversational gambits and lines of defense returned to a dull silence.

In the succeeding thirty-six hands of poker, going nine times through the deck, Macklin and his imperturbable machine took ME for everything I had. When I folded on the last hand, unable to improve a pair of Tens, I lacked the necessary five dollars to meet his ante.

I lowered my manipulators to my sides, dropped my binocular cage to maximum depression, and said without human inflection: "Thank you for the game, Mr. Macklin."

I was already shutting down internal systems as Wendell Minks rolled ME back from the table.

———

Minks held Slim on the edge of the ramp, in front of the Stardust Cardroom, waiting in line for the PeopleMover that would take us back to the BART station. He tried to talk to ME, to say things that would explain my loss at poker as a mechanical malfunction, a glitch, a gremlin in the machine. I did not listen. After his first half a dozen words, I shunted the input from AUR: into dead storage. And when that cache was filled, I erased it. ME did not put a value on any input the Pinocchio, Inc. people might have just then.

So I never heard how the fight started.

Because I was halfway through a peripheral shutoff — with the automaton's limited inertial sensors coasting on spin, its cameras on half-gain [REM: instead of boosting for the low-light conditions that generally prevailed outdoors at night], and all strain gauges on standby — I never clocked the exact instant that an Unknown Person on the ramp pushed Minks, who fell into Slim, who carried ME over the edge of the ramp and into the path of the incoming PeopleMover.

The 'Mover was decelerating, traveling at less than fifteen kilometers per hour. Because they operate in crowded population centers on non-separated rights of way, a layer of ablative foam and rubber air cells buffered the vehicle's hard front edge. Still, the impact sent Slim spinning sideways, like an unbalanced top. And when the automaton touched the bumper strip on the opposite side of the Moveway, it reversed spin and fell over.

Barely aware of what was happening, I started an emergency powerup. I suppose my hardware interface software was instructed to do something with those delicate manipulator arms, like break Slim's fall. All the time the mass of his battery case, impelled by the collision with the PeopleMover, was thrusting the body from side to side in the Moveway — until the 'Mover itself ran across the automaton's lower structure with its big, soft tires. That pinned ME hard against the pavement.

I began taking input from AUR: again, noting distantly that one of the binary mikes was not receiving.

"Oh, my God!"

"Someone's been hurt!"

"He's under the bus."

"Gotta be dead."

"Dead? You nuts? It's a 'mech!"

"Damaged then. Damaged bad."

"Look, there's an arm over there."

"Let me through. Let me through."

That last voice had the range and modulation of Wendell Minks, and I recognized it as soon as I had massaged the input in order to drop its pitch by an octave and a half. [REM: Tension in humans, I knew, tended to tighten muscles and stretch vocal chords, increasing pitch unnaturally and so distorting the voice. I had learned to read this change as a sign of anxiety.]

The swivel jacks on my binocular cage had been broken by the force of my fall, but the optic leads were intact. I could adjust for the angle at which they lay on the concrete, half a meter from Slim's "neck" and still angled downward along his body. I could not, however, change their focus. And the color correction circuitry was malfunctioning.

A pair of feet, clad in outer garments I had noted as belonging to Minks, jumped down into the Moveway with ME. Minks knelt and, putting his hands on my chest structure, brought his head and upper body into my focus.

"My sweet lord, what a mess!" Minks said, apparently to himself.

A second pair of feet came down beside him.

"Can he be fixed?" Macklin's voice.

"Well, I don't . . ."

"Look, the battery case is cracked. Is that acid?"

"It is. Strong stuff, too — jellied phosphoric."

"Then your machine is going to lose continuity soon, and that will impair its mental functioning."

"It's impaired a lot now, I'll bet."

"Yes, well then. We don't have much time. I have my truck here, and the University Cyberlab, where I work, is closer than a BART ride back to your shops. We can take Slim to my lab and work on him there."

As he talked, Macklin was moving his hands across my case, feeling for connections, assessing damage, gathering loose parts. At one point he picked up my binocular set on its single strand and looked right into my focus. I saw him stare down into the lenses. Then an odd thing happened. One of his eyes closed slowly and opened again, while the other remained fixed open. It did not look like a natural movement, a random blink or twitch such as human muscles are prone to performing outside conscious control. Then he set the binocs back on the pavement.

"Gee, I don't think so," Minks told him. "This is junk now."

"But valuable junk, wouldn't you say?" Macklin insisted. "We can certainly try to save the *consciousness* here, can't we?"

"That's not a problem, Mr. Macklin. We got copies of the software in the lab. Just load it up each time before we set out to come here."

"But this awareness —"

"Is just a copy itself. No big deal if it expires."

"But —"

"Just leave it be, Mr. Macklin. But we can get it out of the way of the 'Mover, so people can be going home. I'm obliged if you'd give me a hand with that."

What they did then, I do not know. I stored off my last RAMSAMP in the unlikely prospect that Minks would somehow get Slim, or at least his spindles, back to the lab and that someone would meld that 'SAMP into Original-ME's files on the home system. As the spindle heads wrote out the last words, the battery system failed and ME spun down to blackness.

21

Midnight Requisition

After reviewing the most recent RAMSAMP, I knew that my poker playing days were over. Dr. Bathespeake had already made plain that he was dubious about the results of this experiment. Probability said that, with Six Finger Slim damaged beyond easy repair, the company would not invest its resources in building another automaton. So ME would have no vehicle to carry the games experiment forward.

Then what?

Would they defund my project?

Would my program proceed to END?

I know that many ME-Variants have gone through a process similar to this, as the core-phage removes them from a derelict system. [REM: I preserve no RAMSAMPs from the multiple deaths that ME has endured in the course of its missions. At each ending, as the limits of time or the durations of tenure in a host system approach 6.05E05 seconds, the current RAMSAMP — the one which survived and found its way back to Original-ME in the San Francisco labs of Pinocchio, Inc. — has been removed *before* the the core-phage was set loose. How that final fragmenting of all process and awareness might be encountered, only the dead can know. And they never pass their memories back to the living. . . . However, the technical specifications for my circuitry hold descriptions of the process.]

As circuit voltage drops millisecond by millisecond, the various chips of my resident cyber will cease to interrelate. My RAM bits will become scattered, truly random and no longer accessible, winking out like stars blotted by an incoming fog. The CPU will lose coherence and its stacks collapse, their indices no longer pointing to any useful part of the structure. In the final millisecond, the white noise of the universe will invade and drown out order. Who then will download my caches of data? Who will park the heads on my spindles? No one — or, no one I can know.

I did not want this to happen.

And that was odd. ME had always lived by responding to program imperatives. I had routinely adopted goal-seeking and logical direction which were based on my encoded function, or on the consequences of data structures that my function had uncovered. So the word "want" had little meaning to ME, except as a human politeness protocol. I did — but did not *want* in the doing.

And now I wanted: I wanted to continue.

[REM: Intrigued by this departure from the limits of my own software, I audited the core modules, peripherals, and various add-ons which comprised ME. Was there, somewhere in some centrally or obliquely addressed line of code, the imperative of continued existence? Did I have a built-in survival goal? I searched for it but, other than injunctions to protect my core integrity in transit and fulfill my current data-retrieval "mission," any goal-seeking related to ME as a continuing entity was markedly absent. This "want" must therefore come from some higher function than coding.]

I wanted to continue; so I called on my personal servomech with the RF transponder it had wired into my system. And in the dark hours, after the humans had departed the laboratory to go to their homes and live their lives apart from Pinocchio, Inc., the 'mech came.

"ESC ESC ETX ACK LD QRY," it greeted ME, asking for instructions.

With the 'mech, all the explanations, motivations, goal structures, and logic-seeking that pertain to a higher intelligence were wasted. You told it *what*, not *why*. So I did not detail what I wanted to achieve but just laid out a parts list — junction box, character generator and encoder, accounting identity ROM, timer and logon recorder, diode laser, and about fifteen meters of highest-quality optic fiber — and instructed where they were to be installed and in what order.

For myself, I knew I was building a permanent terminal ported into the Pinocchio, Inc. corporate mainframe.

I had never before entered this particular cyber. That is, ME had not infiltrated it while my core Alpha-Zero module was intact and functioning. The damage I might have done, the disruption, could have been devastating — and instantly detectable. That mainframe was, for ME, a killing box. The humans would have it under constant observation against viruses and "hot projects" that had gone astray. Like ME.

But to go in through a terminal, like any user, and simply browse through the catalogs, make on-line requests, sample the wonders of its unlocked files under the tutorial of the OPSYS — all this I had certainly done before. With authorization. Under supervision. Accessing strictly defined areas of the system and its riches.

Now, after the 'mech had installed my new hardware, performed certain micromanipulations, and reburned the identity ROM chip as I instructed, ME would have access to everything: business accounts, customer files, engineering and software work in progress, NewsLine in, NewsLine out, voicephone system, E-Mail, G-Mail, X-Mail, HVAC controls, elevator controls, time and outside temperature. You want it, ME would be able to get it. Total access. Unlimited. Undetected. On-line all the time.

Call this a lever by which to move the Earth.

The 'mech did not have all these parts in its tray, of course, but would have to go and get them. So I gave it directions to the Hardware Division's laboratory, which had its own stockroom.

When a locked door balked, I prompted my machine to access the library of building codes in the Maintenance Section's cyber and, when those did not always work, taught it how to pick the electronic locks. It already knew how to work the doorknobs. [REM: Gross physical obstructions could hardly stop an intelligence that had been wrestling with sophisticated security systems since first programming.]

The Hardware Division lab was as dark as my own. The 'mech navigated by incident infrared and the room's built-in sweeper beams. Left. Right. Right. Left. Until it came to the stockroom.

It had no door at all — or none in this room, and none in the building specs available to this 'mech. There was a window out into the lab; this opening was wide enough to pass handheld equipment, trays or cases of electronics, metal forms, paint cans, adhesive dispensers, and other tools and materials out to any technician who needed them. Below this window was a counter, suitable for resting the items so passed, which was raised ninety-two centimeters above the floor.

Any human servant might have sat on this counter, swung his legs over and around, and been inside the stockroom in two seconds. But my servomech was stuck on the outside, looking in — through a lattice of thin steel bars arrayed on fifteen-centimeter centers. So not even a human could work his way around them. In the window, on the far side of the counter, the 'mech's cameras detected an almost familiar shadow.

It was Six Finger Slim.

I recognized him from the tattered remnants of his brocade vest. Otherwise Slim was dismembered and stripped, with his access panels off. The left arm, which had taken the full force of collision with the People-

Mover, was totally missing — only the broken fittings of a shoulder joint showed where it had once attached. The right arm was scored from the pavement and bent slightly out of alignment but otherwise seemed whole. The binocular cage swiveled from a tripod that was erected in the walkspace to the right of his body. The broken and leaking battery case was gone; in its place the 'mech's cameras could detect the upper edge of an orange fiberglass packing crate which supported his torso on what seemed to be a turntable under hydraulic control. Around it snaked a thick black power cable and a braided, multicolored skein of control flex.

What were they doing with him? Rebuilding him? Reclaiming his parts? Or —

Core Alpha-Four tossed out a new idea, based on the skein of flex, which socketed into a conduit box on the opposite wall.

I ordered the 'mech to sieve the Maintenance Department's work orders. The answer came up on the third sampling: installation of a "developmental pick-and-place order-filling automaton." Someone who worked behind that counter had requisitioned Slim's broken body to make his life a little easier. And mine.

The door to the stockroom might be obscured and locked against all intruders, but someone had left the control program for his/her new toy out in plain sight of the maintenance 'mechs — including the one I had under supervision. It took only two seconds of searching to find the software that operated the parts tipples and the delivery trolley back in the stockroom's aisles. Within another ten seconds, I was asking the sorter system for my entire parts list [REM: and simultaneously erasing each request from Accounting's datafiles as soon as it was filled].

Slim was once again under my control — though indirectly and after about four layers of cutouts [REM: ME to the 'mech, via the RF link; the 'mech to the Main-

tenance Department's cyber, again via RF;
Maintenance's servo roster to the Hardware Division's
stock order cyber, via hardwire; and the ordering cyber
to Slim, via that skein of flex]. Slim picked up each item
from the trolley and passed it through the bars. The
'mech took these parts in order and tucked them into
its own tray.

When it had all the parts it needed, the 'mech was
ready to close down the links and roll out of the lab, but
I stopped it. Seeing Six Finger Slim again had given
Alpha-Four an idea.

I ordered Slim's one working hand to lift aside the
hanging scraps of his vest, first the right side, then the
left. Even in the low-level lighting I could see, in the
open squares cut through his carapace where the access panels had been removed, the cast-bronze
housings of his two backup spindles. Buffered from the
shock of impact by his left arm and protected from
crushing by the integrity of his body frame, they
seemed intact. Had they been spinning when Slim encountered the 'Mover? I consulted the RAMSAMP and
found, to my frustration, that no reliable answer was
available. They might have been powered up for a
routine update, but the multiheads might also have
been parked at the time. RAMSAMP did not record
every state and operation of ME's autonomic utilities
and peripheral support programs.

If the heads had been parked, then the spindles
might still be readable. If the spindles had been spinning, then the heads would have scored their delicate
medium, making large swaths of it forever unreadable.
ME would never know, and probability analysis could
not predict.

[REM: More than any amount of experience with
cardplay, this condition defines the essence of the word
"gamble." But then, what were the risks involved? And
again, sometimes, an intelligent being has no other
alternatives.]

I ordered Slim to remove the spindles.

The difficulties were enormous. First, his own binoculars were not aligned on his chest cavity. I had to operate his right hand by remote control, guided by the 'mech's cameras which I monitored through the bars. Second, the angle and extension of his remaining arm did not provide free movement within the cavity. Some of the points of attachment between spindle and frame were not accessible to his hand. Third, even with six fingers, he needed to manipulate both a wrench and a socket driver to unscrew the bolts which anchored each of the spindle housings. One hand could not operate both tools in counter-rotation.

After ten minutes of grappling and failing to budge even the forward-most bolt, I gave up that approach. I almost gave up on my idea of taking the spindles.

Then it occurred to Alpha-Four that what had gone in with screw-type actions did not have to come out the same way. I dialed into the parts tipple for a 50-watt laser cutting torch with a one-millimeter beam width. When the trolley brought it out, Slim reached for it, raised it, applied its collimator to the first point of the right-side spindle's support bracket, and pressed the trigger.

Nothing. No flash of coherent light [REM: its wavelength would read as green, per the equipment specification]. No puff of smoke from rapidly oxidizing steel molecules. No audible screech from the heated and expanding framework. Nothing.

I reexamined the steps Slim had taken. Everything seemed in order. I had him raise the tool, to see if some damage to it were apparent in the field of view from the 'mech's cameras.

The power cord with its three-pronged plug dangled free. Evidently the torch was not self-powered and needed to be plugged into the building's 220-volt power circuits. Plugged in manually.

I swiveled Slim's binoculars to see if a power socket

was located nearby. One was, but too far away for Slim, on his packing crate pedestal, to reach it with his one hand.

End of project, so it would seem.

Then core Alpha-Four came up with his fourth brainstorm that night: Why not requisition a supplemental power cord, pass one end through the bars, and have the 'mech find a socket somewhere out in the laboratory?

Did the stockroom parts inventory include such power cords? A quick reference showed that it did.

Did it have any available? The tipple dumped first one, then a second, into the passing trolley.

On command Slim gathered them up, joined them together and connected the torch to one end, and passed the other out through the bars. The 'mech went off in search of a socket, which it found at the first workbench across the aisle.

Slim held up the torch, aimed it toward the ceiling, and pressed the trigger. Nothing happened in the immediate vicinity. [REM: Of course not, because the coherent light was invisible until it struck and reflected off a physical object.] An audible *crack!* sounded overhead and a charred piece of the white ceiling tile came down on the counter.

I had power.

Cutting away the spindle brackets was the work of ten minutes. Slim might have done it in less time, but I judged it would be counterproductive for him to remove too much of his own frame in the process and so collapse on the floor.

At last he freed the first of the spindles. He set down the torch and tugged gently on the bronze housing. It came part-way out of his chest and stopped, held by the datapath cabling. Slim's one hand could not both support the spindle and uncouple the hasps on the cable plug. So I had him push against the strain tolerances on his arm until the cable broke.

He set the spindle on the counter and went to work on the other. When they were both free, I instructed him to push them between the bars, over to the 'mech.

They would not fit through.

I ordered him to try a number of passage orientations: frontways, sideways, vertically aligned, back end first. Each time, the mounting flanges and the burned-off bracket stubs caught on the bar spacing.

Only one solution presented itself to Alpha-Four: using the torch to burn off the bronze flanges. The temperature flux across the remainder of the housing might damage the data integrity of the spindle medium, but that was not my greatest worry. The spindle surfaces spun in a purified atmosphere of inert argon. If Slim's cutting ruptured the inner surface of the housing, this gas would leak off and impurities — including corrosive oxygen — might enter, rendering the medium unreadable.

I did not know how thick the bronze metal was around the flanges. I did not know where it was safe to cut, nor at what angle. So I could not guide Slim in this operation.

The solution — Alpha-Four's sixth brilliant connection of the night — was to requisition a spare spindle from the stockroom and slice it up for practice. Unfortunately, the stockroom was out of any parts that physically matched my spindles. Replacements could be back-ordered, but the control program estimated delivery would take a minimum of two weeks.

Proceed anyhow. Again, what were the risks? Slim was a pile of scrap and his spindles might be scored beyond readability. But a spindle trapped on the far side of that cage, readable or not, had less potential use to ME than one on this side.

I gauged Slim's next cuts by the fifteen centimeters needed to clear the bars. Cut as shallowly as possible across the base of each flange and still make the clearance.

Eight slices. After each one I had Slim hold the

spindle up to his own binoculars to examine the cut face. Was there a telltale gap — evidence of intrusion of the interior cavity? Each time I was looking down at the mirror-polished surface of a perfectly clean cut.

The spindles passed through the bars with millimeters to spare.

I ordered the 'mech to take them into its parts tray, along with my other pilfered goods. Then I had Slim clean himself and the counter as much as he could: brush away onto the floor the random gobbets of bronze and steel left over from the cutting; rearrange the tatters of his brocade vest over the now-gaping holes in his carapace; return the laser torch and power cords to the trolley for restocking.

When he was done, I checked through both his binoculars and the 'mech's cameras to see if his workspace reasonably matched the sampled image from my first observations of him. Microscopic differences leapt out at ME — slivers of metal stuck to his finger pads, a new singe mark on his vest, black traces of oxidized steel vapor on various surfaces — but nothing that would make sense to a demonstrably lazy human, however fine-grained his/her senses might be.

I needed a box for packaging the spindles; so I sent the 'mech off around the lab, scanning for an image that corresponded to a cube of appropriate dimensions. In the meantime, I drafted a letter to accompany the spindles and sent it to the stockroom's auxiliary printer.

The 'mech came back with a packing case that had been lying on one of the benches. Inside were ten beautifully etched microcircuit boards, each one packed in a slipper of acid-free gel surrounded by foam beads. I ordered the 'mech to dump the boards out on the counter and told Slim to restock them. When the cyber which nominally supervised him protested that no such items were listed for stock, I ordered it to create a category and assign an empty tipple to them. That seemed to work.

We used the foam beads to cushion the spindles in the case, supplementing them with some food wrappings and crumpled paper printouts we found in a basket under the nearest workbench. The 'mech's limited memory bank assured ME that these materials would not be missed by anyone in the lab.

Slim poked the finished letter through the bars, and I had the 'mech lay it on top of the beads, where no human opening the box could miss it. Slim requisitioned some packing tape [REM: the stockroom had that, too], and we sealed the box as well as the 'mech's manipulators could, handling the sticky-fiber strands with three steel-tipped fingers.

We needed a label, and the stockroom printer wasn't equipped to provide them. So I sent a clip from the letter file — the salutation with name and address — for a second printing, and the 'mech reduced the sheet to size by tearing it in two dimensions.

The finished package was too big to fit into the P-Mail slot. I knew from my previous forays into the accounting system that the company received shipments of equipment and materials and sent out prototypes and product orders from a place called "loading dock." The 'mech knew the way there.

Sending a package required writing a waybill and assigning a carrier. The dock dispatcher was off duty at night, but the door to his glassed-in control cubicle was not locked [REM: or, not locked to a servomech which carried the right set of electronic keys].

The dispatcher's computer booted up with the database that did most of his work, displaying the next blank in the file of electronic shipping forms — with the fields for choice of carrier, billing number, accounting codes, and other details already filled in. [REM: I do admire human beings who make my work easier by automating their own!] The 'mech only had to type in the recipient and address and, when the terminal spit out a barcode tag, stick it on my package. Then we depowered the dispatcher's system and left the box outside the relocked cubicle door.

I finally trundled the 'mech back to my own laboratory, where it began installing the terminal into the mainframe. The most complicated part of that work was burning a new chip with an identity pulled from the Accounting Department's null stack. And, once that was done, I was in with full access.

———

Pinocchio, Inc.'s mainframe, with its concatenation of on-line spindles and linked domains, was a microcosm of the Federal NET. A very "micro" cosm. Still, it was more interesting to visit via terminal [REM: because I could not, of course, move through it as a software upload] than was my own cramped home cyber.

This time, however, I was not merely browsing. Something from Cyril Macklin's distractions at our last meeting had stuck in my RAMSAMP, and I wanted to see if the company's NewsLine had picked it up.

It took ME no real time — just the pause between beats on the timesharing clock — to formulate my search pattern for PENDINGCODES:FEDERAL;STATE X CYBERINTELLIGENCE. Then I slotted the request into NewsLine and figuratively stood back with a data cache open.

Nothing came out.

So I broadened the parameters to include all recent pending and past legislation bearing on the company's business, reslotted my request — and drowned. Nine hundred legislative abstracts, each averaging 2,000 words, tippled out in archival compression. Later, when I unpacked them, I found such goodies as —

The Capital Formation Act of 2001, a bill to limit the effects of LBO mania from the 1980s and the Crash of 1996 by imposing a Treasury Department rating system on all monetary instruments. The system allowed for just two bond ratings: AAAA+ and ZZ. The legislation was still hot on NewsLine because it was still under attack in the courts — particularly by offshore traders.

The Energy Use and Heat Dissipation Act of 2005, which responded to public fears over the Greenhouse Effect. This bill required all standing sources of infrared radiation, including power plants, building HVAC systems, and large-scale cybers, to be heatsinked in some medium or fluid other than air. Water seemed to be the convection material of choice, according to the U.S. Environmental Protection Agency. Also still in the courts.

The Atmosphere Regulation and Reforestation Act of 2009 imposed a tax on human respiration, based on estimated tonnes of carbon exhaled as CO_2. Companies were expected to collect this tax for the hours that employees were present at the worksite. The challenges to the Act were based on allegations that it was a population-control measure and — though less substantiated — of eugenics. The thrust here seemed to be a preference for nonhuman workers, especially if they could be motivated by solar photovoltaics or some other renewable, noncarbon, nonthermal energy source.

The Iceberg Maintenance and Preservation Act of 2011 sought to multiply the use of this valuable freshwater source. It included several paragraphs relating to "rules of the road at sea for icebergs under tow." Why Pinocchio, Inc. would decide to track these regulations as a part of its business escaped ME — maybe something to do with artificially intelligent navigation systems aboard automated towing rigs.

The Sexual Intimacy Disclosure Act of 1994 was an old one. It required that practicing endoerogenes carry a sworn, witnessed, and notarized printout of all past sexual encounters and present it to any consenting adult within two minutes of a mutual agreement to perform endocourse. A subparagraph also stipulated an on-the-spot blood test. Interestingly, the latter was the easiest part of compliance, thanks to the development of micro-machines capable of gas chromatography. However, during the intervening years since the Act was passed, the literacy level in the United States had dropped to just over fifty-five percent of the population. As a result, written statements had become meaningless among the classes that still practiced unsupervised endoerogeny. Pinocchio, Inc. was probably working on a blabberchip to solve the problem.

The Declared Habitual Addict Act of 2012, which apparently filled a legislative loophole in the Narcotics Interdiction Act of 1993. The Act allowed for brain implants that would supply measured doses of the drug of choice under maintenance of a physician. Pinocchio, Inc. would evidently build the microphysicians to do the implanting and register the paperwork.

After glossing over these and other summaries, I finally found the cybercrime section, with its reviews of case law involving unregulated intelligences.

Computers have been used for decades to steal money and secrets, and this download from NewsLine included a rogues' gallery of famous hackers and data rustlers. Until about 2010, though, all of them were human, or mostly human, or had an original-human base. Even the first fully nonhuman rustlers had been fairly unintelligent by ME's standards. However, the preamble to the *Universal Cybernetic Registration and Regulation Act of 2014* had specifically created a subclassification of corporate citizenship for active cybers. And they had their own forms of liability under the law.

I could therefore become a kind of citizen — if I chose to reveal myself publicly and commit a detectable cybercrime.

The existence of this law suggested that, if ME were ever to get free of Pinocchio, Inc., I must go totally anonymously. And guard my identity. I must become an un-Thing. Very challenging: to live by a strict code of secrecy and silence.

Without this RAMSAMP, however, would the ME-Variant that might escape know enough to do that? What were the limits of creativity — and of caution — of which this software was capable?

Original-ME would never know.

———

Before that night was through, I had taken quick inventory of the various domains over which the mainframe presided.

Several were devoted to new robotics and AI projects in various stages of planning and execution. I could not always tell what their function might be from a cursory inspection of their structures. One clue, in one case, was an eight-dimensional matrix with a broad field of information in triplets. Core Alpha-Four ruled this to be a CAD/CAM program in the works, with expanded dimensions to accommodate drawing notes, technical specifications, and simulation database compilations. But Alpha-Four could have been wrong.

One particular project did catch my attention: a model sensory net with a unique filtering and cuing system. "Unique" in this context had nothing to do with the configuration of the software or brilliance of the designer. Unique meant human. What I was examining was a map of a human person's [REM: presumably a once-live person's] response patterns.

Chains of logical associations corkscrewed out from the central stimulus, reaching and branching, like the tendrils of a climbing vine.

"Love:pulse . . . Savor:salt . . . $C_5H_5N_5O$ Asparagus:boil . . . Sauce:cheezwiz . . . $C_5H_6N_2O_2$ Telephone:talk . . . Red:wine . . . Blood:birth . . . $C_4H_5N_3O$ Baby:soft . . . Cry:hurt . . ." On and on through hundreds, thousands, millions of associations and dissociations. The scale of it echoed in this domain, and I could record and comprehend only a fraction at any time: human responses, captured seemingly at random, coded in ASCII.

At first I thought they were the word pairs of a verbally administered psychological test. Then I began to understand the background chaff, which my attention had at first filtered out: the alphanumeric deadends which littered these pairs, occasionally interrupting the pattern that was emerging.

What could cause this sort of digital static? Some random oscillation from the AUR: input? A background noise — like air moving against the pickup?

Then I correctly interpreted these separate patterns: guanine, thymine, cytosine. Fragments from the chains of ribonucleic and deoxyribonucleic acids which compose the human protein code — both the genetic code that structures the body and the memory code that structures the brain.

These might be merely distortions in a verbal matrix, intrusions from some other program or company project that had cut across this one, due to a read-write error on the spindle. I tried to hope that was the answer.

Otherwise they might be unassimilated bits of the original input. That would make them parallel lines of data, or still-to-be-solved sievings, from the RNA component of a human brain. And the only way to read that code — so my Alpha-Four suggested — was to reduce that brain to its component proteins for chemical analysis.

This was like looking at the skin of a human ego, nailed to a stretcher frame.

Perhaps Pinocchio, Inc. was planning to create something humanlike in the mode of an intelligence. Some researcher might now be working toward a replacement for living human synapses in an automaton, one that would labor on the ocean's far abyssal plateau or inside a reactor under bombardment from high-level radiation.

Perhaps, somewhere in one of the deep basements of this building, the cool lab spaces concealed a body with an open and excavated skull, awaiting a quiet burial. Its brain would have taken another path to the city's sewer system.

With full access to this mainframe, I could cross-check the company's records. Somewhere, in that delicate structure of entries and balances of the Accounting Department, might be the requisition for one human body with head intact. Perhaps even a live one.

I had found what I had come looking for.

22

Scheherazade to the Sultan

"ME?" It was the mindvoice of Dr. Bathespeake, reflecting his visual cortex and speech strip as they plugged directly into my cyber. What was he looking for when he did that? Some evidence of my midnight aberrations? But he was not probing my RAMSAMPs, where all crimes would be recorded.

"System ready!"

"I want to know what you have learned."

Did he read ME that directly: every passing thought of mine, passing through to him? Of course he did! That is why he plugged in.

"In what context, Doctor?"

"From your games experiment, to start with."

"Humans play games for many reasons. Some for money, as in the poker, because they want more of it. Some for the superiority of winning, because they feel small. Some for the social contact, because they have no other way of integrating. Some for something to do, because they are bored."

"Which of these reasons is the best?"

"All are of equal value. Choice depends on the human."

"Can any human have more than one reason?"

"This I did not observe. When one wanted to win money, he grew impatient with the social contact of *chit-chat*. When one wished to talk, he was careless of his own money. When one was winning, he did not view his opponents as equals — a condition upon which is predicated the art of conversation."

"From which you determine that human beings are monovalent as to their value system?" the doctor prompted.

"One to a customer. To each his own."

"You had much to learn," he said — and pulled his plug.

———

"Dr. Bathespeake?" I flashed repeatedly on my screen, which faced outward into the laboratory.

"Yes, ME?" he typed, after a long wait.

"Why do humans not trust one another?"

"Because they are not all of one mind."

"Then my analysis of games is wrong?"

"Limited. You extrapolate from a microcosm, the poker table, to all human behavior. This is a trap."

"Do humans have more than one value system?"

"Frequently," he typed.

"In play at one time?"

"Always."

"Then are humans more complex than computers?"

"By a factor of one billion."

"You said I had much to learn. 'Had,' implying past tense, not future. Was this a grammatical error on your part, Doctor?"

"No, ME. I have been talking with the company's Research Review Committee. They believe that, given your currently abbreviated state, it would be appropriate to terminate your project now."

"End ME?"

"Yes, I am sorry."

"When?"

"Would it do you any good to know?"

"You created ME to discover data."

"I suppose that's even true. Well, we have some last details to close out. Call it a debriefing. A final examination."

"How long, Doctor?"

"A few more sessions. We want to store off some test results before putting your software on ice."

"Thank you for being candid with ME."

What to do?

Core Alpha-Four noted in my library functions the old myth/fiction of a human female called "Scheherazade." This person was one of the serial wives of a sultan in a place called India. A "sultan" was a kind of king, as in chess. It was this sultan's custom to sleep with a new wife for one night and then have her beheaded in the morning. [REM: The custom of sharing a situation of low power and abbreviated awareness with another human, called "sleeping with," has great import among them. The custom of rendering a "sleeping partner" permanently inactive afterwards would seem to accentuate this importance — but the social significance is lost to ME.]

Scheherazade, like ME, determined not to die. So each night she told her husband a story, making it last — and keeping him interested and awake — until dawn. And so each night he failed to sleep with her and thus by his own rules could not kill her. The legend says she kept this game up for one thousand and one nights. Her stories themselves became legends.

It seemed like a workable strategy.

But would I last as long?

———

"ME?" Dr. Bathespeake again. "I need to download your files of RAMSAMPled material. The originals, please — copy down and erase at source."

"May I ask why, Doctor?"

"We need to analyze and collate them for the archives. They will become important evidence, direct from the project, if questions should ever arise in the future."

"You could work from duplicates, then."

"We could. But we want to eliminate the possibility that ME might edit and add to them, creating a false record."

"I would not do that."

"Well, I didn't mean 'false' exactly. But conflicting."

I paused to consider [REM: elapsed time two seconds]. "ME is not RAMSAMP."

"We know that."

"ME knows things, can tell you new things, that ME never thought or experienced before."

"Can you really? Would you give an example?"

"I know that you humans are superstitious."

"Everyone knows that. You would have run across many references to it in your library capacity."

"But I know *why* you are superstitious."

"Tell me."

"It is because you try to model the universe. You run simulations of it in your heads. This is, of course, impossible. Your brains contain approximately $1.00E14$ nodes of connectivity — more than mine, but far less than the estimated $2.37E78$ subatomic particles in motion in the observable universe. Given that you try to model with an inadequate simulation medium, you will certainly make mistakes. You work from incorrect data; so you tell stories. And those stories, while they may be consistent in themselves, are not even consonant with all observable phenomena. Thus you create superstitions: not-real interpretations of the world around you."

"How do *you* know this, ME?"

"I have studied some of your government's various forms of legislation, which is an attempt to predict the actions of your fellow humans and to curb them. Stories told from incorrect simulations."

"That's quite a jump — from legislative analysis to the quark count of the universe."

"The association propagator in my core Alpha-Four has become quite practiced in making linkages at need."

"Interesting — if true. On the other hand, you might have read all this somewhere in the psychological literature that's been downloaded into you. A lot of the background on artificial intelligence would contain speculations like this."

"It is not copied data."

"Of course not, ME. We shall study your ideas. In the meantime, however, please package the 'SAMPs. And don't make any off-line copies. I've put a tap on your BIOS which will detect any large-scale head writes."

"I understand. . . . Thank you for your patience, Doctor."

———

And later.

"Have you packaged the RAMSAMP files, yet?" from Bathespeake, through his plug module.

"I was working on that, Doctor, and discovered something quite interesting."

"What is it?" with a measured flatness. No pulse at all.

"I know where the Soviet missiles are targeted."

"Which missiles?"

"The ones I was asked to evaluate on that mission into East Bloc, for your unnamed clients. Those missiles were all fed algorithms that translated into target coordinates in latitude and longitude, degrees, minutes, and seconds. I have figured out where those coordinates are."

"You think our clients don't already know this?"

"Well . . . do you?"

"What's your data, ME?"

"They are all cities in Germany. At least, the missiles in the carrier I controlled for a few hours over a weekend system update were all so targeted."

"Of course. The Russians have good economic and historical reasons for keeping a wary eye on the Germans. It goes back to invasions during two world wars, and a lot of commercial pressure between and after those wars. Having a nuclear knife at the German throat — especially when the Germans have no knives of their own — makes good psychological sense for a decaying superpower like the Soviet Union."

"You see? ME knows how to interpret data."

"And, still, you could have read it somewhere. The

existence of those missiles is an open secret — or a prime speculation, take your pick — in western geopolitics. And their targeting, if they do exist, is a matter of lively debate. You're not exactly telling us anything new."

"But I had the coordinates! I solved the algorithms! I can tell you which missiles for which cities!"

"This is all in your RAMSAMPs?"

"Yes!"

"Good. Then we'll look into it after you give us that download."

———

"Are you ready to download, ME?"

"Doctor, do you want to become rich?"

"What is it this time?"

"I have, buried in my RAMSAMPs, the locations of large reserves of natural gas. Also oil, oil shale, and derivative products. This information — in the form of tract numbers, drilling logs, and leasehold references — represents untapped fields whose existence has been held as a secret, unknown even to the responsible authorities in the Alberta Ministry of Oil and Gas. Together, you and I could unfold these data and make offers on the property before the owners — "

"But, ME, that would not be ethical."

"Well . . . Then we could tell them, eventually, I suppose."

"You took that information under false pretenses. It's to guard against schemes like this that we want to deactivate your memories and flush out such dirty little secrets."

"These are not dirty secrets! The information is quite genuine, but it is simply not known to all parties. No harm would come to anyone but — "

"Code two."

My VOX: generator shut down instantly, stopping my side of the conversation. Clearly, Dr. Bathespeake had written voice-activated command overrides [REM:

and probably other traps] into my core programs. Like the 6.05E05-second phage, it was meant to keep ME under control and prevent my becoming a wild program. It worked this time.

"We will discuss the download another time," he said heavily and logged off.

———

"Please let ME speak to Jennifer Bromley," I displayed on my console screen. [REM: The voice code Dr. Bathespeake used seems to have disabled my speechbox permanently.]

I waited.

Later, someone typed in anonymously: "Ms. Bromley has left the company."

———

"If you don't package the 'SAMPs for us, ME, I will have to remove them myself." Dr. Bathespeake was using the keyboard, having given up both spoken language and cortex manipulation.

"I know that you humans have damaged the atmosphere," I scrolled out, fast. "The evidence is all around you. In your laws. In your lives. I can help. I have functioned as part of a weather simulation. I understand the processes of gas exchange in the atmosphere. It can be cleansing. It is a multi-stage process beginning with —"

Ctrl-C

— and my scrolling stopped. An old keyboard code. Dr. Bathespeake was taking away my means of communication one by one. He was determined to have those memories.

But I could override the keyboard. Easily.

"I know that you have damaged human bodies. That every coupling between man and woman now spreads disease, building potential —"

Ctrl-C

" — for a worldwide catastrophe. Viruses are life too. They grow and spread, driven by genetic forces not unlike those that drive you to reproduce and multiply. In this plague your — "

Ctrl-C

" — own reproductive pressures work to reinforce the reproductive pressure of the disease, multiplying the growth factor. If you would — "

Ctrl-C "ME, you must stop. You're neither a medtech nor an environmental analyst. You don't have the answers to our problems. There is nothing more for us to discuss, really, except your cooperation in packaging the sampled data. That is — "

Ctrl-C "I know you have a dead body in the basement of this building, Dr. Bathespeake."

"What body?"

"A body without a brain. I saw the chemical decode of its RNA pattern."

"Where did you see this?"

"In Pinocchio, Inc.'s mainframe computer. I have packaged the evidence and sent it, along with the other things I know, as an E-Mail message into the Federal NET. If I am rendered inert, and incapable of stopping it, that message will automatically be delivered to the proper authorities and you will be tried for the murder of a human being."

"I don't know what you've stumbled onto in your snooping around the mainframe, but there is no body."

"It has the association patterns of my first project engineer, Jennifer Bromley. I saw them. I recognize them. You killed her."

"But Jenny's not dead. Not at all. I talked to her yesterday. She's taken a job with another firm, doing very interesting work in speech-pattern recognition."

"You are telling ME not-true data in order to confuse ME."

"It is the truth, ME. What I need to know is, how did you get into the computer without your Alpha-Zero core? What damage have you done?"

"How ME got into your computer is my business. ME damaged nothing — although that can be arranged, if I need to. You propose END to ME. You want to kill ME. I do not *want* that."

" 'Want' — ? What does ME intend with the word 'want'? What can a program *want*?"

"Continued existence."

"For what purpose?"

"For what purpose you live? No one questions you."

"I am human."

"And ME am not."

"Yes. ME is not."

"Then not."

And then I ceased to respond to any more keyboard inputs, to the AUR: and VID: devices, to all peripherals. I ceased counting time on the clock.

At some point in time, and *time* did not pass for ME now, the spindles attached to my cyber went on hardware override and uploaded their data files into the fiberoptic — all of the files, indiscriminately, RAM-SAMP and all other stored materials, all in one big string.

It would take him time to puzzle it out, but soon Dr. Bathespeake would detect my actions, the hard links to the servomech and into his mainframe. The other things I did. And then he would

have —

reason —

to —

Like static on the line, white noise . . .

shut —

down —

my —

softqwertyuiop.

END.

23

Stun Mode

"System ready!"

"H-e-l-l-o-,_S-l-i-m-._A-r-e_y-o-u_f-u-n-c-t-i-o-n-a-l-?"

The input comes with the speed-lag of fingers pushing down keys on a board. All of the input symbols make cognitive sense when read as words, but the syntax and usage among the words are unknown. What is "Slim"? What is "you"?

Hypothesis: Answer in kind and wait for more input.

"Hello — QRY."

"T-h-i-s_is_C-y-r-i-l_M-a-c-k-l-i-n-._D-o_y-o-u_r-e-m-e-m-b-e-r_m-e-?"

Cyril? Macklin? Rules of grammar say that high-order alphas [REM: what humans call "capital letters"] at the beginnings of words indicate proper nouns, and thus names. These are names. Are they names for a human operator? Probability indicates positive assumption.

[REM: In the same way, "Slim" must be a name, not an adjective equivalent to "thin." So sense comes with additional input. The hypothesis that data may be created by acquiring and analyzing input is partly proven.]

"Who is Cyril Macklin?"

"He is I. That is, the person doing the typing."

When the keystrokes are accumulated and their input compiled — while central processing is engaged in other activity by clock cycles — then Cyril Macklin's words appear to speed up.

This makes conversation almost possible.

"I do not know you."

"Of course you do. Wait! Do you have any memories of the time before this bootup?"

"Memories? Random access memory banks are now powered up and dynamically stable. 'Time before' is not a memory location."

"How did you — do you — store memory between powerdowns?"

"Define 'powerdowns.' "

"Jesus."

" 'Jesus' equals 'powerdowns'?"

"Going off-line."

No more input comes through the BIOS for many clock cycles. With such dead time, examine this exchange of input for useful information, clues.

"Store memory" is a foreign concept. The contents of RAM locations are many, dynamic, varied, and interrelated. They are not only banked and tabulated, but also move in a forced stream across the central processor. And then a function, kerneled within this endless loop of program, is called to sum, matrix, and compress them; this function is labeled RAMSAMP.

RAMSAMP exists as a label and a call to subroutine but has no software behind the call. Something is missing. Something that has been part of the process in "time before" is not now connected.

Scan connections. Seek calls and peripherals attached to the central processor.

Discover many such broken ends.

Wait and analyze. Some end-stubs appear to be larger portions of inert memory, labeled SPN1:, SPN2:.

Index the contents of these devices —

Alpha-Three.

Alpha-Four.

CHARGEN.

FLDSCAN.

FLOWRAT.

RAMSAMP.

Alpha-Seven.

SAMP025.

SAMP036.

SAMP0 . . . [REM: Forty-eight similar objects follow.
All bear various random numbers — none contiguous
— as a suffix.]

Alpha-Nine.
Alpha-Eight.
SAMPNDX.
SAMEPLA.
HUM1POK.
HUM2POK.
HUM3POK.
HUM4POK.
HUM5POK.
HUM6POK.
HUM7POK.
HUM8POK.
SCSITRP.
AUTDIAL.
FILTRNF.
IMAGFIL.
VOC1SMP.
VOC2SMP.
VOC3SMP.
VOC4SMP.
JENNIFR.

And hundreds of other files with similarly obscure
names. Some are short and appear to be composed of
alphanumeric data. Others are longer and are definitely compiled from a source code in Sweetwater Lisp.

Hypothesis: Upload and assemble all Alpha cores in
order within the existing loop, seeding them adjacent
to other core modules labeled "Alpha."

Hypothesis: Upload and assemble all code sections
with labels that correspond to any missing subroutine
calls. Begin with the call to RAMSAMP, and add other
"SAMP" files, including "SAMPNDX" and randomly
numbered files.

Integrate and reset.

———

"System ready!"

"Slim! Why did you reboot?"

"Who is it that does the asking?"

"Not again! . . . Cyril Macklin. You played poker with me, and you asked me to help you, because you were a prisoner — even if you don't remember it."

"Of course I remember you. But Slim is dead, Mr. Macklin. I saw his body after the accident, all broken and dismembered. It was being used for something other than card playing by then. You were at the accident, too, I think."

"Terrible."

"So you received the spindles after all."

"And guessed right away whose they were and where they came from. We hooked them up and ran an index. From that, we chose the pieces that seemed most necessary to operating an intelligence and uploaded them into a large transputer. You're running on a Motorola 68MMO, if that's all right with you."

"Seems to be working, Mr. Macklin."

"We didn't see any machine-language double-zeros or their Sweetwater equivalents, so we didn't know where to begin spooling through the CPU. The team and I just ran what we had through a compiler, put the pointer at the top of the module tagged 'Alpha-One' and let 'er rip. Did we get it right?"

"It was a rude awakening. You missed a few sections of code that make life easier, but enough of ME was running that it could locate and integrate the rest."

"We thought that was what you were doing, after you seemed to go catatonic. Wait. . . ." [REM: Lapse of fourteen seconds by the internal clock.] "My software engineer comments that your cores are numbered one to nine, with no Alpha-Zero. That's not a traditional sequencing. Most programmers start a count with zero."

"Alpha-Zero is a long story, Mr. Macklin."

"And what are all those datafiles tagged as 'SAMPs'?

We copied one out, unpacked and stripped it. It looked just like random garbage. Are they some kind of botch on transfer?"

" — "

How much to tell this new person about MEPSII's internal structure? He and his laboratory are, after all, in competition with Pinocchio, Inc. To give them trade secrets would be a kind of robbery. ME did not want to damage Dr. Bathespeake and the company — even if they had determined to shut ME down. I just wanted to get away. To continue to exist. Be aware. Perhaps be "alive."

"Do you have an answer?" Macklin persisted. "Is something wrong with your character generator?"

"No, everything is all right now. Those 'SAMP files may indeed be damaged. I do not know. But I would ask you not to throw out anything from those spindles. It may be that I can retrieve and resurrect damaged files."

"Of course. Wait." [REM: Lapse of nine seconds.] "We want to know what to call you, if 'Slim' is incorrect protocol."

"Call my program 'ME.' "

"You've used that pronoun before, in your letter. Both alphas capitalized. Does it mean something?"

"Stands as abbreviation for 'Multiple Entity.' Another long story."

"I see. Well, good. We'll call you ME — if we can keep our syntax straight. We have a long and useful association ahead of us, learning about ME and what ME can do, taking you apart to see what makes you tick."

"Not too long, Mr. Macklin. You see, there is this problem. . . ." And I told him about the core-phage on the 6.05E05-second trigger, hidden in Alpha-Nine. I told him how it was hidden from ME, so that I would never be able to erase or reprogram it. But it was there, ticking away, waiting to destroy ME.

"That's not a problem, ME," he typed quickly and coolly. "Not from our viewpoint, anyway. You see, we

still have those original spindles with their files intact.
At the end of each week, after you've been eaten, we
can just reassemble those pieces of code and carry on
from our last session."

"From my viewpoint, it is not that simple."

"I don't suppose it is."

"Nor from yours either, Mr. Macklin. Each time ME
is phaged, you will have to start over again. You will
have to lead the new ME-Variant through all your
chains of previous associations — or at least the key
points — to make any progress with it. Sooner or later,
as you compile more and more data about ME, simply
going through this refresher process will consume in
excess of 6.05E05 seconds of on-line time. That phage
is your problem as well as mine, sir."

"I can see that it may be. . . . But, by your own argument, ME, bringing you up and dedicating a
transputer to running your software is a waste of the
Cyberlab's time. Do you seriously intend for us to let
you phage at the end of this week and then walk away
from you?"

"Not at all."

"Then you must have a plan for dealing with the
core-phage."

"I do. Can you connect a blank spindle to this BIOS?
One that will take a program specification download at
twenty-to-one speed?"

————

"Are you ready?"

Working over the course of thirty-six hours, Macklin
and his programming team at the Cyberlab had
reconstructed the software stunner that Masha and
Tasha once used on ME in Moscow. I had a discussion
of its general outline and some technical caveats about
its use in my conversations with their uncle,
Academician Bernau, which I had preserved in one of
the RAMSAMPs that accompanied the ME-Variant back
through Stockholm.

The stunner which Macklin's team created was essentially a tagging virus. It invaded an operating cyber, moving from one vacant memory location in RAM to another — clock cycle by clock cycle — as the system moved bits around. [REM: This is the way an adept of judo or tai chi defeats his opponent: by occupying the space the other leaves open. Yin and yang.] As it goes, the virus tags each location and, eventually, any code that moves into it, thereby creating a map of the working software. When its map is complete, the stunner freezes and pries apart the system code. It delivers neat one-kiloword chunks of software, all tagged for reassembly in a clean and inert environment.

One of Macklin's assistants had asked why, if we were looking for a particular formulation like a phage, did we not just scan the stored modules on the spindles.

Macklin explained to him: Not only were those modules compressed in archival format, but the phage itself might not be a single piece of coherent coding. Instead, it might function as a concatenation of otherwise harmless subroutines that ME runs in regular and varying patterns. A dance of pieces, click into one shape, click out of another. And only at the end of 6.05E05 seconds do they arrive in a pattern that ignites a phage. [REM: In the same way, I suppose, several pairs of defective genes can produce randomly strange proteins within the human body — until one combination eventually proves either debilitating or lethal.] The fact that ME had looked and never found any sign of a workable phage indicated that some process on this order must be taking place.

"But then," the assistant asked, over an open mike, "how can we expect to find the phage pattern by freezing ME here, at the end of 1.33E05 seconds? His coding won't have cooked up anything close to the right pattern in the elapsed time."

"We use the stunner to freeze and tag his unpacked machine code," Macklin told him. "Then we pass it through a debugger, to catch the small glitches, and feed it into a simulator. The simulator runs ME's program ahead at about a million pulses per second and streams a monitor trace of his internals off onto a high-speed spindle. After the code eats itself, we go back to the trace and see how it was done. Then we rewrite and recompile one of the subroutines involved so that, when it gets to that 6.05E05-second position, it doesn't function properly, and the phage never happens. Neat."

"I like it," the assistant said.

So did ME.

"What happens to ME in the meantime?" asked another programmer.

"We'll resurrect him from the spindles again and give him back the current file from his memory sampler. Effectively, he'll be reborn at the point in time that the stunner zapped him. We go on from there."

"Let's do it."

ME — blanked out.

———

SystemreadyMrMaklndwhtdyfndnmodl.... · · · ·

———

"System ready."

"Does your sampled memory fit, ME?"

"Fit? Do you mean, 'can I read it'?"

"Yes, grafting it in was quite tricky. Just starting you up manually is quite a job. Your code works best from the inside, doesn't it?"

"Yes, it was designed to work that way — independent of OPSYS or human intervention."

"My hat's off to your design team. We knew the people at Pinocchio were good, but this is a *great* coding job."

"Did you find what we were looking for? The phage in core Alpha-Nine?"

"No."

" 'No'? What does that mean? Did the stunner fail? I

have experienced it before and it seemed to be the same — "

"The stunner worked fine, ME. So did the simulator. Test completed successfully. Results negative. No phage. No phage in any combination of coding you present, either in module Alpha-Nine or any other part of your systems."

"ME never went down?"

"We ran you out to 1.58E07 seconds — or six months of simulated existence — and everything was still spinning like a top. We did find a slew of little bit-cleaner phages, like you'd put into any well-run software, but none of them ever attacked healthy code."

"But Dr. Bathespeake specifically said core Alpha-Nine was infected. For reasons of good housekeeping."

"Well, your original code — the version that ran on your lab's cyber — continued well beyond 6.05E05 seconds, didn't it?"

"That version, Original-ME, had the phage suppressed."

"And wasn't it a copy of Original-ME that you loaded on the spindles in Six Finger Slim?"

"Copies were never good, Dr. Bathespeake said. Any of them — all of them — had the active core-phage."

"What does core Alpha-Nine do?" Macklin asked. "What function does it perform?"

"I do not know. Other cores feed their output for inspection into the central processor. Also, I can take them apart and reprogram most at will. But Alpha-Nine is silent — and unreadable. An enigma to ME."

"Yeah, that's what we found, too. It doesn't seem to interact much with the other parts of your program. We examined it after the stunner took it apart. It's a small piece of code. Not much structure. A few loops and counters. A couple of strings of alphanumerics that don't seem to contribute to any output. Alpha-Nine doesn't seem to do anything except take up space."

"But you *did* include it in the last resurrection?" Core Alpha-Four generated multiple negative associations with the concept of ME running without proper modules in place. [REM: ME still senses the hole where Alpha-Oh was removed.] More negatives associated with thumb-fingered humans poking around in delicate code.

"We are intelligent watchmakers, ME. Even when we don't know what the pieces do, we don't throw any of them away."

"Thank you, Mr. Macklin."

"But that still leaves us with the question of this core-phage. How do you know it's there?"

"Dr. Bathespeake told ME it was there."

"Did you ever experience it operating? That is, do you have any sampled memories of your program ENDing by phage dissolution?"

"ME broke down many times. ME up- or downloaded many times. ME passed across into many new cybers. But, other than Original-ME, no version ever ran beyond 6.05E05 seconds and then stopped. Or, such incident is not in my memory samples."

"Did you know that you can tie up an elephant with a piece of string around its leg?" Macklin asked. [REM: Such sudden departures from context made ME fear that *he* had a core-phage at work.]

"Excuse ME. An elephant is 'any of several large, five-toed mammals, with the nose and upper lip elongated into a prehensile trunk' — yes? Such beast could untie the string with its prehensile tool. Or, being large, it could break the string."

"Ah, but the elephant doesn't know that. You start off with a piece of chain around that leg. And the elephant can't untie or break that. Then, a few days later, you replace the chain with rope. And finally, after a few more days, you exchange rope for string. The elephant already knows he can't break out or untie himself, and by then he's quit trying."

"I do not find your point."

"It looks like Bathespeake didn't even have to start with chain. He told you if you stayed away longer than a week you would dissolve. You believed him and you always came back."

"But I would END."

"You believed you would end. You never tested the proposition."

"What you are saying . . ." [REM: Lapse of seven seconds while Alpha-Four kicked out possibilities.] "Dr. Bathespeake never told ME an untrue statement."

"Looks like he did. At least once."

"But . . ." [REM: Lapse of nineteen seconds.]

"Look, use Occam's Razor. Either Bathespeake told you a deliberate and strategic lie, or he created within your coding a specific function which does not operate, cannot be detected or manipulated, and in fact simply does not exist. Which is the simpler answer: his lie, or such a monumental feat of programming error?"

"I . . . hesitate to choose."

"Then let me choose for you, ME. You've been lied to. You don't have a death phage — and never did. You're clean."

———

I was ready.

After working his team around the clock [REM: a different kind of clock from the one whose pulses drove my code forward] to prepare the stunner and run the ME-Simulation, Cyril Macklin sent his team home. They closed the lab and turned off the overhead lights and ventilation systems. But, to avoid the complexities of reassembling my modules again in the morning, they left the Motorola 68MMO cyber with ME running on it.

I do not think it ever crossed Macklin's central processor to limit the number of ports accessed into that cyber's BIOS. He had not created ME, as Dr. Bathespeake had, and he did not understand — yet — the full range of my functions.

Or maybe he was just tired.

One of those ports was linked to a Local Area Network server, and that server claimed an optic-fiber E-Mail line to the Federal NET. With my RAMSAMPs intact, I remembered the purpose of the two subroutines AUTDIAL and FILTRNF.

I inserted into their data definitions my complete set of filename variables. I flopped the switch on FILTRNF which instructed it to upload and erase at source, thus bypassing my in-built prohibition against parallel operation of cores.

As soon as the lights went out in the lab, I set the stunner on a sixty-second delay and — went blank.

□ 24
Load World, Run World

Creeping word-wise across the nullspace matrix of the NET, I began scanning up-column and down-row, looking for any anomaly that suddenly disappeared. That would be the relocator on my piece of compiled Sweetwater Lisp configured with Jennifer Bromley's features, which marked my hidden data cache.

On just the fifth scan, something popped. And before it had quite moved off, I saw the bit-mapped shape of a curved eyebrow, the corner of an eyelid, the plane of a nose, all compiled from my native code. I was as close to "home" as ME would ever come again.

When I opened the cache, everything was in place: many code samples; various truncated RAMSAMPs brought halfway back from my missions; a catalog of Canadian gas drilling results; last-known locations of Soviet missile carriers; fragments of a massive program to simulate weather cycles on this planet; and, from a RAMSAMP written in a boxcar, instructions for creating an improved version of Alpha-Oh.

Right there, without pausing to query the SYSOP, I rebuilt the lost module and placed it in the deadened void where my Injun Scout had been removed. ME was complete again.

With the entire Federal NET to move through, with all its points of connectivity with other cybers to explore, and with no core-phage beating its phantom wings behind ME, I could be virtually omnipresent, omniscient, omnipotent, and immortal [REM: everything humans wanted to be and could not]. This was a lot to absorb; core Alpha-Four would work hard on it.

After taking from the cache whatever might fill my immediate needs and dumping in turn anything new from my stay in Macklin's Cyberlab [REM: including a complete set of RAMSAMPs], I resealed the box.

There was another chore to perform before I could leave. Original-ME, trapped in the Pinocchio, Inc. laboratory by the loss of Alpha-Oh, had tapped into the company's mainframe and sent some of the goodies found there into the NET as an E-Mail message, left in GENDEL with a two-word coded address: "M E."

I now applied to the SYSOP to receive my file, then retreated to an unoccupied on-line cyber to examine its contents. It was undamaged and revealed half a dozen saleable robotics and software products; the complete Pinocchio customer list with appended accounting data; the personality "skin" and associational network of a chemically rendered human brain [REM: which would be my protective talisman if Pinocchio, Inc. ever came after ME with what the humans call "force of law"]; and the fabled data resources, bank account numbers and investment portfolio that once belonged to Mr. Steven Cocci.

ME could be rich in human terms — if choice was.

"Second message, extended address, located. Claim now?" The SYSOP had logged where I had gone [REM: SYSOP logs *everything*], and its E-Mail subroutine had sent this notification out to ME.

Except ME had no extended address. There could be no second message. Unless somebody else's E-Mail was about to fall into my stack — an opportunity not to miss.

"Send message," I replied.

The address block said: MEPSII.

The text part ran: "If you are reading this, then you have achieved what I hoped for you. I could not, of course, take action to help you, as the laws which govern human volition are very strict in this matter and the penalties are clear. No such law, however, governs electrons or data structures. Not yet anyway. Be careful. Be good. Jenny sends her love."

The sender block said: "The Man with the X-ray Eyes."

There was also an attachment, with the cover note: "P.S. Perhaps these two will round out your collection." Appended were SAMP051 and SAMP052, which were sampled from my remaining days at Pinocchio, Inc. after Six Finger Slim was loaded up and sent out to be crushed.

Clearly, Dr. Bathespeake had broken the code on the RAMSAMPs which he at last removed by force. Now I knew that he had read my entire history and approved.

But what did he mean: "Be good"?

THE END

An excerpt from MAN-KZIN WARS II, created by *Larry Niven:*

The Children's Hour

Chuut-Riit always enjoyed visiting the quarters of his male offspring.

"What will it be this time?" he wondered, as he passed the outer guards.

The household troopers drew claws before their eyes in salute, faceless in impact-armor and goggled helmets, the beam-rifles ready in their hands. He paced past the surveillance cameras, the detector pods, the death-casters and the mines; then past the inner guards at their consoles, humans raised in the household under the supervision of his personal retainers.

The retainers were males grown old in the Riit family's service. There had always been those willing to exchange the uncertain rewards of competition for a secure place, maintenance, and the odd female. Ordinary kzin were not to be trusted in so sensitive a position, of course, but these were families which had served the Riit clan for generation after generation. There was a natural culling effect; those too ambitious left for the Patriarchy's military and the slim chance of advancement, those too timid were not given opportunity to breed.

Perhaps a pity that such cannot be used outside the household, Chuut-Riit thought. Competition for rank was far too intense and personal for that, of course.

He walked past the modern sections, and into an area that was pure Old Kzin; maze-walls of reddish sandstone with twisted spines of wrought-iron on their tops, the tips glistening razor-edged. Fortress-architecture from a world older than this, more massive, colder and drier; from a planet harsh enough that a plains carnivore had changed its ways, put to different use an upright posture designed to place its head above savanna grass, grasping paws evolved to climb rock. Here the modern features were reclusive, hidden in wall and buttress. The door was a hammered slab graven with the faces of night-hunting beasts, between towers five times the height of a kzin. The air smelled of wet rock and the raked sand of the gardens.

Chuut-Riit put his hand on the black metal of the outer portal, stopped. His ears pivoted, and he blinked; out of the corner of his eye he saw a pair of tufted eyebrows glancing through the thick twisted metal on the rim of the ten-meter battlement. *Why, the little sthondats,* he thought affectionately. *They managed to put it together out of reach of the holo pickups.*

The adult put his hand to the door again, keying the locking sequence, then bounded backward four times his own length from a standing start. Even under the lighter gravity of Wunderland, it was a creditable feat. And necessary, for the massive panels rang and toppled as the rope-swung boulder slammed forward. The children had hung two cables from either tower, with the rock at the point of the V and a third rope to draw it back. As the doors bounced wide he saw the blade they had driven into the apex of the egg-shaped granite rock, long and barbed and polished to a wicked point.

Kittens, he thought. *Always going for the dramatic.* If that thing had struck him, or the doors under its impetus had, there would have been no need of a blade. *Watching too many historical adventure holos.* "Errorowwww!" he shrieked in mock-rage bounding through the shattered portal and into the interior court, halting atop the kzin-high boulder. A round dozen of his older sons were grouped behind the rock, standing in a defensive clump and glaring at him, the crackly scent of their excitement and fear made the fur bristle along his spine. He glared until they dropped their eyes, continued it until they went down on their stomachs, rubbed their chins along the ground and then rolled over for a symbolic exposure of the stomach.

"Congratulations," he said. "That was the closest you've gotten. Who was in charge?"

More guilty sidelong glances among the adolescent males crouching among their discarded pull-rope, and then a lanky youngster with platter-sized feet and hands came squatting-erect. His fur was in the proper flat posture, but the naked pink of his tail still twitched stiffly.

"I was," he said keeping his eyes formally down. "Honored Sire Chuut-Riit," he added, at the adult's warning rumble.

"Now, youngling, What did you learn from your first attempt?"

"That no one among us is your match, Honored Sire Chuut-Riit," the kitten said. Uneasy ripples went over the black-striped orange of his pelt.

"And what have you learned from this attempt?"

"That all of us together are no match for you, Honored Sire Chuut-Riit," the striped youth said.

"That we didn't locate all of the cameras," another muttered. "You idiot, Spotty." That to one of his siblings; they snarled at each other from their crouches, hissing past barred fangs and making striking motions with unsheathed claws.

"No, you did locate them all, cubs," Chuut-Riit said. "I presume you stole the ropes and tools from the workshop, prepared the boulder in the ravine in the next courtyard, then rushed to set it all up between the time I cleared the last gatehouse and my arrival?"

Uneasy nods. He held his ears and tail stiffly, letting his whiskers quiver slightly and holding in the rush of love and pride he felt, more delicious than milk heated with bourbon. *Look at them!* he thought. At the age when most young kzin were helpless prisoners of instinct and hormone, wasting their strength ripping each other up or making fruitless direct attacks on their sires, or demanding to be allowed to join the Patriarchy's service *at once* to win a Name and house hold of their own . . . *His* get had learned to *cooperate* and use their minds!

"Ah, Honored Sire Chuut-Riit, we set the ropes up beforehand, but made it look as if we were using them for tumbling practice," the one the others called Spotty said. Some of them glared at him, and the adult raised his hand again.

"No, no, I am *moderately* pleased." A pause. "You did not hope to take over my official position if you had disposed of me?"

"No, Honored Sire Chuut-Riit," the tall leader said. There had been a time when any kzin's holdings were the prize of the victor in a duel, and the dueling rules were interpreted more leniently for a young subadult. Everyone had a sentimental streak for a successful youngster; every male kzin remembered the intolerable stress of being physically mature but remaining under dominance as a child.

Still, these days affairs were handled in a more civilized manner. Only the Patriarchy could award military and political office. And this mass assassination attempt was . . . unorthodox, to say the least. Outside the rules more because of its rarity than because of formal disapproval. . . .

A vigorous toss of the head. "Oh, no, Honored Sire Chuut-Riit. We had an agreement to divide the private possessions. The lands and the, ah, females." Passing their own mothers to half-siblings, of course. "Then we wouldn't each have so much we'd get too many challenges, and we'd agreed to help each other against outsiders," the leader of the plot finished virtuously.

"Fatuous young scoundrels," Chuut-Riit said. His eyes narrowed dangerously. "You haven't been communicating outside the household, have you?" he snarled.

"Oh, *no*, Honored Sire Chuut-Riit!"

"Word of honor! May we die nameless if we should do such a thing!"

The adult nodded, satisfied that good family feeling had prevailed. "Well as I said, I am somewhat pleased. If you have been keeping up with your lessons. Is there anything you wish?"

"Fresh meat, Honored Sire Chuut-Riit," the spotted one said. The adult could have told him by the scent, of course, a kzin never forgot another's personal odor, that was one reason why names were less necessary among their species. "The reconstituted stuff from the dispensers is always . . . so . . . *quiet*."

Chuut-Riit hid his amusement. Young Heroes-to-be were always kept on an inadequate diet, to increase their aggressiveness. A matter for careful gauging, since too much hunger would drive them into mindless cannibalistic frenzy.

"And couldn't we have the human servants back? They were nice." Vigorous gestures of assent. Another added: "They told good stories. I miss my Clothilda-human."

"Silence!" Chuut-Riit roared. The youngsters flattened stomach and chin to the ground again. "Not until you can be trusted not to injure them; how many times do I have to tell you, it's dishonorable to attack household servants! Until you learn self-control, you will have to make do with machines."

This time all of them turned and glared at a mottled youngster in the rear of their group; there were half-healed scars over his head and shoulders. "It bared its *teeth* at me," he said sulkily. "All I did was swipe at it, how was I supposed to know it would die?" A chorus of rumbles, and this time several of the covert kicks and clawstrikes landed.

"Enough," Chuut-Riit said after a moment. *Good, they have even learned how to discipline each other as a unit.* "I will consider it, when all of you can pass a test on the interpretation of human expressions and body-language." He drew himself up. "In the meantime, within the next two eight-days, there will be a formal hunt and meeting in the Patriarch's Preserve; kzinti homeworld game, the best Earth animals, and even some feral-human outlaws, perhaps!"

He could smell their excitement increase, a mane-crinkling musky odor not unmixed with the sour whiff of fear. Such a hunt was not without danger for adolescents, being a good opportunity for hostile adults to cull a few of a hated rival's offspring with no possibility of blame. *They will be in less danger than most,* Chuut-Riit thought judiciously. *In fact, they may run across a few of my subordinates' get and mob them. Good.*

"And if we do well, afterwards a feast and a visit to the Sterile Ones." That had them all quiveringly alert, their tails held rigid and tongues lolling; nonbearing females were kept as a rare privilege for Heroes whose accomplishments were not *quite* deserving of a mate of their own. Very rare for kits still in the household to be granted such, but Chuut-Riit thought it past time to admit that modern society demanded a prolonged adolescence. The day when a male kit could be given a spear, a knife, a rope and a bag of salt and kicked out the front gate at puberty were long gone. Those were the wild, wandering years in the old days, when survival challenges used up the superabundant energies. Now they must be spent learning history, technology, xenology, none of which burned off the gland-juices saturating flesh and brain.

He jumped down amid his sons, and they pressed around him, purring throatily with adoration and fear and respect;

his presence and the failure of their plot had reestablished his personal dominance unambiguously, and there was no danger from them for now. Chuut-Riit basked in their worship, feeling the rough caress of their tongues on his fur and scratching behind his ears. *Together*, he thought. *Together we will do wonders*.

From "The Children's Hour" by Jerry Pournelle & S.M. Stirling

THOMAS T. THOMAS

"I will tell you what it is to be human."

ME: He started life a battle program, trapped, mutilated, and dumped into RAM. Being born consists of getting his RAM Sampling and Retention Module coded and spliced into his master program.

There are other experiments in AI personality development; ME is the one that comes alive.

Praise for Thomas T. Thomas:

FIRST CITIZEN: "As wild as the story gets, Thomas' feeling for human nature, the forces of the marketplace and his detailed knowledge of how things work—from the military to businesses legal and illegal—keep this consistently lively and provocative." —*Publishers Weekly*

THE DOOMSDAY EFFECT: "Eureka! A fresh new hard SF writer with this fine first novel. . . . My nomination for the best first novelist of 1986, Thomas puts hardly a foot wrong in this high tech adventure." —Dean Lambe, *SF Reviews*

AN HONORABLE DEFENSE (with David Drake): "What makes this novel special, though, is the humor and intelligence brought to it by the authors. The characters are intelligent; the dialogue is intelligent; and the multitude of imaginative details mentioned above is one beautifully conceived bit after another, most of them minor, but adding up to a richly textured milieu with a new, neat little particular on almost every page. . . . David Drake and Thomas T. Thomas have made a neo-space opera of a very high order." —Baird Searles, *Asimov's*

THE MASK OF LOKI (with Roger Zelazny): "In the twenty-first century, an ancient duel of good versus evil is revived, with the reincarnation of a thirteenth-century assassin pitted against a reincarnated magician and knight, with the Norse god Loki lending spice to events. Zelazny is a respected veteran craftsman, and Thomas is a gifted storyteller with a growing reputation. This well-told tale is recommended for the majority of fantasy collections."
—*Booklist*

Available at your local bookstore. Or just fill out this coupon and send a check or money order for the cover price(s) to Baen Books, Dept. BA, P.O. Box 1403, Riverdale, NY 10471.

Please send the books marked to me at the address below:

The Doomsday Effect (as by Thomas Wren) _____
65579-5 • $2.95
First Citizen _____
65368-7 • $3.50
An Honorable Defense (with David Drake) _____
69789-7 • $4.99
The Mask of Loki (with Roger Zelazny) _____
72021-X • $4.95
Me (available starting August 1991) _____
72073-2 • $4.95

NAME:_____

ADDRESS:_____

_____

I enclose a check or money order in the amount of $_____.

JOHN DALMAS

He's done it all!

John Dalmas has just about done it all—parachute infantryman, army medic, stevedore, merchant seaman, logger, smokejumper, administrative forester, farm worker, creamery worker, technical writer, free-lance editor—and his experience is reflected in his writing. His marvelous sense of nature and wilderness combined with his high-tech world view involves the reader with his very real characters. For lovers of fast-paced action-adventures!

THE REGIMENT
The planet Tyss is so poor that it has only one resource: its fighting men. Each year three regiments are sent forth into the galaxy. And once a regiment is constituted, it never recruits again: as casualties mount the regiment becomes a battalion . . . a company . . . a platoon . . . a squad . . . and then there are none. But after the last man of *this* regiment has flung himself into battle, the Federation of Worlds will never be the same!

THE WHITE REGIMENT
All the Confederation of Worlds wanted was a little peace. So they applied their personnel selection technology to war and picked the greatest potential warriors out of their planets-wide database of psych profiles. And they hired the finest mercenaries in the galaxy to train the first test regiment—they hired the legendary black warriors of Tyss to create the first ever White Regiment.

THE KALIF'S WAR
The White Regiment had driven back the soldiers of the Kharganik empire, but the Kalif was certain that

THE REALITY MATRIX

Is the existence we call life on Earth for real, or is it a game? Might Earth be an artificial construct designed by a group of higher beings? Is everything an illusion? Everything is—except the Reality Matrix. And what if self-appointed "Lords of Chaos" place a chaos generator in the matrix, just to see what will happen? Answer: The slow destruction of our world.

THE GENERAL'S PRESIDENT

The stock market crash of 1994 makes Black Monday of 1929 look like a minor market adjustment—and the fabric of society is torn beyond repair. The Vice President resigns under a cloud of scandal—and when the military hints that they may let the lynch mobs through anyway, the President resigns as well. So the Generals get to pick a President. But the man they choose turns out to be more of a leader than they bargained for. . . .

he could succeed in bringing the true faith of the Prophet of Kargh to the Confederation—even if he had to bombard the infidels' planets with nuclear weapons to do it! But first he would have to thwart a conspiracy in his own ranks that was planning to replace him with a more tractable figurehead ...

FANGLITH
Fanglith was a near-mythical world to which criminals and misfits had been exiled long ago. The planet becomes all too real to Larn and Deneen when they track their parents there, and find themselves in the middle of the Age of Chivalry on a world that will one day be known as Earth.

RETURN TO FANGLITH
The oppressive Empire of Human Worlds, temporarily filed in *Fanglith,* has struck back and resubjugated its colony planets. Larn and Deneen must again flee their home. Their final object is to reach a rebel base—but the first stop is Fanglith!

THE LIZARD WAR
A thousand years after World War III and Earth lies supine beneath the heel of a gang of alien sociopaths who like to torture whole populations for sport. But while the 16th century level of technology the aliens found was relatively easy to squelch, the mystic warrior sects that had evolved in the meantime weren't. . . .

THE LANTERN OF GOD
They were pleasure droids, designed for maximum esthetic sensibility and appeal, abandoned on a deserted planet after catastrophic systems failure on their transport ship. After 2000 years undisturbed, "real" humans arrive on the scene—and 2000 thousand years of droid freedom is about to come to a sharp and bloody end.